OSLG

THE ABSENT ONE

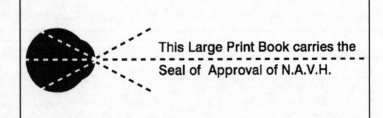

This Large Print Book carries the
Seal of Approval of N.A.V.H.

THE ABSENT ONE

JUSSI ADLER-OLSEN

WHEELER PUBLISHING
A part of Gale, Cengage Learning

GALE
CENGAGE Learning®

Detroit • New York • San Francisco • New Haven, Conn • Waterville, Maine • London

GALE
CENGAGE Learning®

LIBRARY OF CONGRESS CATALOGING-IN-PUBLICATION DATA

Adler-Olsen, Jussi.
  [Fasandræberne. English]
  The absent one / by Jussi Adler-Olsen ; translated by K. E. Semmel.
    pages ; cm.
  ISBN-13: 978-1-4104-5362-4 (hardcover)
  ISBN-10: 1-4104-5362-6 (hardcover)
    1. Police—Denmark—Fiction. 2. Murder—Investigation—Fiction.
  3. Copenhagen (Denmark)—Fiction. 4. Large type books. I. Semmel, K. E.
  II. Title.
  PT8176.1.D54F3713 2012b
  839.81'38—dc23   2012034495

Published in 2012 by arrangement with Dutton, a member of Penguin Group (USA) Inc.

Printed in the United States of America
1 2 3 4 5 6 7 16 15 14 13 12

Dedicated to the three Graces
and iron ladies:
Anne, Lene, and Charlotte

Prologue

Another shot echoed over the treetops.

The beaters' calls had grown clearer. A throbbing pulse was thundering against my eardrums, the damp air forcing its way into my lungs so fast and hard that it hurt.

Run, run, don't fall. I'll never get up again if I do. Fuck, fuck. Why can't I get my hands free? Oh, run, run . . . shhh. Can't let them hear me. Did they hear me? Is this it? Is this really how my life is going to end?

Branches slapped against my face, drawing streaks of blood, the blood mixing with sweat.

The men's shouts were all around now. It was at this moment that I was seized by the fear of death.

More shots. A bolt whistled through the chill air so close that sweat poured off me, settling like a compress beneath my clothes.

In a minute or two they'll catch me. Why won't my hands behind my back obey? How can the tape be that strong?

Frightened birds suddenly flew from the treetops, wings beating the air. The dancing shadows beyond the dense line of spruces grew clearer. Maybe they were only about a hundred yards away. Everything was more distinct now. The voices. The hunters' bloodlust.

How would they do it? A single shot, a single arrow, and it would be over? Was that it?

No, no, why would they settle for that? Those bastards were not that merciful. That wasn't their way. They had their rifles and their blood-splattered knives. They had shown how efficient their crossbows were.

Where can I hide? Is there any place? Can I make it back? Can I?

I searched the forest floor, looking back and forth. But it was difficult since my eyes were nearly covered over with tape, and my legs continued their stumbling flight.

Now I'll see for myself how it feels to be in their snares. They won't make any exceptions for me. This is how they get their kicks. It's the only way to get this over with.

My heart was hammering so hard now that it hurt.

1

When she ventured down the pedestrian street called Strøget, she was poised as if on the edge of a knife. With her face half covered by a dirty green shawl, she slipped past well-lit shop windows, alert eyes scanning the street. It was vital to know how to recognize people without being recognized. To be able to live in peace with her demons and leave the rest to those who hurried past her. Leave the rest to the fucking bastards who wanted to harm her, to those whose blank stares shunned her.

Kimmie glanced up at the streetlights, which threw an icy brightness across Vesterbrogade. She flared her nostrils. The nights would soon grow cold. She had to prepare her winter lair.

She was standing in a crowd by the crossing, among a group of frozen people emerging from Tivoli Gardens, looking toward the central train station, when she noticed the woman beside her in the tweed jacket. The woman squinted at her, wrinkled her nose, and then eased away. It was only a few inches, but more than enough.

Take it easy now, Kimmie, the warning signal flashed in her head as the rage tried to take hold.

Her eyes glided down the woman's body until they reached her legs. The woman's stockings gleamed, her ankles taut in high-heeled shoes. Kimmie felt a treacherous smile curling at the corners of her mouth. With a hard kick she could crack those heels. The woman would topple over, and she would learn how even a Christian Lacroix dress gets soiled on a wet pavement. That would teach her to mind her own business.

Kimmie looked directly at the woman's face. Heavy eyeliner, powdered nose, a meticulous haircut, fashioned one strand at a time. Her expression was rigid and dismissive. Yes, Kimmie knew her type better than most people did. She had once been like her. Arrogant upper-class snobs who were thunderously hollow inside. Back then her so-called women friends had been like that; her stepmother, too.

She loathed them.

So do something, the voices in her head whispered. *Don't let her get away with it. Show her who you are. Do it!*

Kimmie stared at a group of dark-skinned boys on the other side of the street. Had it not been for their roving eyes, she would have shoved the woman just as the 47 bus whizzed past. She saw it clearly in her mind's eye: what a wonderful bloodstain the bus would leave behind. What a shock-wave the snooty woman's crushed body would send through the crowd. What a delicious sense of justice it would give her.

But Kimmie didn't push the woman. In a swarm of people there was always a watchful eye; plus there was something inside her that held her back. The frightening echo from a time long, long ago.

She raised her sleeve to her face and took a deep breath. It was true what the woman beside her had noticed: her clothes stank terribly.

When the light turned green, she made her way over the crossing, her suitcase knocking along behind her on its crooked wheels. This would be its final trip, because the time had come to toss out the old rags.

It was time to slough her skin.

In the center of the train station, a placard

displayed the day's newspaper headlines in front of the railway kiosk, making life bitter for both the hurried and the blind. She'd seen the poster several times on her way through the city, and it filled her with disgust.

"Pig," she mumbled when she passed the sign, gazing steadfastly ahead. Still, she turned her head and caught a glimpse of the face on *Berlingske Tidende*'s placard.

The mere sight of the man made her tremble.

Under the PR photo it read: "Ditlev Pram buys private hospitals in Poland for 12 billion kroner." She spat on the tile floor and paused until her body grew calmer. She hated Ditlev Pram. Him and Torsten and Ulrik. But one day they'd get what they deserved. One day she'd take care of them. She would.

She laughed out loud, making a passerby smile. Yet another naive idiot who thought he knew what went on inside other people's heads.

Then she stopped abruptly.

Rat-Tine stood at her usual spot a little farther ahead. Crouched over and rocking slightly, with dirty hands, drooping eyelids, and a hand outstretched in mind-blown faith that at least one person in the swarming anthill would slip her a ten-krone coin. Only drug addicts could stand like that hour after hour. Miserable wretches.

Kimmie tried to sneak past her, heading directly for the stairwell to Reventlowsgade, but Tine had spotted her.

"Hi, Kimmie. Hey, wait up, damn it," she managed in a sniffling moment of lucidity, but Kimmie didn't respond. Rat-Tine wasn't good in open spaces. Only when she sat on her bench did her brain function reasonably.

She was, however, the only person Kimmie could tolerate.

The wind whipping through the streets that day was inexplicably cold, so people wanted to get home quickly. For that reason, five black Mercedes idled in the taxi queue by the train station's Istedgade entrance. She thought there'd be at least one remaining when she needed it. That was all she wanted to know.

She dragged the suitcase across the street to the basement Thai shop and left it next to the window. Only once before had a suitcase been stolen when she'd put it there. She felt certain it wouldn't happen in this weather, when even thieves stayed indoors. It didn't matter anyway. There was nothing of any value in the suitcase.

She waited only about ten minutes at the main entrance to the station before she got a bite. A fabulously beautiful woman in a mink coat, with a lithe body not much larger than a size 8, was leaving a taxi with a suitcase on hard rubber wheels. In the past Kimmie had always looked for women who wore a size 10, but that was many years ago. Living on the street didn't make anyone fat.

While the woman concentrated on the ticket machine in the front entrance, Kimmie stole the suitcase. Then she made off toward the back exit and in no time was down among the taxis on Reventlowsgade.

Practice makes perfect.

There she loaded her stolen suitcase into the boot of the first taxi in the queue and asked the driver to take her for a short ride.

From her coat pocket she pulled out a fat bundle of hundred-krone bills. "I'll give you a few hundred more if you do as I say," she told him, ignoring his suspicious glance and quivering nostrils.

In about an hour they would return and pick up her old suitcase. By then she would be wearing new clothes and another woman's scent.

No doubt the taxi driver's nostrils would quiver for an entirely different reason then.

2

Ditlev Pram was a handsome man, and he knew it. When flying business class, there were any number of women who had no objections to hearing about his Lamborghini and how fast it could drive to his domicile in the fashionable suburb of Rungsted.

This time he'd set his sights on a woman with soft hair gathered at the nape of her neck and glasses with heavy black frames that made her look unapproachable.

It aroused him.

He'd tried speaking to her, with no luck. Offered her his copy of *The Economist*, the cover of which featured a backlit nuclear reactor, only to be met with a dismissive wave. He ordered her a drink that she didn't touch.

By the time the plane from Stettin landed on the dot at Kastrup Airport, the entire ninety valuable minutes had been wasted.

It was the kind of thing that made him aggressive.

He headed down the glass corridors in Terminal 3 and upon reaching the moving walkway he saw his victim. A man with a bad gait, headed determinedly in the same direction.

Ditlev picked up his pace and arrived just as the old man put one leg on the walkway. Ditlev could imagine it clearly: a carefully placed foot would make the bony figure trip hard against the Plexiglas, so that his face — glasses askew — would slide along the side as the old man desperately tried to regain his feet.

He would have gladly carried out this fantasy in reality. That was the kind of person he was. He and the others in the gang had all been raised that way. It was neither invigorating nor shameful. If he'd actually done it, in a way it would have been that bitch's fault. She could have just gone home with him. Within an hour they could have been in bed.

It was her bloody fault.

His mobile rang as the Strandmølle Inn appeared in the rearview mirror and the sea rose once again, blindingly, in front of him. "Yes," he said, glancing at the display. It

16

was Ulrik.

"I know someone who saw her a few days ago," he said. "At the pedestrian crossing outside the central train station on Bernstoffsgade."

Ditlev turned off his MP3 player. "OK. When exactly?"

"Last Monday. The tenth of September. Around nine P.M."

"What have you done about it?"

"Torsten and I had a look around. We didn't find her."

"Torsten was with you?"

"Yes. But you know how he is. He wasn't any help."

"Who did you give the assignment to?"

"Aalbæk."

"Good. How did she look?"

"She was dressed all right, from what I'm told. Thinner than she used to be. But she reeked."

"She reeked?"

"Right. Of sweat and piss."

Ditlev nodded. That was the worst thing about Kimmie. Not only could she disappear for months or years, but you never really knew who she was. Invisible, and then suddenly alarmingly visible. She was the most dangerous element in their lives. The only one who could truly threaten them.

"We've got to get her this time, do you hear me, Ulrik?"

"Why the hell do you think I phoned?"

3

Not until he stood outside Department Q's darkened offices in the basement of police headquarters did Carl Mørck fully realize his holiday and summer were definitively over. He snapped on the light, letting his gaze fall on his desk, the top of which was covered in swollen stacks of case files; the urge to close the door and get the hell out of there was powerful. It didn't help that, in the midst of all this, Assad had planted a bunch of gladioli big enough to obstruct a medium-size street.

"Welcome back, boss!" said a voice behind him.

He turned and looked directly into Assad's lively, shiny brown eyes. His thin black hair flared in all directions in a sort of welcoming way. Assad was ready for another round at the police station's altar, worst luck for him.

"Well, now!" Assad said, seeing his boss's

blank look. "A person would never know you've just returned from your holiday, Carl."

Carl shook his head. "Have I?"

Up on the third floor they'd rearranged everything again. Bloody police reform. Carl would soon need a GPS to find his way to the homicide chief's office. He had been away for only three lousy weeks, and yet there were at least five new faces glaring at him as if he were an alien.

Who the hell were they?

"I've got good news for you, Carl," Homicide Chief Marcus Jacobsen said as Carl's eyes skated over the walls of his new office. The pale green surfaces reminded him of a cross between an operating room and a crisis-control center in a Len Deighton thriller. From every angle, corpses with sallow, lost eyes stared down at him. Maps, diagrams, and personnel schedules were arranged in a multicolored confusion. It all seemed depressingly efficient.

"Good news, you say. That doesn't sound good," Carl replied, dropping into a seat opposite his boss.

"Well, Carl, you'll have visitors from Norway soon."

Carl gazed up at him from under heavy eyelids.

"I'm told a five-person delegation is coming from Oslo's police directorate to have a peek at Department Q. Next Friday at ten A.M. You remember, right?" Marcus smiled, blinking. "I've been asked to tell you how much they're looking forward to meeting you."

That sure as hell made them the only ones.

"With this visit in mind I've reinforced your team. Her name is Rose."

At this, Carl straightened up a little in his seat.

Afterward he stood outside the homicide chief's door, trying to lower his arched brow. It's said that bad news comes in clusters. Bloody right it does. At work for only five minutes and he'd already been informed that he'd have to serve as mentor for a new employee. Not to mention act as some kind of hand-holding guide for a herd of mountain apes, which he'd happily forgotten all about.

"Where is this new girl who's supposed to be joining me?" he asked Mrs. Sørensen, who sat behind the front desk.

The hag didn't glance up from her keyboard.

21

He knocked lightly on the desk. As if that would help.

Then he felt a tap on his shoulder.

"Here he is in the flesh, Rose," someone said behind him. "May I introduce you to Carl Mørck."

Turning, he saw two surprisingly similar faces. Whoever invented black dye hadn't lived in vain, he thought. They both had tousled, coal-black, and ultra-short hair, with jet-black eyes and somber, dark clothes. The resemblance was damned uncanny.

"Blimey! What happened to you, Lis?"

The department's most competent secretary slid a hand through her previously elegant blond hair and flashed him a smile. "I know. Isn't it pretty?"

He nodded slowly.

Carl shifted his attention to the other woman, who stood on mile-high heels. She gave him a smile that could have taken anyone down a peg. Once again he glanced at Lis, noting the striking likeness between the two women, and wondered whose image had inspired whom.

"This is Rose. She's been here for a few weeks, cheering us secretaries up with her infectious humor. Now I'll entrust her to you. Take care of her, Carl."

■ ■ ■ ■

Carl stormed into Marcus's office with his arguments at the ready, but after twenty minutes he realized he was fighting a losing battle. He managed to win a week's reprieve and then he would have to welcome the girl down in Department Q. Right beside Carl's office was the utility closet that housed lengths of traffic spikes and equipment they used to cordon off crime scenes. Marcus Jacobsen explained how it had already been cleaned and furnished. Rose Knudsen was his new colleague in Department Q, and that was final.

Whatever the homicide chief's motives were, Carl didn't like them.

"She received top marks at the police academy, but she failed the driver's test, and that means you're done for, no matter how talented you are," Jacobsen said, spinning his swollen cigarette pack around for the fifteenth time. "Maybe she was also a little too thin-skinned to work in the field, but she was determined to join the police, so she learned how to be a secretary. And she's been at Station City for the past year. Then the last few weeks she's been Mrs. Sørensen's substitute, who of course is back now."

"Why didn't you send her back to City, if I may ask?"

"Why? Well, there was some internal hullabaloo. Nothing that relates to us."

"OK." The word "hullabaloo" sounded ominous.

"At any rate, Carl, you now have a secretary. And she's a good one."

He said that pretty much about everyone.

"She seemed very, really nice, I think," said Assad under the fluorescent lights in Department Q, trying to make Carl feel better.

"She started a hullabaloo down at City, I'll have you know. That's not so nice."

"Hulla . . . ? You'll have to say that one more time, Carl."

"Forget it, Assad."

His assistant nodded. Then he gulped a substance smelling of mint tea that he'd poured into his cup. "Listen to this, Carl. The case you put me on top of while you were away, I couldn't get very far with. I looked here and there and all impossible places, but the case files have all gone missing during the moving mess upstairs."

Carl looked up. Gone missing? No shit? But all right — something good had happened today, after all.

"Yes, completely gone. But then I looked a little through the piles of folders and found this one. It's very interesting."

Assad handed him a pale green case file and stood as still as a pillar of salt, an expectant expression on his face.

"Are you planning on standing there while I read?"

"Yes, thanks," he said, setting his cup down on Carl's desk.

As he opened the file, Carl puffed his cheeks with air and slowly exhaled.

The case was quite old. From the summer of 1987, to be exact. The year he and a mate had taken the train to the Copenhagen Carnival and a red-headed girl who couldn't get the rhythm out of her loins had taught him how to samba — which, when they ended the evening on a blanket behind a bush in Rosenborg Castle Gardens, was heavenly. He had been twenty-odd years old then, and nothing was virgin territory after that.

It had been a good summer, 1987. The summer he was transferred from Vejle to the Antonigade Police Station.

The murders had to have been committed eight or ten weeks after the carnival, at roughly the same time as the redhead decided to throw her samba body across the next country bumpkin. Yes, it was precisely the period when Carl was making his first nightly rounds in Copenhagen's narrow streets. Actually, it was odd that he didn't recall anything about the case; it was certainly bizarre enough.

Two siblings, a girl and a boy aged seventeen and eighteen respectively, were found beaten to a pulp in a summer cottage not far from Dybesø, near Rørvig. The girl's body was badly bruised, and she had suffered terribly during the beating, as evidenced by the defensive wounds.

He scanned the text. No sexual assault, nothing stolen.

Then he read the autopsy report once more and riffled through the newspaper clippings. There were only a few, but the headlines were as large as they could get.

"Beaten to death," wrote *Berlingske Tidende*, providing a description of the bodies that was unusually detailed for this old, highbrow newspaper.

They were found in the living room, by the fireplace, the girl in a bikini and her brother naked, a half bottle of cognac gripped in his hand. He had been killed by a single blow to the back of his head, with a blunt object later identified as the claw hammer discovered in a tuft of heather somewhere between Flyndersø and Dybesø.

The motive was unknown, but suspicion quickly fell on a group of young boarding-school pupils who were staying at the lavish summer residence of one of their parents near Flyndersø. On numerous occasions they had been involved in skirmishes at the local nightclub, the Round, where a few locals got seriously hurt.

"Have you caught up to where it says who the suspects were?"

From beneath his eyebrows, Carl glanced up at Assad. That ought to be enough of an answer, but Assad wouldn't give up.

"Yes, of course you have. And the report also suggests that their fathers were all the kind who earned lots of money. Didn't many do that in the gold-eighties, or whatever it was called?"

Carl nodded. He'd now reached that part of the report.

Yes, Assad had it right. Their fathers were all well known, even today.

He skimmed the group's names a few times. It was enough to produce beads of sweat on his brow, because it wasn't just their fathers who'd earned enormous sums and become well-known figures. Years later some of their offspring had become famous, too. Born with silver spoons in their mouths, they now held the golden spoon. They were Ditlev Pram, founder of numerous exclusive private hospitals, Torsten Florin, internationally recognized designer, and stock market analyst Ulrik Dybbøl Jensen. All stood on the top rung of Denmark's ladder of success, as had the now deceased shipping magnate Kristian Wolf. The final two members of the gang stood out from the rest. Kirsten-Marie Lassen had also been a part of the jet set, but no one knew where she was today. Bjarne Thøgersen, the one who'd pleaded guilty to killing the siblings and now sat in prison, came from more modest means.

When Carl was done reading, he tossed the file on the table.

"Right. So I don't understand how this case got down to us," Assad said. Normally he would have smiled at this point, but he didn't.

Carl shook his head. "I don't, either. A man is in prison for the crime. He confessed, got a life sentence, and is now behind bars. As a matter of fact, he turned himself in, so why the doubts? Case *closed*!" He clapped the file shut.

"Except . . ." Assad bit his lip. "He didn't

turn himself in until nine years later."

"So what? He *did* turn himself in. When he committed the murders he was only eighteen years old. Maybe he realized, as he grew older, that a bad conscience never fades."

"Fades?"

Carl sighed. "Yes, fades. Withers, dies. A bad conscience doesn't go away with time, Assad. On the contrary."

Assad was clearly puzzled about something. "The Nykøbing Sjælland and Holbæk police worked on the case together. And the Mobile Investigation Unit, too. But, who sent it to us, I can't tell. Can you?"

Carl lowered his eyes to the file's cover. "No, it doesn't say anywhere. Very peculiar." If one of those three units hadn't sent them the file, who had? And if the case had ended in a conviction, why bother reopening it at all?

"Could it have something to do with this?" Assad asked. He riffled through the file until he found a document from Revenue and Customs, and handed it to Carl. "Annual Report," it said at the top. It was addressed to Bjarne Thøgersen, residing in Albertslund County in Vridløselille State Prison. The man who had killed the two youths.

"Look!" Assad was pointing at the gigantic figure in the stock revenue line. "What do you think?"

"I think he comes from a wealthy family, and now he's got enough time to play with his money. Apparently he's done pretty well with it. Where are you going with this?"

"I'll have you know, Carl, that he doesn't come from a wealthy family. He was the only member of the boarding-school gang who attended on a scholarship. You can see that he was quite different from the others. Take a look." He turned the pages back.

Carl propped up his head with one hand.

That was the thing about holidays.

They came to an end.

4

Autumn 1986

Although they were six very different people, the fifth-form students had something in common. When classes were over, they would meet in the forest or on the nature paths and light their hash pipes, even if rain was bucketing down. They kept the paraphernalia within reach in the hollow of a tree trunk; Bjarne made sure of that. Cecil fags, matches, tinfoil, and the finest dope money could buy on the square in Næstved. Standing in a cluster, they would mix fresh air with a few quick drags, careful not to get so stoned that their pupils would give them away.

Because it wasn't about getting high. It was about being their own masters and defying the authorities in the biggest way possible. And smoking hash right next to the boarding school was pretty much the worst you could do.

So they passed the pipe around and mocked the teachers, trying to outdo one another imagining what they would do to them if they could.

And that's how they spent most of the autumn until the day Kristian and Torsten were nearly caught with hash on their breath, which not even ten cloves of garlic could hide. After that they decided to eat it, because then there was no scent.

It was shortly afterward that everything began in earnest.

When they were caught in the act, they were standing beside a thicket close to the stream, high as kites and acting silly, while melting frost dripped from the leaves.

One of the younger boys suddenly appeared from behind a bush, staring straight at them. He was a blond, ambitious little shit, an irritating Goody Two-shoes on the prowl for a beetle he could display in biology class.

Instead, what he found was Kristian busily shoving the whole works back into the hollow of the tree, while Torsten, Ulrik, and Bjarne giggled like idiots and Ditlev's hands rummaged inside Kimmie's shirt. She, too, was laughing like a lunatic. This shit was some of the best they'd ever had.

"I'm telling the headmaster!" the boy screamed at them, noticing too late how quickly the older students' laughter fell silent. A sprightly boy who was used to taunting others, he could have easily outrun them, given how loaded they were. But the thicket was overgrown and the danger he'd put them in too great for them to let that happen.

Bjarne had the most to lose if he were kicked out, so once they got hold of the little twit, he was the one Kristian pushed forward. And it was he who landed the first blow.

"You know my father can crush your father's business, if he wants to," the boy shouted, "so bugger off, Bjarne, you pile of shit! Otherwise it'll be worst for you. Let go of me, you idiot."

They hesitated. The boy had made life terribly difficult for many of his classmates. His father, uncle, and big sister had been pupils at the school before him and were regular contributors to the school fund. Giving the kind of donations Bjarne was dependent on.

Then Kristian stepped forward. He didn't have the same financial concerns. "We'll give you twenty thousand kroner to keep your mouth shut," he said, meaning it.

"Twenty thousand kroner!" the boy snorted mockingly. "All I have to do is phone my father once, and he'll send me double that amount." Then he spat in Kristian's face.

"Damn you, you little shit," Kristian said, punching him. "If you say anything, we'll kill you." The boy fell backward against a tree trunk, breaking a pair of ribs with an audible crack.

For a moment he lay there, gasping in pain, but his eyes remained defiant. Then Ditlev came forward.

"We can choke you right now, no problem. Or we can hold you under water in the stream. Or we can let you go and give you the twenty thousand kroner to keep your mouth shut. If you go back now and tell everyone you fell, they'll believe you. What do you say, you little shit?"

The boy didn't respond.

Ditlev went and stood right over him, curious, searching. The little bastard's reaction fascinated him. With a sudden movement he raised his hand as if to strike, but the boy still didn't react, so he whacked him hard on the head. When the boy crumpled in fright, Ditlev struck again, smiling. It was a tremendous feeling.

Later he told the others how that slap had

been the first real rush of his life.

"Me too." Ulrik grinned, shuffling toward the shocked boy. Ulrik was the biggest of them all, and his clenched fist put an ugly mark on the boy's cheek.

Kimmie protested weakly, but was neutralized by a fit of laughter that flushed all the birds from the underbrush.

They carried the boy back to school and watched as the ambulance came to pick him up. Some of the gang were concerned the boy would rat on them, but he never did. In fact, he never returned. According to rumor, his father took him back to Hong Kong, but that might not have been true.

A few days later, they attacked a dog in the forest, beating it to death.

After that, there was no turning back.

5

On the wall above the three panorama windows was inscribed the word "Caracas." The manor had been constructed using vast sums earned in the coffee trade.

Ditlev Pram had instantly recognized the building's potential. A few pillars here and there, walls of icy green glass elevated yards in the air. Straight rows of water basins trickling water and manicured lawns with futuristic sculptures stretching toward the Sound were all that was required to create the newest private hospital on the Rungsted coast. Dental and plastic surgery were the specialties here. It wasn't an original idea, but it was incredibly lucrative for Ditlev and his Indian and Eastern European staff of doctors and dentists.

After his older brother and two younger sisters inherited the enormous fortune their father had accumulated through stock speculation and a series of hostile takeovers in the eighties, Ditlev managed his money craftily. By now his empire had expanded to include sixteen hospitals, with four new ones on the drawing board. He was making good progress toward realizing his ambition to channel fifteen percent of the profits from all of northern Europe's breast-implant operations and facelifts into his account. It was hard to find one wealthy woman north of the Black Forest who hadn't had nature's caprices adjusted on one of Ditlev Pram's steel tables.

In short, life was good.

His only concern was Kimmie. Eleven years with her rudimentary existence in the back of his mind was long enough.

He straightened his Mont Blanc fountain pen, which was slightly askew on his desk, and glanced at his Breitling watch again.

There was plenty of time. Aalbæk would arrive in twenty minutes. Five minutes after that, Ulrik would pay him a visit, and maybe Torsten, too, but who knew?

He rose and made his way down ebony-clad corridors, past the hospital wing and the operating rooms. He nodded agreeably to everyone who knew he was the unchallenged man at the top and pushed through the swing doors into the kitchen on the lowest level, with its fine view of the ice blue sky over the Sound.

He shook the cook's hand and praised him until he blushed, patted his assistants on the shoulder, and then disappeared into the laundry.

After many calculations, he knew that Berendsen Textile Service could deliver the bed sheets faster and cheaper, but that wasn't the point of having your own on-site laundry facility. It was handy, of course, but so was having easy access to the six Philippine girls he'd hired to do the work. What did money matter?

He noted how the young, dark-skinned women recoiled at the sight of him, and, as always, it amused him. So he grabbed the nearest one and dragged her into the linen cupboard. She looked frightened, but she'd been through it before. She had the narrowest hips and the smallest breasts, but she was also the most experienced. Manila's brothels had given her a solid training, and whatever he did to her now was nothing by comparison.

She pulled his trousers down and, without being told, latched on to his cock. While she rubbed his belly with one hand and masturbated him in her mouth with the other, he punched her shoulders and arms.

With this one he never came; his orgasm

settled into his tissue in another way. His adrenaline was pumping fast as he landed his blows, and after a few minutes his tank was full.

He stepped back, hoisted her up by the hair and rammed his tongue deep in her mouth, yanking her underwear down and forcing a pair of fingers into her vagina. By the time he thrust her back on the floor, they'd both had more than enough.

Then he straightened his clothes, shoved a thousand-krone bill in her mouth and departed the laundry, giving a friendly nod to all. They seemed relieved, but they shouldn't have been. He was going to be at the Caracas clinic for the whole of the following week. The girls would come to know who was boss.

The private detective looked like shit that morning, in stark contrast to Ditlev's shiny office. It was all too clear that the scrawny man had spent the entire night on the streets of Copenhagen. Yet wasn't that what they paid him for?

"What's the word, Aalbæk?" Ulrik grunted next to Ditlev while stretching his legs under the conference table. "Any news in the case of the missing Kirsten-Marie Lassen?" Ulrik always opened his conversations with Aalbæk that way, Ditlev thought as he stared with annoyance at the dark gray waves beyond the panorama windows.

He wished to hell this would all be over soon, so that Kimmie wouldn't be gnawing at his memory all the time. When they got hold of her, they would make her vanish forever. He was sure he would figure out a way.

The private detective craned his neck and suppressed a yawn. "The locksmith at the central train station has seen Kimmie a few times. She goes around dragging a suitcase, and last time he saw her she was wearing a tartan skirt. The same outfit she wore when the woman near Tivoli spotted her. But as far as I'm aware, Kimmie isn't a regular at the train station. In fact, there's nothing about her that's regular. I've asked everyone in the station. Security, police, homeless people, shopkeepers. A few of them know of her, but they don't know where she lives or even who she is."

"You'll have to set up a team to observe the station day and night until she turns up again." Ulrik rose from his seat. He was a large man but seemed smaller when they were discussing Kimmie. Maybe he was the only one among them who'd seriously been in love with her. Perhaps it still pained Ulrik that he'd been the only one who'd never had her, thought Ditlev for the thousandth time, and laughed to himself.

"Round-the-clock surveillance? That will cost you an arm and a leg," Aalbæk said. He was about to pluck a pocket calculator from his ridiculous little shoulder bag, but he didn't get that far.

"Stop that," Ditlev barked. He considered throwing something at him, then leaned back in his chair. "Don't discuss money as though it's something you know anything about, you got that? What are we talking about here, Aalbæk? A few hundred thousand kroner? How much do you think Ulrik, Torsten, and I have made while we've been sitting here discussing your pathetic hourly wages?" Then he picked up his fountain pen anyway and threw it at him. He aimed for the man's eyes, but missed.

After Aalbæk's thin corpus had closed the door behind him, Ulrik picked up the Mont Blanc and put it in his pocket. "Finders keepers," he said, laughing.

Ditlev said nothing. Ulrik had better think twice before doing that again. "Have you heard from Torsten today?" he asked.

At this, the energy drained from Ulrik's face. "Yes, he went up to his country estate in Gribskov this morning."

"Doesn't he care at all about what's going on here?"

Ulrik shrugged his shoulders, which were beefier than ever. That's what happened when you hired a chef specializing in foie gras. "He's not at his best right now, Ditlev."

"I see. We'll have to take care of it ourselves then, won't we?" Ditlev clenched his teeth. They'd have to expect that Torsten would have a complete breakdown someday. And then he would be as big a threat as Kimmie.

Ditlev felt Ulrik scrutinizing him.

"You won't do anything to Torsten, will you, Ditlev?"

"Of course not, old boy. Not Torsten."

For a moment they watched each other like beasts of prey, with lowered heads and measured glances. In the sport of stubbornness, Ditlev knew he would never outlast Ulrik Dybbøl Jensen. His father had founded the family's stock market research firm, but Ulrik had expanded its influence. When he doggedly pursued something, he would invariably get his way. Even if that meant forcing it through by any means necessary.

"Well, Ulrik," Ditlev said, breaking the silence. "We'll let Aalbæk do his job, and we'll see what happens."

Ulrik's expression changed. "Is the pheasant hunt set?" he asked, eager as a child.

"Yes. Bent Krum has gathered the entire team. Thursday morning at six we meet at Tranekær Inn. We have to invite the local wallies, but that'll be the last time."

Ulrik laughed. "You have a plan for the hunt, I imagine."

Ditlev nodded. "Yes, the surprise is ready."

Ulrik worked his jaw muscles. The thought clearly excited him. Excitable and impatient, that was his true nature.

"What do you say, Ulrik? Do you want to come with me and see how it's going with our Philippine wenches down in the laundry?"

Ulrik raised his head. His eyes narrowed. Sometimes it meant yes, other times no — it was impossible to tell. The man had too many contradictory impulses.

6

"Lis, do you know how this case ended up on my desk?"

She glanced at Carl's file as she adjusted her new, stylishly messy hair. Her frown suggested she didn't.

Carl gave the file to Mrs. Sørensen. "Do you know, then?"

It took the woman five seconds to scan the first page. "I'm afraid not," she replied, eyes triumphant. She liked to see Carl struggle. Moments such as these were among her finest.

Deputy Commissioner Lars Bjørn didn't know, either, nor did any of the investigative officers. Apparently the file had somehow placed itself on his desk.

"I've called Holbæk Police!" Assad shouted from his shoebox-size office. "As far as they know, the file is in their archives as it is supposed to be. But they'll check when they have the time."

Carl raised his legs and planted his size 11 shoes in the center of the table. "What do they say in Nykøbing Sjælland?"

"Just a second, I'll call them." While tapping in the number, Assad whistled a few notes of one of his native country's melancholic songs. It sounded as though he were whistling backward.

Not good.

Carl studied the noticeboard on the wall. Four newspaper headlines echoed one another: the Merete Lynggaard case had been expertly solved. Department Q, the newly established department for cases of special focus, led by Detective Superintendent Carl Mørck, was described as an absolute success.

He stared at his tired hands, which hardly had the stamina to hold a lousy one-inch file, the origins of which were unclear. The word "success," at this moment, gave him a hollow feeling. He sighed and continued reading the file. Two young people murdered, a very brutal double murder, with several children of prominent families as suspects, and nine years later one of these kids suddenly turns himself in, admitting his guilt. He was the only one of the gang who didn't actually come from a wealthy family. In less than three years, this Thøgersen would be released. He would be rich as hell, too, having earned a fortune on the stock market during his incarceration. Were people in prison even allowed to invest like that? It was a damned scary thought.

He read copies of the interrogation reports thoroughly and then, for the third time, skimmed the documents in the case against Bjarne Thøgersen. The killer apparently hadn't known his victims. Even though the convicted man claimed he had met them several times, there was no corroborating evidence to prove it. Indeed, the reports suggested otherwise.

Carl glanced again at the cover of the file. "Holbæk Police," it said. Why didn't it say "Nykøbing"? Why didn't the Mobile Investigation Unit work with the Nykøbing Police? Were the officers in Nykøbing too close to the case? Could that be the explanation? Or were they just incompetent?

"Hey, Assad!" he shouted across the brightly lit hallway. "Call the department in Nykøbing and ask if anyone there knew the victims."

There was no response from Assad's cubbyhole, just his murmuring on the telephone.

Carl stood and walked across the corridor.

"Assad, ask if anyone at the station —"

Assad stopped him with a hand movement. He was already in full swing. "Yes, yes, yes," he said, followed by another series of yeses in the same vein.

Carl exhaled heavily and scanned the room. More framed photographs had appeared on Assad's shelf. A picture of two elderly women now competed with the other family snapshots. One of the women had a trace of a mustache, the other was podgy, with hair so thick it resembled a scooter helmet. Assad's aunts, if he were to hazard a guess.

When Assad hung up, Carl pointed at the photos.

"Those are my aunts from Hamah. The one with the hair is dead now."

Carl nodded. The way she looked, any other answer would have surprised him. "What'd they say in Nykøbing?"

"They didn't send us the file, either, Carl. For good reasons they couldn't. They never got it."

"I see. That's peculiar, because the documents suggest that the police in Nykøbing, Holbæk, and the Mobile Investigation Unit all worked together."

"No. They say that Nykøbing was in charge of the inquest, but left the case to

47

the others."

"Really? I find that rather odd. Do you know if anyone in Nykøbing knew the victims personally?"

"Yes and no."

"What does that mean?"

"The two victims were the son and daughter of one of the officers." He pointed at the notes he had just taken. "His name was Henning P. Jørgensen."

Carl pictured the savagely beaten girl. It was any police officer's worst nightmare to find his own children murdered.

"How awful. But I suppose that explains why the case was handed over to another station. I'll bet you there is a personal motivation behind it. But you said yes and no. Why?"

Assad leaned back in his chair. "I did it because there is no longer anyone at the station who is related to those children. Right after the discovery, the officer drove back to the police station in Nykøbing Sjælland. He greeted the guy at the front desk, went straight to the weapons depot, and pulled the trigger on his service revolver like this." He pointed at his temple with two short, thick fingers.

The Danish police reform brought many

strange results. Districts were renamed, titles were changed, and archives were moved. All in all, most personnel had difficulty finding their footing in all this lunacy. Plenty used the opportunity to jump off the merry-go-round, accepting the title of "early retiree."

In the old days, retirement for a police officer hadn't exactly been a walk in the park. The average number of years they had left to live after such an exhausting career didn't even reach two digits. Only reporters had worse prospects, but then again, many more pints probably passed through that profession. Death had to have a cause, after all.

Carl knew officers who hadn't even made it to their first anniversary as a pensioner before they kicked the bucket, leaving the world in the hands of freshly minted lackeys. But thankfully things were changing. Even police officers wanted to see the world, wanted to see their grandchildren get their A levels. As a consequence, many left the force. Like Klaes Thomasen, a retired cop from Nykøbing Sjælland who stood before them now with his potbelly, nodding. Thirty-five years in blue was enough, he said. These days his wife exerted a stronger pull on him. Even though the part about the wife gnawed at Carl a little, he knew what Klaes meant. Technically, of course, he, too, still had a wife, but it had been ages since she'd left him, and her undersized lovers with their long Vandykes would no doubt protest if he insisted on having her back.

As if he would ever try.

"A very lovely place you've got," Assad said. Impressed, he stared through the double windows at the fields surrounding Klaes Thomasen's well-tended garden and the town of Stenløse beyond.

"Thanks for taking the time to see us, Thomasen," Carl said. "There aren't many officers left who knew Henning Jørgensen."

Klaes's smile vanished. "The best friend and colleague anyone could ask for. We were neighbors. That's one reason we moved. After all that happened, his widow took ill and started acting batty and we no longer liked living there. Too many bad memories."

"I understand that Henning Jørgensen was unprepared for who the victims were in that summer cottage?"

Thomasen shook his head. "We got a call from a neighbor who'd stopped by the cottage and discovered the dead kids. I was the one who answered. Jørgensen was off that day. But when he drove out to pick up his children he saw all the police cars. They would have begun their final school year the following day."

"Were you there when he arrived?"

"Yes, along with the crime-scene techs and the head of the investigation." He shook his head again. "He's dead, too, now. Car accident!"

Assad pulled out a pad and took notes. Before long, Carl's assistant would be able to do everything on his own. Carl looked forward to that day.

"What did you see in the cottage?" he asked. "Just the general outline would be fine."

"The doors and windows were wide open. There were several footprints. We never found the shoes, but we did find sand that we later traced back to the terrace of the parents of one of the suspects. And then we entered the living room and found the bodies on the floor." He sat down on the sofa by the coffee table, gesticulating to the others to join him.

"The girl was a sight I would rather not remember," he said, "if you know what I mean. I knew her, after all." His wife poured coffee. Assad declined, but she ignored him.

"I've never seen a body so badly beat up," he continued. "She was so small and thin. I don't understand how she could've survived as long as she did."

"What do you mean?"

"The autopsy showed that she was alive for perhaps an hour after they left. The bleeding in her liver amassed in her abdominal cavity until her blood loss became too severe."

"That's quite a risk the killers took."

"Not really. Had she lived, her brain would have been so damaged she would never have been able to help the investigation. That was obvious straightaway." With the thought of this, Thomasen turned his face toward the fields. Carl knew the feeling. Some inner images made you want to see beyond this world.

"The killers knew this?"

"Yes. An open skull fracture like that, in the middle of the forehead, leaves no doubt. It was quite extraordinary. So it was plain to see."

"And the boy?"

"Well, he lay next to her. He had a surprised yet peaceful expression on his face. He was a good lad. I'd met him many times, both at home and at the station. He wanted to be an officer like his father." His gaze focused on Carl. It was rare to see a seasoned officer with such grief-stricken eyes.

"Then the father arrived and saw everything?"

"Unfortunately, yes." He shook his head. "He wanted to take the bodies with him straightaway. He was in such a state he walked around the crime scene and probably ruined all kinds of evidence. We had to forcefully drag him out of the house. I truly regret that now."

"And then you gave the case to the Holbæk Police?"

"No, it was taken from us." He nodded to his wife. There was plenty of everything on the table now. "Biscuit?" he asked, but seemed as though he really wanted them to say no and just leave.

"So it was you who put the case in our hands?"

"No, it wasn't." Thomasen sipped his coffee and glanced at Assad's notes. "But I'm happy the case has been reopened now. Every time I see those bastards on the telly — Ditlev Pram, Torsten Florin, and that stockbroker — I feel like rubbish the rest of the day."

"You've formed an opinion about who the perpetrators were, I see."

"You're damned right."

"What about the man who was convicted, Bjarne Thøgersen?"

53

The retired officer's foot traced circles on the parquet floor under the coffee table, but his face remained placid. "That damn flock of rich-folks' kids, they were all in it together, believe me. Ditlev Pram, Torsten Florin, the stockbroker, and that girl they had along. That little shit Bjarne Thøgersen was probably there, too, but they were all in on it. And Kristian Wolf, the sixth member of the gang. And he didn't just die from some heart attack. If you want to know my theory, the others had him liquidated because he got cold feet about something or other. That was homicide, too."

"As far as I know," said Carl, "Kristian Wolf was killed in a hunting accident, wasn't he? The report states he accidentally shot himself in the thigh and bled to death. None of the other hunters were in the vicinity."

"Bollocks. It was murder."

"You base that theory on, well, what?" Assad leaned across the coffee table and snatched a biscuit, eyes focused on Thomasen.

The man shrugged. Copper's intuition. What would Assad know about that, he was probably thinking.

"Well," Assad went on, "do you have anything for us to look at around the Rørvig murders? Something we maybe can't find other places?"

Klaes Thomasen pushed the plate of biscuits toward Assad. "I don't think so."

"Who might have something then?" Assad pushed the plate back. "Who can help us move along here? If we don't find out, the case will end up back in the pile."

A surprisingly independent observation.

"I'd get hold of Henning's wife, Martha Jørgensen. She pestered the investigators for months after the murders and her husband's suicide. Yes, try Martha."

7

The light over the rail tracks appeared gray in the mist. On the opposite side, beyond the spiderweb of overhead wires, the yellow postal vans had been active for hours. People were on their way to work, and the S-trains that made Kimmie's home shake were brimming with passengers.

It could be the start of an average day, but inside her the demons were on the loose. They were like feverish hallucinations: ominous, ungovernable, and unwanted.

For a moment she sank to her knees and prayed for the voices to stay quiet, but the higher powers had the day off, as usual. So she took a long swig from the whisky she kept next to her makeshift bed.

When half the bottle had burned its way through her body, she decided to leave the suitcase behind. She had enough to carry. The hatred, the loathing, the anger.

First in line was Torsten Florin. That's

how it'd been since Kristian Wolf's death.

This was a thought she'd had frequently.

She had seen Torsten's fox-face in a celebrity news magazine, proudly posing in front of his newly renovated and award-winning glass palace of a fashion house at Indiakaj in the old free port. That is where she would confront him with reality.

She eased out of the ramshackle bed, her lower back throbbing, and sniffed her armpits. The smell wasn't pungent yet, so her bath in DGI City's municipal swimming center could wait.

She rubbed her knees, ran her hand under the bed, pulled out the little chest, and opened the lid.

"Did you sleep well, my little darling?" Kimmie asked, stroking the minute head with her finger.

Every day she thought, *The hair is so soft and the eyelashes are so long*. Then she smiled warmly at her dear little one, closed the lid carefully, and put the chest back. As always, it was the best moment of the day.

She riffled through the pile of clothes to find the warmest pair of tights. The mildew growing up under the tarpaper was a warning. This autumn the weather was unpredictable.

When she was done, she carefully opened

the door of her brick house and stared directly out at the rail tracks. Less than two yards separated her and the S-trains, which whipped past at practically all hours of the day.

No one saw her.

So she slipped out, locking the door and buttoning her coat. She walked the twenty steps around the steel-gray transformer that the railway engineers rarely checked, along the asphalt path to a wrought-iron gate that exited on to Ingerslevsgade, and unlocked it.

Back when she could reach the railway building only by walking on the rubble alongside the fence all the way from Dyb-bølsbro Station — and doing it at night because she'd have been caught otherwise — it had been her greatest dream to have the key to this gate. Three or four hours of sleep were all she could get before having to vacate the little round house. If she were spotted even once, she knew they would throw her out and make sure she didn't come back. So the night became her companion until the morning she discovered the LØGSTRUP FENCE sign on the gate.

She called the factory and introduced herself as Lily Carstensen, the Danish State Railway's supplies manager, and arranged to meet the locksmith at the gate. For the occasion she wore a newly pressed blue trouser suit and could have passed for middle management in the state bureaucracy. She had two copies of the keys made and got a bill — which she paid in cash — and now she could come and go as she pleased. If she took precautions, and the demons left her alone, everything would be OK.

On the bus to Østerport she was mumbling to herself and people were staring. *Stop it, Kimmie*, she told herself. But her mouth wouldn't obey.

Sometimes she listened to herself as if she were someone else talking, and that's how it was on this day. She smiled at a little girl, and the girl returned the kindness by making a face at her.

So it must be especially bad.

With ten thousand eyes drilling into her, she got off a few stops early. That was the last time she would take the bus, she promised herself. People were simply too close. The S-train was better.

"Much better," she said aloud, as she made her way along Store Kongensgade. There were almost no people on the street. Almost no cars. Almost no voices in the back of her head.

Kimmie reached the building at Indiakaj straight after the lunch hour. At Brand Nation she discovered the yawningly empty parking spot, which, according to an enamel sign, belonged to Torsten Florin.

She opened her handbag and glanced inside. She had stolen the handbag in the foyer of the Palace Cinema from a girl who'd been preoccupied with herself and her reflection in the mirror.

According to her health insurance card, the bimbo's name was Lise-Maja Petterson. Probably another victim of numerology, she thought, pushing the hand grenade aside and pulling out one of Lise-Maja's insanely tasty Peter Jackson fags. "Smoking Causes Heart Disease" the packet read.

Lighting up, she laughed aloud, then inhaled deeply into her lungs. She had been smoking ever since she'd been kicked out of boarding school and her heart still beat just fine. It wouldn't be a heart attack that would do her in, she knew that much.

After a couple of hours she'd emptied the pack, smudging the butts all over the flagstones. Then she grabbed one of the young women sashaying in and out of Brand Nation's glass doors.

"Do you know when Torsten Florin will

be back?" she asked, and was answered with silence and a disapproving glare.

"Do you?" she said more emphatically, tugging at the girl's arm.

"Let go!" the girl shouted, twisting Kimmie's arm around with both hands.

Kimmie narrowed her eyes. She hated it when people touched her, hated it when they wouldn't answer, and hated their stares. In one fluid movement, she swung her free arm until it struck the girl's cheekbone.

The girl dropped like a rag doll. It was a good feeling, and yet it also wasn't. Kimmie knew this wasn't how people were supposed to act.

"Tell me," she said, leaning over the shocked woman. "Do you know when Torsten Florin's coming back?"

When the woman stuttered no for the third time, Kimmie turned on her heel, fully aware she couldn't return for a while.

She ran into Rat-Tine on the crumbling concrete corner outside of Jacob's Full House on Skelbækgade. She was standing underneath the proprietor's sign that read THE SEASON'S MUSHROOMS, with her plastic bag and her makeup long since smeared. The first johns she blew in the alleys had been rewarded with sharply drawn eye makeup and rouged cheeks, but the remaining customers would have to settle for less. Her lipstick was now blotched and it was clear she'd removed semen from her face with her sleeves. Tine's customers didn't use condoms. It had been years since she'd been in a position to demand that. Years since she'd been in a position to demand anything at all.

"Hi, Kimmie! Hi, sweetie! Fucking great to see you," she snuffled, wobbling toward Kimmie on legs as thin as a crane fly's. "I've been looking for you, sweetie," she said, waving her freshly lit fag. "Did you know that people are asking about you down at the central station?"

She seized Kimmie by the arm and escorted her to the benches across the street at Café Yrsa.

"Where have you been? I've missed you so fucking much," Tine said, fishing a couple of beers from her plastic bag.

As Tine opened the bottles, Kimmie glanced toward the Fisketorv Shopping Center.

"Who asked about me?" she said, pushing the bottle back to Tine. Beer was the drink of the proletariat. She'd learned that growing up.

"Oh, just some blokes." Tine set the extra bottle under the bench. She was happy sitting there, Kimmie knew, in that spot where she felt most at home; beer in one hand, money in her pocket, and yellowed fingers pinching a fresh cigarette.

"Tell me everything, Tine."

"Oh, Kimmie, I don't remember so well, you know. It's the junk, innit? Then it doesn't work so good in here." She patted her head. "But I didn't say anything. Just told 'em I didn't know a fucking thing about who you were." She smiled, shaking her head. "They showed me a picture of you, Kimmie. My God, but you were fine in those days, Kimmie, love." She took a long drag on her fag. "I was nice-looking, too, once, I was. Someone told me that once. His name was . . ." She stared into space. That was also gone.

Kimmie nodded. "Was there more than one who asked for me?"

Tine nodded and took another gulp. "There were two, but not at the same time. One of them came at night, just before the station closed. So maybe it was around four in the morning. Could that be right, Kimmie?"

Kimmie shrugged. Now that she knew there were two, it didn't really matter.

"How much?" The question came from a man standing right in front of Kimmie, but she didn't react. This was Tine's business.

"How much for a blow job?" he repeated.

She felt Tine's elbow in her side. "He's asking you, Kimmie," she said, gone from the world. She'd already earned all she needed for the day.

Kimmie raised her head and saw an ordinary-looking man with his hands in his coat pocket, wearing a pathetic expression on his face.

"Sod off," she said, giving him a murderous glare. "Sod off before I smack you."

He stepped back and straightened up, then smiled crookedly, as if the threat alone were satisfaction enough.

"Five hundred. Five hundred if you wash your mouth first. I won't have any of your slime on my cock, you hear?"

He pulled money from his pocket and flashed the bills, and the voices in Kimmie's head grew louder. *Come on*, whispered one. *He's asking for it*, sounded the rest. She grabbed the bottle under the bench and put it to her mouth as the man tried to stare her down.

When she threw her head back and spat in his eyes, he lurched backward, shock etched into his face. He glanced down at his coat, furious, and leveled his gaze at her again. She knew he was dangerous now. There was no shortage of assaults on Skelbækgade. The Tamil handing out free newspapers up at the next corner was unlikely to intervene.

So she got to her feet and smashed the bottle down on the man's skull. Shards of glass slid across the street to a buckled post box. A delta of blood spread from his ear and dripped down the collar of his coat. As the man stared at the jagged bottle aimed at him, his mind was no doubt racing. How would he explain this to his wife, his children, his colleagues? He began running toward the central station, presumably aware that he'd need a doctor's attention and a new coat in order to return to normal.

"I've seen that cocksucker before," Tine snuffled at Kimmie's side as she stared at the beer stain spreading on the pavement. "Bloody hell, Kimmie. Now I need to go to Aldi for another one, don't I? Poor fucking beer. Why did that idiot have to come wading by when we're sitting here, having a good time?"

Kimmie relaxed her gaze and her grip on the bottleneck as the man disappeared down the street. Then she stuck her fingers in her trousers, fished out a chamois-leather neck purse, and opened it. The newspaper clippings were very new. On occasion she exchanged them with fresh ones so that she could stay updated on how the others looked. She unfolded the clippings and held them in front of Tine's face.

"Was this guy one of the men asking about me?" She put her finger on the press photo. At the bottom it read: "Ulrik Dybbøl Jensen, director of the stock market research firm UDJ, rejects partnership with conservative think tank."

Ulrik had gradually become a big man, in both the physical and figurative meanings of the word.

Tine studied the clipping through a blue-white cloud of cigarette smoke and shook her head. "They weren't that fat."

"How about this one?" It was from a women's magazine she'd found in a rubbish bin on Øster Farimagsgade. With his long hair and shiny skin, Torsten Florin came across as a queer, but he wasn't. She could confirm that.

"I've seen that one before, on TV-Denmark or something. He does something in fashion, right?"

"Was it him, Tine?"

Tine giggled as if it were a game. So it wasn't Torsten, either.

When she'd also rejected the Ditlev Pram clipping, Kimmie packed them all up and stuffed them back in her trousers. "What did the men say about me?"

"They just said they were looking for you, sweetie."

"If we went down there to find them someday, would you recognize them?"

She shrugged. "They're not there every day, Kimmie."

Kimmie gnawed at her lip. She had to be careful now. They were getting close. "You tell me if you see them again, got it? Pay close attention to what they look like. Write it down so you can remember." She rested her hand on Tine's knee, which protruded like the edge of a knife under her threadbare jeans. "If you have information, stick it under the yellow sign over there." She pointed at the sign that read CAR RENTAL — DISCOUNT.

Tine coughed and nodded simultaneously.

"Every time you give me solid information I'll give you a thousand kroner for your rat. What do you say to that, Tine? You can get it a new cage. You still have it up in your apartment, don't you?

She stood for five minutes by the parking sign in front of the landmark C. E. Bast Tallow Refinery until she was certain that Tine wasn't watching her.

No one knew where she lived, and she wanted to keep it that way.

Crossing the street, angling toward the wrought-iron door, she felt a headache emerging along with a prickling sensation under her skin. Anger and frustration at the same time. The demons inside her hated it.

Sitting on her narrow bed, holding the bottle of whisky and peering through the small room's faint light, a sense of calm washed over her. This was her real world. Where she felt safe, where she could find everything she needed. The chest containing her most precious treasure lay under the bench, the poster depicting children playing tacked on the inside of the door, the photograph of the little girl, the newspapers she'd attached to the wall for insulation. The stack of clothes, the piss bucket on the floor, the pile of newspapers in the back, two battery-driven mini-fluorescent tubes, and a pair of extra shoes on the shelf. She could do whatever she pleased with all this, and if she wanted something new, she had plenty of money.

When the whisky began to take effect, she laughed and inspected the nooks behind the three loose bricks in the wall. She checked these spaces nearly every time she returned to her house, starting with the one containing her credit cards and last ATM receipts, then moving on to the one where she kept the cash.

Each day she tallied up how much was left. For eleven years she'd lived on the street, and there were still 1,344,000 kroner left. If she continued as before, she would never use it up. Her daily needs, including her clothes, were met more or less through her thievery. She didn't eat much, and thanks to the so-called health-conscious government, alcohol cost next to nothing. A person could now drink himself to death at half-price. What a terrific society Denmark had become. She snorted, removed the hand grenade from her bag and set it in the third nook with the others. Then she replaced the brick so carefully that it was nearly impossible to see the cracks.

Her anxiety came without warning this time, which was unusual. Normally, internal images alerted her. Hands poised to strike, sometimes blood and mutilated bodies. Other times she caught fleeting glimpses of carefree moments from long, long ago. Promises whispered that were later broken. This time, however, the voices failed to notify her.

She began to shake. Cramps in her pelvis squeezed her insides. Like tears, nausea was an unavoidable side effect. Previously she'd tried drowning her emotional distress with alcohol, but it only made her pain worse.

At moments like these she just had to wait for the hours to pass, until darkness returned.

When her head was clear, she would get up and go to Dybbølsbro Station. She would take the lift down to Platform 3 and wait at the far end until one of the trains rushed by. She'd stand on the edge, stretch out her arms, and shout: "You won't get away with this, you bastards."

After that she would let the voices decide.

8

Carl had hardly settled in his office before the clear plastic folder resting squarely on his desk caught his eye.

What the hell, he thought, and called for Assad.

When Assad was at the door, Carl pointed at the folder. "Do you know where that came from?" Assad shook his head. "Don't touch it, OK? There may be fingerprints."

They stared at the topmost sheet. "Boarding-School Gang Attacks," read the heading in laser print.

Underneath was a list of violent crimes with times, places, and names of victims. The attacks seemed to have been committed over a long period of time — all the way up to 1992. A young man on a beach near Nyborg. Twin brothers on a football pitch in broad daylight. A husband and wife on the island of Langeland. There were at least twenty recorded attacks. It wasn't unusual for pupils to be in school until they were twenty back in the eighties, Carl thought, but the later attacks must've been carried out *after* they'd graduated.

"We've got to find out who's putting these files here, Assad. Call the crime-scene techs. If someone here at the station is doing this, then matching fingerprints will be an easy matter."

"They didn't take *my* fingerprints." Assad seemed almost disappointed.

Carl shook his head. Why hadn't they done that? Yet another irregularity in a veritable catalogue of irregularities connected to Assad's hiring.

"Find us the Rørvig victims' mother's address, Assad. She's moved several times over the last few years and apparently doesn't reside at the address listed in Tisvilde's Civil Registration System. So be a little creative, Assad, OK? Call her old neighbors. The telephone numbers are right there. Perhaps they know something." He pointed at a mess of notes he'd just pulled from his pocket. Then he got a notebook and wrote a to-do list.

He had the distinct sense that a new case was unfolding.

"Honestly, Carl, don't waste your time on a

case that has already led to a conviction." Homicide Chief Marcus Jacobsen was shaking his head as he pawed through the notes on his desk. In just eight days there were four new, gruesome cases. In addition to that, there were three requests for leave of absence and two officers had called in sick, one of whom was probably out for good. Carl was well aware what the homicide chief was thinking: who could he transfer, and from which case? But that was his problem, thank God.

"Focus on your visitors from Norway instead, Carl. Everyone up there has heard about what you did in the Merete Lynggaard case, and they want to know how you structure and prioritize your assignments. I think they have a bunch of old cases they'd like to put a lid on. Concentrate on cleaning up your office and instructing them on solid Danish police work. If you do that, they'll have something to take with them when they go to the minister's later in the day."

Carl let his head slump. Would his visitors be going to a coffee klatsch afterward with the country's blow-hard justice minister and gossiping about his department? That was certainly not encouraging.

"I need to know who is tossing cases on

my desk, Marcus. Then we'll see what happens."

"Fine, Carl. You make your own decisions. But if you take up the Rørvig case, we'll stay completely out of it. We don't have even one man-hour to squander."

"Just relax," Carl said, rising to his feet.

Marcus leaned toward the intercom. "Lis, come here a moment, will you? I can't find my calendar."

Carl's eyes roamed to the floor. There lay the homicide chief's calendar. More than likely it had fallen off the desk.

With the tip of his toe he gave it a nudge so that it disappeared under the desk's drawer unit. Maybe his meeting with the Norwegians would vanish the same way.

He glanced at Lis affectionately as she eased past him. He preferred the premetamorphosis version of her, but hey, Lis was Lis.

From over by her desk, Rose Knudsen and her dimples, deep as the Mariana Trench, seemed to be saying, *I'm looking forward to joining you down in Department Q.*

He didn't return the show of dimples, but then again, he didn't have any.

Down in the basement Assad was ready, afternoon prayers completed. He wore an

74

oversized Windbreaker and held a small leather briefcase under his arm.

"The mother of the murdered siblings lives with an old friend in Roskilde," he said, adding that they could get there in less than half an hour if they stepped on the gas. "But they've also called from Hornbæk, Carl. It wasn't such good news."

Carl pictured Hardy. Eighty-one inches of lame flesh, face turned toward the Sound, watching the pleasure boatmen sailing for the final time that season.

"What's happened?" he asked. He felt awful. It had now been more than a month since he'd last visited his old colleague.

"They say he cries so very often," Assad replied. "Even though they give him a lot of pills and all, he still cries."

It was a completely ordinary detached house at the end of Fasanvej. The names Jens-Arnold and Yvette Larsen were etched onto the brass plate, and below that a small cardboard sign in block letters: MARTHA JØRGENSEN.

A woman fragile as fairy dust and quite a few years beyond the age of retirement greeted them at the door. She was the kind of attractive old woman who brought a slight smile to Carl's lips.

"Yes, Martha lives with me. She has since my husband died. She's not feeling so well today, I should say," she whispered in the corridor. "The doctor says it's progressing rapidly now."

They heard her friend coughing before they stepped into the conservatory. She sat staring at them with deep-set eyes. There was a variety of pill bottles in front of her. "Who are you?" she asked, flicking ash from her cigarillo with a trembling hand.

Assad made himself comfortable in a chair covered with faded wool blankets and wilted leaves from the potted plants on the windowsill. Without hesitation, he reached out and took Martha Jørgensen's hand. "Let me tell you, Martha. The way you are feeling right now, I have also seen my mother go through that. And it was not much fun."

Carl's mother would have withdrawn her hand, but not Martha Jørgensen. *How did Assad know to do that?* Carl thought as he considered what role he would play in this production.

"We have time for a cup of tea before the home help arrives," Yvette Larsen said, smiling insistently, and afterward Martha wept softly as Assad explained why they had come.

They drank tea and ate cake before she

gathered her wits to speak.

"My husband was a policeman," she finally said.

"Yes, we know that, Mrs. Jørgensen." It was the first time Carl spoke to her.

"One of his old colleagues gave me copies of the case file."

"I see. Was it Klaes Thomasen?"

"No, not him." She wheezed, and with a deep drag on her cigarillo quelled a coughing fit. "It was someone else. Arne he was called. But he's dead now. He gathered everything in a folder."

"May we have a look at it, Mrs. Jørgensen?"

She raised a nearly transparent hand to her head, her lips trembling. "I'm afraid not. I don't have it any longer." Her eyes narrowed. Apparently she had a headache. "I don't know who I loaned it to last. Quite a few people have had a glimpse at that folder."

"Is this it?" Carl handed her the pale green folder.

She shook her head. "No. It was gray, and it was much bigger. It was impossible to hold in one hand."

"Are there other materials? Anything you can let us have?"

She glanced at her friend. "Can we tell

them, Yvette?"

"I don't really know, Martha. Do you think we should?"

The ailing woman fixed her deep-set blue eyes on a double portrait on the windowsill, resting between a rusty watering can and a tiny sandstone figure of St. Francis of Assisi. "Look at them, Yvette. What did *they* ever do?" Her eyes grew moist. "My little ones. Can't we do it for them?"

Yvette placed a box of After Eight mints on the table. "I suppose we can." She sighed and moved toward the corner where old, crumpled-up Christmas paper and recyclable, corrugated cardboard boxes were stacked: a mausoleum to old age and those days when scarcity was an everyday word.

"Here," she said, pulling out a Peter Hahn box, stuffed to the brim.

"Over the past ten years Martha and I have added newspaper clippings to the files. After my husband died, it was just the two of us, you see."

Assad accepted the box and opened it.

"They're about unresolved assault cases," Yvette went on. "And the pheasant killers."

"The pheasant killers?" Carl said.

"Yes, what else would you call people like that?" Yvette rummaged around a bit in the box to find an example.

Yes, pheasant killers did seem a fitting description. Standing together in a large PR photo from one of the weeklies were a couple of members of the royal family, some bourgeois riffraff, and Ulrik Dybbøl Jensen, Ditlev Pram, and Torsten Florin — each holding a broken-open shotgun, with one foot triumphantly planted before scores of dead pheasants and partridges.

"Oy," Assad exclaimed. There wasn't much more to say on the matter.

They noticed something stirring in Martha Jørgensen, but couldn't tell where her agitation was leading.

"I won't stand for it!" she suddenly cried out. "They must be got rid of, every single one of them. They beat my children to death and killed my husband. To hell with them, I say."

She tried to get up, but instead fell forward under her own weight, crashing forehead-first against the edge of the table. It seemed almost as though she hadn't noticed.

"They, too, must die," she hissed, with her cheek on the tablecloth. Then she proceeded to lash out with her arms, knocking over the teacups.

"Calm down, Martha," Yvette said, ushering the gasping woman back to her stack of pillows.

When Martha got her breathing under control and once again sat passively puffing on her cigarillo, Yvette led them into the dining room next door. She apologized for her friend's behavior, explaining that the tumor in her brain was now so large that it was hard to know how she would react. She hadn't always been that way.

As if they deserved an apology.

"A man came to visit and told Martha he'd known Lisbet well." Yvette raised her almost nonexistent eyebrow a smidgen. "Lisbet was Martha's daughter, and the boy was called Søren. You know that, right?" Assad and Carl nodded. "Maybe Lisbet's friend still has the file, I don't know." She gazed toward the conservatory. "Apparently he expressly promised Martha he'd bring it back someday." She looked at them so sadly, one felt the urge to give her a hug. "He probably won't be able to do so before it's too late."

"This man who took the case file, can you remember his name, Yvette?" Assad asked.

"I'm afraid not. I wasn't there when she gave it to him, and her memory isn't what it used to be." She patted the side of her head. "The tumor, you know."

"Do you know if he was a policeman?" Carl added.

"I don't think so, but maybe. I don't know."

"Why didn't he take this with him then?" Assad asked, referring to the Peter Hahn box under his arm.

"Oh, that. It was just something Martha wanted to do. Someone has already confessed to the murders, haven't they? I helped her collect newspapers clippings because it was good for her. The man who borrowed the case file probably didn't believe they were especially important. And they most likely aren't."

They asked about the key to Martha's summer cottage, which Yvette told them about, and made inquiries about the days around the time of the murders. But Yvette had nothing else to add. As she explained, it had happened twenty years ago. And besides, it wasn't the kind of thing anyone wanted to remember.

When the home help arrived, they said good-bye.

Hardy kept a photograph of his son on his bedside table, the only hint that this prostrate figure with matted, greasy hair and tubes in his urinary tract had once had a life other than that which the respirator, the permanently turned-on television, and the busy nurses provided for him.

"Took your bloody time to get your arse here," he said, eyes fixed on an imaginary point a thousand yards above the Clinic for Spinal Cord Injuries in Hornbæk. A place with a 360-degree view, and from which a person could fall so hard and far that he'd never wake up again.

Carl racked his brain for a good excuse, but gave up. Instead he picked up the framed photo, saying, "I hear Mads has begun studying at the university."

"Who told you that? Are you banging my wife?" he said, without even blinking.

"No, Hardy. Why the hell would you say such a thing? I know because . . . because, oh, I don't fucking remember who at headquarters told me."

"Where's your little Syrian? Have they thrown him back into the sand dunes?"

Carl knew Hardy. This was just small talk.

"Tell me what's on your mind, Hardy. I'm here now, OK?" He breathed deeply. "In the future I'll visit you more often, old boy. I've been on holiday, I'm sure you understand."

"Do you see the shears on the table?"

"Yes, of course."

"They're always there. They use them to cut the gauze. And the tape that secures my

82

probes and syringes. They look sharp, don't you think?"

Carl looked at them. "Sure, Hardy."

"Couldn't you take them and stab me in my carotid artery, Carl? It'd make me very happy." He laughed briefly, then stopped suddenly. "My arm is twitching, Carl, right below my shoulder muscle, I think."

Carl frowned. So Hardy felt some twitching, the poor man. If only it were so. "Do you want me to scratch it for you, Hardy?" Pulling the blanket a bit to the side, he considered whether he should yank the shirt down or scratch over it.

"Damn it, you dumb bastard. Listen to what I'm saying. It's twitching. Can you see it?"

Carl moved the shirt. Hardy had always made it a point to look attractive. Well groomed and tanned. Now, apart from delicate, pale blue veins, his skin was white as a maggot's.

Carl touched Hardy's arm. There wasn't a muscle left; it felt like tenderized hung beef. And he didn't notice any twitching.

"I can feel you in one small spot, Carl. Take the shears and prick me, but not too fast. I'll tell you when you hit it."

Poor man. Paralyzed from the neck down. Just a touch of feeling in one shoulder was all that was left. Everything else was just the hope of a person in despair.

But Carl did as Hardy asked. Quite systematically, from his elbow down and then up and all the way round. When he neared the back of Hardy's armpit, he gasped.

"There, Carl. Use your pen to mark it."

He did. A friend was a friend, after all.

"Do it again. Try to trick me. I'll tell you when you hit the mark. I'm closing my eyes."

When Carl reached the spot again, Hardy grinned, or perhaps it was a grimace. "There!" he cried. It was goddamn unbelievable. Enough to give you the shivers.

"Don't tell the nurse, Carl."

Carl wrinkled his brow. "Huh? Why not, Hardy? This is wonderful news. Maybe there's a glimmer of hope in spite of everything. Then they'll have something to work from."

"I'm going to try to enlarge the spot. I want my one arm back, do you hear?" Only then did Hardy look at his old colleague for the first time. "And what I use the arm for isn't anyone's business, got it?"

Carl nodded. Whatever improved Hardy's mood was fine with him. The dream he had of picking up the shears by himself and stabbing himself in the throat was apparently all he'd been living for.

The question was whether or not that little sensitive spot on Hardy's arm had been there the whole time. But it was better to let it lie. In Hardy's case, it hardly made any difference.

Carl adjusted Hardy's shirt and pulled the blanket up to his chin. "Do you still see that lady psychologist, Hardy?" Carl imagined Mona Ibsen's delectable body. A vision that was balm for his soul.

"Yes."

"And? What do you talk about?" he asked, hoping his name would be wedged somewhere in the response.

"She keeps poking around in the shooting episode out in Amager, though I don't know what good it'll do. But whenever she visits, that damn nail-gun case is what interests her most."

"Yes, I suppose it is."

"You know what, Carl?"

"What?"

"She's got me thinking, in spite of myself. I mean, what's the fucking use? And yet, the question lingers."

"Which question, Hardy?"

He looked directly into Carl's eyes. In the same way they would cross-examine a suspect. Not accusatory, and not the opposite — just unsettling.

"You and I and Anker were out at the shed at least ten days after the man was murdered, right?"

"Right."

"The culprits had oceans of time to remove any traces. Oceans. Then why didn't they? Why did they wait? They could have set the fucking house on fire. Taken the body and burned the place down."

"Yes, it does make you wonder. I do, too."

"But why did they come back to the house right when we were there?"

"Yes, that also makes you wonder."

"Wonder? Do you know what, Carl? I don't wonder so much. Not anymore." He tried to clear his throat, but didn't succeed.

"Maybe Anker could have said more if he were still alive," Hardy continued.

"What do you mean?" Carl hadn't thought of Anker in weeks. Only eight months had passed since their best colleague had been shot before their eyes in that rotten house, yet he had already floated out of Carl's consciousness. It made him wonder how long he would be remembered if the same happened to him.

"Someone was waiting for us at the house, Carl. What happened there doesn't make sense any other way. I mean, it wasn't a typi-

86

cal investigation. One of us was involved, and it wasn't me. Was it you, Carl?"

9

Ditlev stuck his head out the passenger window and signaled the drivers of the six four-wheel-drives parked in front of the yellow-washed facade of Tranekær Inn to follow him.

The sun was wavering on the horizon as they reached the forest, and the beaters disappeared behind the hedgerow boundary of the hunting ground. The drivers knew the routine and after a few minutes they were standing beside Ditlev with their coats buttoned and their gun barrels broken open. A few had dogs trotting at their sides.

As always, the last to step forward was Torsten Florin. Plaid knickerbockers and a tailored, snug-fitting hunting coat was his unique combination for the day. He could attend a formal ball in that get-up.

Ditlev looked warily at a bird dog that had hopped from the rear of one of the four-wheel-drives at the last moment, and then he scanned the faces at the gathering. There was one participant he certainly hadn't invited.

He leaned close to Bent Krum. "Who invited her, Krum?" he whispered. Bent Krum, lawyer for Ditlev Pram, Torsten Florin, and Ulrik Dybbøl Jensen, was also the one who coordinated their hunts. He was a versatile man who'd been putting out their fires for years and was now totally dependent on the ample sum they transferred into his bank account each month.

"Your wife invited her, Ditlev," he responded softly. "She said Lissan Hjorth was welcome to come with her husband. Just so you know, she's also a better shot than Hjorth."

Better shot? Bloody hell, that had nothing to do with it. There were plenty of reasons why women weren't allowed on Ditlev's hunts — as if Krum didn't know. Thelma, that bitch.

Ditlev put his hand on Hjorth's shoulder. "I'm sorry, old boy, but your wife can't come with us today," he said. Though he knew it would cause problems, he asked Hjorth to give the car keys to his wife. "She can drive down to the inn. I'll call ahead and have them open up. And have her take your unruly dog with her. This is a special battue, Hjorth. You ought to know that."

A few of the others tried to mediate, as if they had any say in the matter. They were old-money idiots without proper fortunes. But maybe they didn't know what that damned bird dog was like.

He kicked the toe of his boot against the ground and repeated: "No women. Good-bye, Lissan."

Ditlev handed out orange scarves and avoided Lissan Hjorth's eyes when he skipped her. "Remember to take that creature with you," was all he said. He was sure as hell not letting them change his rules. This was not going to be your average hunt.

"If my wife can't come with us, Ditlev, then neither will I," Hjorth tried to argue. He was a pathetic little man in a pathetic, worn Moorland coat. Had he not felt Ditlev Pram's wrath once before when he'd tried to contradict him? Didn't his relationship to Ditlev benefit his business? And didn't he almost go bankrupt when Ditlev rerouted his granite purchases to China? Would Hjorth really want Ditlev to punish him again? He could of course do that.

"That's your decision." He turned his back on the couple and looked directly at the others. "Each of you knows the rules. What you experience today is no one else's business, do you hear?" They nodded, as he expected. "We've put out two hundred pheasants and partridges, both cocks and hens. Enough for everyone." He grinned. "OK, so it's a little too early in the season for the hens, but does anybody care?" He turned toward the men from the local hunting club. They would certainly keep quiet. Everyone worked for him in one way or the other. "But why bother discussing the poultry? You'll score some kills, no matter what. What's more interesting is the other game I've brought for the lot of you today. I won't tell you what it is. You'll see for yourselves."

Eager faces followed his movements as he turned and accepted a bundle of sticks from Ulrik. "Most of you know the routine. Two of you will draw a shorter stick than the others. These lucky individuals get to lay down their shotguns for a rifle. There'll be no birds for them. Instead, they'll have the opportunity to bring home the prey of the day. Are we ready?"

A few of the men tossed their cigars on the ground and stamped them out. Everyone had his own method of preparing for the hunt.

Ditlev smiled. This was the ruling class at its best: merciless and selfish — by the book.

"Yes, normally the two chosen riflemen share the kill," he said, "but that's up to the one who downs the animal. If Ulrik bags the trophy, we all know what will happen." All of them laughed, except for Ulrik. Whether it was shares of stock, women, or boars released in the wild, Ulrik shared with no one. They knew him.

Ditlev leaned over and picked up two rifle cases. "Look," he said, dragging the rifles into the morning light. "I've taken our old Sauer Classics back to Hunter's House so we can try these two small wonders." He raised one Sauer Elegance rifle above his head. "They're broken in, and they're damn lovely to hold. You can look forward to it!"

He thrust out the bundle of sticks, ignoring the heated exchange taking place between the Hjorths, and gave the two lucky winners the rifles.

Torsten was one. He seemed agitated, but Ditlev knew it was hardly because of the hunt. This was something they would have to discuss afterward.

"Torsten has done this before, but not Saxenholdt, so congratulations are in order." He nodded at the young man and raised his hip flask to him along with the others. With his cravat and pomaded hair, Saxenholdt was a real boarding-school lad, and would be until his dying day. "You two are the only ones who may shoot at today's special game, so it's your responsibility to see to it that it is done properly. Remember to keep firing until the animal is no longer moving. And remember that whoever downs it receives the prize. . . ."

He took a step back and removed an envelope from his inner coat pocket.

"The deeds to a fine little three-bedroom flat in Berlin with a view of the landing strips at Tempelhof Airport. But don't worry, the airport will be gone soon, and you'll have the pier right under your window." When the men began clapping, he smiled. His wife had pestered him for months to buy that damned flat, but had she bothered to visit it even once? Hell, no. Not even with her bastard lover. Now was his chance to rid himself of it.

"My wife is leaving, Ditlev, but I'm taking the dog with me," a voice behind him said. Ditlev turned and looked directly into Hjorth's stubborn visage. Clearly, he was trying to negotiate so that he wouldn't lose face.

Ditlev glanced over his shoulder, catching Torsten's eye for a split second. No one overruled Ditlev Pram. If he told a man he couldn't take his dog with him, then that man would have to suffer the consequences of disobeying.

"You insist on taking the dog along, Hjorth? OK, then," Ditlev said, avoiding Hjorth's wife's stare.

He didn't care to argue with the bitch. This was exclusively between him and Thelma.

When they reached the clearing at the top of the hill, the smell of humus from the undergrowth decreased. Fifty yards below was a little fog-enshrouded grove, and behind it a thicket extended all the way to a dense forest, which lay like a wide sea before them. It was a magnificent sight.

"Everyone spread out a little," Ditlev said, and nodded with satisfaction when there were seven or eight yards between each of them.

The noise of the beaters in the grove wasn't loud enough yet. Just a few of the released pheasants had taken flight before softly gliding back into the undergrowth. The footfalls of the hunters near Ditlev were muted but expectant. Some of the men were thoroughly addicted to the kick they got out there in the morning fog. Squeezing the trigger could satisfy them for days. They earned millions, but it was the killing that made them feel alive.

Young Saxenholdt, pale with agitation, walked at Ditlev's side. His father had been the same, back when he was a regular participant in the hunts. The son walked cautiously, his sights set on the grove, the thicket behind it, and the forest a few hundred yards farther ahead, knowing full well that a good shot could reward him with a love nest his parents would have no control over.

Ditlev held up his hand, and everyone stopped. Hjorth's bird dog whined and spun around with excitement while its dolt of a master tried to shush it. Just as he'd expected.

Then the first birds flapped up from the grove and there was a volley of gunfire followed by the thud of dead fowl hitting the ground. Hjorth could no longer manage his dog. When the man beside him shouted "Fetch!" to his hound, Hjorth's ran off, tongue lolling from its mouth. At that moment hundreds of birds flew up at once, and the hunting party ran amok. The gunfire, and the echo it made in the thicket, was deafening.

This was what Ditlev loved: ceaseless gunfire, ceaseless killing, flapping specks in the sky terminated in an orgy of color. The slow drizzle of birds' bodies falling from above. The eagerness of the men to reload their weapons. He detected Saxenholdt's frustration at not being able to shoot along with those who carried shotguns. His glance shifted from the grove, to the edge of the forest, and then across the flat, thicket-overgrown terrain. Where would his quarry come from? He didn't know. The more bloodthirsty the hunters became, the tighter he held his rifle.

Hjorth's dog suddenly leaped for the throat of another dog, which let go of its quarry and retreated, whining. Everyone except Hjorth noticed. Having yet to score a kill, he continued to reload and fire, reload and fire.

When Hjorth's hound returned with a third bird and again snapped its jaws at the other dogs, Ditlev nodded to Torsten, who was already watching. The combination of its muscle, instinct, and lousy training were terrible traits in a hunting dog.

Everything happened just as Ditlev had predicted. The other dogs had caught on and no longer let Hjorth's dog retrieve the birds falling in the clearing, and so it disappeared into the forest to ferret out what it could.

"Take care now," Ditlev called to the two

riflemen. "Remember, there's a fully furnished flat in Berlin at stake." Laughing, he discharged both chambers at a new flock that soared from the hedgerow. "The best shot wins the big prize."

At that point, Hjorth's hound was just trotting out of the dark underbrush with another bird. A single shot from Torsten's rifle felled the animal before it reached the open. Probably only Ditlev and Torsten had seen what happened, because the hunters' only reaction to the blast was Saxenholdt's gulping for breath, followed by a chorus of laughter — with Hjorth leading the way — when they thought the rifle shot had missed its mark.

But in a little while, when Hjorth found his dog with a hole in its cranium, the laughter would come to an end, and hopefully he'd have learned his lesson. There would be no poorly trained dogs on their hunts when Ditlev Pram said so.

Ditlev caught Krum shaking his head at the same moment they heard new sounds emerging from the thicket behind the grove. So he, too, must have seen Torsten kill the dog.

"Don't shoot until you're certain, understand?" he quietly told the men at his side. "The beaters cover the entire area behind the grove, so I imagine the animal will come out of the thicket down there." He pointed at some towering junipers. "Aim a yard or so above the ground, directly at the target's midsection. In that way a missed shot will hit the ground."

"What is that?" whispered Saxenholdt, nodding at a cluster of overgrown trees that had suddenly begun to shake. There was the sound of crackling twigs, faint at first, then stronger, and the beaters' shouts behind the creature grew more and more shrill.

And then it jumped.

Saxenholdt and Torsten fired simultaneously, and the dark silhouette stumbled a little to one side before bounding clumsily forward. Not until it was out in the open could they see what it was. Everyone cheered as Saxenholdt and Torsten sighted their weapons for another round.

"Stop!" Ditlev shouted as the ostrich halted and glanced around, disoriented. It was about a hundred yards away. "Shoot it in the head this time," he said. "One shot at a time. You go first, Saxenholdt."

The hunters stood still as the lad, holding his breath, raised his rifle and fired. The shot was a little low, so the animal's neck was torn off at once and its head disappeared backward. But the crowd roared its approval, including Torsten. What use did he have for a three-bedroom flat in Berlin, anyway?

Ditlev smiled. He had expected the animal to drop to the ground, but for a few seconds it ran about, headless, until the uneven terrain made the dead body topple. There it lay, twitching momentarily before its head sank to the ground. All in all, it was quite a sight.

"Bloody hell!" the young man groaned as the group fired a few salvos at the remaining pheasants. "An ostrich, I've shot a fucking ostrich! I'm getting some pussy tonight at Victor's Bar. And I know exactly whose."

The three of them met at the inn and were given the drink Ditlev had ordered. It was clear that Torsten needed it.

"What's wrong, Torsten? You look like shit," Ulrik said, swallowing the Jägermeister in one gulp. "Are you angry that you didn't win? You've shot ostriches before, for Christ's sake."

Torsten spun his glass a few times. "It's Kimmie. It's serious now." Then he drank.

Ulrik poured another round and toasted them. "Aalbæk is on the case. We'll get her soon. Relax, Torsten."

Torsten Florin pulled a box of matches from his pocket and lit a candle that was on the table. There's nothing sadder than a candle without flame, as he often said. "I hope you're not assuming that Kimmie is just some silly little woman walking around in dirty old rags, waiting for your daft private detective to find her. He won't, Ulrik. For God's sake, it's Kimmie we're talking about. You know her. They won't find her, and it's a problem that'll cost us dearly. Do you understand that?"

Ditlev set his glass down and glanced up at the inn's rafters. "What do you mean?" He hated Torsten when he was like that.

"She attacked one of our models in front of the fashion house yesterday. She'd waited for hours. There were eighteen cigarette butts stamped out on the pavement. Who do you think she was waiting for?"

"What do you mean by 'attacked'?" Ulrik seemed worried.

Torsten shook his head. "Take it easy, Ulrik. It wasn't all that bad, just a single punch. The police weren't called in. I gave the girl a week off and a pair of tickets to Kraków."

"Are you sure it was her?"

"Yes. I showed the girl an old picture of Kimmie."

"No doubt?"

"No." Torsten looked irritated now.

"We can't allow Kimmie to be apprehended," Ulrik said.

"You're bloody right we can't. And we can't have her getting close to us, either, now, can we? She's capable of anything, I'm sure."

"Do you think she still has the money?" Ulrik asked as a waiter stopped by, wanting to know if there was anything he could bring them.

Ditlev nodded at the man, still drowsy at this early hour of the day. "We have everything we need, thank you," he said.

They were silent until the waiter bowed and left the room.

"Oh, for God's sake, Ulrik. How much did she get off us back then? It was almost two million. How much do you think she spends on the street?" Torsten sneered at him. "Nothing. That means for sure she has enough money to buy whatever she wants. Even weapons. If she hangs out in the inner city, there are plenty to choose from, I know."

Ulrik's bulky frame began to fidget. "Maybe we should reinforce Aalbæk's team."

10

"Who did you say you wished to speak to? Assistant Detective el-Assad? Is that what you said?" Carl glanced at the handset. Assistant Detective el-Assad?! That was one hell of a promotion.

He transferred the call and, a second later, heard the telephone ringing on Assad's desk.

"Yes?" Assad replied, in his broom closet.

Carl raised his eyebrows and shook his head. Assistant Detective el-Assad. How dare he?

"Holbæk Police called to say they searched for the Rørvig murder file all morning." Assad stood in Carl's doorway, scratching the stubble on his dimple. They had been studying files now for two days, and he looked pretty knackered. "And do you know what then? They just don't have it anymore. It's blown away with the wind."

Carl sighed. "So let us assume someone removed it, OK? I wonder if it was that Arne fellow, the one who gave Martha Jørgensen the gray folder with reports about the murders? Did you ask whether they could remember what color it was? Did you ask if it was gray?"

Assad shook his head.

"Oh, well, it's not important. The man who took it is dead, according to Martha, so we can't talk to him anyway." Carl's eyes narrowed. "And there's something else I'd like you to answer honestly, Assad: can you please tell me when you were promoted to assistant detective? You should be really careful, going around impersonating a police officer. There's a section of the criminal code that is very strict on this point, actually. Section 131, if you would like to know. You could get six months in prison."

At this, Assad tilted his head back slightly. "Assistant detective?" he said, holding his breath for a second. He raised both hands to his chest as if to protest his innocence, which was draining from him at that moment. Carl had not seen such indignation since the prime minister's reaction to press allegations that Danish soldiers had indirectly participated in torture in Afghanistan.

"That would never occur to me," Assad said. "On the contrary, so. I have said I am assistant assistant detective. People don't listen properly, Carl." He dropped his hands to his side. "Is that my fault?"

Assistant assistant detective! God in heaven! This sort of thing could give a man an ulcer.

"It would probably be more accurate if you called yourself assistant detective vice-superintendent or, even better, assistant police vice-superintendent. But if you must use that title, then it's OK with me. Just make sure you enunciate it very clearly, do you understand? Now go to the car park and bring the old banger round. We're going to Rørvig."

The summer cottage was in the center of a cluster of pine trees. Over the years, it had slowly chewed itself into the sand. To judge from the windows, no one had stayed here since the murders. Broad, opaque surfaces showed between decaying beams. A depressing scene.

They looked up and down the tire tracks that wound their way among the other cottages in the area. This late in September, of course, there wasn't a soul for miles.

Assad shielded his eyes with his hands and tried in vain to peer through the largest of the windows.

"Come on, Assad," Carl said. "The key is supposed to be hanging back here."

He stared up under the eaves at the rear of the cottage. For twenty years the key had been hanging where everyone could see it — on a rusty nail right above the kitchen window, precisely where Martha Jørgensen's friend Yvette had said it would be. But then again, who would have taken it? Who would wish to enter the house? And the burglars who ravaged these summer cottages every single year during the off-season would have to be blind not to notice there was nothing to find here. Everything about the cottage signaled that one might as well just turn around and leave.

He reached for the key and unlocked the door. It surprised him how easily the old lock turned and the door yielded.

He stuck his head inside and recognized the stench of days past: mold, mustiness, and abandonment, the smell that inhabits old people's bedrooms.

Carl felt around for the light switch in the small entryway and found the electricity had been disconnected.

"Here," Assad said, waving a halogen torch in Carl's face.

"Put that away, Assad. We don't need it."

But Assad had already stepped back into

the past, the cone of light dancing from side to side above wooden settle beds painted in old-fashioned colors and traditional blue enamel kitchenware.

It wasn't entirely dark in the cottage. Weak gray sunlight managed to penetrate the dusty windows, making the room look like a night scene from an old black-and-white film. A large stone fireplace. Swedish rag rugs criss-crossing broad wooden floorboards. And then there was the Trivial Pursuit game, still resting on the floor.

"Just as it says in the report," Assad said, tapping the Trivial Pursuit box. At one time it had been navy blue, but now it was black. The board itself was not quite so filthy, but almost, as were the two pie game pieces still lying on it. In the heat of the struggle the pies had been knocked from their squares, but probably not significantly. The pink pie had four wedges, while the brown pie had none. Carl guessed that the pink pie was the girl's. If so, she'd no doubt had a clearer head than her brother that day. Perhaps he'd drunk too much cognac. The autopsy report suggested as much.

"It's been here since 1987. Is the game really that old, Carl? I can't believe it."

"Maybe it took a few years before it made

its way to Syria. Can you actually buy it in Syria?"

He noticed how quiet Assad had become, and then glanced at the two boxes filled with question cards. A single, loose card lay in front of each box. The final questions the siblings answered in life. It was rather sad, when you thought about it.

Carl let his eyes wander across the floor.

Obvious traces of the murders were still visible. There were dark stains where the girl had been found. It was clearly blood, as were the dark specks on the game board. In a few places he could see the crime-scene techs' circles around fingerprints, though the numbers accompanying each circle had faded. And he could barely make out the powder used by the forensics team, but that was understandable.

"They didn't find anything," Carl said to himself.

"What?"

"They didn't find any fingerprints that couldn't be traced back to the siblings or their father and mother." He looked at the board again. "It's strange that the game is still here. I would have thought the crime-scene techs would've taken it with them for closer examination."

"Yes." Assad nodded, tapping his forehead. "Well put, Carl. I remember it now. The game was actually presented in the prosecution of Bjarne Thøgersen, so they *did* take it with them then."

They both stared at the game.

What was it doing here?

Carl frowned. Then he pulled his mobile from his pocket and called headquarters.

Lis didn't sound terribly excited. "We've been expressly notified that we're no longer at your disposal, Carl. Do you have any idea how busy we are? Have you heard about the police reforms? Or should I jog your memory? And now you're stealing Rose from us."

That one they could damned well keep, if it was any help.

"Hey now, hold on a minute. It's me! Carl! Take it easy, OK?"

"You've got your own little slave now, so why don't you talk to her? One moment, please . . ."

He looked confusedly at his mobile and didn't return it to his ear until he heard an easily recognizable voice on the other end.

"How can I help you, boss?"

Carl furrowed his brow again. "Oh, who is this? Rose Knudsen?"

Her hoarse laughter could make anyone worry about the future.

He asked her to find out if a blue Genus Edition of Trivial Pursuit was still among the articles taken from the Rørvig murder. And no, he didn't have a clue where she should search. And yes, possibilities abounded. Whom should she ask first? She would have to figure that out on her own — just as long as she was quick about it.

"Who was that, Carl?" Assad asked.

"It was your competitor, Assad. Be careful she doesn't nudge you back to wearing green rubber gloves and driving a mop bucket."

But Assad wasn't listening. He'd already squatted down to inspect the blood splatter on the game board.

"Isn't it strange there isn't more blood on the board, Carl? After all, she was beaten to death right here," he said, pointing at the stain on the rag rug beside him.

Carl pictured the bodies in the crime-scene photographs he'd seen earlier at headquarters. "Yes," he said, and nodded. "You're absolutely right."

She'd been struck so many times, and had lost so much blood, yet there was very little of it on the game board. Christ, it was a shame they hadn't brought the case file with them so they could compare the photographs with the scene of the crime.

"As I remember, there was a lot of blood on the board in the photos," Assad said as he poked the hexagonal mark at the board's center.

Carl kneeled beside him, carefully inserted a finger under the board and lifted it. Sure enough, it'd been moved a tad. Contrary to the laws of nature, additional splatters of blood had stained the floor an inch or so in under the board.

"It's not the same game, Assad."

"No, I don't think so, also."

Carl gingerly let the board fall back to the floor and then cast a glance at the box and the light outline of fingerprint powder around it. Twenty years ago it'd been a shiny box. The powder could be just about anything, now that he really saw it. Flour, white lead — anything.

"I wonder who put that game here then," Assad said. "Do you know the game, Carl?"

Carl didn't respond.

He was looking at the shelves bordering the room, just below the ceiling, where Eiffel Towers of nickel and Bavarian steins with pewter lids recalled a time when such objects were typically brought home from travels abroad as trophies. At least a hundred souvenirs bore witness to a family with a caravan and familiarity with the Brenner

Pass and the wild forests of Harzen. Carl pictured his father, who would have gone into nostalgia overdrive.

"What are you looking for, Carl?"

"I don't know." He shook his head. "But something tells me we ought to pay close attention. Can you open the windows, Assad? We need more light."

Carl stood up and once more studied the entire floor surface while his hand searched his breast pocket for his pack of cigarettes and Assad banged on a window frame.

Except for the fact that the bodies were gone, and that someone had tampered with the game, everything was apparently as it had been.

As he lit his fag his mobile rang. It was Rose.

The game was in the archives at Holbæk, she said. The file was gone, but the game was still there.

So she wasn't completely hopeless after all.

"Call them again," Carl said, inhaling a deep drag of smoke into his lungs. "Ask them about the pies and wedges."

"Wedges?"

"Yes, that's what they call the tiny thing-amabobs you get when you answer correctly. You put them in the pies. Just ask them which wedges are in which pie. Note which, pie for pie."

"Pies?"

"Yes, damn it. They're also called wheels. Wheels or pies, it's all the same thing. The round pieces that the small triangles fit into. Don't you know Trivial Pursuit?"

She emitted that ominous laughter again. "Trivial Pursuit? Today, in Denmark, it's called Bezzerwizzer, Gramps!" Then she hung up.

They would never be best friends.

He took another puff to calm his racing pulse. Maybe he could exchange Rose for Lis. Lis probably wouldn't mind gearing down to his speed. Punk hair or not, she sure would be a major aesthetic improvement to the basement, next to the photos of Assad's aunts.

At that moment the extraordinary sound of splintering wood and breaking glass was followed by a few of Assad's foreign phrases that clearly had nothing to do with afternoon prayers. But the shattered window had quite a stunning effect: light poured into every nook and cranny, leaving no doubt that spiders had lived like kings in this house. Cobwebs hung like festoons from the ceiling; on the long shelves, souvenirs sat in dust so thick that all colors melded into one.

Carl and Assad went through the events they'd read about in the reports.

In the early-afternoon hours someone entered the house via the open kitchen door and killed the boy with a single blow from a hammer, which was later found a few hundred yards away. The boy probably never felt a thing. Both the coroner's report and the autopsy indicated he died on the scene. His rigid grip on the cognac bottle attested to that.

The girl had certainly tried to get away, but the attackers had gotten to her first. Then she'd been pummeled to death, exactly where the dark stains were on the rug — which was where they'd also found the remains of the victim's brain mass, spit, urine, and blood.

The investigators had presumed that the killers had removed the young man's bathing trunks in order to humiliate him. The trunks were never found, but the notion that the siblings had been playing Trivial Pursuit with the girl in her bikini and the boy naked had never been a credible one. An incestuous relationship was absolutely unimaginable. Each had a sweetheart, and each lived a harmonious life.

The brother's and sister's sweethearts had

slept over with them in the cottage the night before the assault, but in the morning had driven to Holbæk, where they attended school. They were never suspects. They had alibis. Besides, they were completely devastated by the murders.

His mobile rang again. Carl glanced at the number on the display and fortified himself by taking another deep drag from his cigarette. "Yes, Rose."

"They thought your question about pies and wedges was very strange."

"And?"

"Well, they had to go look, didn't they?"

"And?"

"The pink pie had four wedges. A yellow, a pink, a green, and a blue."

Carl glanced down at the pie. That was what he had at his end, too.

"The blue, yellow, green, and orange pies weren't used. They were in the box with the rest of the wedges, and they were empty."

"OK. What about the brown pie?"

"The brown pie had a brown and a pink wedge in it. You following me?"

Carl didn't respond. He just looked down at the empty brown pie sitting on the board. How very odd. "Thanks, Rose," he said. "Well done."

"What's new, Carl?" Assad asked. "What

did she say?"

"There should be a brown and a pink thingamajig in the brown pie, Assad. But it's empty."

They both stared at it.

"Should we be looking for the two small thingies that are missing, I wonder, then?" Assad said. He bent down and peered under an oak bench that was pushed up against the wall.

Carl drew yet another deep pull of smoke into his lungs. Why had someone replaced the original Trivial Pursuit game with this one? It was so obvious that something was off. And why was the locked kitchen door so easy to open after all these years? Why had this case been tossed on his basement desk in the first place? Who was behind it?

"They celebrated Christmas in the cottage once," Assad said. "That must have been cold then." He yanked a festive paper heart from the depths under the bench.

Carl nodded. It couldn't have been colder in this house than it felt now. Everything in it was saturated with the tragedy of the past. Who was even left from that time? An old woman who would soon die of a tumor in her brain, that was about it.

He focused on the panel doors leading to the bedrooms. *Father, mother, and child we see. Count them quickly: one, two, three.* He peeked into each room, one after the other. As expected, he saw the usual pine beds and small night tables draped with what resembled remnants of checkered tablecloths. The girl's room was adorned with posters of Duran Duran and Wham!, the boy's with Suzy Quatro wearing tight black leather. In these bedrooms, beneath the sheets, the future had seemed bright and infinite. And in the living room behind him, that future had been brutally torn from them. Which meant that he was standing on the very axis upon which life revolved.

The threshold where hope had met reality.

"There's still alcohol in the cupboards, Carl," Assad called out from the kitchen. So there had been no burglars in the house, in any case.

Observing the house from the outside, a strange unease came over Carl. This case was like grabbing at quicksilver: poisonous to touch, impossible to hold. Liquid and solid at the same time. The many years that had passed. The man who'd turned himself in. The gang formed at school, now roaming the upper echelons of society.

What did he and Assad have to go on? Why bother continuing at all? he asked himself, turning toward his partner. "I think we should give the case a rest, Assad. C'mon, let's go."

He kicked at a tuft of grass in the sand and pulled out his car keys to emphasize his decision. But Assad didn't follow. He simply stood there, gazing at the living room's smashed window as if he'd opened the route to a holy place.

"I don't know, Carl. We are then the only ones who can do anything for the victims now, do you realize that?"

Do anything for, Assad had said, as though somewhere inside of him, his Middle Eastern soul had a lifeline to the past.

Carl nodded. "I don't think we'll find anything else out here," he said, "but let's head up the road a little way." He lit another fag. Breathing fresh air through puffs of cigarette was simply the best.

They walked for a few minutes against a soft breeze that carried the scent of early autumn, until they came to a summer cottage from which they heard sounds indicating that the last retiree hadn't yet retreated to his winter abode.

"That's right, there aren't many of us left up here now, but it's only Friday, you know," said a ruddy man who they found behind the cottage, wearing a belt hitched all the way up to his chest. "Just come back tomorrow. Saturdays and Sundays it's teeming with people around here, and it'll be like that for at least another month."

Then, when he caught sight of Carl's badge, his mouth began to run. Everything gushed out in one long litany: thefts, drowned Germans, speed demons down around Vig.

As though the old geezer had been trapped in an extended Robinson Crusoe–like state of silence, Carl thought.

At this point Assad seized the man's arm. "Was it you, then, who killed the two children in the house down on that road called Ved Hegnet?"

He was an old man. In the middle of a breath, he seemed to shut down. He stopped blinking and his eyes glossed over like a dead man's; his lips parted and turned blue, and he couldn't even bring his hands to his chest. He simply stumbled backward, and Carl had to leap to his assistance.

"Good God Almighty, Assad! What the fuck do you think you're doing?" was the last thing Carl said before loosening the man's belt and collar.

Ten minutes passed before the old man recovered. In all that time his wife — who'd hurried in from the scullery — didn't utter a single peep. They were ten very long minutes.

"Please, please excuse my partner," Carl said to the stunned man. "He's here on an Iraqi-Danish police-exchange program and doesn't understand all the nuances of the Danish language. Sometimes our methods are at loggerheads."

Assad said nothing. Perhaps the word "loggerheads" threw him off.

"I remember the case," the man said at last, following a few squeezes from his wife and three minutes of deep breathing. "It was terrible. But if you want to ask someone about it, then ask Valdemar Florin. He lives here on Flyndersøvej. Just fifty yards farther, on the right. You can't miss the sign."

"Why did you say that about the Iraqi police, Carl?" Assad asked, chucking a stone into the water.

Carl ignored him and stared instead at Valdemar Florin's residence, which towered above the hill. Back in the eighties, that bungalow had been a regular feature in the weekly magazines. This was where the jet set came to let their hair down. Legendary parties where anything went. Rumors circulated that whoever tried to match Florin's parties would have a mortal enemy for life.

Valdemar Florin had always been an uncompromising man. He trod a fine line at the edge of the law, but for inscrutable reasons had never been arrested. Granted, he'd been involved in a few settlements over rights and sexual harassment of young girls in his workplace, but that was it. When it came to business, Florin was a jack-of-all-trades. Buildings, weapons systems, colossal pallets of emergency foodstuffs, sudden ventures in the Rotterdam oil market; he could do everything.

But that was all history now. When his wife, Beate, killed herself, Valdemar Florin lost his grip on the rich and beautiful. From one day to the next, his houses in Rørvig and Vedbæk became fortresses no one wished to frequent. Everyone knew he was into very young girls and had driven his wife to suicide. Even in those circles something like this was unforgivable.

"Why, Carl?" Assad repeated. "Why did you say that about the Iraqi police?"

Carl looked at his diminutive partner. Beneath his brown skin his cheeks were flushed, though it was unclear whether it was from indignation or the cold breeze from Skansehage.

"Assad, you cannot threaten anyone with those kinds of questions. How could you

120

accuse the old man of something he so clearly hadn't done? What good did it do?"

"You've done that yourself."

"Let's leave it at that, shall we?"

"And the Iraqi police, what about that?"

"Forget it, Assad. I made it up." But when they were shown into Valdemar Florin's living room, he could feel Assad's eyes on his neck, and he filed this in the back of his mind.

Valdemar Florin was sitting in front of his panorama window, from which they could see across Flyndersøvej and farther out in an almost endless view across Hesselø Bay. Behind him, four double glass doors opened onto a sandstone terrace and a swimming pool that lay in the middle of the garden like a dried-up, desert reservoir. At one time this place had buzzed with activity. Even members of the royal family had visited.

Florin sat calmly reading a book. His legs rested on a footstool, there was a fire in the woodstove, and a dram on the marble table. All told it was a very tranquil scene, if one disregarded the many, many book pages spread across the wool carpet.

Carl cleared his throat a couple of times, but the old financier kept his concentration trained on his book, and didn't turn his attention to them until he'd finished the page, torn it out, and tossed it on the floor with the others.

"That way, I know how far I've got," he said. "To whom do I owe the pleasure?"

Assad glanced at Carl, eyebrows quivering. There were some idioms he still could not immediately process.

When Carl showed him his badge, Valdemar Florin's smile vanished. And when Carl explained that they were from the Copenhagen Police, and why they were there, he asked them to leave.

He was close to seventy-five years old, and still the thin, arrogant weasel that snapped at people. But behind his bright eyes was a latent, easily roused peevishness itching to get out. It just needed a little encouragement, then it had free reign.

"Yes, we've come unannounced, Mr. Florin, and if you wish us to go, we will. I have enormous respect for you, so naturally I will do as you request. If it suits you better, I can also return early tomorrow."

Somewhere behind Florin's armor a reaction flickered. Carl had just given him what everyone wishes for. To hell with caressing people, flattering them, and showering them with gifts. The only thing people really long for is respect. Give your fellow humans respect and they'll dance, his teacher at the police academy had said. Bloody right.

"I don't fall for compliments," the man said. But he had.

"May we sit, Mr. Florin? Just for five minutes?"

"What is this about?"

"Do you believe Bjarne Thøgersen acted alone when he killed the Jørgensen siblings back in 1987? Someone is making a different claim, you should know. Your son is not a suspect, but a few of his companions could be."

One of Florin's nostrils flared as if he were about to mutter a curse, but instead he threw the rest of his book on the table.

"Helen," he called over his shoulder. "Fetch me another whisky." He lit an Egyptian cigarette without offering them one.

"Who? Who claims what?" he said with a peculiar alertness in his voice.

"I'm afraid I can't tell you. But it seems pretty evident that Bjarne Thøgersen wasn't alone."

"Oh, that little nobody." His tone of voice was scornful, but he didn't elaborate.

A girl of about twenty entered the room wearing a white pinafore over a black uniform. She poured whisky and water as if it were something she did perpetually. She didn't acknowledge their presence.

When she slipped around behind him her hand brushed through Florin's thin hair. She'd been trained well.

"Quite honestly," Florin said as he sipped, "I would like to offer my assistance, but it has been a long time, and I think it's better to let the case rest."

Carl disagreed. "Did you know your son's friends, Mr. Florin?"

A crooked smile spread over Florin's face. "You are so young, but I can tell you, if you didn't already know, that I was rather busy back then. So no, I didn't know them. They were just some youths Torsten had met at boarding school."

"Did it surprise you that they were suspects? I mean, they were nice young people, right? They all came from good homes."

"I don't know if it bloody surprised me or not." He squinted at Carl over the rim of his glass. They had seen a great deal, those eyes. Including challenges far greater than Carl Mørck.

He set his glass down. "But during the investigation back in 1987, a few of them stood out," he said.

"What do you mean?"

"Well, my lawyer and I made certain we

were present at Holbæk Police Station when the young men were interrogated. My lawyer acted for all six of them throughout the investigation."

"Bent Krum, right?"

Assad had asked the question, but Valdemar Florin gazed straight through him.

Carl nodded to Assad. Bull's-eye. " 'Stood out,' you said. Who do you think stood out during the hearing?"

"Perhaps you should call Bent Krum instead and ask him, since you know him. He still has an excellent memory, I'm told."

"Is that so? Who says?"

"He's still my son's lawyer. And Ditlev Pram's and Ulrik's."

"I thought you said you didn't know the youths, Mr. Florin. But still you name Ditlev Pram and Ulrik Dybbøl Jensen in such a way that one might believe otherwise."

He nodded curtly. "I knew their fathers. That's how it was."

"And Kristian Wolf and Kirsten-Marie Lassen — did you know their fathers, too?"

"Barely."

"And Bjarne Thøgersen's?"

"An insignificant man. Didn't know him."

"He owned a lumberyard in northern Zealand," Assad interjected.

Carl nodded. He remembered that himself, actually.

"Listen," Valdemar Florin said, staring through the skylights at the crystal-clear sky. "Kristian Wolf is dead, OK? Kimmie disappeared and has been missing for years. My son says she wanders around the streets of Copenhagen, toting a suitcase. Bjarne Thøgersen is in jail. What the hell are we discussing?"

"Kimmie? Kirsten-Marie Lassen, is that who you're talking about? Is that what she's called?"

He didn't respond. Simply took another sip and reached for his book. The audience was over.

When they left the house, they could see Florin through the veranda windows as he slammed his mistreated book on the table and reached for the telephone. He seemed angry. Maybe he was warning his lawyer that they might turn up. Or calling Securitas to find out if they sold a warning system that ensured guests like them were rejected at the gate.

"He knew all kinds of things, Carl," Assad said.

"Yes, perhaps. With people like him it's hard to tell. They've been taught their entire lives to be careful what they say. Did you know Kimmie was living on the street?"

"No, it's not noted anywhere in the files."

"We need to find her."

"Yes. But we could talk to the others first, couldn't we?"

"Yes, maybe." Carl gazed across the water. Of course they should talk to all of them. "But when a woman like Kimmie Lassen turns her back on her rich family and ends up on the street, there's a reason. Those kinds of people could have unusually deep wounds that are well worth poking, Assad. So we need to find her."

When they got to the car by the summer cottage, Assad pondered things for a moment. "I don't understand the part about that Trivial game, Carl."

Great minds think alike, Carl thought. He said: "We'll make another pass through the cottage, Assad. I was just about to suggest it. In any event, we have to bring the game home to have it examined for fingerprints."

This time they inspected everything. The outbuildings, the garden behind the house where weeds were a yard high, the storage hut that housed the gas flasks.

By the time they returned to the living room, they had made no progress.

127

As Assad dropped to his knees again to search for the two wedges missing from the brown pie, Carl scanned the souvenir shelves and all the furniture.

Finally his attention settled on the pies and the Trivial Pursuit board.

It was obvious that one should take another look at the pies lying there on the central hexagon. Tiny flashes of a larger picture. One pie containing exactly the wedges it should, the other with two missing. A pink and a brown.

Then it dawned on him.

"Here's another Christmas heart," Assad mumbled, pulling it from under a corner of the rug.

But Carl said nothing. He bent over slowly and picked up the cards that lay in front of the card boxes. Two cards with six questions each, each question marked with a color corresponding to the colors of the wedges.

At this moment he cared only about the brown and pink questions.

He flipped the cards over and looked at the answers.

He felt as though he'd just taken a giant leap, causing him to heave a deep sigh. "Here. I've got something, Assad," he said as quietly and as composed as he possibly could. "Have a look."

With Christmas heart in hand, Assad rose and peered over Carl's shoulder at the cards. "What?"

"A pink and a brown wedge were missing, right?" He gave one card to Assad, then the other. "Look at what's been written over the pink answer on this card and the brown answer on this one. What do they say?"

"It says 'Arne Jacobsen' on the one card and 'Johan Jacobsen' on the other."

They stared at each other a moment.

"Arne? The same name as the police officer who took the file from Holbæk and gave it to Martha Jørgensen. What was his surname? Do you recall?"

Assad's eyebrows shot up. He lifted his notebook from his breast pocket and skimmed his notes until he found the conversation with Martha Jørgensen.

Then he whispered a few unintelligible words and glanced up. "No, she didn't give a surname."

He whispered a few more words in Arabic and looked down at the game. "If Arne Jacobsen is a policeman, who is the other one then?"

Carl got his mobile out and phoned Holbæk Station.

"Arne Jacobsen?" the duty officer said.

129

No, he'd better talk to one of their older colleagues. It took him a moment to transfer the call.

After that, only three minutes passed.

Then Carl clapped his mobile shut.

11

It often happens the day a man turns forty. Or the day he earns his first million. Or, at the very least, when the day comes where his father retires to a life of crossword puzzles. On that day, most men will know what it's like to finally be free of patriarchal condescension, overbearing comments, and critical glares.

But that's not how things had gone for Torsten Florin.

He had more money than his father and had distanced himself from his four younger siblings, who, unlike him, hadn't managed to make anything significant of themselves. He had even been on television and in the newspapers more often than his father. All of Denmark knew him. He was admired, especially by the women his father had always hankered after.

Yet whenever he heard his father's voice on the telephone, he still felt awful. Like a difficult child, inferior and scorned. It gave him this indefinable knot in his stomach that would only disappear if he slammed the phone down.

But Torsten didn't slam the phone down. Never when it was his father.

And after such a conversation, no matter how short, it was nearly impossible for Torsten to drive the anger and frustration from his body.

"The eldest child's lot," was how the only decent teacher at boarding school had once put it, and Torsten had hated him for it. For if it were true, how could a man change anything? The question had occupied his thoughts day after day. Ulrik and Kristian had felt the same way.

This painful, shared hatred of their fathers had united them. And when Torsten helped beat their blameless victims to a pulp or twisted the necks of his teacher's carrier pigeons — or later in life, when he gazed into a competitor's horrified eyes just as they realized he'd created another new, unsurpassed collection — his thoughts turned toward his father.

"Bloody arsehole," he said, trembling, when his father hung up. "Bloody arsehole," he hissed to his diplomas and the myriad hunting trophies mounted on the walls. Had it not been for the designers, his chief purchaser, and four-fifths of the firm's best clients and competitors in the adjacent room, he would have bellowed out his rage. Instead, he grabbed the old yardstick he'd been given on the fifth anniversary of the firm's founding and smashed it into the mounted head of a chamois.

"Arsehole, arsehole, arsehole!" he whispered fiercely, hacking the small goat-antelope trophy again and again.

When he noticed the sweat gathering at the nape of his neck, he stopped and tried to think clearly. His father's voice and what he'd told him filled his mind more than was healthy.

Torsten looked up. Outside, where the forest met the garden, a few hungry magpies flitted about. They cawed cheerfully while pecking at the carcasses of birds that earlier had felt his wrath.

Fucking birds, he thought, and knew that now he was growing calmer. He lifted his bow from the wall hook, grabbed a few arrows from the quiver behind his desk, opened the terrace door, and shot at the birds.

By the time their chattering had quieted, the rush of anger burning inside his head had vanished. It worked every time.

He walked across the lawn, pulled the arrows from the birds, kicked the cadavers into the forest with the others, went back to his office, listened in on his guests' ceaseless jabber, hung his bow back on its hook, and tossed the arrows back in the quiver. Only then did he phone Ditlev.

"The police were up in Rørvig talking to my father," was the first thing he said when Ditlev answered.

There was a moment of silence on the other end. "OK," Ditlev replied, emphasizing the last syllable. "What did they want?"

Torsten breathed deeply. "They wanted to know about the brother and sister up at Dybesø. Nothing specific. If the old fool understood correctly, someone contacted the police and sowed doubt on Bjarne's guilt."

"Kimmie?"

"I don't know, Ditlev. As I recall, they didn't say who."

"Warn Bjarne, OK? Immediately. What else?"

"Dad suggested the police contact Krum."

The laughter on the other end of the line was classic Ditlev: totally ice-cold. "Krum? They won't get anything out of him," he said.

"No. But apparently they've begun some

sort of investigation, and that's bad enough."

"Were they from Holbæk Police?" Ditlev asked.

"I don't think so. The old man thought they were from Copenhagen's Homicide Division."

"Jesus Christ. Did your father get their names?"

"No. As usual, the arrogant bastard wasn't listening. But Krum will get them."

"Forget it. I'll phone Aalbæk. He knows a couple of blokes at police headquarters."

After the conversation, Torsten sat staring blankly into space for a while as his breathing grew deeper. His brain was permeated with images of terrified people begging for mercy, screaming for help. Memories of blood, and the laughter of the others in the gang. Them all talking about it afterward. Kristian's photo collection that brought them together night after night, smoking until they were high or pumped up with amphetamines. In such moments he recalled everything and he both reveled in it and hated himself for doing so.

He opened his eyes wide to sink back into reality. Typically it took a few minutes for him to get the frenzy of rage out of his bloodstream, but the erotic arousal always remained.

He put his hand to his crotch. His cock was hard again.

Shit! Why couldn't he control these feelings? Why did it continue, on and on?

He locked the door to the adjacent suites, from which the voices of half of Denmark's fashion barons and baronesses could be heard.

He inhaled sharply and sank slowly to his knees.

Then he folded his hands and let his head fall forward. Sometimes it simply felt necessary. "Our Father who art in heaven," he whispered a couple of times. "Forgive me. For I cannot help myself."

12

Ditlev Pram quickly updated Aalbæk on the situation, ignoring the fool's complaints about late nights and lack of manpower. So long as they paid his price, he better just keep his trap shut.

Then he swiveled his office chair and nodded pleasantly at his trusted colleagues around the conference table.

"Excuse me," he said in English. "I have a problem with an old aunt who's always straying from home. This time of year, we obviously need to find her before nightfall."

They smiled agreeably, understanding what he meant. Family comes first. That's how it was where they came from, too.

"Thank you for a good briefing." He smiled broadly. "I'm very pleased that this team has become a reality. Northern Europe's best doctors congregated in one place — could one wish for anything more?" He smacked his palms on the tabletop. "Let's get started, shall we? Will you begin, Stanislav?"

His head of plastic surgery nodded, flicking on the overhead projector. Stanislav showed them a man's face on which lines had been drawn. "We will make incisions here, here, and here," he said. He'd done the procedure before. Five times in Romania and twice in the Ukraine. In every case but one the feeling in the facial nerves had returned startlingly fast. He made it sound uncomplicated. A facelift, he claimed, could now be done with just half the incisions doctors typically used.

"Take a look here," he said, "right at the top of the sideburns. A triangular area is removed and the skin is pulled up and sewn together with only a few stitches. Simple and straightforward."

At this point Ditlev's hospital director interrupted. "We have submitted descriptions of the operation to the journals." He pulled out one American and three European journals. Not the most prestigious, but they were good enough. "It will be published before Christmas. We call the treatment 'The Stanislav Facial Correction.' "

Ditlev nodded. There was bound to be a great deal of money in this, and they were smart, these people. Ultra-professional

138

scalpel technicians. Each earned a salary equal to that of ten doctors in their homeland. It didn't make them feel guilty, and in that way all those present were equals: Ditlev, who made money from their labor; and the doctors, who made money from everyone else. An unusually advantageous hierarchy, especially since he was the one at the top. And right now he was objectively calculating that one failed operation out of seven was completely unacceptable. Ditlev avoided unnecessary risk. His time at boarding school had taught him that. If you were headed into a shitty situation, you steered clear of it. For that reason he was about to reject the entire project and fire his director for having submitted the articles for publication without his approval, and it was for the same reason that, deep down, he couldn't think of anything else but Torsten's telephone call.

The intercom behind him beeped. He arched backward to push the button. "Yes, Birgitte?"

"Your wife is on her way."

Ditlev glanced round at the others. The dressing-down would have to wait, and the secretary would have to put a stop to the articles.

"Ask Thelma to stay where she is,"

he said. "I'm coming over. We're finished here."

A glass walkway snaked from the clinic a hundred yards across the landscape to the villa, so you could walk through the garden without getting your feet wet and still enjoy the view of the sea and the beech trees. He got the idea from the Louisiana Museum of Modern Art. But at his house, no art adorned the walls.

Thelma was prepared to make a big scene. Just the kind of thing he wouldn't want others to be witness to in his office. Her eyes were full of hate.

"I spoke to Lissan Hjorth," she said bitingly.

"Hmm, that took a while. Weren't you supposed to be with your sister in Aalborg by now?"

"I didn't go to Aalborg, I was in Gothenburg, and not with my sister. You shot her dog, Lissan says."

"What do you mean, 'you'? I assure you, it was an accident. The dog was utterly unmanageable and ran in among the quarry. I'd warned Hjorth. What were you doing in Gothenburg, by the way?"

"It was Torsten who shot the dog."

"Yes, it was Torsten, and he's very sorry.

Should we buy a new pup for Lissan? Is that what this is all about? Now tell me, what were you doing in Gothenburg?"

Shadows fell across her forehead. Only an unusually heated temperament was capable of creating wrinkles in her ridiculously tight facial skin, the result of five facelifts, but Thelma Pram succeeded. "You gave my apartment in Berlin away to that little nobody, Saxenholdt. *My* apartment, Ditlev." She aimed a finger at him. "That was your last hunt, do you hear me?"

He approached her. It was the only way he could get her to step back. "You never used that apartment anyway, did you? You couldn't get your lover to go with you, could you?" He smiled. "Aren't you getting a little old for him, Thelma?"

She raised her head, admirably adept at taking insults. "You've no idea what you're saying, you realize that? Did you forget to sic Aalbæk on me this time, since you don't know who he is? Did you, Ditlev, since you don't know who I was in Gothenburg with?" Then she laughed.

Ditlev was stopped in his tracks by the unexpected question.

"It'll be an expensive divorce, Ditlev. You do bizarre things — the kind of things that will cost you when lawyers enter the picture.

Your perverse games with Ulrik and the others. How long do you think I'll keep them secret for nothing?"

He smiled. It was a bluff.

"Don't you think I know what's on your mind right now, Ditlev? *She doesn't dare*, you're thinking. *She has it too good with me.* But no, Ditlev, I've grown away from you. I don't care about you. You can rot in prison for all I care. And you'd have to do without your slaves down in the laundry in the meantime. Do you think you can handle that, Ditlev?"

He stared at her throat. He was well aware how hard he could strike. And he knew where.

Like a civet cat, she sensed it and retreated.

If he were going to strike, he'd have to do it from behind. No one was invincible.

"You're sick in the head, Ditlev," she said. "I've always known that. You used to be sick in a fun way, but not anymore."

"Then get a lawyer, Thelma."

Her smile was like Salome's when she requested that Herod bring John the Baptist's head on a platter.

"And face Bent Krum on the other side of the table? No way, Ditlev. I've got other plans. I'm just waiting for the right opportunity."

"Are you threatening me?"

Her hair was slipping out of her hairband. She thrust her head back and flashed her bare neck, showing him she wasn't afraid of him. Mocking him.

"You think I'm threatening you?" There was fire in her eyes. "I'm not. When I'm ready, I'll pack my clothes and leave. The man I've found is waiting for me. A mature man. You had no idea, did you, Ditlev? But he's older than you. I know my appetites. A boy cannot satisfy them."

"I see. And who is he?"

She smiled haughtily. "Frank Helmond. Quite a surprise, isn't it?"

Several thoughts collided in Ditlev's head.

Kimmie, the police, Thelma, and now Frank Helmond.

Be careful what you're getting involved in, he told himself, and considered for a moment going down to see which of the Filipinas was working the evening shift.

A new cloud of loathing sank over him. Frank Helmond, she'd said. How degrading! A chubby local politician. A member of the underclass. A complete nobody.

He searched for Helmond in Krak's directory and found the address, even though he already knew it. Helmond wasn't one to hide his light under a bushel, as was evident from the address. But that's how the man was, and everyone knew it. Lived in a villa he couldn't afford, in a neighborhood where no one would ever dream of voting for his worthless party.

Ditlev went to his bookshelf, removed a thick volume, and opened it. It was hollow inside, with just enough room for his small plastic bags of cocaine.

The first line blurred the image of Thelma's pinched glare. The second line caused him to straighten his shoulders, look at the telephone, and forget that the word "risk" wasn't in his dictionary. He simply wanted to put a stop to it. Why not do it the right way? Together with Ulrik. In the dark of night.

"Shall we watch movies at your place?" he asked, the very instant Ulrik picked up the receiver. He heard a contented sigh from the other end.

"Do you mean that?" Ulrik asked.

"Are you by yourself?"

"Yes. Damn it, Ditlev, are you serious?" He was already excited.

It was going to be a brilliant evening.

They had seen the film countless times. Life

wouldn't have been the same without it.

The first time they'd watched *A Clockwork Orange* was at boarding school, at the beginning of their second year. A new teacher had misunderstood the school's cultural diversity code and had shown the class both that film and another one called *If*, which was about a rebellion at an English boarding school. The larger theme had been British cinema from the sixties, which, it was believed, was very fitting for a school with British traditions. But no matter how interesting this teacher's choice was, it was also utterly misguided, the school's leadership decided after close scrutiny. The new teacher's career was therefore brief.

The damage was already done, however, because Kimmie and the class's newest pupil, Kristian Wolf, lapped up the films' messages without qualm. Through them they discovered new possibilities for release and revenge.

Kristian was the one who took the lead. Since he was nearly two years older and completely unruly, the entire class looked up to him. He always carried a lot of cash with him, even though it was against school policy. He was always on the lookout, and with great care he selected Ditlev, Bjarne, and Ulrik to be part of his gang. They were all alike in so many ways. They were outsiders, and they were filled with hatred for the school and any authority figure. Yes, that — and *A Clockwork Orange* — glued them together.

They found the film on video and watched it time after time on the sly in Kristian and Ulrik's room. And as a result of this fascination they made a pact. They would be just like the gang in the film. Indifferent to their surroundings. Constantly on the hunt for excitement and ways to transgress. Devil-may-care and merciless.

When they assaulted the boy who caught them smoking hash, everything suddenly came together. Only later did Torsten, with his usual flair for histrionics, suggest they wear masks and gloves.

Ditlev and Ulrik drove from Fredensborg with several lines of cocaine in their veins and the pedal to the metal. Dark sunglasses and long, cheap trench coats. Hats, gloves. Cold, clear heads. Disposable gear for a lively evening under the cloak of anonymity.

"Who are we looking for?" Ulrik asked when they stood before the JFK café's saffron yellow facade on the town square in Hillerød.

"Wait and see," Ditlev said, opening the

door to a rowdy Friday crowd. Noisy people in every corner. Not a bad place to be if you liked jazz and casual company. Ditlev hated both.

They found Helmond in the back. Full face glistening, he was standing in the company of another inferior local politician, gesticulating eagerly under the bar's chandelier. Here, in this public space, they were engaged in their own little crusade.

Ditlev discreetly pointed him out to Ulrik. "It may take a while before he leaves, so let's get a beer and wait," he said, heading to one of the bars farther away.

But Ulrik stood still and observed their prey with enormous pupils behind tinted glasses, obviously quite content with what he saw. His jaw muscles were already quivering.

Ditlev knew him well.

The evening was foggy and mild, and Frank Helmond talked to his companion for a long time outside the café before they finally went off in separate directions. Frank doddered farther up Helsingørsgade, and they followed him at a distance of fifteen yards, knowing that from here to the local police station was two hundred yards at most. Another parameter that made Ulrik pant with lust.

"We'll wait until we reach the alley," Ulrik whispered. "There's a secondhand shop on the left. No one walks through the alley this late."

Farther on, an elderly couple strolled up the fog-shrouded lane, headed toward the end of the street, their shoulders drooping. It was way past their bedtime.

Ditlev wasn't concerned with them in the slightest; that's how the coke operated. Apart from the couple, the street was deserted and conditions were perfect. The pavement was dry. A moist breeze embraced the shopfronts and the three men who were each about to play a role in a carefully orchestrated and thoroughly practiced ritual.

When they were a few yards from Frank Helmond, Ulrik handed Ditlev a mask. By the time they reached him, the latex masks were in place. Had they been at a carnival, people would have smiled at them. Ulrik had a huge cardboard box stuffed with these masks. As he said, they needed a selection to choose from. This time he'd chosen model numbers 20027 and 20048. They could be purchased on the Internet, but Ulrik didn't do that. He brought them home from abroad. The same masks each time, the same numbers. Impossible to trace. Here were just two old men with the deep furrows of life chiselled into their skin. Very lifelike, and quite different from the faces they hid.

As always it was Ditlev who struck first. It was he who made the victim fall sideways slightly with a quiet gasp. Then Ulrik grabbed him and hauled him into the alley.

It was here that Ulrik punched him for the first time. Three direct blows to the forehead and one to the throat. Depending on their strength, the victims were often unconscious by now. But he hadn't landed any hard blows this time. Ditlev had instructed him not to.

They dragged the man's half-limp body, legs splayed, through the alley. When they reached the castle lake ten yards farther ahead, they beat him again. First just light punches to the body, then they got a little rougher. When the paralyzed man realized he was in the process of being killed, tiny, inarticulate sounds began slipping from his mouth. He hadn't really needed to say anything; their victims seldom did. Their eyes usually said it all.

At this point Ditlev's body swelled with pulsing streams of warmth. This is what he sought: wonderful surges of heat. Just like in his childhood, sitting under the sun in his parents' garden, when he was so young the world still seemed made of elements that were benign. Whenever Ditlev reached this point, he had to restrain himself in order not to take the victim's life.

With Ulrik it was different. Death was of little interest to him. It was the vacuum between strength and impotence that drew him, and their present prey found himself in that vacuum right now.

Ulrik straddled the man's motionless body and stared into his eyes through the mask. Then he pulled his Stanley knife from his pocket, holding it in such a way that his enormous hand almost hid it. For a moment it looked as though he was discussing with himself whether or not to follow Ditlev's instructions or ramp it up a notch. Their eyes met through the masks.

I wonder if I look as crazy as he does, Ditlev thought.

Then Ulrik put the knife against the man's throat. Let the dull edge glide back and forth across his arteries. As the man began to hyperventilate, Ulrik ran the blade along his nose and across his trembling eyelids.

This wasn't the cat toying with the mouse — it was worse. The prey wasn't waiting for a chance to escape; it had already resigned itself to its fate.

At last Ditlev nodded calmly to Ulrik and turned his attention toward the man's legs. In a moment, when Ulrik cut his face, he would see them jerk in fright.

And now. Now the leg spasms, this wondrous seizure in which the victim's powerlessness was more evident than ever. Nothing else in Ditlev's life could equal this kick.

He watched blood drip onto the gravel, but Frank Helmond didn't utter a peep. He'd acknowledged his role. Ditlev would give him that.

They left him groaning at the edge of the lake. They'd done a good job. He would survive, but he would be dead inside. It would take years before he dared walk the streets again.

The two Mr. Hydes could go home, and the Dr. Jekylls could reemerge.

By the time he got home to Rungsted, half the night was gone and he was relatively clear-headed. He and Ulrik had cleaned up, thrown their hats, gloves, coats, and sunglasses in the fire and hidden the Stanley knife under a stone in the garden. After that they'd called Torsten and agreed on the course of events for the rest of the evening. Torsten, understandably enough, was livid.

Complained that it hadn't been the right time to do something like that, and they knew he was right. But Ditlev didn't need to apologize to Torsten, nor did he need to beg him. Torsten was well aware that they were all in it together. If one went down, they all went down. It was as simple as that. And if the police drew close, it was just a question of having their alibis ready.

For that reason alone Torsten agreed on the story the other two had concocted: Ditlev and Ulrik had met at JFK in Hillerød fairly late in the evening, and after a single beer they'd headed up to Torsten's in Ejlstrup, arriving at 11 P.M. That was the basis of their alibi. In other words, half an hour before the attack occurred. No one could prove otherwise. Maybe someone had seen them in the bar, but would they remember who was where, when, and for how long? Then the three old friends had drunk cognac up at Torsten's place. Talked about the old days. Nothing special. Just a cozy Friday evening together. That was what they'd say, and what they'd stick to.

Ditlev entered the hallway and confirmed to his satisfaction that the entire house was dark, and that Thelma had retreated to her lair. Then he stood by the fireplace and emptied three snifters of Cypriot brandy, one after the other, so the blissful buzz of his act of revenge could gradually return to a more natural level and he could regain control of his thoughts.

He stepped across the ceramic-tiled kitchen floor to open a tin of caviar, which he could consume while picturing Frank Helmond's terrified face. These tiles were the housekeeper's Achilles heel. Thelma's inspections always ended with a scolding, and no matter how much of an effort the woman made, she could never satisfy Thelma. When it came down to it, who could?

So it was as obvious as blinding sunlight that something was wrong as he stared down at the chequered pattern and discovered the footprints. They weren't large, but they weren't a child's, either. Dirt-smudged.

Ditlev pursed his lips. Stood a moment with his senses on high alert. Yet he detected nothing. Neither smell nor sound. He edged to the knife block and chose the biggest of the Misono knives, which could fillet sushi like no other. It would be very unfortunate for anyone who got in its way.

Carefully he stepped through the double doors into the arboretum, instantly aware of a draft coming from the windows, even though they were all closed. Then he noticed the hole in one of the windows. It was small, but there it was.

He scanned the arboretum floor. Additional footprints, more havoc. Chaotically spread shards of glass that bore witness to a simple burglary. Since the alarm hadn't gone off, it must have happened before Thelma had gone to bed.

Suddenly he felt panic spreading through him.

On his way back to the hall he grabbed another knife from the block. The feel of their handles in each hand gave him a sense of security. He didn't fear the force of an attack so much as the sheer surprise of it, so he held the knives raised on each side and glanced over his shoulder with each step.

Then he walked upstairs and stood at Thelma's bedroom door.

A narrow strip of light seeped out from beneath it.

Was someone in there, waiting for him?

Gripping the knives hard, he cautiously pushed the door inward. There sat Thelma in the center of the bed. Wearing her negligee and looking very much alive, her eyes large and angry.

"Did you come to kill me, too?" she said, with intense loathing in her expression. "Is that it?"

Then she drew a pistol from under the duvet and aimed it at him.

It wasn't the weapon but the iciness of her voice that stopped him and caused him to drop the knives.

He knew Thelma. If it had been anyone else it might have been a joke. But Thelma didn't joke. She didn't possess a sense of humor. He stood stock-still.

"What happened?" he said, sizing up the pistol. It looked real, big enough to shut anyone up. "I can see that someone broke into the house, but there's no one here now, so you can put that thing down." He could feel the aftereffects of the cocaine swirling round in his veins. The mixture of adrenaline and drugs was potentially an incomparable combination. Just not right now.

"Where the bloody hell did you get that gun? Come on now, be a good girl and put it down, Thelma. Tell me what happened." But Thelma didn't move an inch.

She looked sexy, lying there. Sexier than she had in years.

He tried to come closer, but she stopped him by clutching the pistol tighter. "You attacked Frank, Ditlev. You just couldn't let him be, could you, you monster?"

How the hell could she know? And so

quickly?

"What do you mean?" he said, trying to hold her gaze.

"He's going to survive, you know. Which is not to your advantage, Ditlev, as I'm sure you understand."

Ditlev took his eyes off her and glanced at the knives on the floor. He shouldn't have dropped them.

"I have no idea what you're talking about," he said. "I was at Torsten's this evening. Call him and ask."

"You and Ulrik were seen at JFK in Hillerød this evening. That's all I need to know, do you hear?"

In the old days he would have felt his defense mechanisms steering him toward telling a lie, but right now he felt nothing. She already had him right where she wanted him.

"That's correct," he said without blinking. "We were there before we went to Torsten's. What about it?"

"I can't be bothered to listen to you, Ditlev. Come here. Sign your name. Otherwise I'll kill you."

She pointed at a few documents lying at the foot of the bed, then fired off a shot that blasted a hole in the wall behind Ditlev. He turned and estimated the extent of the damage. The hole was as big as a man's hand.

Then he cast a quick glance at the top sheet of paper. It was a rather tough pill to swallow. If he signed, she would get a good thirty-five million kroner per year for the twelve years they'd circled each other like beasts of prey.

"We won't report you, Ditlev. Not if you sign this. So do it now."

"If you report me, then you won't get anything, Thelma. Did you consider that? I'll let the fucking business go bankrupt while I'm in prison."

"You'll sign. Don't you think I know that?" Her laughter resounded with contempt. "You know as well as I do that things don't move so quickly. I'll still get my share of the spoils before you go broke. Maybe not as much, but enough. But I know you, Ditlev. You're a practical sort. Why throw away your business and sit in jail when you can afford to rid yourself of the wife in a normal fashion? So you'll sign. And tomorrow you'll admit Frank to the clinic, understand? I want him as good as new in a month. Even better than new."

He shook his head. She'd always been a devil. Birds of a feather flock together, as his mother used to say.

"Where did you get the pistol, Thelma?"

he asked calmly, taking the documents and scrawling his signature on the top two pages. "What happened?"

She stared at the papers, waiting until she had them in her hand before responding.

"It's too bad you weren't here tonight, Ditlev, because then I don't think I would have needed your signature."

"Is that so? And why is that?"

"Some filthy, dirty woman smashed the window and threatened me with this." She waved the weapon. "She was asking for you, Ditlev."

Thelma laughed, and the strap of her negligee slid off one shoulder. "I told her I would gladly let her in the front door next time she passed by. Then she could do whatever she wished without all the bother of smashing windows."

Ditlev felt his skin grow cold.

Kimmie! After all these years.

"She gave me the pistol and patted me on the cheek as if I were a little child. She mumbled something and then she went out the front door." Thelma laughed again. "But don't despair, Ditlev. Your girlfriend will pay you a visit another day, she said to tell you!"

13

Homicide Chief Marcus Jacobsen rubbed his forehead. This was a bloody awful way to start the week. He'd just been handed his fourth request for leave in as many days. Two men from his best investigation unit were off sick, and then this bestial attack right in the middle of a downtown street. A woman had been beaten beyond recognition and then tossed in a rubbish container. The violence was growing more and more raw and, understandably enough, everyone was demanding immediate action. The newspapers, the public, the police chief. If the woman died, all hell would break loose. It was a record year for homicides. One would have to go back at least ten years to see statistics this high, and because of that, and because so many officers were leaving the police force, the brass were calling meetings all the time.

It was one pressure on top of another, and

now Bak had also asked for leave. Bak of all people, for Christ's sake.

In the old days, he and Bak would have lit fags and walked round the courtyard, and they'd have solved their problems right there — of that he was convinced. But the old days were gone, and now he was powerless. Simply put, he had little to offer his personnel. The salary was shit, and so were the working hours. His officers were worn out and their work had become practically impossible to carry out satisfactorily. And now they couldn't even soothe their frustrations with a smoke. A hell of a situation.

"You've got to prod the politicians, Marcus," said his deputy, Lars Bjørn, as the office movers blustered about in the hallway so that everything would appear organized and efficient, as the reforms demanded. But it was merely camouflage, window dressing.

Marcus raised his eyebrows and looked at his deputy with the same resigned smile that had been plastered on Lars Bjørn's face the last few months.

"And when will *you* be asking me for leave, Lars? You're still a relatively young man. Don't you dream of landing another job? Wouldn't *your* wife like you around the house more, too?"

"Hell, Marcus, the only job I'd prefer to

mine is yours." He said it so drily and matter-of-factly it could make a man nervous.

Marcus nodded. "OK. But I hope you have time to wait, because I'm not getting out of here before my time. That's not my style."

"Just talk to the police chief, Marcus. Ask her to put pressure on the politicians so we can have tolerable working conditions."

There was a knock on the door, and before Marcus could react, Carl Mørck was halfway into his office. Could that man do something by the book, just for once?

"Not now, Carl," he said, knowing full well that Mørck's hearing could be surprisingly selective.

"It'll only take a moment." Carl nodded almost imperceptibly to Lars Bjørn. "It's about the case I'm working on."

"The Rørvig murders? If you can tell me who almost killed a woman last night in the middle of Store Kannikestræde, then I'll listen. Otherwise you're on your own. And you know what I think about the Rørvig case. There was a conviction. Find another case, one where the perpetrator is still on the loose."

"Someone here at this station has a connection to the case."

Marcus let his head fall resignedly to his chest. "I see. Who?"

"A detective by the name of Arne Jacobsen removed the case file from Holbæk Police ten to fifteen years ago. Does that ring any bells?"

"Fine surname, but *I* don't have anything to do with it."

"He was personally involved in the case, I can tell you. His son was dating the girl who was murdered."

"And?"

"And today the son works here at the station. I'm bringing him in for questioning. Just so you're aware."

"Who is he?"

"Johan."

"Johan? Johan Jacobsen, our handyman? You're pulling my leg —"

"Hang on, Carl," Lars Bjørn interrupted. "If you're going to bring one of our civilians in for questioning, it's best if you call it something else. I'm the one who has to speak with the union if anything goes wrong."

Marcus saw a quarrel emerging. "That's enough, you two." He turned toward Carl Mørck. "What's this all about?"

"You mean, apart from the fact that an ex-employee removed case materials from the Holbæk Police?" Carl straightened up so that he covered an additional foot of wall. "The fact is that his son put the case on my desk. Furthermore, he broke into the crime scene and deliberately left clues that point back to him. I also believe he's got a lot more material in his goody bag. Marcus, he knows more about this case than anyone else between heaven and earth — if one can put it that way."

"Good God, Carl. That case is more than twenty years old. Can't you just conduct your showdown in the basement nice and quietly? I imagine there are plenty more open-and-shut cases to work on other than that one."

"You're right. It's an old case. And it's the very one that I, at your request, will be presenting on Friday to a team of dimwits from the land of brown cheese. *Remember*? So, please, Marcus, be so kind as to make sure Johan stops by my office in no more than ten minutes."

"I can't do that."

"What's that supposed to mean?"

"As far as I know, Johan is off sick." He looked at Carl over his glasses. It was important he understood the message. "You're not to contact him at home, do you understand? He had a nervous breakdown over the weekend. We don't want any trouble."

"How can you be so certain he was the one who put the case file on your desk?" Lars Bjørn asked. "Did you find his fingerprints on it?"

"No. I got the results of the analysis today and there weren't any fingerprints. I just know it, OK? Johan's the one. If he's not back by this afternoon I'll be going over there. Then you can say whatever you like."

14

Johan Jacobsen lived in a co-op flat on Vesterbrogade, across from the Black Horse Theater and the now defunct Mechanical Music Museum. In fact, he lived right where the decisive battle between the anarchist squatters and police occurred in 1990. Carl remembered those days all too well. How many times had he donned riot gear and beaten up girls and boys nearly his own age?

Not exactly the best memories from the good old days.

They had to ring the buzzer on the brand-new intercom a few times before Johan Jacobsen let them in.

"I didn't expect you this soon," he said softly, showing them into his living room. From here there was a view of the old tiled roofs of the theater and adjacent inn.

The room was large, but not a very pretty sight. Clearly untouched by a woman's

165

expert hand and critical eye for quite some time. Gravy-caked plates were stacked on the kitchen worktop, Coke bottles were strewn on the floor. It was a dusty, greasy pigsty.

"Please excuse the mess," the man said, removing dirty clothes from the sofa and coffee table. "My wife left me about a month ago." His face made the nervous twitch they'd seen so many times at the police station. As if sand had blown in his face and he'd just managed to keep it from getting in his eyes.

Carl shook his head. It was too bad about the wife. He knew the feeling.

"You know why we're here?"

He nodded.

"So you admit straightaway that you were the one who put the Rørvig file on my desk, Johan?"

He nodded again.

"Why didn't you simply give it to us, then?" Assad said, thrusting out his lower lip. If he put on a military-style cap, he would resemble Yasser Arafat.

"Would you have accepted it?"

Carl shook his head. Hardly. A twenty-year-old case with a conviction? No, he was certainly correct on that score.

"Would you have asked me where I got it?

Would you have inquired why I was interested in the case? Would you have bothered to take the time to have your interest aroused? I've seen the piles on your desk, Carl."

Carl nodded. "And so you put the replacement Trivial Pursuit box in the cottage as a lead. It couldn't have been very long ago, since the lock on the kitchen door opened so easily. Am I right?"

Johan nodded.

Just as Carl thought. "OK, so you wanted to know whether we'd get properly hooked on the case. I can understand that. But you took quite a risk doing it that way, didn't you, Johan? What if we hadn't noticed the game? What if we hadn't discovered the names written on the cards?"

He shrugged. "You're here now."

"I don't understand it so well." Assad sat down in front of one of the windows facing Vesterbrogade. With the light cascading in behind him, his face turned completely dark. "So you're not satisfied that Bjarne Thøgersen admitted he'd done it?"

"If you had been in the courtroom during sentencing, you wouldn't be satisfied, either. Everything was predetermined."

"Yes, of course," Assad said. "Hardly strange when the man turns himself in —"

"What do you find unusual about the case, Johan?" Carl interrupted.

The man avoided Carl's eyes and looked out the window, as if the gray sky might calm the storm inside him.

"They were smiling the whole time," he said, "every single one of them. Thøgersen, the defense lawyer. The three arrogant bastards sitting in the public gallery."

"Torsten Florin, Ditlev Pram, and Ulrik Dybbøl Jensen. Are they who you're referring to?"

He nodded while stroking his quivering lips in an attempt to still them.

"They sat there smiling, you say. That's a very weak basis for pursuing the case, Johan."

"Yes, but I know more now than I did then."

"Your father, Arne Jacobsen, worked the case?" Carl asked.

"Yes."

"And where were you at the time?"

"I was at Holbæk Technical College."

"Holbæk? Did you know the victims?"

"Yes." He said it almost inaudibly.

"So you also knew Søren?"

He nodded. "Yes, a little. But not as well as Lisbet."

"You listen now, you," Assad broke in. "I

can tell from your face that Lisbet had told you she wasn't in love with you anymore. Isn't that right, Johan? She didn't want you after all." Assad's eyebrows formed a frown. "And when you couldn't have her, you killed her, and now you want us to figure it out so we can arrest you, so you don't have to commit suicide. Isn't that right?"

Johan blinked rapidly a few times, then his face hardened. "Does he need to be here, Carl?" he asked in a measured tone.

Carl shook his head. Assad's outbursts were unfortunately becoming a habit. "Go into the other room, Assad. Just for five minutes." He pointed at a side door behind Johan.

At this Johan jerked like a jack-in-the-box. There were many indicators of fear, and Carl knew most of them.

So he looked at the closed door.

"No, not in there. It's too messy," Johan said, standing in front of the door. "Go and sit in the dining room, Assad. Or have a cup of coffee in the kitchen. I just made some."

But Assad had also noticed Johan's reaction. "No thanks, I prefer tea," he said, squeezing himself behind Johan and throwing the door wide open.

Behind the door was another high-ceilinged room. There was a row of tables along one wall, covered with stacks of files and loose papers. But most interesting was the face hanging on the wall, staring down at them with melancholy eyes. It was a yard-high photostat of a young woman, the girl who'd been murdered in Rørvig. Lisbet Jørgensen. Unruly hair on a cloudless background. A real summer snapshot with deep shadows across her face. Had it not been for her eyes, the size of the photo and its unusually prominent position, he would hardly have noticed it. He did now.

As Carl and Assad entered the room it became clear to them that this was a shrine. Everything in here was about Lisbet. There were fresh flowers beside one wall with clippings about the murder. Another wall was adorned with characteristic square Instamatic photos of the girl, plus a few letters and postcards, even a blouse. Happy and cruel moments, side by side.

Johan didn't say a word. Simply stood in front of the photostat and let himself be drawn into her eyes.

"Why didn't you want us to see this room, Johan?" Carl said.

He shrugged, and Carl understood. It was too intimate. His soul, his life, his broken dreams — all was laid bare on these walls.

"She broke up with you that night," came

Assad's accusation again. "Tell it like it is, Johan. It would be best for you then."

Johan turned and glared at him. "All I will say is that the girl I loved most in the entire world was massacred by people who right now are looking down on us from the highest ranks of society and laughing. The fact that somebody as fucking insignificant as Bjarne Thøgersen is the one paying the price comes down to one thing, and that's money. Judas money, cold hard cash, filthy lucre, for God's sake. That's what it boils down to."

"And now it has to stop." Carl said. "But why now?"

"Because I'm alone again, and I can't think about anything else. Can't you see that?"

Johan Jacobsen was just twenty when Lisbet said yes to his marriage proposal. Their fathers were friends. The families had visited one another often, and Johan had been in love with Lisbet for as long as he could remember.

He had been with her that night, while her brother had made love with his girlfriend in the next room.

They'd had a serious talk, and then they'd made love — as a parting gesture, as far as

171

she was concerned. At dawn he'd left in tears, and later that same day she was found dead. In just ten hours he'd plummeted from the highest peak of joy into deep lovesickness and finally into hell. He had never really recovered from that night and the following afternoon. He'd found a new girlfriend whom he'd married, and they'd had two children, yet it was only Lisbet he thought about.

When his father, on his deathbed, told him that he'd stolen the case file and given it to Lisbet's mother, Johan had driven up to see her the very next day and retrieved the folder.

Since then, these papers had become his most cherished possessions, and from that day forward, Lisbet filled more and more of his life.

Finally she simply filled too much. And so his wife left.

"What do you mean by 'filled too much'?" asked Assad.

"I talked about her constantly. Thought about her night and day. All the clippings about the case, all the reports. I simply had to read about her all the time."

"And now you want to get rid of it all? That's why you got us involved?" Carl asked.

"Yes."

"And what have you got for us? All this?" Carl spread his arms out over the stacks of paper.

He nodded. "If you read all of it, you'll know that it was the school gang that did it."

"You've made a list for us of other assaults. We've already seen it. Is that what you mean?"

"That's only a partial list. I've got the full one here." He leaned over the table, lifted a stack of newspaper clippings and pulled out a sheet of paper from underneath.

"It starts here, before the Rørvig murders. This boy went to the same boarding school, it states in the article." He pointed at a page in *Politiken* from June 15, 1987. The headline read: "Tragedy in Bellahøj. Man, 19, Falls to Death from Ten-Meter Diving Board."

He ran through the cases, many of which Carl recognized from the list that had been delivered to Department Q. Three or four months separated the different incidents. A couple of them had resulted in deaths.

"It's possible they're all accidents then," Assad said. "What do they have to do with the boarding-school kids? They aren't necessarily connected with one another at all. Do you have any proof?"

"No. That's your job."

Assad swung his head dismissively. "Honestly, there's absolutely nothing in this. You've just become sick in your head because of this case. I feel sorry for you. You should see a psychologist then. Can't you go to that Mona Ibsen at headquarters instead of sending us on a wild duck chase?"

On their drive back to headquarters, Carl and Assad were quiet, each absorbed in thought. Between their ears, the case was moving full speed ahead.

"Make us a cup of tea, Assad," Carl said down in the basement, pushing the plastic grocery bags containing Johan Jacobsen's papers into the corner. "Go easy on the sugar, OK?"

He put his legs up on the desk, turned on the news program on Channel 2, unplugged his brain, and expected nothing more from the day.

The next five minutes changed that.

He picked up the telephone on the first ring and his eyes rolled toward the ceiling when he heard the homicide chief's dark voice.

"I've talked to the police chief, Carl. She sees no reason why you should dig deeper into this case."

At first Carl made a show of protesting, but when Marcus Jacobsen wouldn't give him additional reasons why, he felt the temperature rising around the nape of his neck.

"I'll repeat: why?"

"That's just the way it is. You should prioritize your assignments so that you're concentrating exclusively on cases that haven't resulted in a conviction. The rest you should file away in the metal cabinets down in the archive."

"Aren't I the one who actually decides what to prioritize?"

"Not when the police chief says something else."

So that conversation was over.

"Nice mint tea with a little sugar," Assad said after the conversation ended, handing him a cup. It looked as though the teaspoon could stand upright in the sea of syrup.

Carl accepted the scalding hot and sickeningly sweet beverage, knocking it back in one gulp. Christ, he was getting used to the glop.

"You shouldn't sulk, Carl. We'll let the case rest for a few weeks until this Johan comes back to work. Then we'll quietly pressure him day after day. He'll confess everything sooner or later. You'll see."

Carl studied Assad's cheery face. If he didn't know any better he'd think it was painted on. Just an hour earlier he had been aggressive, insistent, and flushed-faced on account of this case.

"Confesses what, Assad? What the hell are you talking about?"

"That night Lisbet Jørgensen told him she didn't want him anymore then. She probably said she'd found another guy. So he came back that morning and killed them both. If we dig a little deeper we'll probably find out there was some sort of shit between Lisbet's brother and Johan. Maybe he went completely crazy."

"Forget it, Assad. The case has been taken from us. Besides, I don't believe your theory in the slightest. It's too twisted."

"Twisted?"

"Yes, for God's sake, and I'm not talking about a pretzel. If Johan had done it, he'd have fallen apart a hundred years ago."

"Not if he's screwed up in the head." He tapped the bald patch on his crown.

"Someone who's screwed up in the head doesn't give leads like the Trivial Pursuit cards. He throws the murder weapon right in your face and looks the other way. Anyway, didn't you hear what I said? We've been taken off the case."

Assad glanced indifferently at the flat-screen TV on the wall, where the news was reporting on an assault on Store Kannike-stræde. "No, I didn't hear that. I don't want to hear that. Who took us off the case, did you say?"

They could smell Rose heading their way before they saw her. She was suddenly standing there, arms full of office supplies and bakery bags patterned with Christmas elves. In every sense of the word, she was early.

"Knock-knock!" she said, rapping her forehead twice on the door frame. "Here comes the cavalry, tah-dahhhh! Scrumptious pastries for everyone."

Carl and Assad stared at one another. One with a pained expression on his face, the other with Christmas lights in his eyes.

"Hi, Rose, and welcome to Department Q. I've made everything ready for you, you bet," said the little traitor.

As Assad pulled her toward the neighboring room, she gave Carl a telling glance that said, *You can't get rid of me.* But it damned well took two to tango. As if he could be bought for the price of a pastry and a biscuit.

He glanced at the plastic bags in the

corner and then pulled a sheet of paper from the drawer.

Then he wrote:

SUSPECTS:
Bjarne Thøgersen?
One or more of the others in the boarding-school gang?
Johan Jacobsen?
Random murder?
Someone connected to the boarding-school gang?

He frowned in frustration at this meager result. If Marcus had left him in peace, he probably would have simply shredded the paper himself. But Marcus hadn't. He'd given Carl a direct order to let the case go; therefore he was unable to.

When Carl was a boy, his father had been on to him. He gave Carl explicit orders not to plow the meadow, so Carl plowed it. He admonished Carl not to join the military, and Carl enlisted. His crafty father had even tried to steer him toward the lasses. This farmer's daughter and that farmer's daughter weren't good enough, he said, so Carl went after them. That was Carl's way, and always had been. No one was going to make his decisions for him, which actually made him easy to manipulate. He knew this, of course. The question was whether or not the police chief also knew it. It was hard to imagine.

But what the hell was this really about? How did the police chief even know he was involved with the case? Only a handful of people were aware of this.

He imagined the possibilities: Marcus Jacobsen, Lars Bjørn, Assad, the team in Holbæk, Valdemar Florin, the man from the summer cottages, the victims' mother . . .

For a moment he stared off into space. Yes, these people knew, and a bunch of others knew, too, if he really thought hard.

At this point anyone else might have applied the brakes. When names like Florin, Dybbøl Jensen, and Pram became associated with a murder investigation, you could quickly find yourself on thin ice.

He shook his head. He really couldn't give a shit about people's titles and what favors the police chief owed whom. Now that they'd started, no one was going to stop them.

He looked up. New sounds were emanating from Rose's office across the corridor. That guttural, peculiar laughter of hers — booming outbursts of it — plus Assad at full throttle. If they kept at it, someone might suspect there was a rave going on.

He knocked a fag from its packet, lit it, and stared at the cloud of smoke that enveloped the sheet of paper. Then he wrote:

TASKS:
Similar murders abroad at the same time? Sweden? Germany?
Who from the old investigation unit is still active today?
Bjarne Thøgersen/Vridløselille State Prison.
Accident with the boarding-school pupil at Bellahøj Swimming Center. Coincidence?
Who from the boarding-school gang can we speak with?
Lawyer Bent Krum!
Torsten Florin, Ditlev Pram, and Ulrik Dybbøl Jensen: any current cases? Did anyone working for them report them? Psychological profiles?
Find out about Kimmie, alias Kirsten-Marie Lassen: any next of kin we can speak with?
Circumstances of Kristian Wolf's death!

He tapped the paper repeatedly with his pencil, before jotting down:

180

Hardy.

Get Rose the hell out of here.

Thoroughly shag Mona Ibsen.

He glanced at the last line a few times and felt like a naughty pubescent boy scratching girls' names into the surface of his desk. If only she knew how heavy his balls got whenever he fantasized about her backside and bouncing breasts. He took a couple of deep breaths, plucked an eraser from his drawer, and began removing the last two lines.

"Carl Mørck, am I disturbing you?" said a voice at the door, which made his blood boil and turn to ice at the same time. His spinal cord sent five commands through his infrastructure: get rid of the eraser, cover the last line, put away the cigarette, drop the stupid facial expression, close your mouth!

"Am I disturbing you?" she said as his bulging eyes tried to look directly into hers.

They were still brown. Mona Ibsen was back, and he was scared to death.

"What did Mona want?" Rose asked with a silly smile. As if it were any of her concern.

She stood in the doorway, steadily chewing on her custard-filled pastry as Carl attempted to return to reality.

"What was it she wanted, Carl?" asked Assad, his mouth full. Never before had Carl seen so little custard coating so much stubble.

"I'll tell you later." He turned toward Rose, hoping she wouldn't notice his glowing cheeks, which his hammering heart had bombarded with blood. "Have you made yourself comfortable in your new digs?"

"Oh my! You care? Thank you. I suppose if a person hates sunlight and colors on the wall and having friendly people around, then you've found the most perfect place for me." She elbowed Assad. "I'm only joking, Assad. You're OK."

Oh joy. This was going to be such a lovely partnership.

Carl rose and laboriously scribbled the list of suspects and tasks on the whiteboard.

Then he turned toward their newly installed wonder of a secretary. If she thought she already had enough on her plate, she had another thought coming. He'd make her work so hard that a job as cardboard-box presser at the margarine factory would seem like paradise.

"The case we're working on is a little tricky because of who might be involved," he said, glancing at the pastry she was nibbling with her front teeth, like a squirrel.

"Assad will brief you in a moment. Then I'd like you to put the papers in these plastic bags in chronological order and match them with the papers here on the desk. Then make a copy of the whole shebang for you and Assad — except for the folder here. That'll have to wait until later." He pushed Johan Jacobsen and Martha Jørgensen's gray folder to one side. "And when you're done with that, find out everything you can about this item here." He pointed to the line on the whiteboard concerning the diving-board accident at the swimming center. "We're a little busy, so go ahead and make it snappy. You'll find the date of the accident on the summary page that's on top in the red plastic bag. The summer of 1987, before the Rørvig murders. Sometime in June."

Maybe he'd expected her to grunt a bit. Just a tart little remark that would win her a couple more tasks, but she was surprisingly dispassionate. Unmoved, she merely glanced nonchalantly at the hand that held the remainder of her pastry, then shoved it sideways into a mouth that seemed as though it could swallow anything.

He turned to Assad. "How would you like to take a break from the basement for a few days?"

"Does it have something to do with Hardy?"

"No. I want you to find Kimmie. We need to begin forming our own picture of this gang. I'll start on the others."

Assad appeared to be trying to imagine the bigger picture. Himself, hunting for a bag lady on the streets of Copenhagen, while Carl sat, nice and cozy, indoors with the wealthy folks, tossing down coffee and cognac. That was how Carl saw it, at any rate.

"I don't understand, Carl," he said. "Are we continuing with this investigation? Were we not just told to stay away from it?"

Carl furrowed his brows. Maybe Assad should have kept his trap shut. Who knew if Rose was loyal? Why was she down here anyway? He sure as hell hadn't asked for her.

"Well, yes, now that Assad has mentioned it, the police chief has given us a red light on the case. Do you have a problem with that?" he asked Rose.

She shrugged. "It's OK with me. But it means you're the one who buys pastries next time," she said, lifting the plastic bags.

After Assad had received his instructions, he slunk off. Twice a day he was to phone

Carl's mobile to report his findings regarding Kimmie. He had been given a to-do list, which among other things included checking the Civil Registration System, talking to cops on the beat at City Station, Social Services at City Hall, staff at the Red Cross shelter on Hillerødgade and a number of other locations. Quite the assignment for a man who was still wet behind the ears, especially when all they knew so far about Kimmie's whereabouts came from Valdemar Florin. According to him, she walked the streets of downtown Copenhagen with a suitcase, and had done so for years. Even if you could trust what the man said, this wasn't terribly specific. It was probably rather doubtful she was even alive, considering the gang's reputation.

Carl opened the pale green folder and wrote down Kirsten-Marie Lassen's Civil Registration Number. Then he went into the corridor where Rose was already running reams of paper through the copier in unusually irritating and energetic fashion.

"We need some tables out here so I can sort the sheets," she said, without looking up.

"Is that so? Do you have a certain make in mind?" he said, smiling crookedly as he handed her the Civil Registration Number.

"I need all her personal data. Last place of residence, any hospitalizations, welfare payments, education, parents' residence if they're still alive. Hold off on the copying for a bit. I need this quickly. And all of it, thanks."

She rose to her full, stiletto-heel height. Her direct gaze at his larynx didn't feel pleasant. "You'll have the order list for the tables in ten minutes," she said drily. "I'd go with the Malling-Beck catalogue. They have height-adjustable ones priced between five and six thousand apiece."

He swept items into his grocery cart half consciously, with visions of Mona Ibsen swirling in his head. She hadn't worn her wedding ring, which was the first thing he'd noticed. That and how dry his throat got when she looked at him. Another sign that it was getting to be a long time since he'd last been with a woman.

Bloody hell.

He glanced round, trying to orient himself since the Kvickly supermarket's enormous expansion, just like everyone else who was wandering about, searching for toilet paper where there were now cosmetics. This kind of thing could make a person crazy.

At the end of the pedestrian shopping

street, the razing of the old dry-goods shop was nearly complete. Allerød was no longer a quaint little town with small, independently owned shops, and Carl almost didn't give a toss anymore. If he couldn't have Mona Ibsen, then for all he cared they could level the church, too, and build yet another supermarket.

"What the hell did you buy us, Carl?" asked his tenant, Morten Holland, as he unpacked the groceries. He'd had a difficult day, too, he said. Two hours of political science at the university followed by three hours at the video-rental store. Yes, these were indeed hard times, Carl could plainly see.

"I thought you might make chili con carne," Carl said, ignoring Morten's reply that it would've been cool if he had bought a little beans and meat.

Leaving him scratching his head at the kitchen table, Carl went upstairs where the nostalgia renaissance was about to blow Jesper's door out onto the stairwell.

He was in the midst of a Led Zeppelin orgy while splattering soldiers on his Nintendo, as his zombie girlfriend sat on the bed, texting her hunger for contact to the rest of the world.

Carl sighed and thought about how much

more adventurous he'd been with Belinda in his bedroom loft in Brønderslev. Long live electronics. As long as he didn't have to have anything to do with it.

Then he tumbled into his own room and stared blankly at his bed. If Morten didn't call him down to dinner within twenty minutes, the bed would have already won the round.

He lay down, put his hands behind his neck, and gazed at the ceiling, imagining Mona Ibsen stretching her naked body under the duvet. If he didn't pull himself together soon, his goddam nuts would shrivel up. Either Mona Ibsen or a few quick fishing trips at the bodegas, otherwise he might as well just sign up for the police corps in Afghanistan. Better to have one hard ball in his skull than two limp ones in his drawers.

An unusually dreadful cross between gangsta rap and an entire town of collapsing corrugated metal houses thundered through the wall from Jesper's room. Should he go in and complain, or close his ears, or what?

He continued lying where he was, his pillow stuffed against his head. Maybe that was why he came to think of Hardy.

Hardy, who couldn't move. Hardy, who

couldn't even scratch his forehead when it itched. Hardy, who could do absolutely nothing else except think. If Carl were in his position, he would've lost his mind ages ago.

He looked at the picture on the wall of Hardy, Anker, and himself, standing with their arms around each other's shoulders. *Three damn fine policemen*, Carl thought. Why had Hardy thought otherwise when Carl last visited him? What had he meant when he said someone had been waiting for them at the building in Amager?

He studied Anker's face. Though he'd been the smallest of the three, he'd had the strongest gaze. Dead now for almost two-thirds of a year, and yet Carl could still see these eyes so clearly. Did Hardy truly think that either he or Anker could have had anything to do with the people who killed him?

Carl shook his head. It was hard to believe. Then his eyes panned across a framed photo of him and Vigga, back when she still fancied putting her fingers in his bellybutton, then to the picture of the farm in Brønderslev, and finally the photograph Vigga had taken of him the day he'd returned wearing his first, real parade uniform.

He squinted his eyes. It was dark in the corner where the photograph hung, but still he could tell that something about it was not as it should be.

He let the pillow drop and stood up just as Jesper started a new horror orgy of sound on the other side of the wall. Then he slowly approached the photograph. At first the stains appeared to be shadows, but when he drew closer he saw what they were.

Fresh blood like that was hard to mistake. Only now did he see how it streamed down the wall in thin streaks. How the hell had he not seen it before? And what the hell was it doing there?

He shouted for Morten, then went and yanked Jesper from his stupor in front of the flat-screen TV, and showed them the blood spots while they gave him looks of disgust and indignation, respectively.

No, Morten had nothing to do with this revolting mess.

And no, damn it, Jesper had nothing to do with it, either. Nor did his girlfriend, if that was what Carl was thinking. Was he going soft in the head?

Carl glanced at the blood again and nodded.

With the right equipment it would take at most three minutes to break into the house, find an object Carl was sure to see fairly often, rub on a little animal blood, and then hightail it out. Wouldn't it be easy to find three unobserved minutes, given that Magnolievangen — in fact all of Rønneholtparken — was as good as deserted from eight in the morning until four in the afternoon?

If someone thought such shenanigans would make him give up the investigation, then they weren't just unbelievably stupid.

The bastards, in one way or another, were also culpable.

15

The only time she could dream good dreams was after she'd been drinking. Which was one of the reasons she did it.

If she didn't take a couple of generous swigs from the whisky bottle, then the outcome was assured. After dozing for hours with the voices whispering in her head, her gaze would fall from the poster hanging on her door — the one with the children playing — and she'd glide into dark nightmares. Those damn images were always cued up when she drifted off. Memories of a mother's soft hair and a face rigid as stone, of a little girl trying to become invisible in the nooks and crannies of the family mansion. Horrible moments. Faded glimpses of a mother who simply left her. Ice-cold embraces from the women who succeeded her.

And when she awoke with sweat on her forehead and the rest of her body shaking with cold, the dreams had usually reached the point in her life where she turned her back on the bourgeoisie's insatiable expectations and false niceness. She wanted to forget all of that. That, and the time that followed.

The previous evening she had drunk steadily, so the morning was relatively uncomplicated. She could easily handle the cold, the coughing, and the splitting headache. As long as her thoughts and the voices were at rest.

She stretched, put her hand under the bed, and pulled out the cardboard box. It was her pantry, and the procedure was simple. The food on the right side of the box always had to be consumed first. When that side was emptied, she rotated the box 180 degrees and again ate what was on the right. Then she could fill the empty left side with new goods from Aldi. Always the same procedure, and never more than two or three days' at a time in the box. Otherwise the food spoiled, especially when the sun was baking the roof.

She gobbled up yogurt without any real pleasure. It had been years since food had meant anything to her.

She shoved the box back under the bed,

fumbled around until she found the coffin, caressed it a moment, and whispered: "Mommy has to go into town now, my precious. I'll be home soon."

Then she sniffed her underarms and decided that it was time to take a shower. She used to do it in the central train station once in a while, but not anymore; not after Tine had warned her about the men searching for her. If she absolutely had to go back there, she needed to take special precautions.

She licked her spoon and tossed the plastic cup in the rubbish sack beneath her, considering her next steps.

She had been to Ditlev's house the evening before. For one hour she'd waited outside on Strandvejen, watching through the mosaic of luminous mansion windows before her voices gave the green light. It was an elegant house, but clinical and emotionless, like Ditlev himself. What else would one expect? She'd smashed a window and had a good look around before a woman in a negligee suddenly appeared. She had stared anxiously as Kimmie drew her pistol, but her expression became more subdued as soon as she discovered her husband was the target.

So Kimmie had given the woman the

pistol and told her she could use it however she wished. She had looked at it for a moment. Weighed it in her hand, and smiled. Indeed she seemed to know what to use it for. Exactly as the voices had predicted.

And Kimmie had wandered back toward the city with a bounce in her step, assured that by now the message was crystal clear to everyone. She was after them. None of them could feel safe anywhere. She had them in her sights.

If she was right about them, they'd put more people on the streets to track her down, and that thought amused her. The more there were, the greater the evidence of their attentiveness.

She would make them so vigilant they wouldn't be able to think of anything else.

For Kimmie, the worst part about taking a shower around other women wasn't their stares. It wasn't the little girls' curious peeks at the long scar on her back and stomach. Nor was it the unmistakable delight the mothers and their children took in doing something together. It wasn't even the carefree noises and laughter out at the pool.

It was the women's bodies that shone with life. That was the worst. Gold rings on fingers that had someone to caress. Breasts that nurtured. Potbellies waiting to bear fruit. It was sights like these that fueled the voices.

So Kimmie quickly tore off her clothes and heaped them on top of the lockers without looking at anyone, letting the plastic bags filled with new clothes lie on the floor. The whole procedure should be done quick enough that she could be gone before her eyes began to wander on their own.

While she was still in control.

So within twenty minutes she was standing on Tietgens Bridge in a tailored coat, her hair up, an unaccustomed mist of exclusive perfume on her skin, staring across the tracks that vanished inside the central station. It had been quite some time since she'd dressed like this, and she didn't like it one bit. At this moment she was the spitting image of everything she fought against. But it was necessary. She would head slowly down the platform and up the escalator and all the way round inside the central hall like any other woman. If she didn't notice anything unusual in the first pass, she would sit at the corner of Train Fast Food with a cup of coffee, occasionally glancing at the clock. She would resemble anyone waiting to go anywhere. Streamlined, with eyebrows finely drawn above her sunglasses.

Just another woman who knew what she wanted in life.

She'd been sitting for an hour when she saw Rat-Tine waddle past with her head canted sideways, gaze fastened on the empty space a half yard in front of her. The emaciated woman smiled soullessly to everything and nothing; clearly she'd shot some heroin recently. Never before had Tine seemed more vulnerable and transparent, but Kimmie didn't move. Simply watched her until she disappeared somewhere behind McDonald's.

It was during this long, scrutinizing stare that she saw the lean man standing against the wall, talking to two other men in light coats. It wasn't three men huddled together that caught her attention. It was that they didn't look each other in the eye as they spoke, but instead kept stealing glances around the hall. That, and the fact that they were wearing nearly identical clothes, caused her warning lights to flash.

She rose slowly, adjusting the glasses on her nose and, with long, sweeping stiletto-heel steps, walked directly toward the men. When she was close she could see they were all around forty years old. Deep creases at the corners of their mouths indicated a hard life. They were not the kind of lines businessmen earned under the sickly glare of office lights while stacks of paper flowed across their desks during the wee hours of the morning. No, they were more like furrows carved by the wind, the elements, and endless, boring assignments. These were men hired to wait and observe.

When she was a few yards away, they all looked at her in the same instant. She smiled at them and avoided showing her teeth. Then she passed close by and felt the silence cement the men together. When she was a little farther ahead, they began talking once more. She stopped to rummage in her purse. One of them, she overheard, was called Kim. Of course it had to be a name with the letter "K."

They were discussing times and locations and weren't the faintest bit interested in her, which meant she could move around freely. The person she was pretending to be didn't fit the profile they were looking for. Of course not.

She made a pass round the hall, accompanied by whispering voices, bought a women's magazine in the kiosk at the other end and returned to her point of departure. Only one of the men remained. He was leaning against the brick wall, clearly ready for a long wait. Every one of his movements was slow; only his eyes were busy. These were precisely the kind of men Torsten, Ulrik, and Ditlev associated with. Lackeys. Cold-hearted pricks. Men who did almost anything for money.

Jobs you wouldn't read about in the classifieds.

The more she watched him, the closer she felt to the bastards she wanted to destroy. Excitement swelled inside her as the voices in her head contradicted one another.

"Stop it," she whispered, dropping her gaze. She noticed how the man at the neighboring table glanced up from his plate, trying to ascertain the target of her anger.

That was his problem.

Stop, she thought, catching sight of a tabloid headline: KEEP YOUR MARRIAGE ALIVE it read in large capital letters. But it was only the letter "K" she noted.

A big, capital "K" in a curved font. Another "K."

The sixth-form pupils simply called him "K," but his name was Kåre. He was the one who raked in nearly all the fifth-form votes when it was decided which final-year student would be the next prefect. He was the one who resembled a god, the one the girls whispered about on their bunks in the dormitory. But Kimmie was the one who scored him. After three dances at the comedy ball it was her turn, and Kåre felt Kimmie's fingers where none had been before. For Kimmie understood her body and that of the boys, too. Kristian had made certain of that.

Kåre was in her grip, as though caught in a vise.

People commented on how, from that day forward, the popular prefect's average began to slide, and how it was strange that so intelligent and focused a pupil could suddenly begin to lose it. And Kimmie enjoyed it. It was her handiwork, her body shaking this goody-two-shoes's foundation. Her body alone.

Everything had been prepared for Kåre. His future had been determined long ago by parents who never found out who he actually was. All that mattered was keeping their son on track, ensuring he would bring honor to the tenderloin caste.

If a person could make the family happy and harvest success, then that person had found the meaning of life. To hell with the costs.

Or so they thought.

Kåre became Kimmie's first target for that

reason alone. Everything Kåre believed in nauseated her. Winning prizes for diligence. Being the best at shooting birds and the fastest runner on the racetrack. Being an eminent orator at festive occasions. Having hair trimmed a little neater, trousers ironed a little smoother. Kimmie wished all this gone. She wanted to peel him to see what lay hidden beneath.

And when she was through with him, she looked around for more challenging prey. There was plenty to choose from. She wasn't afraid of anything or anyone.

Only occasionally did Kimmie glance up over her magazine. If the man by the wall left, she would feel it. More than eleven years on the street had sharpened her instincts.

These instincts awoke when, one hour later, she observed yet another man moving around the hall in an apparently aimless way, as if he were being led by legs set on automatic pilot while his eyes remained fixed on his surroundings. He wasn't a pickpocket, attentively trying to spot a ripe handbag or loose coat. Nor was he the pickpocket's little helper, sticking his hand out and asking for spare change while his accomplice did the dirty work. No, she knew the type better than most, and he wasn't it.

He was a compact little man in shabby clothes. Thick coat, large pockets. It was wrapped around his body like a snakeskin, suggesting a derelict. But that wasn't quite right. Even there, Kimmie knew better. Men wearing the uniform of the outcast — men who'd given up — didn't look at other people. They had their sights set on the rubbish bins. On the ground in front of them. On corners where they might find an empty bottle. Maybe even on a random shop window or the offer of the week at Sunset Fast Food. They never scrutinized people's faces and behavior like this man was doing from under his bushy eyebrows. Besides, he was dark-skinned, like a Turk or Iranian. Who had ever seen a Turk or Iranian fall so far that he walked Copenhagen's streets as a homeless person?

She watched him until he passed the man leaning against the wall, expecting they would acknowledge one another somehow, but they didn't.

So she sat there, peering over the top of her magazine, imploring the voices in her head to keep out of it. And that's how she was sitting when the little man returned to where he started. Not even on his way back did the two men acknowledge each other.

It was at this point that she rose quietly, pushed the chair carefully under her table and followed the squat, dark man at a distance.

He walked slowly. Now and then he would exit the hall and peer down Istedsgade, but he never walked so far that she couldn't see him from the stairwell near the train station's construction site.

There was no doubt that he was searching for someone, someone who could be her. So she stayed back in the shadows, behind corners and signs.

When he was standing near the train station post office for the tenth time, glancing around, he suddenly turned and stared straight at her. This was something she hadn't prepared herself for, so she turned on her high heels and made her way toward the taxi queue. She would hail one and get away fast; he wasn't going to keep her from doing that.

The other thing she hadn't expected was that Rat-Tine would be standing right behind her.

"Hi, Kimmie!" she called shrilly, her eyes lusterless. "I thought it was you, love. You look smashing today. What's the occasion?"

She thrust her arms toward Kimmie, as if

to make sure she was real, but Kimmie dodged her, leaving Tine with arms raised in the air.

Behind her Kimmie heard the man's running footfalls.

16

The telephone had rung three times during the night, but each time Carl lifted the receiver the line was dead.

At the breakfast table he asked Jesper and Morten whether they'd noticed anything unusual in the house, but only got sleepy glances in response.

"Maybe you forgot to close windows or doors yesterday?" he tried. There had to be some way into their sleep-leaden think tanks.

Jesper shrugged. To get anything from him at this time of the day, you first had to pull the winning number in Utopia's grand lottery. Morten, at least, grunted a sort of answer.

Afterward Carl walked round the house without spotting anything abnormal. The front-door lock had no scratches. The windows were as they should be. The break-in had been committed by a person or people who knew what they were doing.

After a ten-minute investigation, he got in his police car that was parked between the gray concrete buildings and noticed how it stank of petrol.

"Bloody hell!" he shouted. In a split second he ripped open the Peugeot's door and lunged sideways onto the ground, rolling several times before taking shelter behind a van, expecting Magnolievangen to be illuminated by a blast powerful enough to blow in windows.

"What's wrong, Carl?" he heard a calm voice say. He turned toward his barbecuing mate, Kenn, who in spite of the morning chill wore a thin T-shirt and seemed nice and warm.

"Stand still, Kenn," he commanded, staring down toward Rønneholtparken. Apart from Kenn's animated eyebrows, nothing was moving anywhere. Maybe a remote control would activate the explosion the next time he approached the vehicle. Perhaps the spark from the ignition would be enough to set it off.

"Someone has tampered with my car," he said, finally turning his attention from the rooftops and the hundreds of windows in the buildings.

For a moment he considered calling the

crime-scene techs, but decided against it. Whoever was trying to frighten him didn't leave fingerprints or other similar clues. He might as well accept that fact and take the train.

Hunter or hunted? Right now it was all relative.

He hadn't even removed his coat before Rose was standing at his office door with arched brows and charcoal gray lashes.

"The police mechanics are out in Allerød and report that nothing special is wrong with your car. A loose petrol line, how interesting can that be?"

She closed her eyes resignedly and in slow motion, which Carl ignored. Better to assert his authority right away.

"You've given me a lot of assignments, Carl. Are we going to talk about them, or should we wait until the petrol fumes have evaporated from your belfry?"

He lit a cigarette and settled in his chair. "Fire away," he said, hoping the mechanics had enough wits about them to bring his car to headquarters.

"Let's start with the accident at Bellahøj Swimming Center. There's not much to say about it. The guy was nineteen and his name was Kåre Bruno." She stared him

207

down, dimples at full strength. "*Bruno*! Seriously!" She repressed something, maybe a giggle. "He was a good swimmer, very athletic across the board, actually. His parents lived in Istanbul, but his grandparents lived in Emdrup, close to the Bellahøj open-air swimming pool. That's where he usually stayed during his free weekends." She riffled through her papers. "The report states it was an accident, and that Kåre Bruno himself was responsible. Not paying attention on a ten-meter diving board isn't particularly smart, you know." She stuck her pen in her hair where it could hardly stay very long.

"It had rained that morning, so the guy probably slipped on the wet surface while showing off for someone, I'd guess. But he was there by himself, and no one saw exactly what happened. Not until he was lying on the tiles underneath with his head rotated 180 degrees."

Carl looked at Rose with a question on his lips, but she cut him off. "And yes, Kåre went to the same boarding school as Kirsten-Marie Lassen and the others from the gang. He was in the sixth form when the others were in the fifth. I've not spoken with anyone from the school yet, but I can do that later." She stopped as suddenly as a bullet hitting a block of concrete. He would need to get used to her style.

"OK. We'll review it all in a bit. What about Kimmie?"

"You really believe she's very important in this gang," she said. "Why is that?"

Should I count to ten? he thought.

"How many girls were in the gang, in total?" he asked instead. "And how many of them have since disappeared? Only one, am I right? And she's probably also a girl whom one could assume wants to change her current status. So that's why I'm especially interested in her. If Kimmie is still alive, she might be the key to a whole lot of information. Don't you think we ought to consider the possibility?"

"Who says she wants to change her current status? Many homeless people can't be forced to live in a house again, if that's what you think."

If her mouth always ran on like this, it would drive him up the wall.

"I'll ask you again, Rose. What have you found out about Kimmie?"

"Do you know what, Carl? Before we come to that, I'd like to say that you need to buy a chair so Assad and I can sit down in here when we're giving you our reports. Your back starts aching when you have to loll around in the doorway, even when we're discussing the tiniest details."

So loll around somewhere else, he thought, taking a deep drag of his cigarette.

"I'm sure you've seen the perfect chair in some catalogue or other," was what he said.

She didn't bother to respond. He figured that meant there would probably be a chair standing there in the morning.

"There isn't much in the public registry on Kirsten-Marie Lassen. At any rate, she has never been on the dole. She was expelled from school in the fifth form and later continued her education in Switzerland, but I don't have anything more about that. The last registered address I have is at Bjarne Thøgersen's on Arnevangen in Brønshøj. I don't know when she moved out, but it couldn't have been too long before Thøgersen turned himself in, I think. Which would make it any time before September 1996. And before that, from 1992 to 1995, she's listed at her stepmother's on Kirkevej in Ordrup."

"You'll get me the woman's full name and address, right?"

Before he'd completed his sentence she'd handed him a yellow slip of paper.

Kassandra was the woman's name. Kassandra Lassen. He knew the film, *The Cas-*

sandra Crossing, but he'd never heard it as a damn name.

"What about Kimmie's father? Is he still alive?"

"Yes," she replied. "Willy K. Lassen, software pioneer. He lives in Monte Carlo with a new wife and a couple of rather new children. I've got the note somewhere on my desk. He was born around 1930, so either his pistol comes fully loaded or his new wife is a bit of a tart." She fabricated a smile that covered four-fifths of her face, accompanied by that growling laughter, which at some point was going to make Carl lose his composure.

She finished laughing. "It doesn't appear that Kirsten-Marie Lassen slept at any of the shelters we normally check, but it's possible that she rented a room or something else that's not reported to the taxman. What the heck, that's how my sister scrapes by. She has four lodgers at a time. You need something to support three kids and four cats when your husband is a prick who abandons you, don't you?"

"I don't think you should be telling me too many details, Rose. I am a guardian of the law, in case you've forgotten."

She held out her palms. *Good grief*, her expression said, *if he's going to be such a stickler, that's his problem.*

"But I have information about Kirsten-Marie Lassen's admission to Bispebjerg Hospital in the summer of 1996. I don't have the case record because they have to rummage around in their archives even if you need information on something that happened the day before yesterday. I only have the time she was admitted and the time at which she disappeared."

"She disappeared from the hospital? While undergoing treatment?"

"I don't know anything about that part, but in any case there's a notation saying she left against the doctor's wishes."

"How long was she in the hospital?"

"Nine or ten days." Rose riffled through her small yellow slips of paper. "Here. From July 24, to August 2, 1996."

"The second of August?"

"Yes, why?"

"That was the date of the Rørvig murders. Exactly nine years afterward, to the day."

She pouted upon hearing this, clearly irritated that she hadn't noticed the coincidence herself.

"Which department was she in? Psychiatric?"

"No. The gynecological ward."

He drummed on the edge of the desk.

"OK. Get the file. Go over there yourself and offer your assistance, if necessary."

She gave an ultra-quick nod.

"What about the newspaper archives, Rose, have you looked into them?"

"Yes, and there's not much. Court proceedings were closed in 1987, and when Bjarne Thøgersen was arrested, Kimmie was not named."

He breathed deeply. Only now did it occur to him. Not one of the boarding-school gang had ever been publicly named in connection with the case. Unsullied, they had quietly climbed to the top rung of society without anyone having reason to raise an eyebrow. No bloody wonder they tried to keep it that way.

But why the hell had they tried to frighten him in such an amateurish and unacceptable way? Why had they not just come to him and explained themselves if they knew he was the one investigating the case? All else simply created suspicion and resistance.

"She disappeared in 1996," he said. "Wasn't a missing-persons bulletin issued to the media?"

"She wasn't listed as missing. Not even by the police. She simply disappeared. The family did nothing."

Carl nodded. Nice family.

"In other words, there's nothing in the papers about Kimmie," he said. "What about galas? Didn't she go to those? People with her background do that."

"I've no idea."

"Then get to work checking it out, please. Ask the people at the tabloids. Ask them at *Gossip*. They have nearly bloody everyone in their archives. You must be able to find a damned caption or something."

She gazed at him with an expression probably meant to suggest that she was ready to give up on him. "It'll probably take a long time to find her hospital case record. What should I start with?"

"Bispebjerg Hospital. But don't forget the tabloids. People in her circles are prize meat for those vultures. Do you have her registry information?"

She handed the paper to him. There was nothing new in it. Born in Uganda. No siblings. Every other year throughout her childhood a new home address, alternating between England, the United States, and Denmark. When she was seven, her parents divorced, and oddly enough her father was given custody. And she was born Christmas Eve.

"There are two items you've forgotten to

ask about, Carl. I think that's embarrass-ing."

He lifted his eyes toward Rose. From that angle she resembled a slightly chubby ver-sion of Cruella de Vil right before she snatched the 101 little Dalmatians. Maybe it was a good idea to get that chair on the other side of his desk after all, so the perspective could be altered a bit.

"What's embarrassing?" he asked, not car-ing to hear the answer.

"You haven't asked about the tables. The tables out in the corridor. They've already arrived. But they're in boxes and need to be assembled. I'd like Assad to help me."

"That's fine with me, if he can figure out how to do it. But, as you can see, he's not here. He's out in the field searching for the mouse."

"Hmm. What about you, then?"

He shook his head slowly. Assemble tables with her? She must be out of her mind.

"And what is the other item I haven't asked about, if I may be so bold?"

She looked as though she couldn't be bothered to respond. "You know, if we don't put the tables together, I won't copy all that shit you asked me to. One good turn de-serves another."

Carl swallowed hard. In a week she would

be out of here. She could babysit those damned dried-cod eaters who were visiting on Friday, then it would be a good swift kick of his shoe.

"Well, anyway. The other thing was that I spoke to the Inland Revenue. They told me that Kirsten-Marie Lassen had employment from 1993 to 1996."

Carl paused in the middle of a hit on his cigarette. "She did? Where?"

"Two of the places don't exist anymore, but the third one does. She also worked there the longest. A pet shop."

"A pet shop? Did she wait on customers in a pet shop?"

"I don't know. You'll have to ask them. It's still at the same address. Ørbækgade 62 in Amager. Nautilus Trading A/S, it's called."

Carl noted it down. It would have to wait a bit.

She bowed her head toward him, brow arched. "And yes, Carl, that was all." She nodded at him. "And you're welcome, by the way, kind sir."

17

"I'd like to know who halted my investigation, Marcus."

The homicide chief peered over his bifocals. Of course he did not care to respond to the question.

"And, apropos, I think you should know that I've had uninvited guests in my home. Have a look at this."

He produced the old photograph of himself in a parade uniform and pointed at the splatters of blood. "Usually it's hanging in my bedroom. Last night the blood was still pretty fresh."

Carl's boss leaned back slightly to inspect it. He didn't care for what he saw.

"What do you make of it, Carl?" he asked after a moment's pause.

"Someone wants to scare me. What else can I make of it?"

"Every policeman makes enemies along the way. Why do you assume this has anything to do with the case you're on now? What about your friends and family? Are there any practical jokers among them, do you think?"

Carl smirked. It was a nice try. "I got three telephone calls last night. Do you think someone was on the other end when I picked up?"

"I see! And what would you like me to do about it?"

"I'd like you to tell me who's shutting down my investigation. Would you rather I call the police chief myself?"

"She'll be here this afternoon. We'll see what she says."

"Can I count on it?"

"We'll see."

On the way out of the homicide chief's office Carl slammed the door a little harder than usual, then found himself staring directly into Bak's pale, sickly, morning face. The black leather coat that was always glued onto him now hung nonchalantly over his shoulder. *Now I've seen everything,* thought Carl.

"What's up, Bak? I hear you're leaving us. Did you inherit money or something?"

Bak stood a moment, as though considering whether the sum total of their shared working life was ending in a minus or a plus.

Then he turned his head slightly and said: "You know how it is. Either you're a damn good policeman, or you're a damn good family man."

Carl considered putting a hand on his shoulder, but settled on proffering one instead. "Last day today! I wish you luck and happiness with the family, Bak. Even though you're a total arsehole, know that you wouldn't be the worst to have back if you chose to return after your leave of absence."

The tired man looked at Carl, surprised. Or maybe the right word was "overwhelmed." Børge Bak's microscopic emotional displays were difficult to interpret.

"You've never been especially kind, Carl," he said, shaking his head. "But I guess you're all right."

For the two men this was a shocking orgy of compliments.

Carl turned and nodded toward Lis, who stood behind the front desk with at least as many papers as those lying on the basement floor waiting to be put on one of the tables Rose had already assembled.

"Carl," Bak said, his hand resting on the door handle to the homicide chief's office. "Marcus isn't the one stopping your investigation, if that's what you think. It's Lars

Bjørn." He raised his index finger. "You didn't hear that from me."

Carl cast a glance at the deputy commisioner's office. As usual, the blinds were down, but the door was open.

"He'll be back at three. There's a meeting with the police chief, as far as I know," were Bak's final words to him.

He found Rose Knudsen on her knees in the basement corridor. Like a full-grown polar bear sliding across the ice, she lay with her legs splayed out and both elbows on a piece of folded-out cardboard. Around her were table legs and metal brackets and an array of Allen keys and tools. Four inches below her nose lay a jumble of assembling instructions.

She'd ordered four height-adjustable tables, and Carl certainly hoped that after all that effort they would indeed materialize.

"Weren't you supposed to visit Bispebjerg Hospital, Rose?"

Without budging from her patch of floor, she merely pointed at Carl's door. "There's a copy on your desk," she said. Then she was lost in the assembly diagrams once more.

Bispebjerg Hospital had faxed her three

pages and, sure enough, they were lying on Carl's desk. Stamped and dated and exactly what he wanted. Kirsten-Marie Lassen. Admitted July 24, to August 2, 1996. Half the words were in Latin, but their meaning was clear enough.

"Pop in here for a minute, will you, Rose," he called out.

There was a series of groans and curses from the corridor floor, but she did as he asked nonetheless.

"Yes?" she said, with pearls of sweat on her mascara-massacred face.

"They found the case record!"

She nodded.

"Have you read it?"

Again she nodded.

"Kimmie was pregnant and was admitted due to bleeding following a violent fall down a flight of stairs," he said. "She received good care and apparently made a good recovery, and yet she lost the child. There were signs of new injuries. Did you also read that?"

"Yes."

"There's nothing here about the father or any relations."

"That was all Bispebjerg had, they said."

"I see." Again he paged through the file. "So she was four months along when she was admitted. After a few days the doctors believed her risk of miscarriage had passed, but on the ninth day she miscarried anyway. In the follow-up examination they found new bruises from a blow to her abdomen. Kimmie explained them by saying she'd fallen out of bed." Carl fumbled after a cigarette. "That's really hard to believe."

Rose backed a couple of steps away, eyes squinting as she rapidly fanned the air with one hand. So she couldn't tolerate cigarette smoke. All right then! There was something that could keep her at a distance.

"No police report was filed," she said. "But then again, if that had been the case, we would have already known."

"It doesn't say whether doctors performed a D and C on her or anything like that. But what does this mean?" He pointed a few lines down the page. "*Abortus incompletus.* Doesn't that mean 'miscarriage'?"

"I phoned them. It means that not all the placenta passed with the miscarriage."

"How big is the placenta in the fourth month?"

She shrugged. Clearly this had not been part of her curriculum at business college.

"And she never got a D and C?"

"No."

"As far as I know that can be fatal. Infections in the abdominal cavity are no laughing matter. She was also injured by the blows. Badly, I imagine."

"That was why the doctors wouldn't discharge her." She pointed at the surface of his desk. "Did you see the note?"

It was a small, self-adhering yellow thing. How the hell did she expect him to see something that tiny on his desk? Next to it, the needle in the haystack was nothing.

"Call Assad," it read.

"He called half an hour ago. He said he'd probably seen Kimmie."

Carl felt a lurch in his gut. "Where?"

"At the central train station. You're supposed to phone him."

He tore his coat off the hook. "The station's only four hundred yards away. I'm *outta* here!"

Out on the street, people were walking around in short sleeves. The shadows were suddenly long and sharp, and everyone seemed to be trying to out-smile one another. It was late in September and a little more than twenty degrees, so what the hell were people smiling for? They ought to be raising their faces toward the ozone layer in horror. He removed his coat and slung it over his shoulder. Next there would be people wearing sandals in January. Long live the greenhouse effect.

He pulled out his mobile, punched in Assad's number, and realized his battery was dead. This was the second time in just a few days that had happened. Fucking useless battery.

He entered the central station and scanned the crowd. It looked hopeless. So he made a fast, fruitless round of the sea of suitcases.

Son of a bitch, he thought, heading to the train depot's police station near the exit to Reventlowsgade.

He needed to call Rose now to get Assad's number. He could already hear her gravelly, mocking laughter.

The personnel behind the front desk at the police station didn't know him, so he pulled out his badge. "I'm Carl Mørck. Hi. My mobile is dead. Can I use your telephone?"

One of the cops pointed at an old contraption behind the desk while trying to console a young girl who'd wandered away from her big sister. Ages ago Carl had been the cop on the beat, consoling children. It was actually sad to think about.

Just as he was about to dial the number, he spotted Assad through the blinds. He was standing next to the stairwell to the public lavatories, half hidden behind a flock of excited high-school students wearing rucksacks. He didn't look too good, scoping out the territory in his wretched coat.

"Thanks for letting me use the phone," Carl said, and hung up.

Only five or six yards separated them by the time Carl was outside the police office and about to hail Assad, when someone came from behind Assad and grabbed his shoulder. He was dark-skinned, about thirty years old, and didn't seem particularly friendly. In one jerk he spun Assad round and began shouting curses at him. Carl didn't understand what he was saying, but Assad's expression left no doubt. Friends they weren't.

A couple of the girls among the flock of students looked at them indignantly. *Low-life! Tossers!* their faces seemed to say through arrogant masks.

Then the man lashed out at Assad, and Assad struck back with an incredibly precise and devastating blow that stopped the man in his tracks. For a moment he stood wobbling, as the schoolteachers discussed whether or not to get involved.

But Assad didn't care. He grabbed the man roughly and clutched him tight, until he began shouting again.

Then, as the school group angled away from the scene, Assad caught sight of Carl, and his reaction was instantaneous. He shoved the man away and gave him a hand gesture that invited him to fuck off. Before the man reached the stairway to the train platform, Carl managed to get a glance at him. At his razor-sharp sideburns and glistening hair. He was a handsome guy with a hateful gaze. Not the kind of man one wished to see again.

"What just happened?" Carl asked.

Assad shrugged. "I'm sorry, Carl. He's just some idiot."

Assad's eyes roamed all over. Toward the police station behind Carl, toward the schoolchildren, toward Carl, and beyond. This was a completely different Assad to the one who made mint tea in the basement. A man with a score to settle.

"You'll tell me what that was all about when you're ready, OK?"

"It was *nothing*. Just a neighbor of mine." Then he smiled. Not convincingly, but almost. "You got my message then? You know your mobile is completely dead, right?"

Carl nodded. "How do you know it was Kimmie you saw?"

"A junkie prostitute called out her name."

"Where is she now?"

"I don't know. She managed to get away in a taxi."

"Bloody hell, Assad. You followed her, didn't you?"

"Yes. My taxi was right behind hers, but when we reached Gasværksvej, her taxi had stopped just around the corner. She was already gone then. I was just a second too late, and she was gone."

Success and failure, all at once.

"Her taxi driver said that she'd given him five hundred kroner. She'd just hopped in the backseat, shouting, 'Drive to Gasværksvej! Fast. The money's all yours.'"

Five hundred kroner for five hundred yards. That's desperation.

"I searched for her, of course. Went in all the shops to hear if they'd seen anything. Rang doorbells."

"Did you get the taxi driver's number?"

"Yes."

"Bring him in for questioning. There's something fishy about this."

Assad nodded. "I know who the junkie prostitute is. I have her address." He handed him a note. "I got it from this police station ten minutes ago. Her name is Tine Karlsen. She has a bedsit down on Gammel Kongevej."

"Well done, Assad. But how did you get the information from the officers? Who did you say you were?"

"I showed them my ID from headquarters."

"That doesn't allow you to get that kind of information, Assad. You're a civil employee."

"Well, I got it anyway. But it would be good then if I got a badge now that you're sending me out so much, Carl."

"I'm sorry, Assad, but I can't do that." He shook his head. "You said they knew her at the station. Has she been arrested?"

"Oh, yes. Many times. They are rather tired of her. She usually goes around begging for money near the train station's main entrance."

Carl looked up at the yellow building buttressed against Teaterpassagen. Lots of sets of rooms on the lower four floors, attic rooms at the top. It wasn't difficult to guess where Tine Karlsen lived.

The door to the fifth floor was opened by a gruff-looking man in a threadbare blue dressing gown. "Tine Karlsen, you say? Follow me." He led Carl past the stairwell and into a corridor with four or five doors. He pointed at one as he clawed his gray beard.

"We don't like having the police running around up here," he said. "What did she do?"

Carl squinted, drawing one of his acerbic smiles from his goody bag. The man earned wads of cash on these small, crappy rooms. So he could bloody well treat his tenants properly.

"She's an important witness in a renowned case. I request that you give her the support she needs. Do you understand?"

The man let go of his beard. Did he understand? He had absolutely no idea what Carl was talking about. But it didn't matter — so long as it worked.

She didn't open her door until he'd pounded on it for what seemed an eternity. Her face was extraordinarily ravaged.

Inside the room he was met with a pungent, nasty odor, the smell a pet's cage exudes when it isn't cleaned often enough. Carl remembered all too well that phase of his stepson's life — when his hamsters mated day and night on his desk. In no time the number had multiplied fourfold, and that trend would have continued if the boy hadn't lost interest and the animals hadn't begun eating each other. In the months before Carl donated the rest of the critters to a day-care center, the stink was a permanent fixture of the home atmosphere.

"You've got a rat, I see," he said, bending toward the little monster.

"His name's Lasso and he's completely tame. Would you like me to take it out so you can hold it?"

He tried to smile. Hold it? A mini-pig with a hairless tail? He'd sooner eat its fodder.

It was at that point Carl decided to show her his police badge.

She glanced disinterestedly at it and wobbled over to the table. With an experienced hand, she pushed a syringe and some tinfoil fairly discreetly under a magazine. Heroin, if he were to venture a guess.

"I understand you know Kimmie?"

Had she been arrested with a needle in her veins or shoplifting or jerking off a customer on the street she wouldn't have batted an eye. But that question made her jump.

Carl moved to the dormer window and looked out over the soon-to-be barren trees that ringed St Jørgen's Lake. Hell of a nice view this junkie had.

"Is she one of your best friends, Tine? I've heard you two are close."

He leaned right up against the window and gazed down at the footpath alongside the water. Had the girl been normal, she might be jogging around the lake a few times a week like the ones doing so now.

His eyes scanned the bus stop on Gammel Kongevej, where a man in a light-colored coat stood staring up at the building. Carl had seen the guy from time to time during his many years on the force. Finn Aalbæk. A gaunt ghost of a man who used to camp at Antonigade Police Station so his little detective agency could sponge bits of information from Carl and his colleagues. It had been at least five years since Carl had last seen him, and he was still just as ugly.

"Do you know the man in the light-colored coat down there?" he asked. "Have you seen him before?"

She stepped to the window, sighed deeply, and tried to focus on the man. "I've seen someone in the same coat in the central station. But he's too damn far away for me to really see him."

He saw her enormous pupils. Even if the man stood right in her face she would hardly have recognized him.

"And the man you saw at the train station. Who's he?"

She moved away from the window and bumped into the table, so he had to grab her. "I'm not sure I want to talk to you," she sniffled. "What has Kimmie done?"

He escorted her to the settle bed and eased her onto the thin mattress.

Let's try another angle, Carl thought, glancing round. The room was ten square yards and seemed as devoid of personality as possible. Apart from the rat cage and clothes piled in the corners, there were very few objects in the apartment. A few sticky magazines on the table. Stacks of beer-reeking plastic shopping bags. The bed and its coarse, wool blanket. A sink and an old refrigerator, on top of which was a grimy soap dish, a well-used towel, a tipped-over bottle of shampoo and a small collection of hairpins. There was nothing on the walls and nothing on the windowsill.

He looked down at her. "You're growing your hair long, right? I think it'll look good on you."

Instinctively she reached for her neck. So he was right. That was what the hairpins were for.

"You also look nice with shoulder-length hair, but I think long hair will look very good on you. You have fine hair, Tine."

She didn't smile, but behind those eyes of hers she was jubilant. For a brief instant.

"I'd like to hold your rat, but I've become allergic to rodents and the like. I'm very sorry about that, in fact. I can't even hold our little kitty anymore."

Now he had her.

"I love that rat. It's name is Lasso." She smiled with what had once been a row of white teeth. "Sometimes I call it Kimmie, but I haven't told her that. It's because of the rat I'm called Rat-Tine. It's just so cute, don't you think? Especially when you know you've got your nickname from it."

Carl tried to agree.

"Kimmie hasn't done anything, Tine," he said. "We're looking for her because there's someone who misses her."

She bit the inside of her cheek. "I don't know where she lives. But tell me your name. If I see her I'll pass it on."

He nodded. Years of fighting the authorities had taught her the art of caution. Completely wasted on junk and yet still on her guard. Quite impressive, and at least as irritating. It would certainly not help the case if she told Kimmie too much. Then they ran the risk of Kimmie disappearing for good. Eleven years' experience and Assad's hunting her had demonstrated that she was capable of it.

"OK, I need to be honest with you, Tine. Kimmie's father is seriously ill, and if she hears that the police are searching for her, then her father will never see her again, and that would be a terrible shame. Can't you just tell her to call this number? Don't mention the illness or the police. Just have her call."

He wrote his mobile number on his pad and gave her the page. He'd have to make sure to charge the battery.

"And if she asks who you are?"

"Then just tell her you don't know, but that I said it was something that would make her happy."

Tine's eyelids closed slowly. Her hands lay relaxed on her thin knees.

"Did you hear that, Tine?"

She nodded with her eyes closed. "Yeah, OK."

"Good. I'm glad to hear it. I'll be going now. I know there's someone looking for Kimmie at the central train station. Do you know who?"

She looked at him without raising her head. "Just someone asking whether I knew Kimmie. He probably wanted her to contact her father, too, right?"

Down on Gammel Kongevej he grabbed hold of Aalbæk from behind. "An old offender, out getting some sun," he said, resting a heavy fist on his shoulder. "What are you doing here, old boy?" he went on.

"Long time no see, eh?"

Aalbæk's eyes were bright — but not with the joy of recognition.

"I'm waiting for the bus," he said, turning his head away.

"OK." Carl looked at him. Strange response. Why did he lie? Why not just say: "I'm on an assignment. I'm shadowing someone." It *was* his job, after all, and they both knew it. He hadn't been accused of anything. He didn't need to reveal whom he was working for.

No, but now he had revealed himself. No doubt about it. Aalbæk was certainly aware that it was Carl's path he was crossing.

"Waiting for the bus," the man had said. What an idiot.

"You really get around in your job, don't you? You didn't by any chance take a trip to Allerød yesterday and mess up one of my photographs? What do you say, Aalbæk? Did you?"

Aalbæk turned round calmly to face Carl. He was the type of person who you could kick and punch without getting a reaction. Carl knew a guy born with underdeveloped frontal lobes who was simply unable to become angry. If the brain had a similar area that controlled emotion and stress, in Aalbæk's case it had been replaced with an echoing vacuum.

Carl tried again. Why the hell not?

"What are you doing here? Can't you tell me that, Aalbæk? Shouldn't you be up at my place in Allerød instead, drawing swastikas on my bedposts? Because there's a connection between what we're both working on right now, isn't there, Aalbæk?"

His facial expression didn't exactly suggest a desire to oblige. "You're still a sarky old git, eh, Mørck? I really have no idea what you're talking about."

"Why are you standing here, staring up at the fifth floor? It wouldn't happen to be because you hope Kimmie Lassen drops by to say hi to Tine Karlsen, would it? You're the one asking round the central train station for her, aren't you?" He got in Aalbæk's face. "Today you connected Tine Karlsen up there with Kimmie, didn't you?"

The thin man's jaw muscles worked under the skin. "I don't know who or what you're blathering on about, Mørck. I'm here because a father and mother wish to know what their son is doing with the Moonies on the second floor."

Carl nodded, recalling how slick Aalbæk was. Of course he was able to fabricate a cover story when he needed one.

"I think it might be nice to see your business receipts from this last period of time. I wonder if one of your employers is interested in finding this Kimmie? I think so. I'm just not completely sure why. Will you tell me that voluntarily, or do I need to fetch those receipts myself?"

"You can fetch whatever the hell you like. Just remember a warrant."

"Aalbæk, old boy." He thumped him so hard on the back that his shoulder blades collided. "Will you tell your employer that the more they harass me privately, the more I will go after them. Is that understood?"

Aalbæk was trying not to gasp for air, but when Carl was out of sight, he surely would. "I've understood enough to know that you're losing it, Mørck. Leave me alone."

Carl nodded. That was the disadvantage of being the head of the country's unquestionably tiniest investigative unit. If he had a few more men, he'd put a couple of his best magnets on Finn Aalbæk. He had a strong hunch it would pay to tail this stick figure, but who would do it? Rose?

"You'll hear from us," Carl said, heading off down Vodroffsvej. Then, when he was out of sight, he ran as fast as he could down the cross street and back around the Codan Building, ending up on Gammel Kongevej again, near Værnedamsvej. In a few breathless leaps he was on the other side of the street in time to see Aalbæk standing beside the lake, talking into his mobile.

Maybe he was hard to ruffle, but he certainly didn't look happy.

18

During the time Ulrik worked as a stock market analyst he had made many investors richer than anyone else in his line of business, and the key words were "information, information, information." In this field, wealth was created neither through coincidence nor luck. Certainly not luck.

Nobody in the business had as many contacts, and there wasn't a single media conglomerate where he didn't know someone. He was confident and careful, and he scrutinized the publicly traded companies thoroughly and by every imaginable means before he estimated the profitability of their stocks. Sometimes he was so thorough, in fact, that businesses asked him to forget what he'd learned. And his acquaintances with people who were caught in a bind, or who knew someone who knew someone who needed help getting out of an ugly situation, spread like ripples in the water until they eventually covered the entire ocean upon which society's largest platforms floated.

In some less advanced countries this would have made Ulrik an extremely dangerous man who for many would have been a much better ally with his throat slashed — but not here. In tiny Denmark the system was so ingenious that if you knew some dirt about somebody, they also knew something just as bad about you. If it wasn't hushed up, the one person's offense quickly infected the other's. A strange, practical principle that meant that no one would say anything about anyone else, not even if they were caught with their hands in the biscuit tin.

Because nobody wanted to spend six years in prison for insider trading. And nobody wanted to saw off the branch they were sitting on.

Up in his slowly growing money tree, Ulrik spun a spiderweb that in polite circles was called a "network" — this wonderful, paradoxical word that functioned as intended only if the net filtered out more people than it caught.

And Ulrik made exceptionally good catches in his network. The kinds of people others read about. Respected people. The crème de la crème. All of them people who'd risen from their origins and were now soaring toward a stratum where one needn't share the sunlight with riffraff.

These were the people he hunted with. The ones he walked arm in arm with at the Freemasons' lodge. The ones who understood the importance of sticking with their own kind.

Ulrik was thus a vital cog in the boarding-school gang's wheel. He was the gregarious one everyone knew, and behind him stood his childhood pals, Ditlev Pram and Torsten Florin. It was a strong, albeit oddly matched, triumvirate, one that was invited to everything worth being invited to.

This afternoon they had begun their high jinks at a reception in a downtown gallery that had connections to both the theater scene and the royal family. Afterward they'd wound up at a lavish soirée in the company of parade uniforms, medals, and knightly orders. The event featured well-prepared speeches written by underlings who had not been invited, while a string ensemble tried to draw those present into Brahms' world, and the champagne and self-praise flowed generously.

"Is it true what I'm hearing, Ulrik?" the cabinet minister at his side asked, his alcohol-dulled eyes trying to measure the distance to his glass. "Is it really true that Torsten killed a couple of horses with a crossbow on a hunt this summer? Just like that, in an open field?" He tried again to pour a few drops in his much-too-tall glass.

Ulrik reached out in support of the man's efforts. "Do you know what? Don't believe everything you hear. And, by the way, why don't you come and hunt with us sometime? That way you can see for yourself what it's all about."

The minister nodded. This was exactly what he'd wanted, and he would love it. Ulrik knew such things. Another important man snared in his net.

Then he turned to his dinner companion, who'd been attempting to get his attention all evening.

"You look beautiful tonight, Isabel," he said, laying a hand on her arm. In another hour she would learn what she'd gotten herself into.

Ditlev had assigned him the task. They didn't get a bite every time, but this was a sure thing. Isabel would do whatever they asked her to — she seemed to be up for a little of everything. Of course she would whimper along the way, but the years of boredom and lack of satisfaction would certainly be a plus. Perhaps she'd find it more difficult bearing Torsten's method of handling her body than that of the others, but on the other hand they'd seen evidence that it was precisely this way of Torsten's that made them dependent. Torsten understood women's sensuality better than most. In any event, she'd keep it to herself. Rape or not, she wouldn't run her mouth off. Why hazard the risk of losing access to the many millions her impotent husband controlled?

Ulrik stroked her forearm, up along her silken sleeve. This cool fabric, primarily worn by warm-blooded women — he simply loved it.

He nodded to Ditlev at one of the tables across from him. It should have been the signal, but a man was standing at Ditlev's side, stealing his attention. He was whispering something to Ditlev, who sat there holding a forkful of salmon mousse, ignoring all else. His eyes were staring blankly into space as the wrinkles on his forehead deepened into furrows. It was impossible to misinterpret these signs.

With an appropriate excuse, Ulrik stood up and tapped Torsten on the shoulder as he passed his table.

The neglected woman would have to wait until next time.

He heard Torsten excuse himself to his

dinner companion. In a moment he would kiss her hand, which was expected of a man like Torsten Florin. A heterosexual man who dressed women ought to also know how best to undress them.

The three of them met in the foyer.

"Who was the guy you were talking to?" Ulrik asked.

Ditlev's hand fidgeted with his bow tie. He hadn't fully recovered from what he'd just heard. "That was one of my people from Caracas. He came to tell me that Frank Helmond has told several of the nurses that we were the ones who attacked him."

It was precisely this kind of mess Ulrik hated. Hadn't Ditlev sworn he'd had the situation under control? Didn't Thelma promise that she and Helmond would keep their mouths shut if the divorce and his plastic surgery went smoothly?

"Shit!" Torsten exploded.

Ditlev looked at each of them in turn. "Helmond was still under the influence of the anaesthetic. No one will believe him." He glanced at the floor. "It'll work out. But there's something else. My man also got a telephone message from Aalbæk. Apparently none of us has our mobiles on."

He gave them the note and Torsten read

over Ulrik's shoulder.

"I don't understand the last part," Ulrik said. "What does it mean?"

"Sometimes you can be so damned dim-witted, Ulrik." Torsten glared at him disrespectfully. Ulrik hated that.

"Kimmie's out there somewhere," Ditlev cut him off. "You've not heard, Torsten, but she was seen at the central station today. One of Aalbæk's men heard a junkie calling her name. He only saw her from behind, but he'd observed her earlier in the day. She was wearing expensive clothes and she looked good. She'd been sitting at a café for an hour or an hour and a half. He just thought it was someone waiting for a train. At one point she also walked past them at close range while Aalbæk was briefing his men."

"Bloody fucking hell!" Torsten blurted.

Ulrik hadn't heard this last part, either. It wasn't good news. Maybe she knew they were after her.

Damn. Of course she knew. It was Kimmie, after all.

"She'll get away from us again," he said. "I know it."

They all knew that.

Torsten's fox-face narrowed even more. "Aalbæk knows where the junkie lives?"

Ditlev nodded.

"He'll take care of her, right?"

"Yes. The question is whether or not it's too late. The police already paid her a visit."

Ulrik massaged the back of his neck. Ditlev was probably right. "I still don't understand the final line of the message. Does it mean that whoever's investigating the case knows where Kimmie lives?"

Ditlev shook his head. "Aalbæk knows the policeman well. If the cop had known where Kimmie lived he would have taken the junkie back to headquarters after paying her a visit. Of course he could still do that later on. We'll have to consider that possibility. Look at the line above it, Ulrik. What do you think it means?"

"That Carl Mørck is after us. But we've known it all along."

"Read it again, Ulrik. Aalbæk writes: 'Mørck saw me. He's after us.'"

"What's the problem?"

"That Mørck's begun to connect Aalbæk and us and Kimmie and the old case up into one big patchwork. Why, Ulrik? How does he know anything about Aalbæk? Did you do anything we don't know about? You talked to Aalbæk yesterday. What did you tell him?"

"Just the usual, when people get in the

way. That he ought to give the policeman a warning."

"Bloody fool," muttered Torsten.

"And this warning — when did you think you'd get around to telling us about it?"

Ulrik looked at Ditlev. Since the attack on Frank Helmond it had been difficult to come back down to earth. He'd gone to work the next day feeling invincible. The sight of the deathly frightened and bleeding Helmond had been like an elixir. Every trade and index went his way that day. Nothing could or would stop him. Not even some stupid copper digging into matters that didn't concern him.

"I just told Aalbæk he could apply a little pressure," he said. "Drop a warning or two somewhere where they would make an impression on the man."

Torsten turned his back to them and stared across the marble staircase that sliced through the foyer. His thoughts on the situation were stirring inside him.

Ulrik cleared his throat and explained what had happened. It was nothing special. Just a few telephone calls and a few splats of chicken blood on a photograph. A little Haitian voodoo. Like he said: nothing special.

Then the other two looked directly at him.

"Get Visby, Ulrik," snarled Ditlev.

"Is he here?"

"Half the ministry is here. What the hell do you think?"

Section Chief Visby from the Justice Ministry had long been in pursuit of a better job. Despite his obvious qualifications, he couldn't count on becoming department head. And since he'd stepped off the beaten path for top lawyers ages ago, thereby eliminating his chances of securing a judgeship in the higher courts, he was now searching high and low for new bones to chew on before age and misdeeds caught up with him.

He'd met Ditlev on a hunt, and their agreement was that he, in exchange for a couple of favors at work, could prepare himself for assuming the job as their lawyer when Bent Krum soon departed for the eternal happiness of retirement and red wine. The job didn't come with fine titles, but it did offer short working days and unusually high wages.

On several occasions Visby had proved to be a good man for them. Quite the right choice.

"We need your help again," Ditlev said, when Ulrik led him into the foyer.

The section chief looked around furtively, as if the chandeliers had eyes and the wallpaper ears. "Right here and now?" he said.

"Carl Mørck is still investigating the case. He needs to be stopped. Do you understand?" Ditlev said.

Visby fumbled with his dark blue tie with the scallop insignia, the boarding school's coat of arms, while his eyes skated round the hall. "I've done what I could. I can't issue any more directives in other people's names without the minister getting suspicious. As it stands now, it could still seem like an honest mistake."

"Do you need to go through the police chief?"

He nodded. "Indirectly, yes. I can't do anything more with that case."

"Do you understand what it is you're saying right now?" asked Ditlev.

Visby pressed his lips together. Ulrik could read in his face how he'd already planned his life. His wife expected something more at home. Time and holidays and everything people dream about.

"We may be able to get Mørck suspended," the section chief said. "For a short while, anyway. It won't be easy after his work on the Merete Lynggaard case. But that shooting incident a few months ago really affected him, so maybe he could have a relapse — on paper, at least. I'll look into it."

"I can get Aalbæk to accuse him of assault and battery," Ditlev said. "Is that something you can use?"

Section Chief Visby nodded. "Assault and battery? Not bad at all! But we'll need witnesses."

19

"I'm quite certain it was Finn Aalbæk who broke into my house the day before yesterday, Marcus," Carl said. "Are you the one who authorizes warrants for timesheets, or do I do it?"

The homicide chief didn't glance up from the photos of the bloodied woman who'd been assaulted on Store Kannikestræde. She looked like hell, to put it mildly. The blows sat like blue tracks on her face, the region around her eyes terribly swollen. "Am I right to assume your request is connected to the Rørvig murders, Carl?"

"I just want to know who hired Aalbæk, that's all."

"You're not investigating that case anymore, Carl. We discussed it."

First-person plural? The dimwit said "we"? Wasn't the homicide chief familiar with first-person singular? Why the hell didn't they just leave him be?

He took a deep breath. "That's why I'm coming to you, of course. What if it turns out that Aalbæk's clients are the same people who were suspects in the Rørvig case? Doesn't that seem significant to you?"

The chief set his bifocals on the table. "Listen up, Carl. First of all, follow the police chief's order. The case led to a conviction; they prioritize differently further up the system. Second, don't walk in here and play dumb. Do you really think people like Florin and Pram and that stock market analyst are so foolish as to hire someone like Aalbæk through normal channels? *If*, and let me emphasize that, *if* they've hired anyone at all. Now leave me alone. I've got a meeting with the police chief in a few hours."

"I thought that was yesterday."

"It was, and today. Now go, Carl."

"Damn, Carl!" Assad shouted from his office. "Come have a look."

Carl heaved himself out of his chair. Since Assad had returned, Carl hadn't noticed anything peculiar about him, but he could still picture it: that cold glare of the man who'd lashed out at Assad at the central station, a look that seemed to have been built up over many years of hatred. How could

Assad tell an experienced detective that it meant nothing? Nothing whatsoever?

He waded across Rose's half-finished tables, which lay like beached whales on the basement floor. It was time she got them out of the way. At any rate, Carl wasn't going to be the one held accountable if someone came downstairs and tripped over all the clutter.

He found Assad beaming.

"Yeah? What is it?" Carl asked.

"We have a picture, Carl. We have simply a picture then."

"A picture? Of what?"

Assad tapped the computer's space key, and a photograph emerged on the screen. It wasn't in focus and it wasn't a frontal shot, but it was Kimmie Lassen. Carl recognized her at once from the old photographs. Here was Kimmie as she looked now. A quick side glimpse of a fortyish-year-old woman turning her head. Very distinct profile. Straight nose with slight ski-jump. Full lower lip. Lean cheeks and tiny wrinkles clearly visible through the shield of makeup. With a little ingenuity they could manipulate the old photos of her to accommodate for her aging. She was still an attractive woman, albeit careworn. If they got the computer folks to play with the photo programs, then they would have excellent material for instigating a search.

They just needed a valid reason to get the search started. Maybe someone in her family could request it. He would have to check it out.

"I have a new mobile, so I didn't know whether I'd got the shot in the box," Assad explained. "When she ran away from me yesterday I just pressed the button. Reflexes, you know. I tried to get something up on the screen last night, but I did something wrong."

Was that actually possible?

"What do you say? Isn't it fantastic, Carl?"

"Rose!" Carl shouted, twisting his head toward the corridor.

"She's not here. She's out on Vigerslev Allé."

"Vigerslev Allé?" Carl shook his head. "What's she doing there?"

"Didn't you tell her to investigate whether or not the tabloid magazines had anything on Kimmie?"

Carl glanced at Assad's dour-looking old aunts in the picture frames. Soon Assad would be looking like them, too.

"When she gets back, give her the image so she can have it manipulated along with some of the old photos we have. It was good that you took that picture, Assad. Well done." He clapped his partner on the shoulder and hoped in return that Assad wouldn't offer him any of that pistachio glop he was chewing on. "We have an appointment out at Vridsløselille State Prison in half an hour. Shall we get going?"

Already on Egon Olsens Vej, which was the new name of the street to the prison, Carl noticed his partner's obvious discomfort. Not that he broke into a sweat or was reluctant. But he grew unusually quiet, and stared blindly at the front gate towers as if they were waiting to crush him.

Carl didn't feel that way. For him Vridløselille was a convenient drawer into which some of the country's worst arseholes could be shoved. If one combined the sentences the nearly two hundred and fifty inmates were serving, the total figure would be somewhere over two thousand years. A complete waste of life and energy, that's what it was. It was pretty much the last place a person would want to draw a breath, but most of them damned well deserved to be there. That was still his firm conviction.

"We need to head to the right," Carl said, after they'd arrived and gone through the formalities.

Assad hadn't uttered a word the whole time and emptied his pockets without being asked, following instructions automatically. Apparently he knew the procedure.

Carl pointed across the courtyard at a gray building with a white sign that read VISITORS.

Here Bjarne Thøgersen awaited them, no doubt armed to the teeth with dodging tactics. In two or three years he'd be out. He wasn't going to get himself into any trouble.

He looked better than Carl had expected. Eleven years in prison normally takes a thorough toll. Bitter lines at the corner of the mouth, unfocused eyes, and a fundamental recognition of not being any use to anybody, which eventually settles in the body's posture. Yet here was a man with clear, teasing eyes. Skinny for sure, and on guard, but unusually upbeat nonetheless.

He stood up and extended his hand to Carl. No questions or explanations. Someone had evidently told him what was in store. Carl noticed these things.

"Deputy Detective Superintendent Mørck," he said anyway.

"This is costing me ten kroner an hour," the man replied with a wry smile. "I hope it's important."

He didn't greet Assad, but then again, Assad hadn't encouraged it. He just pulled his chair back and sat down at a slight distance.

"You spend time in the workshop?" Carl glanced at his watch. Quarter to eleven. Yes, it was smack in the middle of the workday.

"What's this about?" Thøgersen wanted to know, sitting down a trifle too slowly. Also a telltale sign. So he was a tad nervous, after all. Good.

"I don't hang out much with the other inmates," he continued, unsolicited. "So I can't give you any information, if that's what you're here for. Otherwise I'd be happy to strike a little deal, if it could get me out sooner." He grinned briefly, trying to assess Carl's low-key attitude.

"Twenty years ago you killed two young people, Bjarne. You've confessed, so that part of the case we won't need to discuss, but I do have a missing person you're more than welcome to tell me about."

Bjarne nodded, raising his eyebrows — a nice blend of a bit of goodwill with a pinch of surprise.

"I'm talking about Kimmie. I've heard you two were good friends."

"That's correct. We were at boarding school together, and we also dated at one point." He smiled. "A fucking awesome lady." He would say that about anyone after eleven years without having real sex. The guard had told him that Bjarne Thøgersen never had any visitors. Never. This was his first visit in years.

"Let's start at the beginning. Is that OK with you?"

He shrugged, glancing down for a moment. Of course it wasn't.

"Why was Kimmie expelled from boarding school? Do you recall?"

He put his head back and stared at the ceiling. "Something about her getting involved with one of the teachers. That wasn't permitted."

"What happened to her afterward?"

"She rented an apartment in Næstved for a year. She worked at a grill bar." He laughed. "Her folks didn't know anything about it. They thought she was still in school. But they found out, of course."

"She was sent to boarding school in Switzerland?"

"Yes. She was there for four or five years. Not just boarding school, but also the university. What the hell was it called again?" He shook his head. "Never mind. I can't remember the bloody name. At any rate, she was studying to be a veterinarian.

Hey, wait. It was Berne. The University of Berne."

"So she spoke very good French?"

"No, German. Lectures were in German, she said."

"Did she finish her studies?"

"No, not completely. I don't know why, but she had to quit for some reason."

Carl glanced at Assad, who jotted it down in his notebook.

"And then what? Where did she live after that?"

"She came home. Lived for a while in Ordrup with her parents — that is, with her father and stepmother. And then she moved in with me."

"We know she worked at a pet shop. Wasn't that beneath her level of training?"

"Why? She never finished her studies to become a vet."

"And you, what did you do for a living?"

"I worked at my father's lumberyard. That's all in the report, you know that."

"Wasn't there something in the report about you inheriting the lumberyard in 1995, and then it burned down shortly afterward? After that you were unemployed, right?"

Apparently the man could also appear hurt. "The unloved child has many faces," as Kurt Jensen, his old colleague who now sat twiddling his thumbs in parliament, always said.

"That's utter rubbish," Bjarne protested. "I was never accused of starting that fire. And what would I have got out of it? My father's business wasn't insured."

No, Carl thought. *He should probably have checked that out first.*

Carl sat for a while, staring at the walls. He'd sat in this room countless times before. These walls had lent an ear to tons of lies. Tons of tall tales and assurances no one believed.

"How did she get along with her parents?" he asked. "Do you know?"

Bjarne Thøgersen stretched, already calmer. They'd entered the small-talk zone. The conversation wasn't about him, and he liked that. He felt safe.

"Terribly," he said. "Her folks were a couple of arseholes. I don't think her father was ever home. And the slag he was married to was a mean bitch."

"What do you mean?"

"Yeah, you know. The type of person who only cares about money. A gold-digger." He savored the word. It wasn't one that was regularly used in his world.

"They argued?"

"Yes. Kimmie said they fought like hell."

"What was Kimmie doing while you killed the two teenagers?"

The sudden shift back in the sequence of events caused the man's eyes to freeze on Carl's shirt collar. If there had been electrodes attached to Bjarne Thøgersen, all the gauges would be flipping out.

For a moment he sat in silence, seemingly unwilling to respond. Then he said: "She was with the others at Torsten's father's summer cottage. Why do you ask?"

"Didn't they notice anything about you when you returned? You must have had blood on your clothes."

Carl instantly regretted the last question. He hadn't meant to be so direct. Now the interrogation would come to a standstill. Thøgersen would say he'd told the others how he'd tried to save a dog that had been hit by a car, just as it stated in the report. Damn it.

"Did she think it was cool with all that blood?" Assad asked from the corner, before the man was able to respond to Carl's question.

Bjarne Thøgersen looked confusedly at the little man. A reproachful glare might have been expected, but not this naked, exposed manner indicating that Assad had hit the mark. He didn't need to say anything. Whether the story held or not, they now knew that Kimmie had thought the blood was cool. Very unbecoming for someone who later wanted to dedicate herself to saving the lives of small animals.

Carl gave Assad a quick nod that was intended just as much to show Thøgersen that he'd noted his reaction. A reaction that had been too strong — and miscalculated.

"Cool?" Thøgersen said, trying to recoup. "I don't think so."

"But she moved in with you," Carl went on. "That was in 1995, right, Assad?"

Assad nodded from his corner.

"Yes, in 1995. The twenty-ninth of September. We'd been seeing each other for a while. An awesome lady."

He'd said that before.

"Why do you remember the exact date? It was very many years ago."

He spread his hands. "Right, and what's been happening in my life since then? For me, it's still one of the last things that happened before I was sent here."

"I see." Carl tried to appear obliging. And then he changed his expression. "Were you the father of her child?"

Thøgersen glanced at the clock. His fair skin flushed slightly. Apparently one hour suddenly seemed endless to him.

"I don't know."

Carl considered flaring up in anger, but he checked himself. It was neither the time nor the place. "You say you don't know. What do you mean by that, Bjarne? Was she seeing others besides you when you lived together?"

He tilted his head to the side. "Of course not."

"So it *was* you who got her pregnant?"

"She moved away, didn't she? How the hell would I know who she went to bed with?"

"From what we've determined, she miscarried at around eighteen weeks. Wasn't she living with you when she became pregnant?"

Thøgersen lurched up from his seat and spun the chair round. This was the kind of jaunty attitude prison taught its inmates. Strolling nonchalantly through the central building. The laid-back waving of limbs to indicate indifference. Holding fags loosely between the lips out on the pitch. And then this habit of turning the chair round and taking the next questions with arms on the backrest, legs spread. *Ask me your bullshit, I don't care*, the posture said. *You'll get nothing from me anyway, dumb copper pig.*

"Does it really make any fucking difference who the father was?" he asked. "The kid died, after all."

Ten to one he knew it wasn't his.

"And then she disappeared."

"Yeah, she just took off from the hospital. Really stupid."

"Was it like her to do such a thing?"

He shrugged. "How the hell should I know? She'd never had a miscarriage before, as far as I know."

"Did you go looking for her?" came Assad's voice from the corner.

Thøgersen glowered at him as if it were none of his business.

"Did you?" Carl asked.

"It had been a while since we split up. So no, I didn't."

"Why weren't you together anymore?"

"We just weren't. It didn't work out."

"Was she unfaithful?"

Thøgersen glanced once more at the clock. Only a minute had passed since the last time he'd checked. "Why do you think she was the one who was unfaithful?" he said, and gave his neck a couple of stretch exercises.

They discussed the relationship back and forth for five minutes. It was fruitless. He was slippery as an eel.

Meanwhile, Assad had been slowly edging his chair closer. Each time he asked a question, he inched forward, until he was nearly beside the table. No doubt about it, he was irritating Thøgersen.

"We see you've had a bit of luck on the stock market," Carl said. "According to your tax documents you're a wealthy man. Isn't that right?"

He curled his lips. Smugly. This was something he would love to discuss. "I can't complain," he said.

"Who gave you the investment capital?"

"You can see that in the tax documents."

"I've not actually been carrying your tax documents in my back pocket for the last eleven years, so I think you should just tell me yourself, Bjarne."

"I borrowed the money."

"Well done. Especially considering you were behind bars. Someone who wasn't afraid to give a risky loan, that's for sure. One of the drug kingpins in here, perhaps?"

"I borrowed the money from Torsten Florin."

Bingo, Carl thought. He would have loved to see Assad's face at this moment, but he kept his eyes trained on Thøgersen.

"Well, well. So you were still friends, despite your secret? That it was you who killed those kids. The abominable crime that Torsten, among others, had been suspected of committing. That's what I'd call a friend, I must say. But perhaps he owed you a favor?"

Bjarne Thøgersen realized where this line of questioning was headed and fell silent.

"You are good at stocks then?" Assad had pulled his chair right next to the table. As imperceptibly as a reptile, he'd slithered into position.

Thøgersen shrugged. "Better than many, yes."

"Fifteen million kroner it's turned into." Assad looked dreamy. "And still growing. Maybe I should get tips from you then. Do you give tips?"

"How do you follow the market, Bjarne?" Carl added. "Aren't you rather limited in communicating with the outside world, and vice versa?"

"I read newspapers and send and receive letters."

"So you know the buy-and-hold strategy, maybe? Or the TA-7 strategy? Is that how you do it?" Assad asked calmly.

Carl slowly turned his head toward Assad. Was that poppycock, or what?

Thøgersen smiled curtly. "I follow my nose and KFX stocks. Nothing can go too wrong then." He smiled again. "I've had a good stretch."

"Do you know what, then, Bjarne Thøgersen?" Assad said. "You should have a chat with my cousin. He started with fifty thousand kroner, and now, three years later, he *still* has fifty thousand kroner. He'd like you, I think."

"I'd say your cousin should refrain from trading stocks," Bjarne said, annoyed, and turned back to Carl. "I thought we were supposed to be talking about Kimmie? What does she have to do with my stock trading?"

"That is true, but I have just one more question, for my cousin," Assad insisted. "Is Grundfos a good stock in KFX?"

"Yes, it's decent."

"OK. Thank you then. I didn't think that Grundfos was traded at all, but you probably know better."

Touché, Carl thought, as Assad blinked overtly at him. It wasn't hard to imagine how Bjarne Thøgersen felt right now. It was Ulrik Dybbøl Jensen who invested for him. No doubt about it. Thøgersen didn't know jack about stocks, but he needed enough to live on once he was out of prison. Quid pro quo.

They didn't really need to know any more than that.

"We have a picture we'd like you to see," Carl said. He put Assad's photo on the table. They'd altered the image a bit, and now the focus was sharp as a knife.

They both watched Thøgersen. Of course they'd anticipated a certain kind of curiosity. It's always a special moment to see how an old flame looks after so many years. What they hadn't counted on, however, was the depth of reaction from a guy who had been living among the worst criminals in Denmark. Eleven years of debasement surrounded by all kinds of wretchedness: the pecking order, the homosexuality, assaults, threats, blackmail, brutalization. The man who had made it through all that, looking five years younger than his contemporaries, now turned ashen-faced. His eyes shifted back and forth — from Kimmie's face to the wall, and back again. Like a spectator at an execution who doesn't want to watch, but can't resist, either. A terrible inner conflict that Carl would give anything to understand.

"You're not happy to see her. She looks pretty good," Carl said. "Don't you think?"

Bjarne nodded slowly, his Adam's apple gliding visibly up and down. "It's just strange," he said.

He tried to smile as though he were feeling sad. But it wasn't sadness.

"How can you have a picture of her if you don't know where she is?"

In and of itself the question was reasonable enough, but his hands shook. His words came slowly. His eyes darted back and forth again.

He was afraid. That's what it was.

Simply put, Kimmie scared him to death.

"You have to go and see the homicide chief," the duty officer said as Carl and Assad passed his cage at headquarters. "The police chief is there, too," he added.

Carl took the stairs, formulating his arguments with each step. He was damn well going to give as good as he got. They all knew the police chief. And what did she amount to other than a run-of-the-mill solicitor who'd simply stumbled on the path to a judgship?

"Uh-ohhh," Mrs. Sørensen muttered encouragingly from behind the front desk. He'd return her "uh-ohhh" right back some other time.

"Good that you've come, Carl. We've just been discussing everything," the homicide chief said, pointing at an empty seat. "It doesn't look good, you know."

Carl frowned, wondering if Marcus had

laid it on a little too thick. He nodded at the police chief, who was sitting in full regalia and sharing a pot of tea with Lars Bjørn. Tea, for God's sake.

"You're probably aware of what this is about," Marcus said. "I'm just a little surprised you didn't mention it yourself when we met this morning."

"What are you talking about? That I'm still investigating the Rørvig murders? Isn't that what I've been asked to do? To choose the cases I wish to work on? What about letting me run my own show?"

"Damn it, Carl. Be a man and stop evading the point." Lars Bjørn straightened his slender frame in his chair, so that the police chief's imposing corpus didn't overshadow him. "We're talking about Finn Aalbæk, the proprietor of Detecto, who you assaulted on Gammel Kongevej yesterday. We have his solicitor's breakdown of the incident, so you can read for yourself what the matter is."

The incident? What were they talking about? Carl grabbed the piece of paper and glanced at it. What the hell was Aalbæk up to? In black-and-white it said Carl had assaulted him. Did they really believe that dumb piece of shit?

"Sjölund & Virksund" he read on the letterhead. Quite a proper bunch of bloody high-society bandits, to polish and cleanse the tall tales of such a loser.

The time frame was good enough. Exactly when Carl startled Aalbæk at the bus stop. The dialogue, too, was relatively accurate, but the thump on the back had been turned into repeated hard blows to Aalbæk's face with his fist and the shredding of his clothes. There were photos of his injuries. Aalbæk sure as hell didn't look too good.

"That meathead is being paid by Pram, Dybbøl Jensen, and Florin," he said in self-defense. "They've made him let someone beat him up in order to get me away from the case, no doubt about it."

"That may well be your view, Mørck, but we must address this, nevertheless. You know the procedure whenever there's a report of violence committed on duty." The police chief looked at him with the same pair of eyes that had helped her rise to that stratum where there was really something to see. He, too, was neutralized by them for a moment.

"We won't suspend you, Carl," she continued. "You've never previously abused anyone, now, have you? But earlier this year you suffered both traumatic and sad events. Maybe it's all affected you more than you think. Don't get the impression we're not sympathetic."

Carl gave her a lopsided smile. "Never previously abused anyone," she'd said. It was good that she believed that.

The homicide chief looked at him thoughtfully. "There will be an investigation, of course, and during the investigation we'll use the opportunity to let you go on an intensive treatment program so you can get to the bottom of what you've been through these past few months. In the meantime you will not be allowed to do anything here but administrative tasks. You can come and go as you please, but naturally — and I'm sorry about this — we'll have to ask you to turn in your badge and your pistol during this period." He extended his hand. It was a suspension, pure and simple.

"You'll find the pistol up in the weapons depot," Carl said, handing over his badge. As if not having it would keep him from doing anything he wanted. They ought to know that. But perhaps it was exactly what they wanted him to do — be reckless and stupid. Get caught in dereliction of duty. Was that it? Did they want him to do something dumb so they could get rid of him?

"Aalbæk's solicitor Tim Virksund and I

know each other," the police chief said, "and I will explain to him that you're no longer on the case, Mørck. That will satisfy him, I suspect. He's well aware of his client's provocative style, and nobody will benefit if this ends up in court. It also solves the problem of your difficulty in following orders, doesn't it?" She pointed her finger at him. "Because this time you'll have to. And in the future, Mørck, I'll have you know I won't accept any disruptions in the chain of command. I hope you understand. The Rørvig case ended with a conviction, and you've been told we want you to work on other cases. How clearly and how often do we need to tell you?"

He nodded and glanced out the window. He hated this kind of shitty explanation. For all he cared, the three of them could clear off right now and stuff it.

"Is it unreasonable to ask the real reason why this investigation has to be halted?" he asked. "Who gave the order? Politicians? On what grounds? As far as I know there's a principle of equality before the law in this country. I presume that also goes for people under suspicion of a crime. Or am I misunderstanding something?"

They all gazed sternly at him, as if they were Inquisition judges.

What would they do next? Toss him in the harbor to see if he would float like the Antichrist?

"You'll never guess what I have for you, Carl," Rose said excitedly. He peered down the basement corridor. It wasn't that the height-adjustable tables had been assembled, in any case.

"Your resignation, I hope," he said drily, planting himself on his chair in his office.

That statement seemed to make her mascara look even heavier. "I have two chairs for your office," she said. He cast a glance at the other side of his desk, wondering how in the world five square inches of space could suddenly house two chairs instead of one.

"We'll wait on them," he said. "What else?"

"And I've got a few photos from *Gossip* and *Her Life*," she said in an even tone of voice, but tossed the clippings down a little more brutally than she ordinarily would have.

Carl glanced at them disinterestedly. Now that the case had been taken from him, what did he care about the clippings? In reality he should be asking her to pack away the whole mess and find some guileless soul to assemble her bloody tables in exchange for a kind word and a pat on the cheek.

Then he picked up the copies of the articles.

One of them dated back to around Kimmie's childhood. *Her Life* had drawn a portrait of the Lassen family, and the title read: "No Success without the Security of Home." It was a paean to Willy K. Lassen's beautiful wife, Kassandra Lassen, but the photograph showed something else. The father in a gray suit with tapered legs and the stepmother in bold colors and severe late-seventies makeup. Well-groomed people in their mid-thirties. Self-confident, with stern faces. That little Kirsten-Marie stood clamped between them didn't seem to register for them in the slightest. But it clearly affected Kimmie. With her large, frightened eyes, she was a girl who was simply there in body, not in spirit.

Then, in the *Gossip* photograph seventeen years later, she had a totally different look.

It was from January 1996, the same year as she disappeared. It was taken somewhere along the "death route" of downtown Copenhagen bars. Probably outside the Electric Corner, but it could also be Café Sommersko or maybe even Café Victor. This was a Kimmie in good spirits. Tight jeans, feather boa around her neck, and pissed to the gills. Showing a lot of cleavage in spite of the snow on the pavement. Her face was frozen in a rapturous roar, surrounded by high-society types, among them Kristian Wolf and Ditlev Pram, all wearing enormous overcoats. The caption was gracious: "The jet set pulls out the stops. Twelfth Night party gets its own queen. Has Kristian Wolf, 29, Denmark's most eligible bachelor, finally found a life companion?"

"They were awfully nice at *Gossip*," Rose added. "Maybe they'll find more clippings for us."

He gave a quick nod. If she believed those vultures at *Gossip* were nice, then she was incredibly naive. "You'll have the desks in the corridor assembled in the next few days, OK, Rose? Whatever you find for me regarding this case, you'll put out there and I'll bring it in here myself when I need it. You understand?"

Judging by her facial expression, she didn't.

"What happened up in Jacobsen's office, boss?" came Assad's voice at the door.

"What happened? Well, I'm suspended. But they want me to stay down here. So if you two want to talk to me about anything involving this case, write it on a note and put it on the table just outside the door. You can't talk to me about it, because they'll just send me home. And, Assad, help Rose get those ridiculous tables assembled." He pointed into the corridor. "And keep your ears open: if I want to say anything to you about the case or give you orders, I'll write it down on one of these." He motioned to his sheets of ledger paper. "I'm only allowed to administrate when I'm here, just so you know."

"Crappy arrangement," Assad said. A more grandiose way to express it would be hard to find.

"And on top of it all, I've got to go to therapy. So perhaps I'm not going to be in the office the whole time. Let's see which idiots they stick me with this time."

"Yes, let's see," a voice in the corridor said unexpectedly.

He had misgivings as he turned toward the door.

Of course it was Mona Ibsen. Always on the scene when the bullfrog croaked. Just as he was standing there with his trousers as far down as they could go.

"We'll be going through a longer course of treatment this time, Carl," she said, squeezing her way past Assad.

She held out her hand to him. It was

warm and hard to let go of.
Smooth, and without a wedding ring.

20

As they'd agreed, she found Tine's note
behind the car-rental company's drab sign
on Skelbækgade. It was right on top of the
black panel's bottom screw, and moisture
had already made the letters bleed together.

It had been difficult for the unschooled
girl to find enough room to fit all the big,
block letters on the little slip of paper, but
Kimmie was used to deciphering people's
scribbles.

**HI. THE POLICE CAME BY MY PLACE
YESTERDAY — CARL MØRKE HE WAS
CALLED — ALSO ANUTHER DOWN ON
THE STREET WHO'S LOOKIN FOR YOU
— THE ONE FROM THE CENTRAL STA-
TION. DON'T KNOW WHO HE IS — BE
CAREFULL — SEE YOU ON THE BENCH.
T. K.**

She read the note several times, halting

each time she reached the letter "K," like a freight train at a railroad crossing barrier. The letter was frozen onto her retina. Etched into it. Where did the "K" come from?

The policeman's name was Carl. Carl with a "C." That was a better letter. Better than "K," even though it sounded the same. Him, she wasn't afraid of.

She leaned against the wine red Nissan that had been parked under the sign for ages. Tine's words injected her with an overwhelming weariness. Like there were devils whirling around inside, sucking the life out of her.

I won't leave my house, she thought. *They're not gonna get me.*

But how could she know it wouldn't happen anyway? Apparently Tine had spoken with people who were looking for her. People were asking Tine things. Things that only Tine knew about Kimmie. Lots of different things. So she was no longer just Rat-Tine, a danger to herself. She was now also a danger to Kimmie.

She mustn't speak to anyone, she thought. *When I give her the thousand kroner I'll have to tell her so she understands it.*

Turning round instinctively, she caught sight of the pale blue nylon vest of the bloke distributing free newspapers.

Did someone put him up to keeping an eye on me? she wondered. *Was it possible?* They knew where Tine lived now. Presumably they also knew she and Tine were in contact. Who's to say that Tine hadn't been followed all the way to the rent-a-car sign when she placed the note? What would have stopped the people who followed Tine from reading the note?

She tried to gain control of her thoughts. Wouldn't they have removed it? Of course they would have. And yet: would they?

She glanced again at the newspaper guy. Why wouldn't the dark-skinned man trying to make a living from his thankless job delivering piles of newspapers to busy, pampered people welcome the opportunity to make a few extra pennies? After all, he would just have to watch her go down Ingerslevsgade and along the railway tracks. If he moved a little closer to the stairwell down to Dybbølsbro Station, it would be easy. There wasn't a better lookout spot. Standing that high up, the man would be able to see exactly where she was going and where she ended up. At most it was only five hundred yards down to her iron gate and the little house. At most.

She chewed her upper lip, cinching her

wool coat tighter.

Then she went over to him. "Here," she said, handing him fifteen thousand-krone notes. "You can go home now, right?"

Only early sound movies showed black men with wide eyes so large and white as this man's now. As if the bony hand giving him money were no less than the materialization of a dream. The deposit on a flat of his own. Or a small shop. His ticket home. To a life among other black men under the burning sun.

"Today's Wednesday. How about calling your employer and telling him you won't be coming back till next month? Do you catch my drift?"

Fog was settling over the city and Enghave Park, enshrouding her like an alcoholic haze. Her surroundings were disappearing in a white cloak. The tall windows of Kongens Brewery went first, then the blocks before it, the gazebo at one end of the park, and finally the fountain. Damp air with the scent of autumn.

"Those men must die," said the voices in her head.

That morning she'd opened one of the hollow spaces in the wall and removed the hand grenades. She had studied the devilish devices and seen everything so clearly. They would die individually. One at a time, so fear and remorse would have time to devastate each of those remaining.

She laughed to herself, shoving her ice-cold hands deep in her coat pockets. They were already afraid of her, that had been proven. And now the bastards would do anything to find her. And they were getting closer. Cost what it may. Being the cowards they were.

Then she stopped laughing. She hadn't thought through the last part.

They *were* cowards. That was a fact. And cowardly people didn't wait. They ran for their lives while there was still time.

"I'll have to take them all at once," she said aloud. "I'll have to find a way, otherwise they'll disappear." She knew she could, but the voices inside her demanded something else. They were stubborn, they were. It was enough to make a person crazy.

She rose from the park bench and kicked at the seagulls gathered round her.

Which way to go?

Mille, little Mille, flowed her inner mantra incessantly. This was a bad day. There was too much to consider.

She looked down, saw how the fog put moist droplets on her shoes, and thought once again of the letters at the end of Tine's note. "T. K." Where did the "K" come from?

They were coming up to the break prior to fifth-form exams. Not long after Kimmie had cut Kåre Bruno loose and let him sink, crushed by the lecture she had given him on how mediocre he was, both in terms of intelligence and personality.

It was during the following days that Kristian began to tease her.

"You don't have the guts, Kimmie," he whispered each day during morning assembly.

And each day he would nudge her and clap her on the shoulder as the rest of the gang formed a ring round her. "You wouldn't dare, Kimmie!"

But Kimmie did dare, and they knew it. They watched her movements closely. Cultivated her zeal during class. Her legs sprawled between rows of chairs, her dress inching up. Dimples on display as she sashayed up to the teacher's desk. The see-through blouses and the bedroom voice. Two weeks went by before she awakened desire in the only teacher at the school whom practically everyone liked. Wakened it so emphatically that a person had to laugh.

He was the most recent addition to the faculty. Baby-faced, yet a real man. The year's highest final exam scores in Danish at the University of Copenhagen, so the story went. But he was not the archetypal boarding-school teacher, not at all. He expounded on society beyond the school grounds in nuanced terms. The texts he had them read ranged widely.

Kimmie went to him to ask if he would tutor her for exams. Before the end of the first session he was a lost cause, martyred by the sight of the curves her thin cotton dress so generously revealed.

His name was Klavs with a "v," a name he was at pains to explain as the result of his father's poor judgment and overblown interest in the world of Walt Disney.

None dared to call him Klavs Krikke, the Danish version of Horace Horsecollar from *Donald Duck*, but she managed to bring out his inner steed anyway. After three sessions, he no longer kept a record of tuition hours. He received her in his flat, already half undressed and with the radiators at full blast. Captured her with uncontrollable kisses, restless hands against her bare skin. Lit by a tireless lust that burned his brain empty, he was indifferent to pricked-up ears and envious glances. To rules and regulations.

She was going to tell the headmaster that he'd forced her, curious to see where it would lead. See if she could regain control of the situation.

But it didn't work.

The headmaster called them to his office at the same time. Let them sit silently and uncomfortably next to each other in the waiting room with the secretary as their chaperone.

And after that day, Klavs and Kimmie never spoke again.

What happened to him afterward was none of her concern.

The headmaster told Kimmie to pack her things, the bus to Copenhagen was leaving in half an hour. She needn't bother wearing her school uniform. In fact, he asked her not to. From now on she could consider herself expelled.

Kimmie studied the headmaster's flushed cheeks for some time before meeting his eyes.

"It's possible that you . . ." she paused a moment, stretching out the unforgivable insult of using the familiar form to address him ". . . that *you* don't believe he forced me. But can you be certain that tomorrow's tabloids will see it the same way? Can you imagine the scandal? 'Teacher rapes pupil at . . .' Can you see it?"

She would stay quiet on one simple condition. Yes, she would go. Simply pack her things and leave the school immediately. She didn't care, as long as the school didn't notify her parents. *That* was her condition.

He protested, saying it was improper for the school to receive money for a service it didn't provide, so Kimmie disrespectfully tore the corner from a page of the nearest book on the headmaster's desk and jotted something down.

"Here is my bank account number," she said. "You just transfer the money into my account."

He sighed regretfully. With that slip of paper, decades of authority vanished.

Raising her eyes in the fog, she felt a calm wash over her. Over at the playground, children's voices shrieked lightheartedly, prodding her.

In the entire playground there were only two small children and their nanny. The children were bumbling about, playing tag between autumn-silenced jungle gyms.

She approached them through the mist

and silently observed the girl, who held something in her hand that the boy wanted.

She'd once had a little girl like that.

She felt how the nanny was watching her. How her warning bells had rung the instant Kimmie emerged from the bushes in filthy clothes, her morning hair wild.

"I didn't look this way yesterday," she shouted to the nanny, "you shoulda seen me."

If she'd been wearing the get-up she had on at the central station, things would have been different. Everything would have been different. Maybe the nanny would've even talked to her.

Listened to her.

But the nanny didn't listen. She sprang forward, resolutely blocking Kimmie's path to the children, her arms outstretched. She called for the children to come to her this instant, but they didn't want to. Didn't the woman know that little trolls like these didn't always listen? It amused Kimmie.

So she thrust out her chin and laughed in the nanny's face.

"Come *here*!" the nanny screamed at the kids hysterically, glaring at Kimmie as if she were pure filth.

Which is why Kimmie stepped forward and punched her. She wasn't going to let this person make her out to be some kind of monster.

The nanny lay on the ground yelling at Kimmie that she bloody well better not hit her, that she would bloody well fix her good and proper. She knew plenty of people who could.

Then Kimmie kicked her in the side. Once, and then again, so she fell silent.

"Come over here, little girl, and show me what you have in your hand," she lured. "Is that a little stick you have there?"

But the children were frozen in place. Standing with their fingers held out stiffly, howling for the nanny to come.

Kimmie moved closer. She was such a cute little girl, even though she was crying. And she had such long, pretty hair. Brown hair, just as little Mille had had.

"Come here, my dear, show me what you've got in your hand," she said again, approaching cautiously.

She heard a hissing from behind, and though she whirled around, she couldn't ward off the hard, desperate blow to her neck.

She fell face first into the gravel and felt her abdomen slam against a rock that marked a fork in the path.

Meanwhile, the nanny flew silently around

her and grabbed the children, one in each arm. A real Vesterbro hussy. Tight jeans and greasy hair.

Kimmie raised her head and watched as the two screaming children's faces in the woman's arms disappeared behind the bushes and farther into the open.

She'd once had a little girl like that. Who now lay in a coffin at home under the bed. Waiting patiently.

Soon they would be reunited.

21

"This time I'd like for us to talk completely openly to each other," Mona Ibsen said. "Last time we didn't make it as far as we should have, did we?"

Carl surveyed her world, the posters of beautiful nature scenes, palms, mountains, and the like. Bright, sun-splashed colors. Two chairs made of precious wood, wispy plants. Such astonishing tidiness. There were no accidental elements here. No small thingamajigs to distract. And still, lying on the sofa with his mind opening up, there was this enormous distraction that made him able to think only about tearing the woman's clothes off.

"I will try," he said. He would do everything she asked of him. He wasn't that busy.

"You assaulted a man yesterday. Can you explain why?"

He protested, as was to be expected. Proclaimed his innocence. Still, she looked at him as if he were lying.

"We probably won't get anywhere unless we go backward a little in the sequence of events. It may make you uncomfortable, but it's what we need to do."

"Shoot," he said, eyes squinting just enough so he could watch what her breathing did to her breasts.

"You were involved in a shooting in Amager in January. We discussed it before. Do you remember the exact date?"

"It was the twenty-sixth of January."

She nodded as if it were an especially good date. "You managed to get off relatively unharmed, but one of your colleagues, Anker, died, and another is currently lying paralyzed in the hospital. How are you coping with all this now, Carl, eight months later?"

He stared at the ceiling. How was he coping? He really had no idea. It just never should have happened.

"Of course I'm sorry it happened." He pictured Hardy at the spinal clinic. Sad, silent eyes. Two hundred and sixty-four pounds of dead weight.

"Does it upset you?"

"Yeah, a little." He tried to smile, but she was looking down at her papers.

"Hardy told me he suspects that whoever

shot the three of you had been waiting for you in Amager. Did he tell you that?"

Carl confirmed that he had.

"Did he also tell you that he thinks it was either you or Anker who alerted them?"

"Yes."

"How do you feel about that?"

Now she was sizing him up. In his mind, her eyes flashed with eroticism. Carl wondered if she was aware of this, and how wildly distracting it was.

"Maybe he's right," he replied.

"Of course it wasn't you, I can see that by looking at you. Am I right?"

If it had been him, could she expect any response other than a denial? How dumb did she think people were? How well did she think she could read a face?

"No, it wasn't me. Of course not."

"But if it was Anker, then something must've gone horribly wrong in his life, wouldn't you say?"

I may have the hots for you, Carl thought, *but if I'm going to continue with this, ask me some proper questions, damn it.*

"Yes, of course," he said, hearing his own voice like a whisper. "Hardy and I will have to consider that possibility. Once I'm through being the victim of a little, snot-nosed private detective's lies, and once the powers that be stop putting obstacles in my path, we'll see what we can find out."

"At police headquarters they call it the 'nail-gun case' because of the murder weapon. The victim was shot in the head, was he not? It looked like an execution."

"Possibly. Given the situation, I didn't manage to see much. I've not been involved in the case since. It also had an offshoot, but you probably already know that. Two young men were killed in Sorø the same way. It is believed that the perpetrators are one and the same."

She nodded. Of course she knew. "The case plagues you, doesn't it, Carl?"

"No, I wouldn't say it plagues me."

"What plagues you then, Carl?"

He clutched the side of the leather sofa. Now was his chance. "What plagues me is how every time I try to invite you out, you say no. *That* plagues me, damn it."

He left Mona Ibsen's office feeling buoyant. Granted, she had reprimanded him and then forced him to run the gauntlet of a series of questions oozing with doubts and accusations. Many times he'd had the desire to spring angrily from the sofa and demand that she believe him. But Carl stayed put and answered politely, and the end result was that she — without affection but with a harried smile — agreed they could go out to dinner *when* she was finished with him as a client.

Maybe she thought that making this vague promise protected her. That he would forever live with the suspicion that his treatment had not been completed. But Carl knew better. He would have that promise realized.

He glanced down Jægersborg Allé and through Charlottenlund's mangled city center. All it took was a five-minute walk to the S-train and a half-hour ride later he'd again find himself passively sitting in his adjustable office chair in his corner of the basement. Not exactly the best setting for his newly won optimism.

He needed something to happen, and at headquarters there was simply *nada*.

When he reached the start of Lindegårds-vej, he looked up the street. He was well aware that at the opposite end the city name changed to Ordrup, and that it would make sense to take that walk now.

He punched in Assad's number on his mobile and glanced automatically at the battery's power level. He'd just charged it, and yet it was already half-dead. Irritating.

Assad sounded surprised. Were they allowed to talk?

"Rubbish, Assad. We just shouldn't parade it around that we're still in business. Listen, could you do a little research and find people we can speak with at the boarding school? There's an old yearbook in the big folder. In it you can see who was in their class. Either that, or find one of the teachers who was there during the years 1985 to 1987."

"I've already checked it out," he said. Hell, of course he had. "I have a few names then, but will go further, boss."

"Good. Transfer me to Rose, would you?"

A minute passed, then he heard her breathless voice. "Yes!" There was not a hint of him being addressed as "boss" in her rhetoric.

"You're putting tables together, I gather?"

"Yes!" If such a short word could express frustration, accusation, iciness, and tremendous annoyance at being interrupted in the midst of more important objectives, then Rose Knudsen really had the touch.

"I need Kimmie Lassen's stepmother's address. I know you gave me a note, but I don't have it with me. Just give me the address, OK? Don't ask me lots of questions, please!"

He was standing right outside Danske

Bank, where well-preserved men and women patiently waited in long queues. Just as they did in working-class suburbs like Brøndby and Tåstrup on paydays like today, but that made more sense. Why in the world would people with deep pockets like those who lived in Charlottenlund queue up in front of a bank? Didn't they have people to pay their bills for them? Didn't they use Internet banking? Or was there something he didn't know about wealthy people's habits? Perhaps they purchased stocks with all their payday pocket change, just as the vagrants in Vesterbro bought fags and beer?

Well, everyone does what they can with what they've got, he thought. He glanced over at the chemist shop's facade and noticed Bent Krum's sign in the window of the building: BARRISTER WITH AUDIENCE BEFORE THE SUPREME COURT. This right to higher audience might definitely come in handy with clients such as Pram, Dybbøl Jensen, and Florin.

He sighed.

To walk past Krum's office would be like ignoring every temptation in the Bible. It was almost as though he could hear the Devil laughing. If he rang the doorbell, walked up and interviewed Bent Krum, not ten minutes would pass before he would have the police chief on the line, and that would mean the end of Department Q and Carl Mørck.

He stood a moment trying to decide between involuntary retirement and postponement of the confrontation until a better occasion presented itself.

It would be best to just walk on by, he thought, but his finger had a will of its own and pressed the doorbell in as far as it could go. He'd be damned if anyone was going to stop his investigation. Bent Krum was going to end up in the hot seat. Better sooner than later.

He shook his head and took his finger off the doorbell. He was right where he'd been a thousand times before: once more the curse of his youth had caught up with him. If anyone was going to decide anything, it was going to be him, and only him, damn it.

A gruff, female voice curtly announced that he would have to wait a moment, which he did until he heard footfalls on the stairs and a woman came into view behind the glass door. Fashionably dressed, with a designer shawl around her shoulders and a rustic fur coat just like the one Vigga had ogled in front of Birger Christensen's on Strøget for at least four-fifths of their life together. As if it would ever have looked as good on Vigga. If she had bought it, by now it most likely would've suffered the sad fate of being cut to shreds so that one of her wild artist lovers could have a little drapery for his outlandish paintings.

The woman opened the door and gave him a blinding white smile, which couldn't have been obtained without money.

"I'm terribly sorry, but I'm on my way out the door. My husband isn't here on Thursdays. Maybe you can set up an appointment another day."

"No, I . . ." he reached instinctively for the police badge in his pocket and found only bits of lint. He would have said that he was in the midst of an investigation. Something along the lines that her husband only had to answer a few routine questions, and might he not return in an hour or two if that was suitable, and it wouldn't take long. But he said something else.

"Is your husband at the golf course, ma'am?"

She looked at him with incomprehension. "As far as I know, my husband doesn't play golf."

"OK." He inhaled. "I'm sorry to have to tell you, ma'am, but you and I are both being deceived. Your husband and my wife are having an affair, unfortunately. And now I would like to know where I stand." He tried to seem forlorn as he noticed how painfully he'd blindsided the blameless woman.

"You'll have to forgive me," he said. "I'm very sorry." Carefully he touched her arm. "That was truly wrong of me, I apologize again."

Then he withdrew to the pavement and joined the flow of people heading toward Ordrup, a little shocked at how he'd been infected by Assad's impulsiveness. He'd said it had been "wrong" of him. That was putting it mildly, to put it mildly.

She lived across from the church on Kirkevej. Three carports, two stair turrets, one brick groundskeeper's cottage, hundreds of yards of newly plastered garden walls, and five to six thousand square feet of mansion, with more brass on the doors than on the entire Danish royal yacht. Modest and humble would be a thoroughly miserable description.

He was pleased to see shadows moving around behind the windows on the ground floor. So there was a chance.

The housekeeper looked worn out, but agreed to bring Kassandra Lassen to the door, as far as that was possible.

The expression "bring to the door" would prove to be more apt than he could have predicted.

A loud stream of protest from inside was interrupted with the exclamation, "A young man, you say?"

She was the very incarnation of a high-society shrew who'd seen better days and better men. A far cry from the well-polished, slender woman in the *Her Life* article. A lot can change in nearly thirty years, that was for sure. She was wearing a kimono that hung so loosely that her satin underwear became an integral part of her overall presentation. Sweeping gestures with long fingernails gesticulated at him. She had immediately perceived that he was a real hunk of a man — something she had apparently not outgrown.

"Do come in," she greeted. Her boozy breath was day-old, but of quality origin. Malt whisky, Carl guessed. The air was so thick with it, an expert would probably be able to determine the vintage.

She led him by the arm, or rather, directed the way while clinging to him, until they reached the area of the first floor that, lowering her voice, she called, "My Room."

He was offered a seat in an armchair nestled next to hers, directly facing her heavy eyelids and even heavier breasts. It was a memorable scene.

Here, too, her friendliness — or interest, one could say — lasted only until he explained the purpose of his visit.

"So you wish to know about Kimmie?" She laid her hand on her breast, which was meant to indicate that either he left or she'd leave her senses.

Then his country-boy self took over.

"I'm here because I've heard that this establishment is the epitome of good manners," he tried. "That a person can expect to be treated well here, regardless of the reason for the visit." It had no effect.

He picked up the carafe and filled her glass with whisky. Maybe that would thaw her out.

"Is that chit even alive?" she asked, devoid of empathy.

"Yes, she lives on the streets of Copenhagen. I have a picture of her. Do you wish to see it?"

She closed her eyes and looked away, as if he'd shoved dog poop under her nose. Good grief, she obviously could really do without this.

"Can you tell me what you and your husband at the time thought when you heard what Kimmie and her friends were suspected of back in 1987?"

Once again she lifted her hand to her chest. This time, apparently, to gather her thoughts. Then her facial expression changed and she avoided his eye. Common sense and whisky were joining forces. "Do you know what, my dear, we really weren't very involved in all that. We traveled a bit, you see." Suddenly she turned her head back toward him. It took her a moment to regain her equilibrium. "As they say, travel is the elixir of life. And my husband and I made so many wonderful friends. The world is a lovely place, wouldn't you agree, Mr. . . . ?"

"Mørck. Carl Mørck." He nodded. To find the likes of such a callous being one would have to turn to Grimm's fairy tales. "Yes, you're absolutely right." She didn't need to know that, apart from a bus trip to the Costa Brava — where Vigga frequented the local artists while Carl lay frying on a beach with a bunch of retirees — he'd never ventured farther than around six hundred miles from Copenhagen.

"Do you think there is any real substance in the suspicion being laid on Kimmie?"

The corners of her mouth drooped. An attempt to appear concerned, he supposed. "Do you know what? Kimmie was a wicked girl. She wasn't averse to hitting people. Yes, even as a little girl. If she didn't get her way, her arms would flail like drumsticks. Like this." She tried to illustrate as the malt juices sloshed everywhere.

What normal child didn't do that? Carl thought. *Especially with a mother and father like hers.*

"I see. Was she also like that when she was older?"

"Ha! She was nasty. Called me the worst names. You can't imagine."

Actually he could.

"And she was loose."

"Loose? How so?"

She rubbed the fine, blue veins on the back of her hand. Only now did he see how arthritis had dug itself into her wrist. He glanced again at her nearly empty glass. *Pain relief has many faces*, he thought.

"After she came home from Switzerland, she dragged just about anybody home with her and . . . yes, I'll be blunt . . . fucked them like an animal with her door open — while I was up and about in the house." She shook her head. "It wasn't at all easy being alone, Mr. Mørck." She looked at him earnestly. "By that time Willy, Kimmie's father, had already packed his bags and left." She took a sip from her glass. "As if I wanted to hold on to him. That ridiculous . . ."

Then she turned to him again with a redwine-stained set of teeth. "Are you alone in this life, Mr. Mørck?" Her shoulder twist and obvious invitation were straight out of a lady's romantic novel.

"Yes. I am," he said, and accepted the challenge. Stared right at her and held her gaze until she slowly arched her brows and took another sip. Her short, blinking eyelashes were all that peered over the rim of the glass. It had been a long time since a man had looked at her that way.

"Did you know Kimmie had been pregnant?"

She took a deep breath and for a moment seemed far away, but with pensiveness etched across her forehead. As though it were the word "pregnant" more than the memory of a profoundly failed human relationship that caused her pain. As far as Carl was aware, she herself had never managed to give life.

"Yes," she said with a cold glare, "I did. The tart. How would that surprise anyone?"

"What happened then?"

"She wanted money, of course."

"Did she get it?"

"Not from me!" She dropped the flirtation and replaced it with profound disgust. "But her father gave her ten thousand kroner and asked her to stop contacting him."

"And you? Did you hear from her?"

She shook her head. The eyes said it was just as well.

"Who was the father of the child? Do you know?"

"Oh, I suppose it was that little nobody who burned down his father's lumberyard."

"Bjarne Thøgersen, you mean? The one who was convicted of the murders?"

"Probably. I really don't remember his name anymore."

"I see!" He was certain she was lying. Whisky or not, a person didn't just forget something like that. "Kimmie lived here for a while. You say it wasn't easy for you?"

She gazed at him in disbelief. "I hope you don't think I put up with that meat market for very long. No, during that time I preferred living on the coast."

"The coast?"

"Costa del Sol, you know. Fuengirola. Lovely roof terrace right above the promenade. Delightful place. Do you know Fuengirola, Mr. Mørck?"

He nodded. No doubt she went there on account of her arthritis, but otherwise it was where the maladjusted semi-wealthy with skeletons in their closet went. If she had said Marbella, he would have better understood. She must have been able to afford it.

"Is there still anything of Kimmie's left in the house?" he asked.

At that moment something inside her fell apart. She simply sat there, silently emptying her glass at her own leisurely pace, and when it was empty, so, too, was her head.

"I think Kassandra needs to rest now," said the housekeeper, who'd been hovering in the background.

Carl held up his hand to cut her off. He'd begun to grow suspicious.

"May I see Kimmie's room, Mrs. Lassen? I understand that it was left exactly as it had been."

It was a wild shot from the hip. The kind of question an experienced policeman has lying in the box labeled "Worth a try." A question that was always introduced with the phrase: "I understand that . . ."

In a tight spot it was always a good way to begin.

The housekeeper got two minutes to lay the queen of the house in her gilded bed, then Carl started looking around. Kimmie's childhood home or not, it wasn't fit for raising children. Not a single corner to play in. There were too many knick-knacks, too many Japanese and Chinese vases. If a person happened to wave his arms, he risked a seven-digit insurance claim. It had a very uncomfortable atmosphere, which Carl was certain hadn't changed over the years. A children's prison, that's how he saw it.

"Yes," the housekeeper said on their way up to the third floor. "Of course Kassandra just lives here; the house actually belongs to the daughter. So everything on this floor is exactly how it was when she lived here."

So Kassandra Lassen lived in this house at Kimmie's mercy. If Kimmie rejoined society, Kassandra's refuge here would probably be a thing of the past. What a switch of fates. The rich woman lived on the streets and the poor woman enjoyed the high life. That was the reason Kassandra Lassen stayed in Fuengirola and not Marbella. It wasn't of her own free will.

"It's a mess, I should warn you," the housekeeper said, opening the door. "We choose to keep it this way. That way the daughter won't be able to return and accuse Kassandra of prying, and I think that's a smart move."

He nodded from the end of the red-carpeted hallway. Where did one find such blindly loyal servants these days? She didn't even speak with an accent.

"Did you know Kimmie?"

"God, no. Do I look as though I could have been here since 1995?" She laughed heartily.

But in fact she did.

It was practically a separate flat. He had expected a few rooms, but not this veritable facsimile of a loft apartment in Paris's Latin Quarter. There was even a French balcony. The small-paned bay windows set into the sloping walls were filthy, but otherwise quite charming. If the housekeeper thought this place was a mess, she would collapse if she saw Jesper's room.

Dirty clothes were scattered about the floor, but other than that, nothing. Not even a piece of paper on the desk or anything in front of the television on the coffee table to suggest that a young woman had once lived here.

"You can have a look around, but I would actually like to see your police badge first, Mr. Mørck. That's standard procedure, is it not?" asked the housekeeper.

He nodded and fished around in all his pockets. What a meddlesome little busybody. At last he found a tattered business card that had been in his pocket for a hundred years. "I'm sorry, but my badge is back at headquarters. My apologies. You see, I'm the head of the department, so I don't leave the office that often. But here, please, my card. So you can see who I am."

She read the number and the address and felt the card, as if she were an expert in forgeries. "Just a moment," she said and lifted the receiver of a Bang & Olufsen telephone on the desk.

She introduced herself as Charlotte Nielsen and asked if anyone knew of a deputy detective superintendent by the name of Carl Mørck. Then she shuffled her feet for a moment as the call was transferred.

She inquired again, and then asked for a description of what this Mørck looked like.

She laughed briefly, scrutinizing him, then hung up with a smile on her lips.

What the hell was so funny? he wondered. *Ten to one she'd talked to Rose.*

She didn't elaborate on the reason for her chuckle, but exited the room and left him alone with all his unanswered questions in a young girl's abandoned flat that seemingly had nothing to tell.

■ ■ ■ ■

He inspected everything a number of times, and just as many times the housekeeper appeared in the doorway. She had taken on the role of guard, and she believed she could do that best by watching him as one eyes a hungry mosquito sitting on one's hand. But nothing bit her. Carl had neither made a mess nor put anything in his pocket.

Apparently Kimmie had been in a rush to leave. She had vacated the flat in a fast, yet thorough, fashion. Things she didn't want others to see had no doubt been deposited in the rubbish bins by the house's cobblestone driveway, which he could see from the balcony.

The same was true of her clothes. There were small piles on the chair beside her bed, but no underwear. Shoes were scattered about in the corners of the room, but no dirty socks. She had considered what was OK to leave behind, and what was too intimate. And that was precisely what characterized the search: nothing intimate remained.

Even decorations on the walls, which normally could give an indication of attitude or taste, were missing. There was no toothbrush in the small marble bathroom. No tampons in the chest or cotton swabs in the wastebasket next to the toilet. Not the slightest trace of anything in the toilet bowl or the sink.

Kimmie had left the place so clinically devoid of personality that all he could tell was that it had once been occupied by a female. But she could just as well have been a spinster in the Salvation Army as a hip, upper-class girl from the expensive end of the postal codes.

He gently lifted the bed sheets and tried sniffing out her scent. He raised her blotting pad to see if she'd forgotten a little note beneath it. He fished around the bottom of the empty wastebasket, looked in the back of the kitchen drawers, put his head in the hollow space under the sloping roof. Nothing.

"It'll be dark soon," said Charlotte, the housekeeper, implying that he should consider finding another place to play police officer.

"Is there an attic or anything else above here?" he asked hopefully. "A hatch or some stairs I can't see from here?"

"No, there's just this."

Carl looked up. OK, so an attic above the flat didn't exist.

"I'll just make one more pass," he said.

He lifted all the rugs and searched for loose floorboards. Gently removed the spice posters in the kitchen to see if they covered up a hollow space. Knocked on the furniture and on the bottoms of the wardrobe and kitchen cupboards. There was simply nothing there.

He shook his head, reprimanding himself. Why *would* there be anything?

He closed the door of the flat behind him and remained on the landing a moment, partly to see if anything out there was of interest, and when there wasn't, partly to drive away the irritating feeling that he had in fact overlooked something.

Then his mobile rang, and he snapped back to reality.

"It's Marcus," came the voice. "Why aren't you in your office, Carl? And why does it look the way it does down there? The corridor is overflowing with pieces of I don't know how many tables, and your office is covered with yellow sticky-notes. Where are you, Carl? Have you forgotten that you have visitors from Norway tomorrow?"

"Shit!" he said a little too loudly. Yes, he'd happily forgotten all about it.

"OK?" came from the other end of the

line. He knew the homicide chief's OKs. They weren't the kind of thing a person went looking for.

"I'm on my way to headquarters now." He looked at the clock; it was already past four.

"Now?! No, don't you worry about anything at all." He didn't sound as though it were up for discussion. He sounded angry. "I'll take care of the visit you have tomorrow, and they *won't* be coming down to that mess of yours."

"What time did you say they're coming?"

"They're coming at 10 A.M., but you can save yourself the trouble, Carl. *I'm* taking over, and you'll make yourself available for questions, *if* we want your commentary."

Carl stared at his mobile for a moment after Marcus Jacobsen hung up. Right up until that second those dried-cod sheiks could have kissed him in a particular place, but now his attitude had changed completely. If the homicide chief wanted to take over, then Carl damned sure wouldn't let him.

He cursed a few times and glanced out the skylight that topped off the impressive stairwell. The sun was still out and beamed through the glass panes. Even though it was knocking-off time, he didn't have any desire to go home.

His head was in no way ready to make the trip up Hestestien, along the fields, and home to Morten's culinary concoctions.

He noticed the shadows falling sharply through the window, and he felt his forehead forming a frown.

In houses of this vintage, the window frames in rooms with slanting roofs were usually set twelve inches into the wall. But here they were set in much deeper, by almost another ten inches. That meant, if he should venture a guess, that the house had been given additional insulation at a later date.

He craned his neck and discovered a slim crack in the transition from the ceiling above the stairwell to the sloping wall. His eyes followed the crack all the way round the landing and ended where he started. Yes, the sloping walls had settled a tad; the house hadn't been born with such well-insulated walls, that much was clear. There were at least six inches of extra insulation, finished off with gypsum plasterboard. It had been smoothed out with putty and painted quite nicely, but it was common knowledge that after a certain amount of time cracks were inevitable.

He turned around, opened the door to the

flat again, went directly to the outer wall, and scanned all the sloping surfaces. Here, too, cracks had appeared in the join along the ceiling, but otherwise there was nothing remarkable.

The hollow space was there, somewhere, but apparently it wasn't possible to hide anything inside it. Not from the inside anyway.

He repeated the words to himself. "Not from the inside anyway!" He saw the balcony door. He grabbed the handle, pushed the door open, and stepped outside, where the slanted roof tiles formed a picturesque background.

"Remember, it was a long time ago," he whispered to himself and let his eyes roam from one row of tiles to the next. He was on the north side of the house; moss had collected all the rainwater's nutrients and now covered most of the roof like stage scenery. He turned toward the tiles on the other side of the balcony door and recognized the irregularity immediately.

The roof tiles were positioned evenly and firmly, and here, too, there was moss everywhere. The difference, however, was that one of the tiles right at the spot where the top row connected to the apex was slightly staggered from the others. The roof was constructed with pantiles, the kind of tiles that overlap one another, where each one has a small knob on the underside to prevent it from falling off the wooden cross-beams. But this particular tile was about to slide; almost as if the knob had been hacked off, it lay loosely on the beam between the other tiles.

When he lifted it, it loosened without any difficulty.

Carl took a deep drag of the chill September air.

A rare feeling of standing before the brink of something exceptional spread through his body. Kind of like what Howard Carter must have felt when he made the small hole in the grave-chamber door and suddenly found himself in Tutankhamun's tomb. Because lying before Carl in a hollow of insulation material under the tiles was a shoebox-sized, unpainted metal box wrapped in transparent plastic.

Suddenly his heart started pounding furiously. Then he called out to the housekeeper.

"Do you see that box?"

She came in and bent reluctantly to peer under the tiles. "There's a box. What is it?"

"I don't know, but you're my witness that I found it there."

She looked at him sullenly. "OK, I do have eyes in my head, if that's what you're asking?"

He held his mobile toward the hollow space and snapped a few images. Then he showed them to her.

"Do we agree that it was this hollow space I've just photographed?"

She set her hands on her hips. Evidently he wasn't to ask her any more questions.

"Now I'm going to remove it and take it to headquarters." It wasn't a question, but a confirmation. Otherwise she would scurry down and wake Kassandra Lassen, and that would probably create a scene.

Then he allowed her to go. She went off, shaking her head, her trust in the intelligence of authority having suffered a setback.

For a moment he considered calling in the crime-scene techs, but thought better of it when he envisioned the miles of plastic crime-scene tape and men in white jumpsuits everywhere. They had enough to do, and he couldn't wait. Plain and simple.

So he put on his gloves, lifted the box out carefully, put the tile back in place, took the box inside, set it on the table, unwrapped it, and opened it — all in one fluid, unconscious movement.

On top was a little teddy bear, not much bigger than a box of matches. It was a very pale color, almost yellowish, with worn plush on its face and limbs. Maybe it had been Kimmie's most cherished possession at one time, her only friend. Maybe someone else's. Then he pulled out a piece of newspaper from beneath the teddy bear. *Berlingske Tidende*, September 29, 1995, it said in the corner. The same day she moved in with Bjarne Thøgersen. Beyond that, there was nothing of interest. Just endless job announcements.

He looked in the box expecting to find a diary or letters that would shed light on earlier thoughts and deeds. Instead he found six small plastic pockets, the kind used to collect stamps or put recipes in. He hefted the whole lot from the metal box.

Why hide these things so well? he thought to himself, and knew the answer the instant he saw the contents of the bottom two pockets.

"Fuck me!" he blurted out.

There were two cards from a Trivial Pursuit game. One in each pocket.

After five minutes of deep concentration, he grabbed his notepad and carefully described the position of the plastic pockets relative to the rest of the box's contents.

Afterward he scrutinized each of them carefully, one at a time.

One pocket contained a man's wristwatch, one an earring, another had something that resembled a rubber band, and finally a handkerchief.

Four pockets in addition to the ones with the Trivial Pursuit cards.

He chewed on his lip.

That made six in all.

22

Ditlev raced up the stairs to Caracas in four strides. "Where is he?" he shouted to the secretary, and dashed off in the direction her finger pointed.

Frank Helmond lay in his room alone, having fasted and been prepped for his second operation.

When Ditlev entered the room, Helmond didn't look at him with respect.

Strange, Ditlev thought, letting his eyes wander up the sheet to his bandaged face. *This idiot's lying here, showing me no respect. Has he learned nothing? Who was it that hurt him, and who patched him together again?*

When it came down to it, they had agreed on everything. Treatment of the numerous deep gashes in Helmond's face would be accompanied by a light facelift and tightening of the skin around the neck and chest. Liposuction, surgery, and capable hands — that's what Ditlev could offer him. And when you added his wife and a small fortune into the bargain, the point had been reached where it was surely reasonable to demand from Helmond, if not appreciation, then at least that he regard their agreement with a certain degree of humility.

But the bargain hadn't been kept, because Helmond had talked. There were nurses at this moment who must be wondering about what they'd heard, and who needed to be made to see sense.

Because regardless how drugged the patient had been, the words had been uttered: "It was Ditlev Pram and Ulrik Dybbøl Jensen who did this."

He had said *that*.

Ditlev didn't bother making an introduction. The man had no choice but to listen to him anyway.

"Do you know how easy it is to kill a man under anesthetic without being detected?" he asked. "Oh, don't you? In any case, you're now ready for your next operation tonight, Frank. I just hope the anaesthetists have a steady hand. In spite of everything, I am paying them to do their work properly, you know." He aimed a finger at Helmond. "And just one more, simple matter. I'm assuming that we now agree you'll keep your trap shut and stick to our agreement?

Otherwise you're risking having your organs end up as spare parts for people who are younger and fitter than you, and that wouldn't please you very much, would it?"

Ditlev tapped the drip that was already fastened to Frank's arm. "I don't hold grudges, Frank. So you shouldn't either, do you understand me?"

He pushed hard on Helmond's bed and turned away. If that didn't do it, then the little loser was asking for it.

On his way out he slammed the door so violently that a passing porter examined it when Ditlev had turned his back.

Then he made his way directly to the laundry. It would take more than a verbal lashing to exorcize the ugly feeling that Helmond's mere presence created in his body.

His newest acquisition, a girl from the part of Mindanao where a man got his head chopped off if he went to bed with the wrong woman, had yet to be tried out. He'd watched her with great satisfaction. She was exactly how he liked them. With shy eyes and a strong sense of her own insignificance. That, combined with her availability, lit a fire in him. A fire that longed to be extinguished.

"I have the Helmond situation under control," he said, later that day. Behind the wheel, Ulrik nodded, satisfied. He was relieved; that much was evident.

Ditlev gazed out across the landscape, where the forest slowly took shape ahead of them. A calm fell over him. All in all, it had been a reasonably good end to an otherwise rather out-of-control week.

"What about the police?" Ulrik asked.

"That, too. This Carl Mørck has been removed from the case."

They arrived at Torsten's estate, stopping some fifty yards from the gate and turning their faces up to the cameras. In ten seconds the gate between the fir trees a little farther ahead would glide open.

Ditlev dialed Torsten's number on his mobile as they drove into the courtyard. "Where are you?" he asked.

"Drive down past the breeding house and park there. I'm in the menagerie."

"He's in the menagerie," he told Ulrik, already feeling the excitement rising in him. It was the most intense part of the ritual, and definitely the part that Torsten, at least, looked forward to most.

Time and again they had seen Torsten Florin scurrying about among half-naked fashion models. They had seen him bathed in the spotlight and heard the gushing praise

324

of influential people. But never had they seen him exhibit such pleasure as when they visited the menagerie before a hunt.

The next hunt would be on a weekday. Not yet scheduled, but early the following week. On this occasion only those who'd previously won the right to shoot the special prey of the day would be allowed to participate. Only those who had a taste for such experiences, and who had benefitted materially from these hunts. People they could trust; people like them.

Ulrik parked the Rover just as Torsten came out of the building with blood on his rubber apron.

"Welcome," he said, beaming. So he'd just slaughtered an animal.

The hall had been expanded since they'd last been there. It was longer and brighter, with numerous glass partitions. Forty Latvian and Bulgarian workers had done their part, and Dueholt had begun to resemble what Torsten had made his personal ambition for his private home sixteen years earlier, when he'd already made his first millions by the age of twenty-four.

In the hall there were perhaps a hundred or more cages with animals inside them. All of them lit by halogen lights.

For a child, a tour in Torsten Florin's menagerie would be a more exotic experience than a trip to the zoo. For an adult with even a limited understanding of animal welfare, it would be shocking.

"Look at this," Torsten said. "A Komodo dragon."

He was clearly enjoying himself, as though in the midst of an orgasm, and Ditlev understood why. Seeing as these animals were dangerous, and protected species as well, this wasn't your ordinary prey.

"I think we'll take that one to Saxenholdt's estate when the snow comes. Down there the hunting area is easier to survey, and these devils are fantastically good at hiding. Can you imagine it?"

"Their bite is the most infectious on the planet, I've heard," Ditlev said. "So the shot has to be right on target, before it has a chance to lock its jaws onto the shooter."

They saw Florin tremble as if he had the shivers. Yes, it was very good prey he'd procured for them. How had he managed it?

"What will it be next time?" Ulrik asked, curious.

Florin spread his hands. That meant he had an idea, but they would have to discover it for themselves.

"Our choices are over here," he said, pointing at cage after cage containing small animals with big eyes.

It was as clean as a clinic inside the building. With their vast, collective miles of digestive system and correspondingly enormous quantities of metabolic waste, it was thanks to Torsten's excellent, dark-skinned staff that the animals did not leave an overwhelming stench of urine and shit in the hall. Three Somalian families lived on his estate. They diligently swept, prepared food, dusted, and cleaned the cages, but disappeared whenever guests arrived. You couldn't risk people talking.

In the last row, six tall cages stood side by side, silhouettes huddled inside.

Ditlev smiled when he looked into the first two. The chimpanzee was well proportioned, but it had a pair of aggressive eyes that were trained on the animal in the next cage: a wild dingo that stood with its tail between its legs, shaking, while saliva flowed from its bared teeth.

He was just so incredibly creative, Torsten. Far beyond the pale of what society deemed acceptable. If animal rights organizations ever caught a glimpse of his world, he would face prison and fines in the millions. His empire would collapse overnight.

Self-respecting women of means had no problem wearing animal fur, but a chimp frightened half to death by a dingo or forced to run screaming for its life through a Danish deciduous forest — *that* would make them opt out.

The final four cages held more ordinary animals. A Great Dane, a giant billy goat, a badger, and a fox. Except for the fox, these animals lay in the hay, staring out at them as if they had understood their fate. The fox simply stood in the corner, trembling.

"Of course you're thinking, *What's going on here?* But I'll explain." Florin put his hands in his apron's side pockets and nodded at the Great Dane. "You see, that one there has a pedigree going back one hundred years. It cost me the tidy sum of two hundred thousand kroner, but with those nasty, slanty eyes, I don't think it should be allowed to continue passing on its ugly genes."

Ulrik laughed, as could be expected.

"And you should know about this special creature, too." He nodded at the next cage. "You probably recall that my greatest hero is the barrister Rudolf Sand, who kept a strict record of his trophies for almost sixty-five years. He really was a legendary killer." He nodded to himself and drummed on the bars so the animal pulled away, its head lowered and its horn threatening. "Sand dropped 53,276 wild animals, exactly. And a buck like this one was his most important and biggest trophy. It's a corkscrew goat, perhaps better known as a Pakistani Markhor. You see, Sand hunted a male Markhor in Afghanistan's mountains for nearly twenty years until finally, after one hundred and twenty-five days of intensive tracking, he managed to bring down a monstrous, ancient buck. You can read about his experience on the Internet. I recommend it. You'd have to search far and wide to find a hunter his equal."

"And this is a Markhor?" Ulrik's smile was murderous in itself.

Torsten was reveling in it. "It sure as hell is, and just a few kilos lighter than Rudolf Sand's. Two and a half kilos, to be exact. A fine specimen. That's what you get from having contacts in Afghanistan. Long live the war."

They laughed and turned to the badger.

"This one lived for years just south of the estate here, but the other day it came too close to one of my traps. I have quite a personal relationship with this little troll, I'd like you to know."

So that means it's off-limits, Ditlev thought.

Torsten will take care of it himself one day.

"And then there's this one, Fantastic Mr. Fox. Can you figure out what makes him special?"

They studied the quivering fox for a long time. It seemed frightened, but nevertheless stood looking at them, its head completely still, until Ulrik kicked at the cage door.

It bolted at them so fast that its snapping jaws got hold of the toe of Ulrik's boot. Both he and Ditlev jumped. Then they noticed the froth around its mouth, the crazy eyes and recognized that death was about to claim this creature.

"Jesus Christ, Torsten, this here is definitely diabolical. This is the one, isn't it? The animal we're hunting next week, am I right? We're going to set free a fox with advanced rabies." He laughed jovially, so that Ditlev also had to laugh. "You've found an animal that knows the forest inside out, and with rabies no less. I can hardly wait until you tell the other hunters. Damn, Torsten. Why didn't we think of this before?"

At this Torsten joined in the laughter until the hall resounded with the rustling and hissing of animals seeking safety in their prison's deepest corners.

"It's good you're wearing those thick boots, dear Ulrik." He laughed and pointed at the teeth marks that had imprinted themselves in his custom-sewn Wolverine. "Otherwise we'd have to take a trip to Hillerød Hospital, and that would be hard to explain, don't you think?

"One more thing," Torsten said, leading them to the part of the hall with the brightest light. "Have a look!"

He pointed at a shooting range built as an extension of the building. It was a cylindrical tunnel, almost seven feet high and at least fifty yards long. Well marked, yard by yard. With three targets. One for a bow and arrow, one for a rifle, and, finally, one with a steel-plated accumulation box for heavier calibers.

They also inspected the walls inside the tunnel, impressed. At least fifteen inches of soundproofing. If anything outside was capable of hearing shots, it could only be a bat.

"There are air nozzles all the way round, so we can simulate all types of wind conditions in the shooting tunnel." He pushed a button. "This wind force gives a deviation that demands a correction of two to three percent with a bow. You can see the table over there." He pointed at a small computer screen on the wall. "All types of weapons and wind simulations can be keyed in." He stepped into the lock. "But first you need to know how it actually feels. We can't very well take all this equipment out into the forest, now, can we?"

Ulrik followed him. His thick hair didn't move an inch. On that point Torsten probably had a scalp better-suited as a wind-force indicator.

"Now we're getting to the good part," Torsten continued. "We'll let the rabid fox loose in the forest. It's insanely aggressive, as you both saw, and the beaters will be well equipped with leathers all the way up to the groin." He gestured with his hands to illustrate. "We, the hunters, will be the ones exposed. Of course I'll see to it that there's vaccine near by, but even the flesh wounds it can deliver in its crazy frenzy are enough to kill a man. A torn femoral artery! You know what that'll do."

"When are you going to tell the others?" Ulrik asked gleefully.

"Just before we begin. But here's the best part, my friends. Look at this."

He ducked behind a bale of straw and pulled out a weapon. Ditlev was immediately wild about his selection. It was a crossbow with a scope. In no way was this legal in Denmark following the weapons law reform of 1989, but it was truly murderous and superb to aim with. If you could, that is. And you had only one chance to hit the target, because it took time to reload. It would be a hunt with many great, unknown risks. Just as it should be.

"The Relayer Y25, it'll be called. Excalibur's anniversary model, out this spring. Only one thousand will be produced, plus these two. It doesn't get any better than this." He scooped another crossbow from its hiding spot and handed one to each of them.

Ditlev took his with outstretched arm. It weighed next to nothing.

"We managed to sneak them into the country in disassembled pieces. Each part was sent separately. I thought one of the pieces had been lost in the mail, but it turned up yesterday." He grinned. "One year in transit. What do you think?"

Ulrik snapped the string. It sounded like a harp. Sharp and clear-toned.

"The manual states it can pull two hundred pounds, but I think it's more. And with a 2219 bolt, even large animals can't survive a shot at up to ninety yards. Watch this."

Torsten grabbed a crossbow, set the stirrup on the floor, and placed his foot on it. Then he pulled hard, tightened, and locked it. They knew he'd done it many times before.

He pulled a bolt from the quiver under the bow and carefully locked it, accomplishing the task in a single long, lithe, and silent movement, so unlike the explosive force he was about to unleash at the target forty-five yards ahead.

They had expected Torsten would hit the bull's-eye, but not the sizable arc the bolt first described through the air, nor that it would hit the target so forcefully that it disappeared from view.

"When you hit the fox, make sure you're standing higher up, so the bolt doesn't strike one of the beaters when it tears through the fox's body, because unless you hit the shoulder blades, it will. And it would probably be best not to, since it won't die from the wound; it'll just keep running."

He gave them a slip of paper.

"Here's a link online to directions on assembling and using the crossbow. I recommend you watch all the videos very thoroughly."

Ditlev glanced at the link: http://www.excaliburcrossbow.com/demo/listings.php?category-id=47.

"Why?" he then asked.

"Because you two are going to win the draw."

23

Carl returned to the basement to find a single height-adjustable table assembled on wobbly legs. Next to it he found Rose on her knees, cursing at a screwdriver. *Nice rump*, he thought, stepping over her without a word.

He cast a sidelong glance at the table, and saw with foreboding at least twenty yellow notes in Assad's characteristic block letters. Five of them were messages saying that Marcus Jacobsen had called. He crumpled those up immediately. The rest he gathered in a sticky mass and shoved in his back pocket.

He peeked into Assad's little cubbyhole of an office and discovered the prayer rug on the floor and the chair empty.

"Where is he?" he asked Rose.

She didn't bother to respond. Simply pointed behind Carl's back.

He looked into his own office and saw Assad sitting with his legs planted on the paper forest on his desk, reading eagerly, and appearing lost in thought, his head bobbing in rhythm to the buzzing music of indefinable origin streaming from his headphones. A steaming glass of tea sat in the center of a stack of papers that Carl had labeled "Category 1: Cases without perpetrators." It all looked very cozy and organized.

"What the hell are you doing, Assad?" he barked. So brusquely that the man jerked like a marionette, sending file pages floating silently through the air and splashing tea all over the desk.

Assad threw himself across the desk in a flurry, using his sleeves like a tea towel. Not until Carl put a reassuring hand on Assad's shoulder did his look of surprise disappear, replaced by his usual, mischievous grin that implied he was sorry but couldn't help it and besides he had exciting news to share. Only then did he remove his headphones.

"Yes, I'm sorry I'm sitting here, Carl. But inside my office I heard her all the time then."

He motioned with a thumb toward the corridor, where Rose's oaths created as constant a flow of noise as that of all the interesting substances flushing through the basement's sanitation pipes.

"Aren't you supposed to be helping her assemble the tables, Assad?"

Assad put a shushing finger to his full lips. "She *wants* to do it herself. I *did* try."

"Come in here a moment, Rose!" Carl shouted, dumping the most tea-soaked stack of papers on the floor in the corner.

She stood herself before them with a hateful stare and such a savage grip on the screwdriver that her knuckles showed white.

"You get ten minutes to make room for your two chairs in here, Rose," he said. "Assad, you help her unpack them."

They sat before him like two school kids with eager faces. The chairs were OK, though he wouldn't have chosen green metal legs. Those, too, he would probably have to get used to.

He told them about his discovery at the house in Ordrup and put the open metal box on the table before them.

Rose seemed disinterested, but Assad's eyes looked as though they were about to pop out of his skull.

"If we find fingerprints on the Trivial Pursuit cards that match one or both of the victims in Rørvig, then I'd stake everything on the other effects also having fingerprints of others who've been subjected to similar violent experiences," he said, waiting a moment until they appeared to understand what he'd just said.

Carl lined up the little teddy bear and the six plastic pockets. Handkerchief, watch, earring, rubber band, and two cards, each in individual pockets.

"Oh, how cute," Rose said, eyes fastened on the teddy bear. *Typical*, thought Carl.

"Do you two see the most remarkable thing about these pockets?" he asked.

"There are two plastic pockets with Trivial Pursuit cards in them," Rose said, without hesitation. So she was present after all. He could have sworn she wasn't.

"Exactly. Excellent, Rose. And that means . . . ?"

"Well, logically it means then that each pocket kind of represents a person and not an event," Assad said. "Otherwise the Trivial Pursuit cards would have been put in the same plastic thingy, right? The Rørvig murders had two victims. So two plastic pockets." He spread out his hands in a broad, panoramic sweep. Just like his smile. "That is, one plastic pocket to each person then."

"Precisely," Carl said. Assad was a guy one could count on.

Rose put her palms together and slowly

raised them to her mouth. Recognition or shock, or both. Only she knew.

"So, are you saying we might be looking at six murders?" she asked.

Carl pounded his desk. "Six murders. *Bingo!*" he cried. Now they were all on the same page.

Rose stared again at the cute little teddy bear. Somehow she couldn't make it fit with everything else. Nor was it easy to do.

"Yes," he said. "This little guy here most likely has his own significance, since it's not displayed like all the other effects."

They all stared at it for a moment.

"We don't know, of course, whether all the effects are related to a murder, but it's a possibility." He extended his hand across the table. "Assad, give me Johan Jacobsen's list. It's hanging on the board behind you."

He put it on the table so they both could see it, and pointed at the twenty events that Jacobsen had listed.

"It's far from certain that these cases have anything to do with the Rørvig murders. In fact, there might not even be any connection between these, either. But if we explore these cases systematically, maybe we'll find just one among them that we can connect to just one of these effects, and that's enough. We're looking for one more crime

340

the gang could be connected to. If we find it, we're on the right track. What do you say, Rose, are you the one who's going to take on this assignment, or what?"

She let her hands drop and suddenly didn't look too friendly. "You give off incredibly mixed signals, Carl. One moment we're not allowed to talk, the next we're in full swing. Then I'm supposed to assemble tables, and suddenly I'm not. What am I supposed to think? What will you say in ten minutes?"

"Hey, wait. There's something you've misunderstood, Rose. You *will* assemble the tables. You're the one who ordered them."

"It's really too bad that two men make me do it all by myself —"

At this Assad interrupted. "Oh, I wanted to, sure, did I not say it?"

But Rose went on. "Carl, do you have any idea how much it hurts, wrestling with all those metal table legs? There's always some kind of problem with them."

"You ordered them, and they'll be standing in the corridor tomorrow. All put together! We're having guests from Norway. Have you forgotten?"

She cocked her head back as though he had bad breath. "Here we go again. Guests from Norway?" She looked around. "How are we going to have guests from Norway? This place looks like a junkshop. And Assad's office would shock anyone."

"So do something about it, Rose."

"Hello? You want me to do something about *that*, too? That's quite a few tasks all at once. So I guess you expect us to stay here all night long?"

He tipped his head from side to side. It was of course a possibility.

"No, but we can start at five, tomorrow morning," he responded.

"*Five in the morning!*" This just about knocked her over. "Man, you've got to be kidding. Honestly! You must have been born with a screw loose!" she scolded, as Carl wondered whom he could ask at Station City to find out how they'd been able to stand this pain in the neck for more than a week.

"Please, Rose," Assad said, trying to smooth things out. "It's only then because the case is now moving forward then."

At this, she leaped to her feet. "Assad, you bloody well can't butt in and destroy a good row. And stop with all those 'thens.' Take 'em out, mate. I know you can. I've heard you on the telephone. You do fine."

She turned to Carl. "Him," she said, pointing at Assad. "He can assemble the

342

tables. I'll take care of the rest. And I'm not coming until five thirty tomorrow morning, because the bus doesn't run earlier than that." Then she picked up the teddy bear and stuffed it in Carl's breast pocket.

"And this one, you'll find the owner yourself. Agreed?"

Assad and Carl had their eyes trained on the desk as she thundered out of the room. She reminded Carl of some dippy feminist in a TV series.

"Are we then . . ." Assad made a rhetorical pause to assess his use of the word "then." "Are we then officially back on the case, Carl?"

"No, not yet. We'll find out tomorrow." He held the stack of yellow notes in the air. "I can tell from these that you've been busy, Assad. You've found someone we can talk to at the boarding school. Who?"

"It was what I was doing then when you came, Carl." He leaned across the desk and located a couple of photocopies of the old boarding-school students' membership magazine.

"I called the school, but they weren't so happy when I asked to talk to someone about Kimmie and the others. It was the part about the murders they didn't like, I think. I also think they considered throwing

Pram, Dybbøl Jensen, Florin, and Wolf out of school back then on account of the investigation against them." He shook his head. "I didn't get much out of that then. But afterward I got the idea to go after someone who was in the same class as the guy who fell down and died at Bellahøj. And then on top of that I think I've found a teacher who was at the school at the same time as Kimmie and the others. He would maybe like to talk to us, since he hasn't been there so long."

It was almost eight o'clock in the evening when Carl found himself staring at Hardy's empty bed up at the spinal clinic.

He grabbed the first person in white that walked past. "Where is he?" he asked, with foreboding.

"Are you a relative?"

"Yes," he said, having learned from past experience.

"Hardy Henningsen has water in his lungs. We've moved him in here where we can assist him better." She pointed to a room with a sign on the door that read INTENSIVE CARE. "Make it quick," she said. "He's very tired."

There was no doubt that Hardy had taken a turn for the worse. The respirator was running at full throttle. He lay half supine in the bed: naked torso, arms resting atop the blanket, a mask covering most of his face, tubes in his nose, IV and diagnostic equipment everywhere.

His eyes were open, but he was too tired to smile when he saw Carl.

"Hi there, old buddy," Carl said, putting his hand carefully on Hardy's arm. Not that Hardy would feel anything, but still. "What happened? They say you have water in your lungs."

Hardy said something, but his voice vanished behind the mask and the incessant humming of the machines. So Carl leaned closer. "Can you repeat that?" he said.

"I got gastric acid in my lungs," he said in a hollow voice.

Christ, how disgusting, Carl thought, squeezing Hardy's limp arm. "You've got to get better, Hardy, you hear me?"

"The feeling in my upper arm has spread," he whispered. "Sometimes it burns like fire, but I haven't told anyone."

Carl knew why, and he didn't like it. Hardy hoped to have an arm mobile enough that he could raise it, take the gauze scissors, and puncture his carotid artery. So the question was whether one should share his hope.

"I've got a problem, Hardy. I need your help." Carl pulled a chair over and sat beside him. "You know Lars Bjørn much better than I do from the old days in Roskilde. Perhaps you can tell me what's really going on in my department."

Carl briefly explained how his investigation had been brought to a halt. That Bak thought Lars Bjørn was part of it. And that the police chief backed up the decision all the way.

"They've taken my badge, too," he said in conclusion.

Hardy lay staring at the ceiling. If he had been his old self, he'd have lit a cigarette.

"Lars Bjørn always wears a dark blue tie, right?" he said after a moment, and with great difficulty.

Carl closed his eyes. Yes, that was correct. The tie was inseparable from Lars Bjørn, and yes, it was blue.

Hardy tried to cough, but hawked instead, a sound like a kettle about to boil dry.

"He's an old alum from the same boarding school, Carl," he said weakly. "There are four tiny scallops on the tie. It's their school tie."

Carl sat in silence. A few years ago, a rape at the school had nearly destroyed its reputation. What damage might this case cause?

Jesus Christ. Lars Bjørn had been a student at the school. If Bjørn was an active player in all this, was it as the school's lackey and defender? Or what? Once a boarding-school pupil, always a boarding-school pupil. That's what people said.

He nodded slowly. Of course. It was that simple.

"OK, Hardy," he said, drumming on the sheets. "You're simply a genius. But who would ever doubt that?" He stroked his old colleague's hair. It was damp and lifeless to the touch.

"You're not angry with me, Carl?" Hardy said behind his mask.

"Why would you say that?"

"You know why. The nail-gun case. What I told the psychologist."

"Hardy, for God's sake. When you get better, we'll solve the case together, OK? You're lying here getting strange ideas. I understand that, Hardy."

"Not strange, Carl. There *was* something. And there was something about Anker. I'm more and more certain of that."

"We'll solve that together when the time is right. How does that sound, Hardy?"

He lay silently for some time, letting the

respirator do its work, and Carl couldn't do anything but follow Hardy's heaving chest.

"Would you do me a favor?" Hardy said, interrupting the monotony.

Carl pulled back in his seat. It was precisely this moment he feared whenever he visited Hardy. This eternal wish that Carl would help him die. Euthanasia, to use a classy term. Mercy killing, to use another. They were both terrible.

It wasn't the punishment that he feared. It wasn't the ethical considerations, either. He just couldn't do it.

"No, Hardy. Please don't ask me anymore. I don't want you thinking that I haven't considered the possibility. But, I'm really sorry, old boy, I just *can't* do it."

"It's not that, Carl." He moistened his dry lips, as if to give the message an easier time coming out. "I want to ask you if I can come home to yours, instead of being here."

The silence that followed was heart-wrenching. Carl felt paralyzed. All the words were stuck in his throat.

"I've been wondering, Carl," he went on softly. "Can't that guy who lives with you look after me?"

Now his desperation felt like the stab of a dagger.

Carl shook his head imperceptibly. Morten

Holland as a nurse? At his place? It was enough to make him cry.

"You can get a lot of money for home care, Carl. I've looked into it. A nurse will come several times a day. It's a simple matter. You needn't be afraid."

Carl looked at the floor. "Hardy, I don't have the right setup for something like that. My house isn't very big. And Morten lives in the basement, which isn't actually legal."

"I could be in the living room, Carl." His voice was hoarse now. It sounded as if he were fighting hard not to cry, but maybe it was just his condition. "Your living room's large, isn't it, Carl? I just need a corner. No one has to know about Morten in the basement. Aren't there three rooms upstairs? You could just put a bed in one of them, then he could still spend his time in the basement, couldn't he?" The big man was begging him. So big and so small at the same time.

"Oh, Hardy." Carl almost couldn't say it. The idea of this behemoth of a bed and all kinds of medical apparatus in his living room was more than frightening. The difficulties would split his home apart — what little of it remained. Morten would move out. Jesper would be carping constantly about everything. There was no way it could be done, however much he might wish it — in theory.

"You're too ill, Hardy. If only you weren't in such bad shape." He held a long pause, hoping Hardy would release him from his anguish, but he said nothing. "Get a little more feeling back first, Hardy. We'll wait and see what happens."

He watched his friend's eyes slowly close. The busted hope had snuffed out the spark in him.

"We'll wait and see," he'd said.

As if Hardy could do anything else.

Not since his first, green years in the homicide division had Carl got to work as early as he did the next morning. It was Friday, but the Hillerød motorway was devoid of traffic for several long stretches. The officers arriving in the garage at headquarters slammed their car doors sluggishly. The clocking-in desk smelled of Thermos coffee. There was plenty of time.

Entering his basement was something of a shock. A ruler-straight row of tables in the corridor, nicely elevated to elbow height, bid welcome to Department Q's domain. Oceans of paper were lined up in small stacks, apparently sorted according to a system that was bound to create some problems. Three noticeboards hung in a row on the wall with various clippings from the Rørvig case. On the very last table Assad lay in a deep sleep, snoring in the fetal position on a small, lavishly decorated prayer rug.

Farther down the hall, from Rose's office, came a noise that at best could be described as a Bach melody set to unrestrained whistling — all in all, quite an organ concert.

Ten minutes later Rose and Assad were sitting before him, cups steaming, in the office that Carl, the day before, had called his, but now almost couldn't recognize.

Rose watched as he removed his coat and draped it over the back of the chair. "Nice shirt, Carl," she said. "You remembered to put the teddy bear in this one, I can see. Well done." She pointed at the bulge in his breast pocket.

He nodded. It was to remind him to shoo Rose on to a new, unsuspecting department when the opportunity presented itself.

"What do you say then, boss?" Assad said, making a sweeping gesture round a room where nothing seemed visibly out of order. A joy to behold for Feng Shui fans. Clean lines, the floor included.

"We got Johan to come down here and help us. He came back to work yesterday,"

Rose said. "After all, he was the one who set everything in motion."

Carl tried to put a little glow into his frozen smile. It wasn't that he wasn't pleased. Just a little overwhelmed.

Four hours later they sat at their respective desks waiting for the Norwegian delegation to arrive. They all had their roles to play. They'd discussed Johan's list of assaults and had received verification that two easily identifiable fingerprints found on one of the Trivial Pursuit cards matched those of the murdered Søren Jørgensen, and another one, less well preserved, matched the sister. Now the question was, who had taken the cards from the crime scene? If it was Bjarne Thøgersen, then why were the cards in a box found at Kimmie's house in Ordrup? And if others had been in the summer cottage beside Thøgersen, it would really be a radical departure from the court's interpretation of events at the time of sentencing.

The euphoria spread all the way into Rose Knudsen's office, where Bach's mistreatment had now been supplanted by a concentrated effort to dig up facts about Kristian Wolf's death, while Assad tried to get leads on where a "K. Jeppesen" — Kimmie & Co.'s Danish teacher — now lived and worked.

There was quite enough to do before the Norwegians came.

When it got to twenty minutes past ten, Carl knew what that meant.

"They're not coming down here unless I fetch them," he said, setting off with his briefcase.

He trotted up the rotunda's stone steps to the third floor.

"Are they in there?" he shouted to a pair of his weary colleagues, who were busy untying Gordian knots. They nodded.

There were at least fifteen people in the canteen. Besides the homicide chief there was Deputy Commissioner Lars Bjørn, Lis with her notebook, a pair of alert young blokes in boring suits who Carl guessed were from the Justice Ministry, and five colorfully dressed men who, in contrast to the rest of the gathering, received him with polite, toothy smiles. One point for the guests from Oslo-stan.

"Oh my, if it isn't Carl Mørck, what a pleasant surprise," the homicide chief exclaimed, meaning the opposite.

Carl shook hands with everyone, including Lis, and introduced himself extra clearly to the Norwegians. He himself didn't understand a lick of what they were saying.

"Soon we'll continue the tour in the lower chambers," Carl said, ignoring Bjørn's glare. "But first I would like to quickly explain my principles as head of the newly established unit, Department Q."

He stood in front of the whiteboard, the notations on which they'd apparently been discussing, and said: "Do all you guys understand what I'm saying?"

He noted their eager nods and the four scallops on Lars Bjørn's dark blue tie.

For the next twenty minutes he walked them through the Merete Lynggaard investigation, which the Norwegians — judging by their facial expressions — were well acquainted with, and topped it off with a brief account of their current case.

It was clear the chaps from the Justice Ministry were unacquainted with the latter. They'd never heard of that case, he figured.

He turned to the homicide chief.

"During our investigation we've come into the possession, just yesterday, of highly unambiguous evidence that at least one member of the gang, Kimmie Lassen, can be connected directly or indirectly to the crime." He outlined the events, assured everyone there was a reliable witness to his removal of Kimmie's box from the house in Ordrup, and watched as Lars Bjørn's look grew darker and darker.

"She could have got the metal box from Bjarne Thøgersen. She lived with him!" the homicide chief interjected. True enough. They had already discussed that possibility down in the basement.

"Yes, but I don't think so. Look at the date on the newspaper. It's from the day that Kimmie, according to Bjarne Thøgersen, moved in with him. I believe she folded it up and hid it because she didn't want him to see it. But there may be other explanations. We can only hope we track down Kimmie Lassen, so we can interrogate her. To that end we will request an all-points bulletin be sent out, plus reinforcements of a few men to monitor the area around Copenhagen's central station and shadow the drug addict Tine and, not least of all, Messrs Pram, Dybbøl-Jensen, and Florin." Here he glanced at Lars Bjørn with a venomous glint in his eye before turning to the Norwegians. "Three of those pupils who were once suspected of committing the double murder in Rørvig. They are now well-known men in Denmark," he explained, "who today live as respectable citizens in the upper echelons of Danish society."

Now the homicide chief's forehead, too,

was beginning to display a frown.

"You see," Carl said, directly addressing the Norwegians, who were knocking back their cups of coffee as if they had sat through a sixty-hour flight without food or drink, or at the very least came from a country that hadn't seen a coffee bean since the German invasion, "as you know through your and Kripo's generally fabulous work in Oslo, such lucky coincidences often throw light on other crimes that were never solved, or even reveal other cases not previously classified as crimes."

At this point one of the Norwegians raised his hand and asked a question in his sing-song dialect that Carl needed to have repeated a couple of times before a liaison officer came to his rescue.

"What Superintendent Trønnes would like to know is whether a list has been drawn up of the possible crimes that could be linked to the Rørvig murders," came the translation.

Carl nodded politely. How the hell could the man find so much coherent meaning in all that chirping?

He pulled Johan Jacobsen's list from his briefcase and fastened it to the whiteboard. "The homicide chief assisted in this part of the investigation." He glanced appreciatively at Marcus, who in return smiled politely around at the others, while simultaneously resembling a bundle of question marks.

"Our homicide chief has placed a civil employee's personal investigative work at Department Q's disposal. Without fine colleagues like him and his team, and without cross-disciplinary collaboration, it would be impossible to get so far in an investigation in such a short period of time. We must remember that this case, which is more than twenty years old, has been the object of our interest for two weeks only. So thank you, Marcus."

He raised an imaginary glass to Jacobsen, knowing that all this would boomerang on him sooner or later.

Despite attempts — Lars Bjørn's being especially eager — at redirecting Carl's agenda, it was very easy to hustle the Norwegians down to the basement.

The liaison officer made an effort to keep Carl abreast of their Norwegian brothers' commentary. They apparently admired Danish thrift and considered that results should always take precedence over daily demands for resources and fringe benefits. That interpretation would most likely be met with a certain amount of irritation when it made the rounds upstairs.

"There's a guy here who's asking me questions all the time I can't understand a word of. Do you speak Norwegian?" he whispered to Rose, as Assad heaped praises and medals on the Danish police's policy for integrating foreigners and also explained his present slave labor with surprising skill and comprehensiveness.

In the most intelligible and perhaps most attractive-sounding Norwegian Carl had yet to lend an ear to, Rose said, "Here we have the key to our work process," and proceeded to go through a stack of papers she had systematized during the early hours of the morning.

As much as he hated to admit it, the presentation was rather impressive.

When they reached Carl's office, the large-screen TV was displaying a sunny, guided tour of the Holmekollen ski resort. Assad had put in a DVD promoting the wonders of Oslo that he'd purchased around the corner at Politiken's Bookshop ten minutes earlier, and there wasn't a dry eye in the house. The justice minister would be flashing his teeth in an ecstatic smile when they gathered for lunch in another hour.

The Norwegian who'd been asking all the questions, who by now had mumbled his name and was apparently the senior officer, invited Carl over to Oslo with a heartfelt discourse on brotherhood. If he couldn't get Carl to Oslo, then at the very least he would have to join him for lunch, and if he didn't have time for that, either, then, if nothing else, there had to be time for a warm handshake, because he'd earned it.

After they'd gone, Carl looked at his two assistants with something that for a fleeting moment could be construed as warmth and gratefulness. Not because the Norwegians had been shepherded so smoothly through the department, but because he predicted that he would soon be called up to the third floor to continue his brief on the case and have his badge returned. If he got it back, that meant his suspension was a thing of the past, almost before it had started. And if it *was* a thing of the past, then he wouldn't have to attend psychotherapy sessions with Mona Ibsen. And if he didn't have to do that, then they had a dinner date. And if they had a dinner date, then anything was possible.

He needed to offer some nice words of thanks to Assad and Rose, which, while not praising them to the stars, would at least express a promise that in honor of the occasion they could go home an hour early.

The next phone call changed that plan.

The message Assad had left with Rødovre High School had resulted in a return call from one of its senior teachers, a certain Klavs Jeppesen.

He'd agreed to meet with Carl, and, yes, he had indeed taught at that boarding school in the mid-eighties. He remembered the time well.

They hadn't been the best days of his life.

24

She found Tine huddled under the stairwell of a building on Dybbølsgade, close to Enghave Plads. Filthy, bruised, and dying for a fix. She'd been there for almost an entire day and refused to budge, one of the resident vagrants had said.

She was sitting as far back in the stairwell as she could. Totally obscured by darkness.

She lurched in surprise when Kimmie stuck her head in. "God, is it you, Kimmie, love?" she called out, relieved, and threw herself into Kimmie's arms. "Hi, Kimmie. Hey, hey, you're just the person I wanted to see." She shook like a fluttering leaf. Her teeth chattered.

"What happened?" Kimmie asked. "Why are you sitting here? Why do you look like that?" She stroked Tine's swollen cheek. "Who beat you up, Tine?"

"You got my message, didn't you, Kimmie?" She pulled away and looked at Kimmie with yellow, bloodshot eyes.

"Yes, I saw it. Well done, Tine."

"Do I get the thousand kroner then?"

Kimmie nodded, drying sweat from her friend's forehead. Her face was terribly battered. One eye was nearly closed, her mouth was crooked, and there were hematomas and bluish-yellow bruises everywhere.

"You can't go to the places you used to, Kimmie." She crossed her shaking arms over her breast to calm her body. It didn't work. "The men were at my place. It wasn't too good. But now I'll stay here, won't I, Kimmie?"

Kimmie was just about to ask again what had happened when she heard the front door creak open. It was one of the tenants, coming home with the day's trophies clinking in a plastic grocery bag. Not one of those who'd taken over the neighborhood recently. Lots of homemade tattoos covered both his forearms.

"You can't stay here," he said nastily. "Sod off, you dirty whores."

Kimmie stood up.

"I think you should go up to your room and leave us alone," she said, moving a few paces toward him.

"Because otherwise . . . ?" He set the bag between his feet.

"Because otherwise I'll beat the shit out of you."

He loved hearing that, evidently. "Hello, bitch, you sound pretty tasty. Either you can sod off and take your disgusting junkie whore with you, or you can come up to my place. What do you say? For all I care that sow can rot wherever she likes, if you come with me."

He was trying to get his hands on her when his bloated beer belly received her hard fist. Then she punched him again, deforming his surprised expression. There was a crash on the stairway.

"Argh," he groaned, forehead on the floor as Kimmie returned to the stairwell.

"Who came? Some men, you say? Where did they come?"

"The men from the central station. They came to my flat and beat me up when I wouldn't tell them about you, Kimmie." She tried to smile, but the swelling on the left side of her face prevented it. She pulled her knees to her chest. "Now I'm just staying here. Fuck 'em."

"Who are you talking about? The police?"

Tine shook her head. "Them? No way! The cop was kind enough. No, just some arseholes who want to find you because someone's paying them to. You gotta watch

363

out for them."

Kimmie clutched Tine's skinny arm. "They beat you! Did you say anything? Do you remember?"

"Kimmie, please, I need a fix, right?"

"You'll get your thousand kroner, Tine. Did you say anything to them about me?"

"I don't dare go out on the street now. You've got to get it for me, Kimmie, won't you, please? And some chocolate milk and some smokes. And a few beers, you know?"

"OK, OK, you'll get it. Now answer my question, Tine. What did you say?"

"Can't you get it first?"

Kimmie looked at Tine. She was obviously terrified that Kimmie wouldn't give her what she hungered for once she'd told her what had happened.

"Out with it, Tine!"

"You *promised*, Kimmie!" They nodded at each other. "OK. They hit me. They kept hitting me, Kimmie. I said we met on the bench every now and then, and that I'd seen you walk down Ingerslevsgade many times, and that I thought you lived down there somewhere." She looked pleadingly at Kimmie. "You don't really live down there, do you, Kimmie?"

"Did you say anything else?"

Tine's voice grew thick, her shaking more

pronounced. "No, I promise you, Kimmie. I didn't."

"And then they buggered off?"

"Yes. Maybe they'll come back, but I won't say more than I already have. I don't know anything else."

Their eyes met in the semi-darkness. She was trying to make Kimmie believe her, but she'd said the last thing wrong.

So she must have known more.

"Is there anything else you'd like to tell me, Tine?"

The withdrawal symptoms had moved into her legs now, which twitched restlessly on the floor in her bunched-up position. "Just that about Enghave Park, that you sit there watching the children play. That's all."

She had bigger ears and eyes than Kimmie had thought, which meant she picked up tricks farther out than Skelbækgade or the stretch of Istedgade that ran from the train station to Gasværksvej. Maybe it was around here that she gave blowjobs to all those men. There were still enough bushes.

"And what else, Tine?"

"Aww, Kimmie, c'mon. I can't remember everything right now. I just can't think about anything but junk, you know?"

"But afterward, then. When you've had your fix, will you remember more about me?" She smiled at Tine.

"Yes, I think so."

"About where I go and where you've seen me? About my appearance? Where I shop? When I'm on the street? That I don't like beer? That I look in the windows on Strøget? That I'm always here in town? Is it things like that?"

She seemed relieved to have some help. "Yeah, it's things like that, Kimmie. That's the kind of stuff I'm not saying."

Kimmie moved with utmost care. Istedgade was full of nooks and crannies. No one could walk down the street and know for sure that someone wasn't standing ten yards farther ahead, watching closely.

Now she knew what they were capable of. There were probably many of them out looking for her now.

That's why this moment equaled Year Zero. Once again she'd reached the point when everything came to a standstill and new paths had to be opened.

How many times had it happened in her life? The irrevocable change? The big breakup?

You're not gonna get me, she thought, hailing a taxi.

"Drop me off on the corner of Dannebrogsgade."

"What are you talking about?" the taxi driver said, his dark-skinned arm already reaching for the backdoor handle. "Get out," he said, opening the door. "Do you think I can be bothered to drive you three hundred yards?"

"Here's two hundred kroner. Don't bother turning on the meter."

That helped.

She jumped out at Dannebrogsgade and quickly walked to Letlandsgade. Apparently no one was watching her. Then she circled round across Litauens Plads and edged along the house walls until at last she stood on Istedgade, looking directly across the street at the greengrocer's.

Just a couple of leaps and I'm there, she told herself.

"Hi, you. You're back again," the green-grocer said.

"Is Mahmoud out the back?" she asked.

Behind the curtain he and his brother were watching Arabic television. Always the same TV studio and always the same drab production.

"Well," Mahmoud said. He was the smaller of the two. "Have you already chucked the hand grenades? And the gun, it was OK, wasn't it?"

"I don't know, I gave it away. I need a new one now, this time with a silencer. And I need a couple of hits of good heroin. I mean really good, you get me?"

"Right *now*? You're crazy, lady. Do you think you can just barge in off the street and get these things? Silencers! Do you have any idea what you're talking about?"

She pulled a bundle of bills from her trousers. She knew it was more than twenty thousand kroner. "I'll wait out in the shop for twenty minutes. And then you'll never see me again. Agreed?"

A minute later the TV was turned off and the men were gone.

She was given a chair and the choice between cold tea and a Coke, but didn't want either.

Half an hour later a man arrived, no doubt a family member, and he didn't want to take any chances.

"Come in here, then we'll talk!" he commanded.

"I gave the others at least twenty thousand. Do you have the goods?"

"Just a minute," he said. "I don't know you, so raise your arms."

She did as she was told, and gazed steadily into his eyes as he felt up her calves and ran his hands along her inner thighs directly to her groin, where he left his hand a moment. Then he slid his hands farther up over her pelvis, around her back, across her belly, all the way under the fold of her breasts and further round to her neck and hair. Then he relaxed the pressure a little and once again felt her pockets and clothes before finally letting his hands rest on her breasts.

"My name is Khalid," he said. "You're clean. There are no microphones on you. And you have a hell of a fine body."

Kristian Wolf had been the first to recognize Kimmie's great potential and tell her she had a hell of a fine body. This was before the assault on the nature path, before she seduced the prefect, before her expulsion following the scandal with the teacher. Kristian had checked out what she was like, here and there and other places, and realized that without much trouble Kimmie was capable of converting her feelings — feelings that for most people develop into real emotions in the course of time — into huge, hard-hitting sexual explosions.

All he had to do was stroke her neck and declare how wild he was about her, and he would reap deep French kisses and all kinds of other sexual favors a sixteen- or seventeen-year-old dreams about.

And Kristian learned that if you wanted to have sex with Kimmie, you didn't ask. You just got started.

Torsten, Bjarne, Florin, and Ditlev quickly learned the art. Only Ulrik never got the message. Polite and courteous as he was, he seriously believed he needed to court her favor, so he never received it.

Kimmie was conscious of everything that was going on. Even how crazily enraged Kristian became when she later began harvesting blokes outside their circle.

Some of the girls said that he spied on her.

Nothing could surprise her less.

Once both the prefect and the teacher were out of the picture and Kimmie had her own apartment in Næstved, the five lads spent as many of their weekdays with her as they could. The rituals were already prepared. Violent videos, hash, discussing new assaults. And when the weekends came and everyone in theory was on the way home to their indifferent families, they climbed into her faded red Mazda and drove until they no longer knew where they were. Straight out into the blue yonder until they found themselves a park or a strip of forest, pulled on their gloves and masks and took the first person who passed. Age and gender were unimportant.

If it was a man who looked capable of putting up a fight, Kimmie removed her mask and stood in front of the gang with her coat and blouse unbuttoned and her gloved hands on her breasts. Who wouldn't stop, disoriented, in a situation like that?

After a while they learned to tell which types of prey would keep their mouths shut, and which they would have to force into silence.

Tine looked at her friend as if she had saved her life. "Is it good stuff, Kimmie?" She lit a cigarette and dipped her finger in the bag Kimmie held.

"Great," she said after testing it on her tongue. She looked at the bag. "Three grams, right?"

Kimmie nodded.

"First tell me what the police wanted with me."

"Oh, it was just something about your family, Kimmie. Nothing about the other stuff, that's for sure."

"My family? What does that mean?"

"Something about your father being sick, and that you wouldn't contact him if you just sort of found out. I'm sorry to have to tell you this, Kimmie." She tried to squeeze her friend's arm, but couldn't manage it.

"My father?" The words alone were like being given a shot of poison. "Is he even alive? No way. And if he is, he should just die." If that wanker with the bag of beers had still been there, she would have kicked him in the ribs. One for her father, and then one for good measure.

"The copper told me I shouldn't tell you, but now I have. I'm sorry, Kimmie." She stared longingly at the plastic bag in Kimmie's hand.

"What did you say the cop's name was?"

"I can't remember right now, Kimmie. Does it really matter? Didn't I write it down for you in the message?"

"How do you know he was a cop?"

"I saw his badge, Kimmie. I asked to see it, you know?"

The voices in Kimmie's head were whispering, telling her what she should believe. Soon she wouldn't be able to listen to anyone or anything anymore. A policeman sent to find her because her father was ill? Like hell. A police badge, what did that prove? Florin and the others could easily get hold of one.

"How could you get three grams for a thousand kroner, Kimmie? Not so pure, maybe? No, of course it's not. Boy, am I dumb!" She smiled at Kimmie beseechingly. Eyes partly shut, skeletal, and shaking with withdrawal.

So Kimmie returned the smile and gave her the bottle of chocolate milk, the crisps, the beers, the bag of smack, a bottle of water, and the syringe.

The rest she could do on her own.

She waited until twilight had settled in before she ran from the DGI building over to the wrought-iron gate. She knew what had to happen and this really wound her up.

During the next few minutes she emptied the hollow spaces of cash and credit cards, put two of the hand grenades on the bed and one in her bag.

Then she packed her suitcase with the bare necessities, removed the posters on the door and wall, and laid them on top. Last of all she pulled the box out from under the bed and opened it.

The little cloth bundle had become brown and almost weightless. She picked up the whisky bottle, brought it to her mouth, and drank it until it was empty. This time the voices didn't go away.

"OK, OK, I'm hurrying," she said, setting the bundle carefully on top in her suitcase, covering it with her blanket. She gently stroked the fabric a few times and snapped the lid shut.

She dragged the suitcase all the way out to Ingerslevsgade. Then all she'd have to do was grab it.

When she stood in the doorway, she took a good look round inside the house so that this momentous intermezzo in her life had time to imprint itself.

"Thanks for putting me up," she said, backing out of the door while releasing the safety catch on a hand grenade and throwing it next to the other one on the bed.

When the house exploded, she was a good distance beyond the gate.

If she hadn't been, flying chunks of concrete would probably have been the last things she felt in this life.

25

The blast was like a muffled thud against the windows in the homicide chief's office.

He and Carl glanced at each other. This wasn't just premature New Year's fireworks.

"Jesus Christ," Marcus said. "Just as long as no one got killed."

A friendly, empathetic person, who in this instance was probably thinking more of his workforce than potential victims.

He faced Carl again. "That number you pulled yesterday, don't try it again, Carl. I understand what you're saying, but next time you come to me first, otherwise you'll make me look like a fool, understand?"

Carl nodded. Fair enough. Then he told the homicide chief his suspicions regarding Lars Bjørn. That he in all probability had had a personal motivation for interfering with Carl's investigation. "We'll have to call him in, right?"

Marcus Jacobsen sighed.

■ ■ ■ ■

Maybe he knew the party was over, maybe he believed he could maneuver around it. Whatever the case, for the first time ever Bjørn wasn't wearing his customary tie.

The homicide chief got right down to it. "I understand that you were our liaison between the ministry and the police chief in this case, Lars. Would you mind explaining how this adds up before we offer our own interpretation?"

Bjørn sat scratching his chin a moment. A military man by training. A classic, unblemished police CV. The right age. Continuing education courses at the University of Copenhagen. Law, of course. Good administrative abilities. An enormous network of contacts and a good deal of experience in fundamental police work as well. And now this glaringly obvious blunder. He had politicized his job, stabbed his colleagues in the back and helped hinder an investigation he in principle had nothing to do with. And for what? For solidarity with a boarding school he'd left ages ago? For old friendships' sake? What the hell was he supposed to say? One wrong word and he was finished. They all knew it.

"I wanted to spare us a resource-draining fiasco," he said, and instantly regretted it.

"Unless you can produce a better defense, consider yourself out, you hear me?" Carl saw how painful it was for the homicide chief. He and Bjørn were an excellent team, however irritating Carl thought the deputy commissioner was.

Bjørn sighed. "You've no doubt noticed that I have a different tie on."

They both nodded.

"Yes, I went to the same boarding school."

Needless to say, they would have figured it out — and Bjørn could see that.

"There was some very negative press in connection with a rape case at the school a few years ago, so they didn't need the Rørvig case being reopened."

They knew that, too.

"And Ditlev Pram's older brother, Herbert, was one of my classmates. He's on the same school's board of directors today."

That bit of information, on the other hand, had regrettably slipped under Carl's radar.

"His wife is the sister of one of the department heads in the Justice Ministry. And this department head has been a rather good sparring partner for the police chief during the reform process."

Isn't that a nice kettle of fish, Carl thought. It was straight out of one of Morten Korch's sentimental cinematic dramas. Soon they'd probably all turn out to be illegitimate children of some rural landowner.

"I was being pressured on both sides. It's like a brotherhood, all these old boarding-school alums, and I admit I've made a mistake here. But I assumed the department head was doing the justice minister's bidding, and that therefore I wasn't completely in the wrong. She didn't want the case drawing any interest, partly because those who were involved — who aren't exactly nobodies, of course — hadn't been accused of anything when the crime was committed, and partly because there had already been a conviction with an almost-served sentence. To me it seemed as though they wanted to avoid an evaluation of whether or not procedural mistakes had been made and all kinds of other potential problems. I don't know why I didn't check with the minister, but at our lunch yesterday it became clear that she didn't know anything about the investigation, so unfortunately she never took any measures. I know that now."

Marcus Jacobsen nodded. He was ready to do the hard work now. "You didn't notify me of any of these matters, Lars. You just told me the police chief had given us the directive that Department Q was to shut down its investigation. Now I see that it was you who single-handedly advised the police chief to give us this order after you personally misinformed her. What did you tell her, anyway? That there weren't any grounds to reopen the case? That Carl Mørck was messing with it just for fun?"

"I was in her office with the department head from the Justice Ministry. He was the one who informed her."

"Is he also an old pupil from the same boarding school?"

Lars nodded, a pained expression on his face.

"So in reality, Pram and the others in the gang could have set the whole process in motion, Lars, don't you realize that? Ditlev Pram's brother's plea to you! The department head's highly questionable lobbying!"

"Yes, I'm aware of that."

The homicide chief threw his pen down hard on his desk. He was positively furious. "You're suspended from this moment forward. Please write an account that I can present to the minister. Remember to include the department head's name."

Lars Bjørn had never looked so pathetic. If it weren't for the fact that Carl had always found him to be a hemorrhoid in his arse, he would almost have felt sorry for him.

"I've got a suggestion, Marcus," Carl interrupted.

A tiny spark lit up Bjørn's eyes. After all, there had always been such a good, antagonistic understanding between them.

"Let's drop the suspension. We need all the men we can get, don't we? If we make an issue out of this, word will get out. The press and all that crap. You'll have journalists screaming out there in the courtyard, Marcus. Besides, the people we're investigating will be much more careful, and I don't need that."

Bjørn sat nodding mechanically at each of these statements. Poor sap.

"I want Bjørn on the case. Just to lead some of the work in the next few days. Searches, surveillance, everyday legwork. We can't do it all ourselves, and now we have something to work with, Marcus. Do you see? A little effort now and maybe we'll solve some other murders as well." He tapped his finger on Johan Jacobsen's list of assaults. "Damn it, I think it might just happen, Marcus."

No one was injured by the blast at the rail yard near Ingerslevsgade, but Channel 2

News and their infuriating helicopters were already circling the location as if seventeen platoons of terrorists had just demonstrated their strength.

The news anchor was clearly in a state of excitement, although trying hard not to show it. The best news was always the kind that could be delivered with gravity and concern, sensational items especially, and the police were once again in the journalists' hot seat.

Following the events on his TV in the basement, Carl was glad it had nothing to do with him.

Rose entered his office. "Lars Bjørn has activated the Copenhagen Police search team. I sent them a photo of Kimmie, and Assad has filled them in on everything he could from his surveillance. They're also looking for Tine Karlsen. She's caught in the eye of the hurricane, that's for sure."

"What do you mean?"

"The search team's office is on Skelbæk-gade, you know? Isn't that where Tine Karlsen usually turns tricks?"

He nodded, glancing at his notes and directives.

The list of tasks seemed endless. It was a question of prioritizing and working methodically.

"Here are your tasks, Rose. Complete them in order."

She took the paper and read aloud:

1. Find policemen who participated in the Rørvig investigation in 1987. Contact Holbæk Police and the Mobile Investigation Unit on Artillerivej.
2. Find classmates of the gang members. Get eyewitness accounts describing their behavior.
3. Go back to Bispebjerg Hospital. Find a doctor or nurse who was working at the gynecological ward while Kimmie was there.
4. Get details surrounding Kristian Wolf's death.
5. Contact Berne University and get hold of any files they may have on Kimmie.

   Today, thanks!

He thought she'd take the very last word as being conciliatory. She didn't.

"Jesus! Apparently I should have come to work at four o'clock this morning instead of five thirty," she said quite loudly. "You've gone completely batty, man. Didn't you just tell us we could go home an hour early?"

"Yes, but that was a few hours ago."

She spread her arms and dropped them again. "And . . . ?"

"Now things are a bit different. Do you have anything you have to do this weekend?"

"What?"

"Rose, this is your opportunity to prove what you're made of, and to learn what it's like to do real investigative work. And think about how much time off in lieu you'll have when it's over."

She snorted. If she wanted to hear jokes she would make them up herself.

The telephone rang just as Assad walked into the room. It was the homicide chief.

"You were just about to get me four men from the airport, but then you didn't?" Carl fumed. "Is that what you're telling me?"

The homicide chief confirmed it.

"Do you really mean we can't get anyone to help us trail the suspects? If it slips out that the investigation hasn't been shut down after all, then where do you think Pram, Florin, and Dybbøl Jensen will be by tomorrow? Not around here, I can tell you that. Maybe Brazil."

He breathed deeply and shook his head. "I know damned well we don't have any real proof of their involvement, but how about the circumstantial evidence, Marcus? It's there, for God's sake, don't you agree?"

After the call, Carl sat in his office, eyes glued to the ceiling, and rattled off the best countrified curse words he'd learned off a kid from Frederikshavn at a Boy Scout jamboree in 1975. Not something Baden-Powell would have approved of.

"What did Marcus say then, Carl?" Assad asked. "Are we getting help then?"

"What did he say? He said that first they just had to solve the Store Kannikestræde assault and then there'd be more resources to go around. And they have to get that explosion at the rail yard under control." Carl sighed. It was something he'd gotten pretty good at. If it wasn't one thing it was another.

"Sit down, Assad," he said. "We need to find out if Johan's list is worth anything."

He leaned toward the whiteboard and began copying out:

6/14/1987: Kåre Bruno, boarding-school pupil, falls from the ten-meter diving board and dies.

8/2/1987: The murders in Rørvig.

9/13/1987: Assault, Nyborg Beach. Five young men/one girl in the vicinity. The

female victim in shock. Doesn't make a
statement.

11/8/1987: Twins, football pitch, town of
Tappernøje. Two fingers cut off. Thoroughly beaten.

4/24/1988: Elderly couple disappears on
Langeland. Various articles belonging to
them turn up in Lindelse Cove.

When he had written down all twenty
cases, he looked at Assad.

"What's the common denominator? What
would you say, Assad?"

"They all occurred on a Sunday."

"I thought so. Are you sure of that?"

"Yes!"

Logical enough. Of course they must have
started on Sundays. They certainly didn't
have any other possibilities as boarders.
Boarding-school life was restrictive.

"They must have got into the habit of carrying out the attacks on Sundays when they
were at school, and then incorporated that
as part of their ritual after they'd left,"
surmised Carl.

"And they could drive from Næstved to
the crime scenes in a couple of hours," Assad said. "There were no assaults in Jut-

385

land, for example."

"What else do you notice, Assad?"

"During the period 1988 to 1992 none of the victims disappeared."

"What do you mean?"

"As I say — that it was just violent assaults. Beatings and such. No one who was found dead or went missing."

Carl studied the list. A civilian employee at headquarters had compiled it, and he was personally and emotionally involved. How could they know he hadn't been too selective? There were thousands of cases of violence in Denmark each year, after all.

"Bring Johan down here, Assad," Carl said.

In the meantime he would contact the pet shop where Kimmie had worked. That might help him develop her profile, learn something of her dreams and values. Maybe he could arrange a meeting tomorrow morning. Then in the evening he had an appointment with the teacher at Rødovre High School. They were having an alumni party that same evening. "Lasasep," they called it. The last Saturday in September, 9/29/2007. Real cozy, with dinner and dancing, he'd said.

"Johan is on the way," Assad reported, as he mulled over the list on the whiteboard.

"Kimmie was in Switzerland during that period," he said very quietly, a moment later.

"Which period?"

"From 1988 to 1992." He nodded to himself. "No one disappeared or was killed while Kimmie was in Switzerland," he said. "Not anyone on this list, in any case then."

Johan didn't look good. He'd once run around headquarters like a baby calf that had just discovered the paddock's limitless size and abundance. Now he seemed more like the battery calf that had been penned in once and for all. With no room to move or grow.

"Are you still going to the psychologist, Johan?" Carl asked.

He was. "She's good. I just don't feel so well," he replied.

Carl glanced at the photo of the two siblings on the board. Maybe it wasn't so strange.

"How did you select the incidents on your list, Johan?" Carl asked. "How do I know there aren't hundreds and hundreds you didn't include?"

"I started by including all instances of reported violence between 1987 and 1988 that were committed on a Sunday, where the assault wasn't reported by the victims themselves and the distance to Næstved was less than a hundred miles." He looked quizzically at Carl. It was important for him that they were one hundred percent on the same page.

"Listen. I've read a great deal about those kinds of boarding schools. The wants and needs of the individual mean next to nothing. The pupils are kept to a tight schedule where lessons and duties come first, and everything is mapped out. All week long. The goal is to establish discipline and a sense of community. Based on that I concluded that the violent crimes committed during the school year's weekdays or before breakfast on the weekends or at any point after dinner weren't worth looking into. In short, the gang had other activities to keep them occupied at those times. That's how I selected the crimes. Sundays, after breakfast and before dinner. That's when the assaults had to take place."

"They committed their crimes on Sundays in the middle of the day, you say?"

"Yes, I believe so."

"And during that time span they could drive a maximum of a hundred or so miles, if they also had to find their victims and carry out their plan."

"During the school year, yes. Summer breaks were another matter." He looked down at the floor.

Carl checked his perpetual calendar. "But the murders in Rørvig were also committed on a Sunday. Was that just a coincidence, or was it the gang's trademark?"

Johan seemed sad when he replied. "I think it was a coincidence. It was right before the school year began. Maybe they felt they hadn't got enough out of their summer holiday, I don't know. They were psychos, after all."

After that, Johan explained he'd used his intuition to create the list covering subsequent years. Not that Carl thought it was inaccurate. But if they were going to act on intuition, he'd rather it be his own. So for the time being the investigation would focus exclusively on the years before Kimmie went to Switzerland.

After Johan had returned to his daily duties, Carl sat for a bit evaluating the list before calling the police in Nyborg. From them he learned that the twin brothers who'd been attacked on the football pitch in 1987 had emigrated to Canada many years ago. In a voice that might have belonged to an eighty-year-old, the duty officer informed him that they'd inherited a small sum of money and had established a farm-equipment supply business. At any rate, that was what they'd been told at the station. Nobody was familiar with the boys' personal lives. It was, of course, a long time ago.

Carl then looked at the date of the elderly couple's disappearance on the island of Langeland, and let his eyes wander across the case file Assad had requisitioned and put on his desk. It involved two schoolteachers from Kiel who'd sailed to Rudkøbing and then traveled from one bed and breakfast to the next before finally spending the night in Stoense.

The police report stated that they had been seen at the harbor in Rudkøbing the day they vanished, and in all probability had sailed out to sea and sunk. But there were some people who'd seen the couple in Lindelse Cove the same day, and later two young guys were observed in the harbor near where the couple's boat had been moored. The witnesses stressed that they were nice-looking young men. Not the kind of local boys with Castrol or BP caps, but the kind with pressed shirts and neat haircuts. Some suggested they were the ones who'd sailed off in the boat, not the owners.

But that was only local speculation.

The report did also mention some effects that had been found on the beach near Lindelse Cove. Though they couldn't say for sure, relatives thought they might belong to the missing couple.

Carl looked through the whole list of effects for the first time: an empty thermal box with no distinctive labeling; a shawl; a pair of socks; and an earring consisting of two pieces. Amethyst and silver. With a little silver hook. To put through the earlobe and without any locking mechanism.

Not a terribly detailed description, as one might expect from a male police constable, but it sounded like an exact replica of the earring in the little plastic pocket in front of Carl, right next to the two Trivial Pursuit cards.

It was at this astonishing moment that Assad arrived, looking like the incarnation of someone who'd struck gold.

He pointed at the rubber band in the bag next to the earring.

"I've just learned that this type of rubber band was used at the pool at Bellahøj so you could see how long you'd been in the water."

Carl tried to rise to the surface. He was still far away in his thoughts. What could be as important as his truly incredible discovery concerning the earring?

"Those kinds of rubber bands were used everywhere, Assad. They still are."

"Yes," he said. "But in any case, when they found Kåre Bruno smashed on the tiles, he'd lost his."

26

"He's waiting up at the front desk now, Carl," Assad said. "Would you like me here then, when he comes down?"

"No." Carl shook his head. Assad had enough to do. "But bring us some coffee, will you? Just not too strong, please."

With Assad whistling in the Saturday silence, when even the sanitation pipes thundered only at half strength, Carl quickly skimmed *Who's Who* for information about the man he was about to meet.

Mannfred Sloth was his name. Forty years old. Former roommate of Kåre Bruno, the deceased school prefect. Graduated in 1987. Royal Guardsman. Lieutenant in the reserves. MBA. CEO of five companies since his thirty-third birthday. Six board appointments, one of which was in a state-owned organization. Promoter and sponsor of several exhibitions of modern Portuguese art. Since 1994 married to Agustina Pessoa.

Former Danish consul in Portugal and Mozambique.

No wonder that Sloth could add a knighthood and international orders to the list.

"I only have fifteen minutes," he began his handshake with. Sloth sat down, crossed his legs, tossed his autumn coat casually aside, and lifted the creases of his trousers a tad so his knees wouldn't stretch the fabric. It was quite easy to picture him in a boarding-school environment. Much harder to envision him in the sandbox with his children.

"Kåre Bruno was my best friend," he said, "and I *know* he would never have entertained the thought of going to an outdoor public pool, so it's very odd that he was found at Bellahøj. A place such as that was far too close to all kinds of people, you understand." He actually meant it. "Besides, I'd never seen him dive before, and most certainly not from a ten-meter board."

"You don't think it was an accident?"

"How could it be an accident? Kåre was a smart chap. He wouldn't just dawdle about up there when everyone knows falling off would be fatal."

"And it couldn't have been suicide?"

"Suicide! Why? We had just graduated. His father had given him a Buick Regal Limited as a graduation gift. A coupé model, you know?"

Carl nodded hesitantly because he didn't bloody know. He knew that Buick was a type of car, and that would have to do.

"He was set to go to the U.S. to study law. Harvard, right? Why would he do something so idiotic? That doesn't make any sense whatsoever."

"Was he lovesick?" Carl asked cautiously.

"Ha! He could have had whoever he wanted."

"You remember Kimmie Lassen?"

He grimaced. The memory of her didn't please him.

"Was he upset that she'd dumped him?"

"Upset? He was furious. He didn't like being dropped. Who does?" He smiled, teeth gleaming whitely, and swept the hair from his forehead. Hair that was tinted and newly cut, of course.

"And what was he going to do about it?"

Mannfred Sloth shrugged, brushing a few specks of dust from his coat. "I'm here today because I think we both believe he was murdered. That he was pushed over the edge. Otherwise, why would you bother contacting me twenty years later? Am I correct?"

"We're not absolutely certain, but naturally there's a reason we're working on the case again. Who do you think might have pushed him?"

"I have no idea. Kimmie had some sick friends in her class. They ran around her like satellites. She had them in the palm of her hand. Lovely breasts, you know? *Tits rule*, am I right?" He gave a short, dry laugh. It didn't suit him.

"Do you know if he tried to win her back?"

"She already had something going with one of the teachers. One from the suburbs without the common sense to know pupils were off limits."

"Do you remember his name?"

He shook his head. "He hadn't been there terribly long. He taught a few Danish classes, I think. He wasn't the kind of person you noticed if you didn't have him as a teacher. His . . ." He paused and raised a finger in the air, his face radiating remembrance and concentration. "Yes. Now I've got it. His name was Klavs. With a 'v,' for God's sake!" He snorted. The name alone was pathetic.

"Klavs, you say! Klavs Jeppesen?"

He raised his head. "Yes, Jeppesen. I believe that was it." He nodded.

Pinch my arm, I must be dreaming, Carl thought. He was going to meet Jeppesen that very evening.

"Just put the coffee there, Assad. Thank you."

"Well, I must say," Carl's guest said with a crooked smile. "You have humble conditions down here, but at least the help is well trained." He laughed the same dry laugh and Carl could imagine only too well how he had treated the natives in Mozambique.

Sloth tasted the coffee and with the first gulp clearly had had enough.

"OK," he said. "I know he was still keen on the girl. There were many who were. So when she was expelled he wanted her all to himself, naturally. She was living in Næstved then."

"I don't understand how he came to die in Bellahøj."

"When we were done with our exams, he moved in with his grandparents. He had stayed with them before. They lived in Emdrup. Very sweet, fine people they were. I spent a lot of time there back then."

"His parents weren't in Denmark?"

He shrugged. No doubt Mannfred Sloth's children also went to boarding school so he could devote himself to his own affairs. Fuck him.

"Did anyone in Kimmie's circle live near the swimming center?"

He looked right through Carl. Now, finally, he recognized the gravity that the room exuded. The files with the old cases. The photographs on the noticeboard. The list of assault victims, with his friend Kåre Bruno's name at the top.

Shit, Carl thought when he turned round and realized what Sloth was staring at.

"What's that?" Sloth asked, with a menacing seriousness, his finger pointing at the list.

"Oh," Carl said. "The cases aren't connected. We're in the process of categorizing our files in chronological order."

Idiotic explanation, thought Carl. Why in the world would they write on the board what could just as easily be in files on the shelf?

But Mannfred Sloth didn't ask any questions. He wasn't the type who did that kind of slave labor, so how would he know about such basic procedures?

"You must have your hands full," he said.

Carl spread his arms. "That's why it's so important that you answer my questions as precisely as you can."

"What was it you asked?"

"I simply asked if anyone in the gang lived near Bellahøj."

He nodded without hesitation. "Yes,

Kristian Wolf did. His parents owned quite an impressive, functionalist house down by the lake, which he moved into when he threw his father out of the firm. And actually I think his wife still lives there with her new husband."

He didn't get any more out of him. But what he got wasn't so bad.

"Rose," he called, when the hard sound of Mannfred Sloth's Lloyd shoes had faded. "What do you know about Kristian Wolf's death?"

"Hello, Carl?" She tapped her head with her notepad. "Do you have Alzheimer's or what? You gave me five tasks, and that one was number four according to your own prioritization. So what do you suppose I know about it?"

He'd forgotten. "So when can you tell me something? Can't you switch the order around?"

She put her hands on her hips like an Italian mama about to yell at her scoundrel of a husband lounging on the sofa. Then she suddenly smiled. "Oh, to hell with it. I can't keep a straight face anyway." She licked her finger and riffled through her notepad. "Do you think you get to decide everything? Of course I did that one first. It was obviously the easiest."

When he died, Kristian Wolf was only just under thirty years old, but filthy rich. His father had founded the shipping company, but Kristian outmaneuvered and ruined him. People said his father had it coming; he'd raised a son without feelings and when push came to shove, that's what he got in return.

He was a bachelor rolling in money, and for that reason his June marriage to a countess — the third daughter of Baron Saxenholdt, Maria Saxenholdt — caused a sensation. Their wedded bliss lasted barely three months, the press wrote, before Kristian Wolf was killed in a shooting accident on September 15, 1996.

It all seemed so pointless, and maybe that was the reason the newspaper coverage was endless. There were far more articles about his death than about the new bus terminal at Copenhagen's City Hall, and nearly as many as about Bjarne Riis winning the Tour de France a few weeks earlier.

He had gone out alone very early one morning at his weekend estate on the island of Lolland. He was supposed to meet the rest of the hunting party half an hour later, but more than two hours passed before they found him with an ugly gunshot wound in one thigh, his body completely drained of blood. It had to have been a fairly quick demise, the autopsy report concluded.

That was true. Carl had seen it before.

The investigators had been surprised that things could have gone so terribly wrong for such an experienced hunter. But many of his hunting buddies explained that Wolf had a habit of carrying his gun with the safety latch off. Once he'd missed the chance to shoot a polar bear in Greenland because his fingers had been too cold to release the latch, and he wasn't going to let that happen again.

In any event, it was a bit of a mystery how he'd managed to shoot himself in the thigh, but the conclusion was that he had stumbled over a plowed furrow and accidentally fired the shotgun. Reconstructions of the accident showed that it was just possible.

That the young wife didn't make a bigger issue of the accident was more or less unofficially ascribed to the fact that by that time she'd already regretted the marriage. After all, he was older than her, and very different, and the inheritance was a rather nice consolation, all things considered.

■ ■ ■ ■

The country house practically jutted out over the lake. There weren't many properties of its caliber in the vicinity. It was of the kind that makes all those around it appreciate considerably in value.

Carl estimated it was worth 40 million kroner before the real estate market had been brought to its knees. Now this sort of place was just about unsellable. Still he suspected the owners had voted for the very government that had created the conditions for this economic slump in the first place. But what the hell, it was all just words, anyway. A consumer orgy followed by an overheated economy. Who gave a hoot about that around here?

It was people's own fault.

The boy who opened the door was eight or nine years old at most. He had a stuffy, red nose and was wearing a dressing gown and slippers. A quite unexpected sight in this enormous hall where businessmen and finance moguls had held court for generations.

"I'm not allowed to let anyone in," he managed to say, through a couple of highly inflated bubbles of snot. "My mother won't be home for a little while. She's in Lyngby."

"Can you call her and tell her the police would like to speak with her?"

"The police?" He eyed Carl skeptically. It was in these kinds of situations that a long black leather coat like Bak's or the homicide chief's would help develop mutual trust.

"Here," Carl said. "This is what my badge looks like. Ask your mother if I may wait inside."

The boy slammed the door.

For half an hour he stood on the steps, observing people running around on the paths on the other side of the lake. Ruddy-cheeked people with swinging arms and mincing gaits. It was a Saturday morning. The citizens of the Welfare State were out getting their exercise fix.

"Are you looking for someone?" the woman asked, when she'd stepped from her car. She was on her guard. One wrong move and she would throw her purchases on the ground and race to the back door.

Having learned from experience, he flashed his police badge immediately.

"Carl Mørck, Department Q. Your son didn't call?"

"My son is ill. He's in bed." She looked instantly concerned. "Isn't he?"

So he hadn't called, the little scamp.

He introduced himself once again and was reluctantly let in.

"Frederik!" she called upstairs. "I've got a sausage for you." She seemed sweet and natural. Not what you'd expect of a genuine countess.

His shuffling down the stairs came to an abrupt halt when he saw Carl standing in the hall. In an instant it seemed as though childish visions of the kind of punishment he would get for not doing exactly as the police said clouded his snot-streaming face with dread. He was certainly not ready to be confronted with the consequences of his offense.

Carl winked at him to signal that everything was OK. "Oh, so you really are bedridden, huh, Frederik?"

The boy nodded rather slowly, then took his French hot dog and disappeared. Out of sight, out of mind, he probably thought. Wise kid.

Carl got straight to the point.

"I don't know if I can help you with anything," she said, giving him a friendly look. "Kristian and I didn't actually know each other terribly well. So I've no idea what was going on in his head in those days."

"And you remarried, Countess?"

404

"No need to be so formal. Just call me Maria," she smiled. "Yes, I met my husband, Andrew, the same year Kristian died. We have three children now. Frederik, Susanne, and Kirsten."

Very ordinary names. Maybe Carl needed to reconsider his prejudices about the ruling class's signature values.

"And Frederik is the oldest?"

"No, he's the youngest. The twins are eleven." She beat him to his question. "And, yes, Kristian is their biological father, but my present husband has always been there for them. The girls board at a wonderful all-girls school near my in-laws' estate in Eastbourne."

She said it so sweetly and unaffectedly and shamelessly. How the hell did she have the heart to do that to her children? Eleven years old, and they were already exported to the backwaters of England and subjected to relentless discipline.

He looked at her with a freshly cemented foundation under his class prejudices. "While you were married to Kristian, did he ever talk about a Kirsten-Marie Lassen? I'm sure it must be a curious coincidence that she shares your daughter's name, but Kristian knew the woman very well. She went by the name of Kimmie. They were at boarding school together. Does the name mean anything to you?"

A veil descended over her face.

He waited a moment, expecting her to say something. But she didn't.

"Excuse me, but what just happened?" he said.

She raised her palms, fingers splayed. "I don't care to talk about it, that's all I wish to say." She hadn't needed to say that. It was evident.

"Do you think he might have had an affair with her, is that it? Even though you were pregnant at that point?"

"I don't know what he had going on with her, and I don't want to know." She stood with her arms crossed under her breasts. In a second she would be asking him to leave.

"She's a bag lady now. She lives on the street."

That piece of information apparently didn't console her.

"Whenever Kristian had been talking to her, he beat me. Are you satisfied? I don't know why you're here, but you may leave now."

There it was, finally.

"I'm here because I'm investigating a murder," he tried.

The response was instantaneous. "If you

406

think I killed Kristian then you'd better think again. Not that it never crossed my mind." She shook her head and looked out over the lake.

"Why did he hit you? Was he sadistic? Did he drink?"

"Was he sadistic?" She glanced down the hallway to make sure a little head didn't suddenly appear. "You can bet your life he was."

He stood reconnoitering the area before climbing back in his car. The atmosphere in that vast mansion house had been oppressive, as, layer by layer, she had uncovered what a strong, sadistic man could do to a slender woman of twenty-two. How the honeymoon was quickly transformed into a daily nightmare. It started with mean words and threats, then things escalated. He was careful not to leave marks, because in the evening she had to be dressed to the nines, showing off her pedigree. That's why he had chosen her. For that reason only.

Kristian Wolf. A guy she'd fallen in love with in an instant and would spend the rest of her life trying to forget. Him, his deeds, the way he behaved and the people he surrounded himself with. All of it had to be swept away.

Inside the car Carl sniffed for petrol. Then he called Department Q.

"Yeah," Assad simply said. He didn't say "Department Q," or "Vice Police Superintendent Assistant Hafez el-Assad speaking," or anything else. Just a "yeah!"

"You need to identify yourself and the department when you pick up the telephone, Assad," he said, without identifying himself.

"Hi, Carl! Rose has just given me her dictaphone. It looks *so* nice. And then she wants to talk to you."

There was some shouting and loud, echoing footsteps, and then she was on the line. "I've found a nurse from Bispebjerg for you," she said drily.

"OK. Super."

That didn't warrant a response.

"She works at a private hospital up near Arresø," Rose continued, giving him the address. "She was easy to track down once I found her name. It's a *really* peculiar one, too."

"Found it where?"

"At Bispebjerg Hospital, of course. I scoured their old archive filing cabinets. She was working in the gynecological ward when Kimmie was hospitalized. I called her and she remembered the case. Everyone who worked there back then would remember Kimmie, she said."

"Denmark's most beautiful hospital" — as Rose had quoted from the Web site.

Carl looked down at the snow-white buildings and concurred. Everything was exquisitely well maintained. Even this late into autumn, the manicured lawns were worthy of Wimbledon. Absolutely magnificent surroundings. The royal couple had enjoyed the sight only a few months earlier.

Their palace at Fredensborg had nothing on this place.

Head nurse Irmgard Dufner was rather a contrast. Smiling and as big as a vessel putting into port, she cruised out to greet him. People around her stepped quietly to the side as she passed them. A pudding-basin haircut with a fringe, legs like two-by-fours, and shoes that pounded heavily on the floor.

"Mr. Mørck, I presume!" She grinned and shook his hand as if she were trying to empty his pockets of their contents.

Luckily for him, her enormous outward appearance was matched by the size of her memory. A police officer's dream.

She had been senior clinical nurse on Kimmie's ward at Bispebjerg, and even though she'd been off duty when the patient disappeared, the events had been so strange and tragic that she'd never forgotten them, she explained.

"When the woman arrived she was quite beaten up, so we expected her to lose the child, but she actually did all right. She just wanted that child *so* badly. When she'd been at the hospital for a week, we were almost ready to discharge her."

She chewed her lip. "But then one morning when I'd been on night shift, she miscarried suddenly and severely. The doctor said it seemed as though she had provoked it herself. I found that hard to believe, given how much she'd been looking forward to having the baby. At any rate, there were large blue bruises on her abdomen. But it's impossible to know about these things. There are a lot of mixed feelings involved when a woman faces raising an unplanned child on her own."

"What could she have used to cause the bruising? Do you recall?"

"Some said it could have been the chair in her room. That she had pulled it on to her bed and pounded it against her abdomen. In any case, it was lying on the floor when the doctors came in and found her unconscious, with the fetus lying in a pool of blood between her legs."

Carl tried to imagine it. A sad sight.

"And the fetus was big enough for you to see it?"

"Oh yes. At eighteen weeks a fetus resembles a little human being, around five or six inches long."

"Arms and legs?"

"Everything. The lungs haven't fully developed, nor have the eyes. But just about everything else has."

"And it lay between her legs?"

"She had given birth to the child and the placenta in the normal way, yes."

"You mention the placenta. Wasn't there something abnormal about it?"

"It's one of the things everyone remembers. That, and the fact that she stole the fetus. My colleagues had placed it under a sheet while they staunched her bleeding. When they returned after a short break, the patient and the fetus were gone. The placenta, on the other hand, was still there. That was when one of our doctors noticed it had ruptured. Been torn in two, so to speak."

"Couldn't that have happened during the miscarriage itself?"

"Sometimes that happens, but *very* seldom. Maybe the violence inflicted on her abdomen had something to do with it.

Either way, it's quite a serious situation if the woman is not curetted."

"You're referring to potential infections?"

"Yes, in the past, especially, this was a big concern."

"And if this isn't done, what then?"

"Well, the patient risks dying."

"I see. But I can assure you that she didn't. She's still alive. Not in the best condition, since she now lives on the street, but she *is* alive."

She folded her sizable hands in her lap. "I'm relieved to hear that, but it's a shame she's living on the street. Many women never get over that kind of experience."

"You mean the trauma of losing a child might be enough to make her withdraw from society?"

"Ah, you know what? Anything's possible in a situation like that. It happens time and again. They can enter a state of mental derangement and are quite often overwhelmed by self-recrimination."

"I think I'll try to give a brief summary of the case. What do you say to that, friends?" He looked at Assad and Rose, knowing that they both had things they wanted to get off their minds. It would have to wait.

"We have a group of youths comprised of

very strong-minded individuals, which is to say that they always carry out whatever they plan to do. Five guys, each with his own personal attributes, and a girl who appears to be the pivotal figure.

"She's brash and beautiful and initiates a short relationship with one of the top students at the school, Kåre Bruno — who I have a strong hunch dies with a fair amount of assistance from the gang. One of the objects in Kimmie Lassen's hidden metal box points in that direction, in any case. Maybe it was jealousy, maybe a scuffle, but of course it *could* also have been a simple accident, in which case the rubber band she stashed away might just be a kind of trophy. At any rate, the rubber band in itself doesn't tell us anything definite about the question of guilt, even if it arouses suspicion.

"The gang sticks together, despite the fact that Kimmie leaves the school, and their association results directly or indirectly in the murder of two, probably randomly chosen, youths in Rørvig. Bjarne Thøgersen confesses, albeit nine years later, but presumably to cover for one or more of the others. Everything suggests that in this connection he was promised a large sum of money. He came from a relatively poor family and his sexual relationship with Kimmie was over, so it could have been a reasonable solution in his particular situation. In any event, we now know that *someone* in the gang was involved, since we've found effects with the victims' fingerprints in Kimmie's box.

"We in Department Q are drawn into this case following a private citizen's suspicion that Thøgersen's conviction was erroneous. Perhaps the most important element to note in this connection is that Johan Jacobsen supplied us with a list of assaults and disappearances the gang may have been involved in. Furthermore, with this list we can confirm that during the years Kimmie lived in Switzerland there were reports only of physical assaults — not homicides or disappearances. The list is admittedly somewhat speculative, but Johan's general approach seems sound.

"It has come to the attention of the gang that I'm investigating the case. I don't know how, but probably through Aalbæk, and an attempt is currently being made to obstruct the investigation."

At this point Assad raised a finger. "Obstruct? Is that what you said?"

"Yes. Trying to block the investigation, Assad. 'Obstruct' means 'block.' And that tells me the case has more to it than just a few rich men's normal concern for their reputations."

They both nodded.

"As a result, I've been threatened in my home, in my car, and, most recently, at my work, and in all probability people from this gang are behind these threats. They have used old boarding-school chums as go-betweens to get us removed from the case, but now this chain has been broken."

"So we've got to tread cautiously," Rose grunted.

"Correct. We're being left in peace to work for now, and they mustn't know this. Especially because we believe that interrogating Kimmie, given her situation, would be greatly to our advantage. Through her we might get some clarity about what the gang got up to back then."

"She won't say anything, Carl," Assad interjected. "Not the way she looked at me at the central station."

Carl thrust out his lower lip. "Yeah, yeah, we'll see. Kimmie Lassen is probably a few sandwiches short of a picnic. How could she not be, living on the street when she has a palace in Ordrup? A miscarriage in mysterious circumstances, where she was apparently repeatedly subjected to violence — this has probably contributed to the situation." He considered fishing out a cigarette, but Rose's coal-black-mascara glare was resting heavily on his hands. "We also know that one of the gang members, Kristian Wolf, died a few weeks after Kimmie Lassen disappeared, but we don't know whether the two facts are connected. Today, however, I learned from his widow that Wolf had sadistic tendencies, and it was also suggested that he had a relationship with Kimmie Lassen." His fingers were now wrapped around the pack of cigarettes. So far so good.

"But the most important lead in the case is that we now know one or more of the gang committed assaults in addition to the murders in Rørvig. Kimmie Lassen had hidden effects that positively indicate at least four deadly attacks, and two additional plastic pockets with effects give us cause to suspect more.

"So now we'll try to rope in Kimmie, follow the actions of the other suspects, and finish off our other assignments. Do you have anything to add to the summary?" Then he lit his cigarette.

"You still have the teddy bear in your pocket, I see," Rose said, eyes on the cigarette.

"Right. Anything else?"

They shook their heads.

"Good. Fire away, Rose. What did you find out?"

She watched the spiral of smoke creeping toward her. In a moment she would begin fanning it away. "Not very much, and yet a fair amount."

"That sounds cryptic. Let's hear it."

"Besides Klaes Thomasen, I've only been able to locate one policeman involved in the investigation. A Hans Bergstrøm, who was part of the Mobile Investigation Unit back then. Today he has another job, and anyway, he's impossible to talk to." Now she fanned the smoke away.

"There's no one who is impossible to talk to," Assad interrupted. "He's just angry at you because you called him a dumb shit." He smiled broadly when she protested. "Yes, Rose, I heard it."

"I put my hand over the phone. He didn't hear it. It's not my fault he didn't want to talk. He's made a fortune off his patents now, and I've also found out something else about him." She began blinking and fanning again.

"And that is?"

"He is also an old boarding-school pupil. We won't get anything out of him."

Carl closed his eyes and wrinkled his nose.

To show solidarity was one thing, to be thick as thieves quite another. What a bloody nuisance.

"It's the same with the gang's old classmates. None of them will talk to us."

"How many have you got in contact with? They must be scattered to the winds. And the girls might have new surnames."

She fanned so demonstratively now that Assad inched away from her. It *did* look threatening. "Apart from those who live on the other side of the globe, and are getting their beauty sleep right now, I've contacted almost all of them. And I think that's enough now. They refuse to say anything, if they say anything at all. There was only one person who hinted at what they were like."

This time, Carl blew the smoke away from her. "I see. What did that person say?"

"All he said was that they were a wild bunch who bent the school's rules. They smoked hash in the woods and in the parks near the school. But he still seemed to think they were decent enough people. Listen, Carl, can't you put that nicotine bastard away while we're holding a meeting?"

He'd managed ten drags. That would have to do.

"If only we could speak directly with someone from the gang, Carl," Assad interjected. "But I suppose we can't."

"If we contact any of them, I think the whole case will slip through our fingers." He snuffed his cigarette in his coffee cup, which clearly irritated Rose. "No, we'll wait to talk to them. But what do you have for us, Assad? I understand you've looked into Johan's list. Have you come to any conclusions?"

Assad raised his dark eyebrows. He had something — that was plain to see. And he'd had the distinct pleasure of keeping it to himself.

"Out with it, teacher's pet," Rose said, winking at him with coal-black eyelashes.

He glanced down at his notes with a curling smile. "Yes, I've then found the woman who was assaulted in Nyborg on September 13, 1987. Her name is Grete Sonne, and she is fifty-two. She owns a clothing shop down on Vestergade. Mrs. Kingsize, it's called. I haven't talked to her because I thought it was best if we went in person. I have the police report here. There's not much in it about the assault that we didn't already know."

But enough, to judge by his facial expression.

"The woman was thirty-two at the time and had been on the beach at Nyborg walking her dog on that autumn day. The dog had got off its lead and was running toward a treatment center for diabetic children, a place called Skaerven. So she ran as fast as she could to catch it. The dog was a bit snappish, from what I can tell. Then there were some kids who caught up with it before she did, and approached her with the dog. There were five or six of them in all. She couldn't remember any more than that."

"Ugh!" said Rose. "Then it must have been a really heavy battering."

Yes, Carl thought. *Either that or the woman had lost her memory for another reason.*

"It was quite a brutal assault, all right. The report said she had been whipped on her bare skin, several of her fingers had been broken, and the dog was left dead at her side. There were plenty of footprints, but overall the clues led nowhere. There was talk that a medium-sized red car had been parked down in Sommerbyen, outside a brown summer cottage close to the water." Again Assad glanced down at his notes. "Number 50, it was. The car was parked there for a few hours. Some motorists also reported seeing a number of youths running alongside the road around the time of the assault.

"Afterward ferry routes and ticket sales were checked, of course, but that didn't lead anywhere, either."

He shrugged his shoulders regretfully, as if he had been the one leading the investigation.

"And then, after a four-month stay in the psychiatric ward at the university hospital in Odense, Grete Sonne was released and the case was shelved as unsolved. That was that!" He flashed a beautiful smile.

Carl put his head between his hands. "Well investigated, Assad, but honestly, what do you think is so special about all this?"

Again he shrugged. "That I have found her then. And that we can be there in twenty minutes. The shops haven't closed yet."

Mrs. Kingsize was downtown, sixty yards from Strøget, and was very much a clothes shop with a specific aim. Here even the most shapeless woman was able to order flattering, figure-hugging, bespoke gowns in silk, taffeta, and other expensive fabrics.

Grete Sonne was the only one in the boutique with a normal shape. A natural redhead with a little added gleam, she appeared quite lithe and elegant against the shop's imposing backdrop.

She did a double take as they glided in.

She had probably sparred with many drag queens and transvestites of a certain build, but this average-sized man and his little, thickset but not corpulent sidekick didn't fit that category.

"Yes?" she said, glancing at the clock. "We're just about to close, but if I can help you, I'll stay on a bit."

Carl positioned himself between two rows of sumptuousness on hangers. "We'd rather wait until you close, if that's OK with you. We have a few questions."

She looked at his badge when he held it up for her, then grew very serious, as if the flashbacks were always waiting on the firing ramp. "Well, then I'll close up," she said, giving her two plump assistants some instructions for the following Monday and a "have a good weekend" on their way out.

"I'm going to Flensburg on Monday, you see, to do some buying, so . . ." She attempted a smile, fearing the worst.

"We apologize for not calling ahead, but that's partly because it's an urgent matter, and partly because we only have a few questions."

"If this is about the shoplifting in the neighborhood, you should talk to the shopkeepers down on Lars Bjørnsstræde. I'm sure they have their fingers on the pulse more than I do," she said, knowing this was about something else.

"Please listen. I realize the assault you suffered twenty years ago has been hard on you, and that you probably don't have anything to add. So all you have to do is answer 'yes' or 'no' to the questions we ask. Is that OK with you?"

She grew pale, but remained on her feet.

"Just nod or shake your head," Carl continued when she didn't respond. He looked at Assad. He already had his notebook and dictaphone out.

"You didn't remember anything about the assault afterward. Is that still the case today?"

After a short but endless pause, she nodded. Assad noted the movement by whispering into his dictaphone.

"I believe we know who did it. It was six youths from a boarding school in Zealand. Can you confirm there were six attackers, Grete?"

She didn't react.

"Five young men and a girl. Eighteen to twenty years old. Well dressed, I think. I'm going to show you a picture of the girl."

He showed her a copy of the photo in *Gossip* from 1996, where Kimmie Lassen stood in front of a café with Wolf and Pram.

"It was taken a few years later, and the fashion is a little different, but . . ." He observed Grete Sonne. She wasn't paying attention at all. Simply staring at the photo, her eyes flitting between the young jet-setters on a bender in Copenhagen's night-life.

"I don't remember anything, and I don't want to think about that business anymore," she finally said, composed. "I would be very grateful if you'd leave me in peace."

Assad stepped toward her. "I've seen in your old tax returns that you very suddenly then came into money in the autumn of 1987. You had been employed at the dairy in . . ." Assad glanced at his notebook ". . . in Hesselager, it's called. And then some money came. Seventy-five thousand kroner, isn't that right? And then you started your first boutique in Odense, and then here in Copenhagen."

Carl felt his surprise raise one of his eyebrows. How the hell had Assad found that out? And on a Saturday, too? Why hadn't he mentioned it on the way over? There had been time enough.

"Can you explain where that money came from, Grete Sonne?" Carl asked, pointing the eyebrow at her.

"I . . ." She seemed to be searching for

her old explanation, but the magazine photo was stuck in her head and had short-circuited her inner wiring.

"How the devil did you know about that money, Assad?" he said as they walked down the street. "You didn't have a chance to examine old tax returns today, did you?"

"No. I just thought about a saying my father made up: 'If you want to know what the camel stole from your kitchen yesterday, then you shouldn't slit open its stomach. You should stare into its arsehole.' " He smiled broadly.

Carl had to chew on that one. "Which means . . . ?"

"Why make something more difficult than it is then? I just googled whether there was a person in Nyborg called Sonne."

"And then you phoned someone and asked them to spill the beans on Grete's financial situation?"

"No, Carl. You don't understand the saying. You've got to kind of go behind the story, right?"

He still didn't get it.

"Really, Carl! First I called the people who lived *beside* the family named Sonne. What was the worst that could happen? That it was the wrong Sonne family? Or that the

425

neighbor was new?" He spread out his hands. "Honestly, Carl."

"And you got the actual Sonne's actual old neighbor?"

"Yes! Well, not right away, but they lived in a flat, so there were also five other numbers to choose between."

"And?"

"Yes, so I got Mrs. Balder on the third floor. She said she'd lived there for forty years and knew Grete back when she wore plushed skirts."

"Pleated, Assad. Pleated. Then what?"

"Well, the lady told me everything. That the girl had been lucky to get money from an anonymous rich man from Funen who felt sorry for her. Seventy-five thousand kroner. It was just enough to start the shop she wanted. Then Mrs. Balder was glad. Everyone in the building was, she said. Because it had been such a shame for Grete with the assault."

"OK. Well done, Assad."

This, Carl could see, was actually a new and important aspect to the investigation.

When the gang mistreated their victims, there were two possible outcomes: compliant victims like Grete Sonne — who had been permanently frightened out of her wits and scarred for life — they bought off.

Uncooperative victims got nothing. They simply vanished.

27

Carl munched on the pastry that Rose had plonked on his desk. The large-screen TV was showing a news story about the military regime in Burma; the monks' dark crimson robes seemed to be having the same effect as a toreador's red cape on a bull. So the privations of Danish soldiers in Afghanistan were shoved further down the list for the moment.

Something the prime minister was probably not sorry to see.

In a few hours Carl was going to be at Rødovre High School, meeting with one of the former boarding-school teachers. A man Kimmie had had an affair with, according to Mannfred Sloth.

A strange, irrational feeling, experienced by many policemen during an investigation, ran through Carl.

Despite the fact that he'd spoken with Kimmie's stepmother, who'd known her from when she was a little girl, he'd never felt as close to her as he did at this moment.

Staring into space, he wondered where she was.

The image on the TV shifted again, and the story of the blown-up house at the rail yard near Ingerslevsgade was repeated for the gazillionth time. All train traffic had been suspended; a few overhead wires had been blasted to smithereens. Farther down the line were also several of the railway's yellow track-repair cars, which probably meant that rails had been ripped up.

The image of the assistant police commissioner came into focus and Carl turned up the volume.

"All we know is that the house had probably been the residence of a homeless woman for some time. Railroad workers spotted her off and on during the last few months when she slipped out of the house, but we haven't found traces of her or anyone else."

"Is it possible that a crime was committed?" the female reporter asked in that excessively empathetic way that's designed to make inferior news coverage seem earth-shattering.

"What I can say is that, as far as transit authorities are aware, there was nothing in the building that would naturally cause such an explosion, and certainly not of the magnitude that we see here."

The reporter turned to the camera. "The military's explosives experts have been investigating the scene for several hours." Then she turned back to the commissioner. "What have they found? Is anything known at this point?"

"Ahem . . . Well, we don't yet know with certainty if it's the cause, but they have discovered hand-grenade fragments of the type our soldiers are equipped with."

"The house was blown up by hand grenades, in other words?"

She was bloody good at stretching out time.

"Possibly, yes."

"How much more is known about the woman?"

"She was a regular around here. Shopped at the Aldi up there." He pointed up Inger-slevsgade. "Bathed over there once in a while." He turned and pointed toward DGI City. "Naturally we're asking anyone in the area with any information to contact the police. The description has yet to be final-ized, but we believe we're looking for a white woman, thirty-five to forty-five years of age, around five foot six inches, and of average build. Her clothing varies, but is generally a little untidy as a result of her living on the streets."

Carl sat in silence, a hunk of pastry dangling from the corner of his mouth.

"He's with me," he said at the barricade tape, as he and Assad slipped through the chain of police and military technicians.

There were a whole lot of people walking about on the tracks and a lot of questions being asked. Was it an attempt to sabotage a train? And if that was the case, had a specific train been targeted? Had there been prominent people on any of the trains that had just passed by the building? The air buzzed with such queries and speculations, and the journalists' ears were enormous.

"You begin on that side, Assad," Carl said, pointing behind the house. There were bricks everywhere, large and small, in a real hodgepodge. Splinters of wood from doors and roof, tarpaper and roof gutters in shards and pieces. Some of the debris had flattened the chain link fence, behind which photographers and journalists were ready for action if human remains were found.

"Where are the railroad workers who've seen her?" Carl asked one of his colleagues from headquarters, who pointed over his shoulder at a few men who stood clustered together like paramedics in their luminescent uniforms.

As soon as he showed them his badge, two of them began speaking at once.

"Wait! One at a time," he said, aiming a finger at one of the men. "You first. What did she look like?"

The man seemed quite content with the situation. In an hour he would be off work and it had been a wonderfully varied day.

"I didn't see her face, but she usually wore a long skirt and a quilted jacket; but then other times she could be wearing something completely different."

His partner nodded. "Yes, and when she was on the street she often dragged along a suitcase."

"Aha! What kind of suitcase? Black? Brown? On wheels?"

"Yes, the kind on wheels. A big one. The color changed sometimes, I think."

"That's right," the first one said. "I think I've seen both a black one and a green one."

"She always glanced around as if she were being hunted," added the second.

Carl nodded. "And she probably was. How come she was allowed to live in that house anyway, once you discovered her there?"

432

The first man spat on the gravel at his feet. "Hell, we weren't using it. And the way this country is being run, you've got to accept that some people get left behind." He shook his head. "Naw, I didn't want to spill the beans on anyone. What the hell good would that do me?"

His mate agreed. "We have at least fifty such buildings from here to Roskilde. Just think about how many people could live in them."

Carl preferred not to. A couple of drunken vagrants, and there would be chaos on the tracks.

"How did she get into the grounds?"

They each grinned. "Hell, she just unlocked the gate and let herself in," one replied, pointing at what used to be a gate in the fence.

"OK. And how did she get a key for it? Did someone lose a key?"

They shrugged their shoulders up to their yellow helmets and laughed until it spread to the rest of the bunch. How the hell should they know? As if they checked those gates.

"Anything else?" Carl asked, glancing round at the group of men.

"Yes," one of the others said. "I think I saw her up at Dybbølsbro Station the other

433

day. It was a little late, and I was returning with the transporter over there." He pointed at one of the track-repair cars. "She was standing on the platform right up there, facing the tracks. As if she was Moses about to part the sea. I bloody well thought she was thinking of jumping in front of the train, but she didn't."

"Did you see her face?"

"Yes. I was the one who told the police how old I thought she was."

"Thirty-five to forty-five. Wasn't that what you said?"

"Right, but now that I think about it, she was probably closer to thirty-five than forty-five. She just looked so sad. A person seems much older then, don't you think?"

Carl nodded and pulled Assad's photograph from his coat pocket. The laser printout had been slightly battered; the folds were deep now. "Is this her?" he asked, holding the photo in front of the man's nose.

"Yes, damn it, it is." He seemed absolutely flummoxed. "She didn't look quite like that, but hell, that's her all right. I recognize her eyebrows. It's rare that women have such broad eyebrows. Wow, she looks a lot better in that photo."

As the men crowded around the picture and made comments, Carl turned his attention to the leveled building.

What the hell happened here, Kimmie? he thought. If he had just found her a day earlier, they'd be a whole lot further along now.

"I know who she is," Carl said, turning to his colleagues, each of whom was standing around in his black leather coat, lacking precisely the man who could say that exact sentence.

"Would you guys call Skelbækgade Police Station and tell the search team that the woman who lived here is a Kirsten-Marie Lassen, also known as Kimmie Lassen? They have her Civil Registration Number and other information about her. If you find anything out, I'm the first you call, understood?" He was about to go, but stopped. "One more thing. Those vultures over there," he pointed at the journalists, "they mustn't get her name under any circumstances, OK? If they do, it will interfere with an ongoing investigation. Pass it on!"

Carl looked at Assad, who was practically on his knees, searching the rubble. Oddly enough, the crime-scene techs left him alone. Apparently they had already appraised the situation and ruled out any suspicion of terrorism. Now all that remained was to convince the overeager reporters of this.

He was glad that wasn't part of his job.

He leaped over what used to be the door of the building, a wide, heavy, green thing, half-covered with white graffiti, pushed through the hole in the fence and out onto the street. It wasn't hard to find the sign that still hung on one of the galvanized fence posts. GUNNEBO, LØGSTRUP FENCE, it read, along with a list of telephone numbers.

He pulled out his mobile and rang a couple of the numbers without any luck. Fucking weekends. He'd always hated them. How could anyone do police work when people were off hibernating?

Assad will have to talk to them on Monday, he thought. *Someone there might be able to explain how she came into possession of the key.*

He was about to wave Assad over; he wasn't going to find anything the crime-scene techs had overlooked anyway. But then he heard the sound of a car braking, and saw the homicide chief climb out just as it halted halfway onto the curb. Like everyone else, he was wearing a black leather jacket, though his was a bit longer, a little shinier, and probably also more expensive.

What the hell is he doing here? Carl thought, following him with his eyes.

"They haven't found any bodies," Carl called out, as Marcus Jacobsen nodded to a pair of colleagues behind the overturned fence.

"Listen! Can you take a little ride with me, Carl?" he said, when they were facing each other. "We've found the drug addict you're looking for. And she's very, very dead."

This wasn't the first time he'd seen it: a corpse under a stairwell, pale and pathetically hunched over with wispy hair spread out across the remains of tinfoil and filth. An abused creature with a swollen face, resulting from a blow. Hardly more than twenty-five years old.

An overturned bottle of chocolate milk sailing around on a white plastic bag.

"Overdose," the doctor said, pulling out his dictaphone. Of course they would have to do an autopsy, but the medical examiner was familiar with the situation. The needle was still hanging from the mistreated vein on her ankle.

"Agreed," said the homicide chief. "But . . ."

He and Carl nodded to each other. Marcus had had the same thought. Overdose, sure. But how? A seasoned junkie like her?

"You went to talk to her. When was that, Carl?"

Carl turned to Assad, who stood wearing his customary quiet smile. Strangely unaffected by the gloomy atmosphere in the stairwell.

"On Tuesday, boss," Assad replied. He didn't even need to peek at his notebook; it was almost frightening. "Tuesday afternoon, the twenty-fifth," he added. Soon he would say it was at 3.32 or 3.59 or something. If he hadn't seen Assad bleed, Carl would have thought he was a robot.

"That's quite a while ago. A lot could have happened since then," the homicide chief said. He fell to one knee and cocked his head, eyes fixed on all the bruises on the woman's face and throat.

Yes, she'd clearly got those after Carl's meeting with her.

"These injuries were not inflicted immediately before she died. Do we agree on that?"

"A day before, I would say," the medical examiner said.

There were loud noises in the stairwell, and one of the men from Bak's old unit came down the stairs with a person that one would definitely prefer not to count as a family member.

"This is Viggo Hansen. He's just told me something I think you'll want to hear."

The hefty man scowled at Assad and got a suitably haughty glance in return. "Does he have to be here?" he said flat out, revealing a couple of tattooed forearms. A pair of anchors, a swastika, and a KKK. Nice lad.

When he walked past Assad, he bumped his flabby belly into him, and Carl's eyes opened wide. He bloody well hoped Assad wouldn't react.

Assad nodded, absorbing it. Lucky for the sailor.

"I saw that slut with another whore yesterday."

He described her, and Carl retrieved his tattered laser print.

"Was this her?" he asked, contracting his nostrils. The rancid odor of sweat and piss was almost as strong as the stench of alcohol that reeked through the sot's rotten teeth.

He rubbed his sleepy, unappealing eye sockets and nodded, making his double chins flap together. "She pounded away at the junkie there. Look at all the bruises. But I broke it up and kicked her out. She had a big mouth, the bitch," he said, vainly trying to straighten his posture.

What a clown. Why was he lying?

One of their colleagues arrived and whispered something in the homicide chief's ear.

"OK," Marcus Jacobsen said. Hands in his pockets, he stared at the idiot, the expression on his face suggesting he might pull out his handcuffs any second.

"Viggo Hansen. You're a familiar face, I hear. Over ten years in total behind bars for violence and sexual assaults on single women. You claim that you saw this woman beat the deceased. Knowing the police as well as you do, shouldn't you be a little smarter than that?"

He breathed deeply. As if he were trying to spool back to a more appropriate starting point. As if he could just manage it.

"Now tell us what really happened. You saw them standing here, talking, and that was it. OK. Anything else?"

He looked down at the floor, his humiliation palpable. Maybe Assad's presence caused it. "No."

"What time was it?"

He shrugged. The alcohol had destroyed his sense of time. No doubt it had been years since he'd had one.

"Have you been drinking the whole time since you saw them?"

"Just for fun," he tried to smile. Not a

pleasant sight.

"Viggo admits that he swiped a few beers that were lying under the stairwell here," said the officer who'd brought him down from the flat. "Some beers and a bag of crisps."

Things that poor Tine certainly never got much pleasure out of.

They asked him to stay home the rest of the day and try to hold back on the drinking. They didn't get anything out of the rest of the building's tenants.

The long and short of it was that Tine Karlsen had died. Probably alone, and with no one to miss her apart from a large, hungry rat named Lasso that she now and then called Kimmie. She was just another number in the statistics. If it weren't for the police, she would already be forgotten in the morning.

The crime-scene techs turned the stiffened corpse over and found only a dark stain of urine beneath her.

"I wonder what she could have told us," Carl mumbled.

Marcus nodded. "Yes, the incentive to find Kimmie Lassen has certainly not lessened now."

It was just a question of whether this would make any difference.

■ ■ ■ ■

He dropped Assad off at the explosion site, asking him to snoop around to find out if the investigation had led to any discoveries. Afterward he was to go back to headquarters and see if he could help Rose with anything.

"I'll try the pet shop first, then I'll drive out to Rødovre High School," he shouted, as Assad trudged determinedly toward the explosives experts and crime-scene techs who were still swarming about the terrain.

Nautilus Trading A/S stood like a pale green oasis among the other pre-war buildings on a little crooked street that was doubtless next in line to give way to unsellable luxury boxes. Large trees with bright yellow leaves planted in oak barrels stood outside, and posters showing exotic animals were pasted across the entire facade. A considerably larger business than he had imagined, and probably also much larger than back when Kimmie had worked there.

And naturally it was closed. Saturday peace had settled in.

He walked round the buildings and found a recess with an unlocked door. DELIVERIES, it read.

He opened it, walked about ten yards, and found himself in a hellish tropical humidity that immediately made his armpits drip.

"Is anyone here?" he called out in twenty-second intervals, on his wanderings through a land of aquariums and lizards. Then deeper into a paradise of birdsong arising from hundreds and hundreds of cages in a hall the size of an average supermarket.

He didn't find a human being until he was in the fourth hall, among cages housing mammals big and small. It was a man focused on scrubbing an enclosure large enough to house a lion or two.

When Carl drew closer he scented the sharp undertone of a predator in the sickly sweet air. So maybe it *was* a lion's cage.

"Excuse me," Carl said softly, but apparently so heart-attack-inducing that the man in the cage dropped both his bucket and broom.

He stood there in a sea of soapy water, rubber gloves up to his elbows, and looked at Carl as if he had come to tear him to pieces.

"Excuse me," Carl said again, now with his badge thrust out. "Carl Mørck, from Department Q at police headquarters. I ought to have called in advance, but I was in the neighborhood."

The man was most likely between sixty and sixty-five years old, with white hair and large crow's feet around eyes that had no doubt been chiseled there through the years by the delight he took in working with small, furry, baby animals. Just now, however, he seemed less than delighted.

"Big cage to clean," Carl said, to soften him up. He felt the mirror-smooth steel bars.

"Yes, but it has to be picture-perfect. It's to be delivered to the firm's owner tomorrow."

Carl explained the nature of his errand in a backroom where the animals' presence didn't seem quite so intense.

"Yes," the man said. "Of course I remember Kimmie very well. She helped build this place up, you know? I think she was with us close to three years — the same years that we were expanding to become an import and procurement center."

"Procurement center?"

"Yes. If a farmer in Hammer has a place with forty llamas or ten ostriches that he'd like to get rid of, then we enter the picture. Or when mink farmers want to switch to raising chinchillas. Small zoos contact us, too. We actually employ both a zoologist and a veterinarian." Then the crow's feet appeared. "We're northern Europe's largest wholesaler in every type of certified animal. So we get everything from camels to beavers. That was something Kimmie got started, in fact. She was the only one at the time with the necessary animal expertise."

"She was a trained veterinarian, is that right?"

"Yes, well, almost. And she had a good commercial background, so she could evaluate the animals' origins, the trade routes, and all the paperwork."

"Why did she quit?"

He tilted his head from side to side. "Well, it was a long time ago, but when Torsten Florin began to shop here, something changed. Apparently, they already knew each other. And then she met another man through him, I think."

Carl watched the pet-shop manager. He seemed reliable. Good memory. Well organized. "Torsten Florin? The fashion mogul?"

"Yes, him. He's exceedingly interested in animals. In fact, he's our best customer." He tilted his head again slowly sideways. "That's an understatement today because he owns a majority stake in Nautilus, but back then he came in as a customer. A very pleasant and successful young man."

"I see. He must really be interested in animals." Carl looked across the landscape of cages. "They already knew each other, you say. How did you know?"

"Well, I wasn't present when Florin came here the first time. They must have said hello when he was about to pay. She was in charge of that. But in the beginning she didn't seem especially excited about seeing him again. I really can't say what happened later."

"The man you mentioned, the one Torsten Florin knew, was it Bjarne Thøgersen? Do you recall?"

He shrugged. Evidently he didn't remember.

"She moved in with him in September 1995, you know," Carl said. "I'm sure she worked here at that time."

"Hmm. Maybe. She never talked about her private life, actually."

"Never?"

"No. I didn't even know where she lived. She handled her own personnel forms, so I can't help you with that."

The manager stood in front of a cage where a pair of tiny, deep-set, dark eyes was looking at him with fervent trust. "This one is my favorite," he said, and removed a monkey the size of his thumb. "My hand is

446

its tree," he said, holding it up in the air as the Lilliputian creature clung to two of his fingers.

"Why did she stop working at Nautilus? Did she give a reason?"

"I think she just wanted to move on with her life. No particular reason. You know what I mean?"

Carl exhaled so loudly that the monkey sought refuge behind the fingers. To hell with all these questions and to hell with this line of interrogation.

So he put on his mask of annoyance. "I think you know why she quit, so would you be so kind as to tell me?"

The man put his hand into the cage and let the little ape disappear into the deep.

Then he turned to Carl. All that snow-white hair and beard didn't help him seem friendly anymore; now it seemed more like a crowning halo of unwillingness and defiance. Though his face was still soft, his eyes were hardening. "I think you should leave now," he said. "I've tried to be obliging. You've no right to accuse me of standing here feeding you lies."

So that's how you want to play it, Carl thought, smiling his most patronizing smile.

"I was just wondering," he said. "When was a business like this last inspected? Don't these cages seem awfully close together? And is the ventilation system all in order? How many of your animals actually die during transportation? Or here?" He began staring into the cages one at a time, where small, frightened bodies sat, breathing rapidly in the corners.

Now the pet-shop manager smiled, displaying a fine set of dentures. It was clear that for all he cared Carl could say whatever he wished. Nautilus Trading A/S had nothing to worry about.

"You want to know why she quit? Then I think you should ask Florin. After all, he's the boss here!"

28

It was a lethargic Saturday evening, and the radio news gave equal attention to the birth of a tapir in Randers Rainforest and the Conservative Party chairman's threat to abolish the new county delineations he himself had demanded be established.

Carl punched in a number on his mobile, glanced across the water at the sunbeams reflected on the surface, and thought, *Thank God there's still something they can't mess with.*

Assad picked up at the other end. "Where are you, boss?"

"I just crossed Zealand's Bridge on the way to Rødovre High School. Is there anything special I should know about this Klavs Jeppesen?"

When Assad was thinking, one could actually hear it. "He's frust, Carl. That's the only thing I can say."

"Frust?"

"Yes. Frustrated. He sounds slow, but that's probably just emotions blocking the free word."

The free word? Next Assad will be waxing lyrical about the "light wings of thought."

"Does he know why I'm coming?"

"More or less, yes. Rose and I have been working on the list the entire afternoon, Carl. She would like to talk to you about it then."

He was about to protest, but Assad was gone.

So was Carl, in a way, once Rose set her acid tongue in motion.

"Yes, we're still here," she said, shaking Carl out of his train of thought. "We've been studying this list all day and I think we've pinpointed something we can use. Would you care to hear it?"

What the hell did she think?

"Yes, please," he said, almost missing the left-turn lane toward Folehaven.

"Do you recall the case on Johan's list with the couple who disappeared on Langeland?"

Did she think he was suffering from dementia, or what?

"Yes," he replied.

"Good. They were from Kiel, and they vanished. Some effects were found near Lindelse Cove that could have belonged to them, but it was never proven. I've been tinkering around with the case a little."

"What do you mean?"

"I found their daughter. She lives in her parents' house in Kiel."

"And?"

"Take it easy, Carl. Surely someone who's done such damn fine police work is allowed to draw the story out a bit?"

He hoped she couldn't hear his deep sigh.

"Her name is Gisela Niemüller, and she's actually rather shocked by how the case was handled in Denmark."

"What's that supposed to mean?"

"The earring. Do you remember that?"

"Come on, Rose, for Christ's sake. We were just talking about it this morning."

"About twelve years ago she contacted the Danish police and told them she could now identify with absolute certainty the earring found near Lindelse Cove as her mother's."

At this point Carl was as close as humanly possible to torpedoing a Peugeot 106 with four noisy young men inside. "What?" he shouted, as he slammed on the brakes. "One moment," he continued, pulling to the side of the road. "She couldn't identify it back then, so how could she now?"

"The daughter had been at a party with

some relatives in Albersdorff, in Slesvig, and she'd seen some old photographs of her parents at a family gathering. And what do you think her mother was wearing in the photos? Just asking." She emitted a pleasure-filled growl. "Yes, the earrings, damn it!"

Carl closed his eyes and clenched his fists. "Yes!" his brain screamed. Exactly how test pilot Chuck Yeager must have felt the first time he broke the sound barrier.

"I'll be damned." He shook his head. It was a major breakthrough. "Hell's bells. Terrific, Rose. Terrific. Did you get a copy of the photograph showing the mother with the earring?"

"No, but she says that she sent it to the Rudkøbing Police around 1995. I've talked to them, and they say all the old archives are in Svendborg now."

"She didn't send the original to them, did she?" He prayed she hadn't.

"Yes, she did."

Bloody hell. "But she probably kept her own copy. Or a negative. Or someone has it, don't you think?"

"No, she didn't think so. That was one of the reasons she was so angry. She's never heard back from them."

"You'll call Svendborg right away, won't you?"

She let out a noise that sounded mocking. "You evidently don't know me very well, Mr. Deputy Detective Superintendent." Then she slammed down the phone.

In less than ten seconds he'd phoned back.

"Hi, Carl," came Assad's voice. "What did you tell her? She looks strange."

"Never mind, Assad. Just tell her that I'm proud of her."

"Now?"

"Yes, now, Assad."

Assad lay down the receiver.

If the photo of the missing woman's earring was now found in the Svendborg Police archives, and *if* an expert could guarantee that the earring found on the beach near Lindelse Cove matched the one he'd found in Kimmie's stashed metal box and that they were, in fact, the same pair of earrings as in the photograph, *then* they'd have a case. They'd have enough to go to trial. Jesus Christ, they were holding the right end of the stick now. It had taken twenty years, but nevertheless, Florin, Dybbøl Jensen, and Pram were going to be dragged through that long, tenacious process known as the mucky machinations of justice. They just needed to find Kimmie first; after all, he'd found the box at her place. Tracking her down was no doubt easier said than done, and her junkie friend's death didn't exactly make it easier. But she *had* to be located.

"Yes," Assad said suddenly, on the other end of the line. "She was pleased. She called me her little sand worm." He laughed so that it grated in Carl's ear.

Who but Assad would take such a clear insult with such good humor?

"But, Carl, I don't have good news like Rose," he said, after his laughter had subsided. "You shouldn't count on Bjarne Thøgersen being willing to talk to us anymore. Then what then?"

"Did he refuse to let us visit? Is that what you're telling me?"

"In a way that could not be misunderstood then."

"It doesn't matter, Assad. Tell Rose that she has *got* to get hold of that photograph. Tomorrow is our day off, and *that's* a promise."

Carl glanced at his watch as he turned up Hendriksholms Boulevard. He was early, but maybe that was OK. In any event, this Klavs Jeppesen seemed like someone who would rather be too early than too late.

Rødovre High School was a collection of compressed boxes stacked on the asphalt, a chaos of buildings that ran into each other and had probably been expanded many times during the years when a high-school education was taking root among the working class. A walkway here, a gymnasium there, new and old yellow-brick boxes that were supposed to upgrade the privileges of suburban youths to the level north-coast kids had been elevated to long ago.

By following the arrows directing him toward the alumni's "Lasasep" party, he managed to find Klavs Jeppesen outside the assembly hall, his arms full of packages of paper napkins and in conversation with a couple of quite pretty, older students of the opposite sex. He was a nice-looking guy, but dressed in that vapid way of his profession, with a corduroy jacket and full beard. He was a high-school teacher with a capital "H."

He released his audience with an "I'll see you later," spoken in a tone of voice that signaled a free-range bachelor, and led Carl down to the teachers' staff room where other graduates were chatting nostalgically.

"Do you know why I'm here?" Carl asked, and was told that his pidgin-speaking colleague had explained things to Jeppesen.

"What do you want to know?" Jeppesen asked, gesturing for Carl to take a seat in one of the staff room's aged designer chairs.

"I want to know everything about Kimmie and the gang she associated with."

"Your colleague implied that the Rørvig case has been resumed. Is that true?"

Carl nodded. "And we have strong reason to suspect that one or more of this gang are also guilty of other assaults."

Here Jeppesen's nostrils flared as though he lacked oxygen.

"Assaults?" He stared into space and didn't react when one of his colleagues poked her head in.

"Are you in charge of the music, Klavs?" she asked.

He glanced up as if in a trance and nodded absentmindedly.

"I was head over heels in love with Kimmie," he said, when he and Carl were alone again. "I wanted her more than I've ever wanted anyone. She was the perfect blend of devil and angel. So fine and young and gentle like a kitten, yet totally dominating."

"She was seventeen or eighteen when you began having a relationship with her. And a pupil at the school, besides! That wasn't exactly playing by the rules, now, was it?"

He looked at Carl without raising his

head. "It's not something I'm proud of," he said. "I just couldn't help myself. I can still feel her skin today, do you understand? And it's been twenty years."

"Yes, and it was also twenty years ago that she and some others were suspected of committing homicide. What do you think about that? Do you think they could have done it together?"

Jeppesen grimaced. "*Anyone* might be capable of doing something like that. Couldn't you kill a person? Maybe you already have?" He turned his head and lowered his voice. "There were a few episodes that made me wonder, both before and after my affair with Kimmie. In particular, there was a boy at the school I remember very well. A real arrogant little jerk, so maybe he simply got what he deserved. But the circumstances were strange. One day he suddenly wanted to leave the school. He'd fallen in the forest, he said, but I know what bruises look like after a beating."

"What does this have to do with the gang?"

"I don't know what it has to do with them, but I know that Kristian Wolf asked about the boy every single day after he'd left the school: how was he? Had we heard from him? Was he coming back?"

"Couldn't it have been genuine interest?"

He turned to Carl. This was a high-school teacher in whose competent hands decent people entrusted their children's continued development. A person who'd been with his students for years. If he'd ever shown this same expression to anyone at parents' evenings they'd probably be concerned enough to take their kids out of school. No, thank God. It was rare to see a face so embittered by vengefulness, spite, and a loathing of humanity.

"Kristian Wolf showed no genuine interest in anyone but himself," he said, full of contempt. "Trust me, he was capable of anything. But he was terribly afraid of being confronted with his own deeds, I think. That's why he wanted to be sure the boy was gone for good."

"Give me examples," Carl said.

"He started the gang, I am sure of that. He was the activist type, burning with evil, and he quickly spread his poison. He was the one who ratted on Kimmie and me. It was thanks to him that I had to leave the school and she was expelled. He was the one who pushed her toward the boys he wanted to pick on. And when she snared them in her web, he pulled her away again. She was his female spider, and he was the

458

one pulling the strings.

"You're no doubt aware that he's dead? The result of a shooting accident."

He nodded. "You probably think that makes me happy. Not at all. He got off too easily."

There was laughter in the corridor, and he came to himself for a moment. Then the anger settled in his face again, yanking him back down. "They attacked the boy in the forest, so he had to go away. You can ask him yourself. Perhaps you know him? His name is Kyle Basset. He lives in Spain now. You can find him easily. He owns one of Spain's largest contractors, KB Construcciones SA." Carl nodded as he jotted down the name. "And they killed Kåre Bruno. Trust me," he added.

"The thought has crossed our minds, but why do *you* think that?"

"Bruno sought me out when I was fired. We had been rivals, but now we were allies. Him and me against Wolf and the rest of them. He confided in me that he was afraid of Wolf. That they knew each from before. That Kristian lived near his grandparents and never missed an opportunity to threaten him."

Jeppesen nodded to himself. "It's not much, I know, but it's enough. Wolf threatened Kåre Bruno, that's how it was. And Bruno died."

"You sound as though you're certain of these things. But the fact is you'd already broken up with Kimmie when Bruno died, and the Rørvig assaults occurred after you left."

"Yes. But before that I'd seen how the other pupils drew away when the gang strutted down the corridors. I saw what they did to people when they were together. Admittedly not to their classmates, since solidarity is the first thing one learns at that school, but to everyone else. And I just know they attacked the boy."

"How can you know?"

"Kimmie spent the night with me a few times during school weekends. She slept badly, as if there was something inside her that wouldn't let her alone. She called out his name in her sleep."

"Whose?"

"The boy's! Kyle's!"

"Did she seem shocked or tormented?"

He laughed a moment. It came from down where laughter is a defense and not an outstretched hand. "She didn't seem haunted, no. Not at all. That's not how Kimmie was."

Carl considered showing him the teddy

bear, but was distracted by the coffee machine's gurgling. If the coffeemakers kept on like that until the dinner was over, all that would remain would be tar.

"Maybe we could have a cup?" he asked, without expecting an answer. A cup of mocha would hopefully make up for the hundred hours he hadn't eaten properly.

Not for me, Jeppesen gesticulated.

"Was Kimmie evil?" Carl asked, pouring his coffee and practically inhaling it.

He heard no answer.

When he turned round with the cup to his mouth, nostrils titillated by the aroma of a sun that had once shone on a Colombian coffee farmer's fields, Klavs Jeppesen's chair was empty.

The audience was over.

29

She'd walked round the lake from the planetarium to Vodroffsvej and back, taking ten different routes. Up and down the stairs and paths that connected the lake with Gammel Kongevej and Vodroffsvej. Back and forth without getting too close to the bus stop across from Teaterpassagen, where she imagined the men would wait.

Now and then she sat on the planetarium terrace, her back to the window and her eyes focused on the play of light in the lake fountain. Someone behind her marveled at the sight, but Kimmie couldn't have cared less. It had been years since she'd abandoned herself to such things. All she wanted to do was see the men who'd done the job on Tine. Get a sense of who her pursuers were, of who was working for the bastards.

Because she didn't doubt for an instant that they'd return. That was what Tine had been afraid of, and no doubt she'd been right. If they wanted to get hold of Kimmie, they wouldn't just give up.

And Tine had been the link. But now Tine was no more.

She'd gotten away swiftly when the grenades went off and the house blew up. A couple of children might have seen her racing past the swimming center, but that was it. On the other side of the buildings down on Kvægtorvsgade she'd shaken free of her coat and tossed it in her suitcase. Then she'd pulled on a suede jacket and covered her hair with a black scarf.

Ten minutes later she stood at Hotel Ansgar's well-lit reception desk on Colbjørnsensgade, flashing the Portuguese passport she'd found a few years earlier in one of her stolen suitcases. It wasn't a one hundred percent likeness, but on the other hand it was six years old, and who didn't change during that amount of time?

"Do you speak English, Mrs. Teixeira?" the friendly porter asked. The rest was just a formality.

For about an hour she sat in the courtyard under the gas heaters with a couple of drinks. That way the hotel staff would get to know her.

Afterward she slept for nearly twenty

hours with her pistol under her pillow and images of a trembling Tine in her head.

It was from there that her world led her as she walked down to the planetarium and after eight hours of waiting finally found what she was looking for.

The man was thin, almost emaciated, and his focus shifted between Tine's window on the fifth floor and the entrance to Teater-passagen.

"You'll be waiting a long time, you shit," Kimmie mumbled, as she sat on the bench in front of the planetarium on Gammel Kongevej.

When it was approximately 11 P.M. the man was relieved of his watch. There was no doubt that the one replacing him had a lower rank. It was evident from the way he approached. Like a dog that was headed for its food bowl, but first had to sniff around to see if it was welcome.

That was why he was the one who had to do the Saturday-night shift, and not the first man. And that was why Kimmie decided to follow the one who was leaving.

She tailed the thin man at a safe distance, and reached the bus at the same moment its doors were closing.

It was then that she saw how mashed up

his face was. His lower lip was split, and he had a stitched-up gash above one eyebrow and bruises that ran along his hairline from ear to throat, as if he'd dyed his hair with henna and not rinsed it all off properly.

He was looking out the window as she climbed aboard. Just sat scowling out across the pavement, hoping to spy his target in his last glimpse. Only when the bus reached Peter Bangsvej did he begin to relax.

He's off duty now and not busy, she thought, *with no one to come home to.* That was evident by his attitude. His indifference. Had someone been expecting him, a little girl or a puppy or a warm living room where he could hold his girlfriend's hand and they could listen to each other's sighs and laughter, then he would be breathing more deeply and freely. No, he couldn't hide the knots in his soul and stomach. He had nothing to go home to. No reason to hurry.

As if she didn't know what *that* was like.

He got off at the Damhus Inn and didn't ask any questions about the evening's entertainment. He was late, something he apparently already knew. Many of the patrons had already paired off and were on the way out to their one-night stands. So he hung up his coat and walked into the spacious room, evidently without ambitions. And how could he have any, the way he looked? He ordered a pint and sat at the bar, glancing across the tables at the throng to see if there was a woman, any woman, who'd look his way.

She removed her headscarf and suede jacket and asked the cloakroom attendant to watch her handbag carefully. Then she glided into the room, her self-confident shoulders back and breasts softly signaling to anyone who could still focus. Some low-ranking, high-volume band on the stage accompanied the cautiously groping dancers. No one on the dance floor under the crystalline sky of glass tubes seemed to have found their special somebody.

She felt the pack of eyes fastened on her and the tension that had already begun to spread along the tables and barstools.

She wore less makeup than all the other women, she realized. Less makeup and less fat on her bones.

Does he recognize me? she wondered, her eyes wandering slowly past imploring glances, all the way to the thin man. There he was, just like all the other men, coiled and ready to pounce at even the slightest signal. He put his elbow nonchalantly on the bar and lifted his head slightly. Professional eyes weighed whether she was waiting for someone or free prey.

When she was halfway past the tables she smiled at him, causing him to take a deep breath. He couldn't believe it, but Christ, he would sure love to.

Not two minutes passed before she was out on the dance floor with the first sweaty, eager man, bouncing in the same steady rhythm as everyone else.

But the thin man had noticed her glance, and that she had made her choice. He straightened his back, adjusted his tie and tried as best he could to make his lean, beaten face seem relatively attractive in the smoke-colored light.

He approached her in the middle of a dance, taking her by the arm. He clasped her back a bit clumsily and squeezed a little. His fingers weren't practiced, she could tell. His heart was hammering hard against her shoulder. He was an easy catch.

"So this is my place," he said, nodding self-consciously toward his living room, which revealed a lackluster, fifth-story view of Rødovre's S-station and lots of parking spots and streets.

He'd pointed at the nameplate in the lobby beside the lift's lilac-colored doors.

FINN AALBÆK, it read. And then he'd declared that the building was safe, even though it would soon be torn down. He'd taken her hand and led her out onto the fifth-story walkway as if he were a knight leading her safely across a seething river's suspension bridge. He held her quite close, so his quarry wouldn't be allowed to have second thoughts and bolt. Well assisted by anticipation and newly found self-confidence, his imagination already had him groping deep under the blankets, stiff and ready.

He told her she could go out on the balcony to see the view if she wished, and he cleared the coffee table, turned on the lava lamps, put on a CD, and unscrewed the cap on the gin bottle.

It struck her that it'd been ten years since she'd been alone with a man behind closed doors.

"What happened to you?" she asked, running her hand inquiringly across his face.

He raised his wilted eyebrows, a gesture that was no doubt carefully practiced before the mirror. He probably thought it was charming, but it wasn't by a long shot.

"Oh that! I ran into a couple of likely lads on my watch. They didn't get out of the encounter in very good shape." He smiled crookedly. Even the smile was a cliché. He was simply lying.

"What do you do, actually, Finn?" she finally asked.

"Me? I'm a private eye," he answered, in a way that made the word "private" ooze with sleazy snooping and unseemly prying. It conjured up nothing exotic, mysterious, or dangerous, as had doubtlessly been his intention.

She looked at the bottle he was waving about, and noticed her throat tightening. *Take it easy, Kimmie,* the voices whispered. *Don't lose control.*

"Gin and tonic?" he asked.

She shook her head. "Do you have whisky, by any chance?"

He seemed surprised, but not dissatisfied. Women who drank whisky were hardly sensitive types.

"Well, well, aren't you thirsty?" he said, after she'd downed her drink in a single gulp. To keep pace, he poured another glass for her and one for himself.

By the time she'd had three more in succession, he was buzzed and distant.

Unaffected, she asked about the job he was working on and watched his alcohol-suppressed inhibitions lead him closer to her on the sofa. He gave her a fixed smile while his fingers strolled up her thigh.

"I'm trying to find a woman who's capable of making many people's lives miserable."

"Ah, that sounds exciting. Is she an industrial spy or call girl or something like that?" she asked, and illustrated her rapt submissiveness by putting her hand on his and leading it determinedly to her inner thigh.

"She's a little of everything," he said, trying to spread her legs a bit.

She watched his mouth and knew she would throw up if he tried to kiss her.

"Who is she?"

"That's a trade secret, love. I can't tell you."

"Love," he'd said! Again the same pain.

"But what kind of person hires you for such a job?" She allowed his hand to move a little farther up her thigh. His alcohol breath was hot against her throat.

"People in the upper crust," he whispered, as if it would place him higher in the mating hierarchy.

"What do you say to another shot?" she suggested, as his fingers groped their way across her pelvis.

He pulled back slightly, looking at her with a wry smile wrenched into that swollen part of his face. He had a plan, it was clear. She would drink and he would pour, until she was completely lubricated and ready.

For all he cared, she could pass out. He didn't give a hoot what she got out of it. She knew that didn't matter.

"We can't do it tonight," she said as his mouth ran parallel with his frowning eyebrows. "I have my period. We can do it another day, OK?"

It was a lie, of course, but deep within she wished it were true. Eleven years had gone by since she'd bled. Only the stomach cramps remained, and they weren't caused by anything physiological. Years filled with anger and broken dreams.

She had miscarried and almost died. And now she was sterile.

That's what she was.

Otherwise things might have turned out differently.

Carefully she stroked his lacerated eyebrow with her index finger, but failed to mitigate his growing resentment and frustration.

She could see what he was thinking. He had hauled home the wrong bitch, and he wasn't going to stand for it. Why the hell did she go to a singles' night if she was on the rag?

Kimmie watched his facial features harden. Then she pulled her handbag to her and stood up, stepped over to the balcony window and gazed out across the dismal, barren landscape of terraced houses and stark, distant high-rises. There was almost no light, only the cold gleam of the street lamps a little farther up the block.

"You killed Tine," she said softly, reaching into her bag.

She heard him squirm up off the sofa. In a second he would be all over her. He was woozy, but deep inside an instinct of self-preservation stirred.

Then she turned and pulled out the pistol with the silencer.

He saw it as he attempted to maneuver around the coffee table, and stopped in his tracks, astounded at himself and the dent that had been made in his professional pride. It was funny to see. She loved this mix of silent astonishment and dread.

"No," she said, "that probably wasn't very smart. You dragged home your work target without knowing it."

He bent his head and studied her face. Clearly he was adding layers to the image he'd created of a ravaged woman on the streets. Confusedly he ransacked his memory. How could he aim so low? How could he let himself be fooled by clothing and find a bag lady attractive?

Come on, the voices whispered. *Take him. He's nothing but their lackey! Take him now!*

"Without you, my friend would still be alive," she said, now registering the alcohol burning in her belly. She looked over at the bottle, golden and half full. One more slurp and the voices and the fire would die down.

"I didn't kill anyone," he said, his eyes darting from her trigger finger to the safety latch. Looking for anything to give him a sliver of hope that she'd overlooked something.

"Do you feel like a cornered rat?" she asked. The question was superfluous, but he refused to answer. He hated to admit it, but who wouldn't?

Aalbæk was the one who'd beaten Tine. The one who'd really shaken her up, made her vulnerable. Aalbæk was the one who'd made her dangerous to Kimmie. Yes, perhaps Kimmie was the weapon, but Aalbæk was the hand that guided it. That's why he had to pay.

He and the ones who'd given the order.

"Ditlev, Ulrik, and Torsten are behind it. I know," she said, fully absorbed by the proximity of the bottle and its healing contents.

Don't do it, said one of the voices, but she did it anyway. She reached out for the bottle and saw his body first as a vibration in the air, then as a flailing mass of clothes and arms, punching and grabbing hold of her.

In his wild rage he had her thrown to the floor. "Humiliate a man sexually and you have an enemy for life," she had learned. It was true. Now she was going to have to pay for the hungry looks and servile pawing he'd had to perform in order to get her back to his flat. For him having exposed himself and appeared vulnerable.

He threw her against the radiator, the coils bashing against her skull. He grabbed a large wooden figurine that was standing on the floor and slammed it against her hip. He seized her shoulders and twisted her onto her stomach. Pressed her torso down and twisted the arm with the pistol round her back, but she didn't let go of it.

His fingers dug into her arm. She had felt pain many times before and it would take more than that to make her cry out.

"Don't you dare lead me on. Don't you dare try and con me," he said, banging his fist into her lower back. After that he managed to unclasp her grip on the gun and fling it into a corner. Then he got a hand up under her dress, tearing her tights and pushing her underwear aside. "Damn you, bitch, you don't have your period!" he shouted.

He took a hard grip on her, jerked her round and punched her in the face.

They stared directly at each other as he held her down and boxed her with randomly placed blows. Sinewy thighs in worn polyester trousers straddled her chest. Blood-filled veins protruded from his pounding and hammering forearms.

He beat her until her defenses began to wane, and resistance seemed pointless.

"Are you finished, bitch?" he shouted, showing her a clenched fist that was ready to resume her punishment. "Or do you want to end up like your junkie friend?"

Was it "finished" he'd said?

Not finished until I stop breathing.

She understood that better than anyone.

Kristian knew her best. He was the one who sensed when she felt that surge of excitement. This chemical feeling of being lifted off one's base as the belly sends shivers of desire to every cell of the body. And when they sat watching *A Clockwork Orange* in the dark, he showed her where desire could lead.

Kristian was the experienced one. He'd tested girls before. He knew all the code words to their deepest thoughts. Knew which way to turn the key in the chastity belt. And suddenly she was sitting there in the middle of the gang as they lasciviously observed her unveiled body in the flickering light of the horrific images on the TV screen. He showed her and the others how to achieve pleasure in multiple directions at once. How violence and lust went hand in hand.

Without Kristian she never would have learned how to use her body as a lure. Exclusively for the sake of the hunt. What he hadn't bargained for, however, was that she had also learned how to control the events around herself, for the first time in her life. Perhaps not initially, but later.

And when she came home from Switzerland, she mastered the art to perfection.

She slept with random men. Broke them and broke up with them. That's how she spent her nights.

During the day everything was routine. Her stepmother's icy coldness. Her work with the animals at Nautilus Trading. The contact with customers and the weekends with the gang. The occasional assault.

And then Bjarne got close and aroused new feelings in her. Told her that she was worth more than that. That she was someone of value. A person who could enrich him and others. That she was not guilty for

476

her past actions; that her father had been a swine. That she should be wary of Kristian. That the past was dead.

Aalbæk noticed her resignation and immediately began fumbling with his trousers. She smiled briefly at him. Maybe he thought she smiled because she liked it that way. That everything was going according to her plan. That she was more complicated than he'd first assumed. That being knocked about was a part of the ritual.

But Kimmie smiled because she knew he was at her mercy. Smiled when he pulled out his member. Smiled when she felt it on her bare thigh and noticed that it wasn't stiff enough.

"Lie still for a second, we'll get to it," she whispered, looking him in the eyes. "The pistol was a toy. I just wanted to frighten you. But you knew that, didn't you?" She parted her lips slightly so they appeared fuller. "I think you'll like me," she said, rubbing herself against him.

"I think so, too," he said, with sluggish eyes deep in her cleavage.

"You're strong. A wonderful man." She snuggled her shoulders affectionately against him and saw how he relaxed his locked legs so she could free her arm and lead his hand down between her legs. This caused him to completely loosen up so she could take hold of his cock with her other hand.

"You won't say anything about this to Pram and the others, will you?" she said, working him up until he began gasping for air.

If there was anything he wouldn't report to them, it was this.

No one challenged these men. Even he knew that.

Kimmie and Bjarne had lived together for half a year when Kristian would no longer put up with it.

She noticed it one day when he'd tempted the gang into an assault that developed very differently to their usual routine. Kristian had lost control, and in an attempt to restore it had turned the others against her.

Ditlev, Kristian, Torsten, Ulrik, and Bjarne. One for all, all for one.

This she remembered all too clearly when Aalbæk, who was on top of her, could no longer wait and tried to take her by force.

She hated it and loved it at the same time. Nothing could bestow strength like hatred. Nothing could get her going like vindictiveness.

With all her might she lurched backward, lifting herself halfway up against the wall, the hard wooden figurine he'd hit her with underneath her. Once again she took hold of his half-stiff member. It was enough to make him hesitate. Enough so she could work it and tear at it until he was about to cry.

And when he finally came on her thigh, the air got stuck in his lungs. He was a man who'd been taken by surprise many times that night. A man who'd seen better days and who somewhere along the way had forgotten the difference between solitary masturbation and a woman's touch. He was completely lost in the moment. His skin was moist, but his eyes were dry and staring blindly at a point on the ceiling that wouldn't provide an answer as to how she'd been able to slide away from him and suddenly lay with her legs splayed and the pistol aimed directly at his still-throbbing groin.

"Keep that feeling in your body, because it'll be the last time, you bastard," she said, and stood up with semen dribbling down her leg. Filled with contempt and the lingering feeling of having been defiled.

The exact same feeling she'd had when those whom she'd most trusted had let her down.

Like her father's blows when she didn't behave correctly. Like her stepmother's surprise mood swings and boxes on the ear when she spoke enthusiastically about anyone at all. Like the clawing fingers of a wiped-out, drunken mother who didn't know in which direction to direct her punches, or why. She used words like "proper," "silence," and "courtesy." Words that the little girl understood the importance of long before she really understood their meaning.

And then there was what Kristian and Torsten and the others did to her. The ones she'd put her faith in.

Yes, she knew the feeling of defilement, and she craved it. Life had made her dependent on it. It was the way forward. It enabled her to act.

"Get up," she said, opening the balcony door.

It was a quiet, humid evening. Loud voices in a foreign language emanated from the terraced houses across the street and resounded like a pulsating echo in the concrete landscape.

"Get up." She waved the pistol and watched the smile broaden on his swollen face.

"I thought you said it was a toy?" he

asked, moving slowly toward her while zipping up his trousers.

She turned to the figurine on the floor and shot it once. It was surprising how quiet a sound the bullet made as it bored into the wood.

Surprising, too, for Aalbæk.

He shrank back, but again she waved the gun, this time toward the balcony.

"What do you want?" he asked when he was outside, now with a very different degree of seriousness and a good grip on the railing.

She looked out over the edge. The darkness beneath them was like an abyss that could swallow everything. Aalbæk knew it, and he began to shake.

"Tell me everything," she said, retreating to the shadows by the wall.

He did as she asked. It came out slowly, but in the right order. A professional's neatly chronicled observations. Because what was there to hide when it came down to it? It was only a job, after all. But now much more was at stake.

As Aalbæk talked to save his life, Kimmie was picturing her old friends. Ditlev, Torsten, and Ulrik. It's said that powerful men reign over mankind's impotence. As well as their own. History proved it time and again.

And when the man in front of her had nothing more to say, she spoke coldly:

"You have two choices. Jump, or be shot. We're five storys up. You have a good chance of surviving if you jump. There are bushes down there, you know. Isn't that why they're planted so close to the building?"

He shook his head. If something couldn't be happening, this was it. He had seen a lot in his time. But this kind of thing just didn't happen.

He managed a pathetic smile. "There aren't any bushes down there. Just concrete and grass."

"Are you expecting mercy from me? Did you show Tine any?"

He didn't respond, but stood stock-still with furrowed brow, trying to convince himself she didn't mean it. After all, she had just made love to him. Or something that resembled it, in any case.

"Jump, or I'll shoot you in the crotch. You won't survive that, I promise you."

He moved a step closer and followed the pistol with terrified eyes as she leveled it at him and her finger curled round the trigger.

It probably would have ended with a bullet, had it not been for the alcohol pulsing heavily through his veins. Instead he vaulted over the railing, trying to cling to it at the same time, and might have succeeded in slinging himself onto the balcony below if she hadn't slammed the stock of her weapon on his finger joints until they cracked.

There was a dull thud when he landed on the ground. No scream.

Afterward she turned to the balcony door and stared briefly at the broken wooden figurine that lay grinning on the rug. She returned its smile, bent over, gathered up the empty shell casing and put it in her bag.

When she slammed the door behind her after an hour of carefully cleaning glasses and bottles and everything else, she was content. The figurine stood quietly, propped up against the radiator with a tea towel wrapped attractively around its midsection.

Like a chef ready to receive his establishment's next guests.

30

Carl heard thunderous crashings and deep rumbling coming from the living room, as if all the elephants in the world were chewing on his long-suffering IKEA furniture.

So Jesper was throwing a party again.

Carl rubbed his temples and prepared his scolding.

When he opened the door he was met with deafening noise, the light of a flickering television, and Morten and Jesper at each end of the sofa.

"What the hell's going on here?" he shouted, confused by the omnipresent sound and the room's relative emptiness.

"Surround sound," Morten reported with a certain degree of pride, after he'd lowered the volume a bit with the remote control.

Jesper pointed around at the array of loudspeakers hidden behind easy chairs and the bookshelf. *Cool, huh?* his glance said.

Peace was truly a thing of the past for the

Mørck family.

They handed him a tepid Tuborg and tried to smooth out his dark mien by informing him that the stereo was a gift from one of Morten's friend's parents who couldn't use it.

Wise people.

It was at that moment Carl felt the urge to give them a surprise of their own.

"I have some information for you, Morten! Hardy has asked if you'd like to take care of him here, in the house. For pay, I mean. His bed would stand right where your groovy bass speaker is right now. We can always move it behind the bed. That way there's a place to lay his urine bag."

He took a sip, looking forward to their reaction when the information settled into their Saturday-heavy brains.

"For pay?" said Morten.

"Hardy is going to live *here*?" Jesper put in, pouting. "Yeah, well, whatever. I couldn't care less. If I can't get a youth residence down on Gammel Amtsvej asap I'll move in with Mum at her allotment."

He would have to see it to believe it.

"How much do you think it pays?" Morten continued.

Right then Carl's head began pounding again.

Two and a half hours later he awoke staring at his clock radio that said SUNDAY 01:39:09, his head filled with images of earrings made of amethyst and silver and names such as Kyle Basset, Kåre Bruno, and Klavs Jeppesen.

In Jesper's room the gangsta rappers' New York had been resurrected and Carl was feeling as if he'd inhaled a large dose of mutated influenza virus. Dry sinuses, crispy eye sockets, and an overwhelming weariness in his body and limbs.

He lay there struggling for quite some time before he finally hefted his legs over the side of the bed and considered whether a steaming hot shower could scorch off some of the demons.

Instead, he turned to the clock radio and listened to the news report that yet another woman had been found beaten up and half dead in a rubbish container. This time on Store Søndervoldsstræde, but the particulars were exactly the same as on Store Kannikestræde.

It was a strange coincidence of two-part street names, he thought, both beginning with "Store" and ending with "stræde." He tried to recall whether there were other street names like them in Department A's district.

That was mainly why he was already awake when Lars Bjørn called.

"I think it would be a good idea if you got dressed and came out here to Rødovre," he said.

Carl wanted to say something hard-hitting, like how Rødovre wasn't their jurisdiction or something about infections and epidemic diseases, but Bjørn stopped him cold when he reported that private detective Finn Aalbæk had been found dead on the grass, five stories below his balcony.

"His head looks like his, but his body is quite a few inches shorter. He must have landed square on his feet. His spinal column is shoved halfway into his cranium," he said, leaving nothing to the imagination.

Somehow this helped Carl's headache. In any case, he forgot about it.

Carl found Bjørn in front of the high-rise with graffiti behind him as tall as a man. *Kill your Mother and rape your fucking dog!* didn't exactly make him appear more cheerful. Nor was he trying to hide the fact that the area west of Valby Bakke wasn't his turf at all; he was just trying to redeem himself.

"What are you doing out here, Lars?" Carl asked, as he looked across Avedøre Hav-nevej at the glowing windows of some flat buildings that stood behind half-defoliated trees not a hundred yards away. It was Rødovre High School, which he had practically just left. So the party for the school alumni was still going on.

Strange feeling. Just a few hours earlier he'd been over there, talking to Klavs Jeppesen, and now Aalbæk lay dead over here on the other side of the street. What the hell was going on?

Bjørn looked at him gloomily. "I assume you remember that one of headquarter's trusted colleagues, now present, was very recently accused of having assaulted the deceased. So Marcus and I agreed that we ought to be out here to see what this was all about. But maybe you can tell us, Carl?"

That was a hell of a tone to take on a dark, cold September morning.

"If you had put a tail on him as I'd asked, then we'd probably have known a little more, wouldn't you say?" Carl grumbled, as he tried to decipher what was up and what was down on the lump that had bored into the grass ten yards away.

"It was those clowns over there who found him," Bjørn said. He pointed at a hedge surrounding the day-care center and then at a mix of immigrant boys in tracksuits with stripes down the legs and pale Danish girls in ultra-tight jeans. Apparently not all of them thought it was real cool. "They'd just been planning to mess about on the day-care center playground, or kindergarten or whatever the hell it is. But they didn't make it that far."

"When did it happen?" Carl asked the medical examiner, who'd already begun packing up his equipment.

"Well, it's fairly cold tonight, but he's been lying in the lee of the building, so I would venture that it was between one and one and a half hours ago," he said with tired eyes, longing for his duvet and his wife's warm posterior.

Carl turned to Bjørn. "I want you to know that yesterday evening I was right there, at Rødovre High. I spoke with a former boy-friend of Kimmie's. It's a coincidence, pure and simple, but put in the report that I mentioned it."

Bjørn removed his hands from the pockets of his leather jacket and pushed his collar up. "Were you now?!" He looked straight into his eyes. "Have you ever been up in his flat, Carl?"

"No. I assure you I haven't."

"You're completely certain?"

Oh, come on, Carl thought, feeling his headache gloating in its hideout.

"Oh, come on," he said, at the lack of anything better. "That's simply too far-fetched. Have you been up in the flat?"

"Samir and the boys from Glostrup Station are up there now."

"Samir?"

"Samir Ghazi. Bak's replacement. He's from Rødovre Station."

Samir Ghazi. It seemed Assad was getting a kindred spirit with whom he could share his syrupy soup-tea.

"Did you come across a suicide note?" Carl asked up in the flat, after he'd squeezed the calloused fist that every seasoned policeman in Zealand would recognize as Police Superintendent Antonsen's. Just a few seconds in his viselike grip and a person was never the same. One day Carl would tell him he could go easy on the hydraulics.

"Suicide note? No, nothing like that. And you can kick my arse if there hasn't been someone up here to lend a hand."

"What do you mean?"

"There sure as hell aren't very many fingerprints in here. Nothing on the doorknob to the balcony. Nothing on the front row of glasses in the kitchen cupboards. Nothing on the edge of the coffee table. On the other hand, we've got a set of very clear prints on the balcony railing, presumably Aalbæk's, but why the hell would he hold on to the railing if he'd already decided to jump?"

"Second thoughts? It's not unheard of."

Antonsen chuckled. He did that every time he met detectives outside his own district. A highly conciliatory form of condescension if ever there was one.

"There's blood on the railing. Not much, just a bit. And I bet we'll find bruising on his hands from a struggle when we go down and look in a moment. Yup, there's something fishy here."

He sent a couple of crime-scene techs to check the bathroom and pulled an agreeable-looking, dark man in front of Carl and Bjørn.

"One of my best men, and now you're nicking him from me. Look us both in the eye and say you're not ashamed."

"Samir," the man said, introducing himself and extending his hand to Bjørn. So apparently the two hadn't met before now.

"All I'll say is that if you don't treat Samir right," Antonsen said, "you'll have me to deal with." He gave his man a shoulder squeeze.

"Carl Mørck," Carl said, and gave the man a handshake equal to Antonsen's.

"Yes, that's him." Antonsen nodded, in response to the quizzical expression on Samir's face. "The man who solved the Merete Lynggaard case, and who gave Aalbæk a few jabs, so they say." He laughed. Finn Aalbæk had clearly never been a favorite of the other districts, either.

"The splinters here on the carpet don't appear to have been there very long," one of the crime-scene techs said, pointing at some microscopic fragments in front of the balcony door. "They're lying very nearly on top of everything else." He squatted in his white lab coat and observed the fragments at close range. Bizarre lot, these police techs. But clever. Give them credit where credit was due.

"Could it be from a wooden bat or something?" Samir asked.

Carl glanced round the flat and found nothing strange, apart from the fat wooden figurine standing beside the balcony door with a tea towel wrapped around its midriff. A nice, carved Hardy with bowler hat and the whole nine yards. The figurine's partner, Laurel, was all the way over in a corner of the room and didn't seem quite so active. Something didn't seem right.

Carl bent over, removed the towel and tipped the figurine forward a little. It looked promising.

"You'll have to turn it over yourselves, but as far as I can see, this figurine's back has seen better days."

They gathered around it and measured the size of the bullet hole and the mass of the imploded wood.

"A relatively small caliber. The projectile didn't even exit the other side, it's still in there," Antonsen said. The crime-scene techs nodded.

Carl agreed. Most likely a .22. But deadly enough, if that's what the shooter intended.

"Did any of the neighbors hear anything, like shouts, or shots?" Carl asked, sniffing the bullet hole.

They shook their heads.

Strange, and yet not strange. The high-rise was in terrible condition, and mostly abandoned. Scarcely more than a few residents on the entire floor. Probably no one lived directly above or below, either. The days of this red box were numbered. Hardly a loss if the eyesore were to topple in the next storm.

"It smells pretty fresh," Carl said, pulling his head away from the bullet hole. "Fired at a distance of a couple of yards, wouldn't you say? And tonight."

"Absolutely," said the crime-scene tech.

Carl stepped onto the balcony and peered over the railing. Hell of a fall.

He stared out over the sea of lights in the low buildings across the street. There were faces in every window. There was no lack of curiosity, even on a pitch-black early morning.

Then Carl's mobile rang.

She didn't introduce herself and she didn't have to.

"You'll think I'm kidding, Carl," Rose said. "But the night shift down in Svendborg has located the earring. The duty officer knew exactly where it was. Isn't that fantastic?"

He looked at his watch. What was more fantastic was that she thought he was ready for news at this time of day.

"You weren't sleeping, were you?" she asked, not waiting for a response. "I'm heading into headquarters now. They're e-mailing an image of it."

"Can't it wait until daybreak, or Monday even?" His head was pounding again.

"Any idea who would have forced him over the edge?" Antonsen asked, when Carl clapped his mobile shut.

He shook his head. Yes, who could it be? Surely someone whose life Aalbæk had ruined with his snooping. Someone who maybe thought he knew too much. But it could also be someone in the group connected to Kimmie. Carl had plenty of ideas, just none that were substantial enough to broadcast.

"Did you check his office?" Carl asked. "Client files, appointment book, messages on his answering machine, e-mails?"

"We've sent people over there, and they say it's nothing but an old, empty shed with a mailbox."

Carl wrinkled his brow and looked about him. Then he walked over to the desk standing against the wall, picked up one of Aalbæk's business cards, and punched in the number to the detective agency.

Not three seconds passed before a phone rang in the front hall.

"So! Now we know where his office really is," Carl said, glancing around. "Right here."

It was definitely not obvious. No ring binder, no file folder with receipts visible. Nothing of the kind. Only book-club books, some decorative items, and loads of Helmut Lotti CD s and others of the same ilk.

"Turn over every single thing in the flat," Antonsen said. That would probably take some time.

He'd been lying in his bed for no more than

495

three minutes with every conceivable flu symptom circulating through his organism when Rose called back. This time her motor mouth was running at full throttle.

"It *is* the earring, Carl. The one from Lidelse Cove matches the earring found in Kimmie's box. Now we can positively link that earring with the two missing persons on Langeland. Isn't that wonderful?"

It was, of course, but at her tempo it was hard to get a word in edgeways.

"And that's not all, Carl. I just got replies from some e-mails I sent Saturday afternoon. You can talk to Kyle Basset. Isn't that cool?"

Carl drew his shoulders up to his ears and pushed himself wearily toward the head of the bed. Kyle Basset? The boy they'd teased at boarding school. Yeah, that was . . . "cool."

"He can meet you this afternoon. We're lucky, because he's normally not in his office, but Sunday afternoon he happens to be there. You'll meet at two in the afternoon, which just gives you time to get a return flight at 4:20 P.M."

Carl sat up abruptly in bed, as if a spring in his back had been released. "*Flight?!* What the hell are you talking about, Rose?"

"It's in Madrid. He's got an office in

Madrid, you know?"

Carl's eyes opened wide. "*Madrid*! There's no fucking way I'm going to Madrid. You can bloody well go yourself."

"I've already booked the ticket, Carl. You're flying with SAS at 10:20. We'll meet at the airport an hour and a half earlier. You're already checked in."

"No, no, no. I will fly absolutely nowhere." He tried to swallow a thick clump that had gathered in his throat. "Nowhere whatsoever!"

"Wow, Carl! Are you afraid of flying?" She laughed. The kind of laughter that made a decent retort impossible.

Because, truth be told, he *was* afraid of flying. As far as he knew, anyway, because the only time he'd ever tried it, he had flown to a party in Aalborg and, to be on the safe side, had deliberately drunk himself so silly both on the way there and back that Vigga had practically broken her back dragging him around. For the next two weeks he'd clung to her in his sleep. Who the hell could he cling to now?

"I don't have a passport, and I won't do it, Rose. Cancel the ticket."

She laughed again. A really uncomfortable mixture, this combination of headache, gnawing horror, and waves of her laughter in his ears.

"I've fixed the passport issue with the airport police," she said. "They'll have a document for you there for pickup later this morning. Take it easy, Carl, I'll give you some Frisium. You just need to be at Terminal 3 an hour and a half before the flight. The Metro takes you right there, and you don't even need to take a toothbrush. But remember your credit card, OK?"

Then she hung up, and Carl was alone in the dark. Incapable of recalling when it had all gone wrong.

31

"Just take two of these Frisium," she had said, before shoving a couple of tiny pills into his maw and two more into his breast pocket with the teddy bear for the return flight.

He'd glanced confusedly around the terminal and ticket desks for an authoritarian soul who might find some kind of fault with him: the wrong clothes, the wrong look. Anything to deliver him from taking the dreaded escalator to perdition.

She had given him a detailed printout of his itinerary, along with Kyle Basset's business address, a pocket dictionary, and strict orders not to swallow the two remaining pills until he was seated in the plane home. All that and a lot more. A few minutes from now he wouldn't be able to repeat half of it. How could he? He hadn't slept a wink the entire night, and a swiftly developing, explosive case of diarrhea was churning in his nether regions.

"They can make you a little drowsy," she said in conclusion, "but they work, trust me. You won't be afraid of anything after taking them. The plane could crash, for that matter, and you wouldn't even notice."

He saw that she regretted that last part as she guided him to the escalator with his provisional passport and boarding pass in hand.

Already halfway down the runway sweat began trickling from Carl, so that his shirt grew noticeably darker and his feet began to slide in his shoes. The pills had started doing their job, he'd noticed, but the way his heart was presently thumping in his chest, he might just as well die of a heart attack.

"Are you all right?" the woman next to him asked cautiously, extending her hand for him to hold on to.

As the plane climbed thirty thousand feet into the atmosphere he felt as though he were holding his breath. The only thing he sensed was the turbulence and the inexplicable creaking and bumping of the fuselage.

He opened the fresh-air nozzle, then closed it. Leaned his seat back, felt to see if his life vest was under it, and said no thank you each time the stewardess approached.

And then he went out like a light.

"Look, that's Paris down there," the woman beside him said at one point, from far, far away. He opened his eyes and recalled the nightmare, the exhaustion, the influenza aches in all his joints, and finally saw a hand pointing out the shadows of something that the hand's owner believed was the Eiffel Tower and the Place d'Etoile.

Carl nodded and couldn't possibly have cared less. As far as he was concerned Paris could kiss a certain place on his person. He just wanted out of the plane.

She could see how he was feeling so she took his hand again and held it until he awoke with a start as the plane hit Barajas Airport's runway.

"You were completely out of it," she said, pointing at the sign for the Metro.

He patted the little talisman in his breast pocket and then felt his inside pocket where he kept his wallet. For a brief, tired moment he discussed with himself whether his Visa card would be of any use in such a foreign place.

"It's easy," the woman told him, after he'd explained to her where he needed to go. "You buy the Metro card right over there and then you ride the escalator down. Take the train to Nuevos Minesterios, change to the number 6 line and go to Cuatro Caminos, then take the number 2 line to the Opera. After that it's just one stop on the number 5 line and you're at Callao. At which point you only have to go about a hundred yards to the place where you have your meeting."

Carl looked around for a bench that could give his leaden head and legs a little tour in the land of rest.

"I'll show you the way. I'm heading in the same direction. I saw how you were feeling in the plane," a friendly soul said in perfect Danish, and Carl directed his gaze toward a man of obvious Asian ethnicity. "My name is Vincent," he said, shuffling off with his luggage rolling behind.

This wasn't exactly how he'd envisioned a peaceful Sunday as he laid himself ponderously under his duvet only a few hours earlier.

After a smooth, half-unconscious rumbling along on the Metro he emerged from the labyrinthine corridors of Callao Station and stood eyeing Gran Via's iceberglike, monumental structures. Neo-impressionistic, functionalistic, classicistic colossi, if anyone were to ask him to describe them. He had never seen anything like it: the noises, the scents, the heat and the incredible bustle of busy, dark-haired people. There was only one person he saw whom he could identify with. An almost toothless beggar sitting on the pavement right in front of him with a cornucopia of colored plastic lids before him, each of which was open for donations. There were coins and bills in every single one. Currencies from around the globe. Carl couldn't understand half of what was going on, but there was self-irony lurking in the man's flashing eyes. *Your choice*, his eyes said. *Will you donate beer, wine, spirits, or fags?*

The people milling around him smiled. One pulled out a camera and asked if he could snap his picture. The beggar grinned broadly and toothlessly while hefting a sign into view.

It read: PHOTOS, 280 EUROS.

It worked. Not only on the assembled crowd, but also on Carl's wilted state of mind and atrophied funny bone. His eruption of laughter came as a strikingly welcome surprise. This was self-irony at its finest. The beggar even handed him a business card listing his Web site, www.lazybeggars .com. Chortling, Carl shook his head and reached into his pocket in spite of his general aversion to people who begged on the street.

It was at this moment that Carl snapped back to reality, his whole being inflamed with the desire to kick a certain female colleague in Department Q clear off the playing field.

Here he was, feeling like shit in a country he didn't know. Dosed up on pills that muddled his brain. His immune response mechanisms were causing every joint in his body to ache. And now his pocket was gapingly empty as well. He'd always smiled whenever he heard about incautious tourists, and now he — the deputy detective superintendent who spotted danger and suspicious characters everywhere — was one of them. How stupid could a person be? And on a Sunday.

Status quo: no wallet. Not even any lint in his pocket. The price of spending twenty minutes packed into an overfilled Metro. No credit cards, no provisional passport, no driver's license, no crisp banknotes, no Metro tickets, no telephone list, no health-insurance card, no plane tickets.

A person couldn't sink any lower.

They gave him a cup of coffee in a waiting room at KB Construcciones, SA, and let him fall asleep facing dusty windows. A quarter of an hour earlier a desk clerk had stopped him in the foyer of Gran Via 31 and refused to have his appointment verified for several minutes since he was unable to present any form of identification. The guy couldn't stop running his mouth off and his words were incomprehensible. Finally Carl shook his head angrily, found the hardest tongue-twister for foreigners to say in Danish, and yelled: "Rødgrød med fløde!" ("Strawberries with cream!")

That helped.

"Kyle Basset," said a voice miles away, after he had dozed off again.

Carl opened his eyes cautiously, afraid he'd wound up in purgatory, his head and body throbbed so much.

He was handed another cup of coffee in front of the gigantic barred windows in Basset's office, and now with a relatively clear head he saw a face in its mid-thirties that knew very well what it stood for. Wealth, power, and immoderate self-confidence.

"Your colleague briefed me," Basset said. "You're investigating a series of murders that may be connected to the people who assaulted me at my boarding school. Is that correct?"

He spoke Danish with an accent. Carl

looked around. It was an enormous office. Down on Gran Via people were storming out of shops with names like Sfera and Lefties. In these surroundings it was practically a miracle that the man still understood Danish at all.

"It *could* be a series of murders, we don't know yet." Carl drank the coffee greedily. A very dark roast. Not exactly something that helped his fermenting intestines. "You say outright that they were the ones who assaulted you. Why didn't you say so back when there was a case against them?"

He laughed. "I did, and much earlier. To the relevant party."

"And that was?"

"My dad, who was an old boarding-school mate of Kimmie's father."

"I see. And what came out of that?"

He shrugged and opened a chased silver cigarette case. Such things apparently still existed. He offered Carl a cigarette. "How long do you have?"

"My flight leaves at 4:20."

He glanced at his watch. "Oops, then we don't have very long. You're taking a taxi, I assume?"

Carl inhaled the smoke deeply. That helped. "I've got a little problem," he said a bit sheepishly.

He explained how he had been pickpocketed on the Metro. No money, no provisional passport, no plane ticket.

Kyle Basset pushed a button on the intercom. His commands didn't sound friendly. More like the kind he'd say to people he held in contempt.

"I'll give you the short version then." Basset gazed at the white building across the street. Maybe there were painful reminiscences showing in his eyes, but it was hard to tell, petrified and hard as they were.

"My father and Kimmie's father agreed that when the time came, however long that took, she would be punished. I was OK with that. I knew her father well. Willy K. Lassen, yes, and for that matter, I still know him. He owns a flat just two minutes from mine in Monaco and is quite an uncompromising person. Not someone you'd want to provoke, I would say. Not back then, in any case. He's gravely ill now. Not much life left in him." He smiled. It seemed a rather odd reaction.

Carl pursed his lips. So Kimmie's father *was* seriously ill, as he'd tried to convince Tine. Well, how about that? As he'd learned over the course of time, reality and fantasy have a tendency to blend together.

"Why Kimmie?" he said. "You only name

her. Weren't the others equally guilty? Ulrik Dybbøl Jensen, Bjarne Thøgersen, Kristian Wolf, Ditlev Pram, Torsten Florin? Weren't they all there?"

Basset folded his hands as the burning cigarette dangled from his lips. "Are you saying you think they consciously selected me as their victim?"

"I don't know anything about that. I don't know much about the incident."

"Well, I'll tell you then. I was a completely random victim, I'm convinced of that. And how it turned out was just as random." He put his hand on his chest and leaned forward slightly. "Three of my ribs were broken, the rest were separated from my collarbone. I peed blood for days afterward. They could've easily killed me. The fact they didn't was also totally accidental, I can assure you."

"Uh-huh, but where are you going with this? It doesn't explain why your revenge should only be exacted on Kimmie Lassen."

"You know what, Mørck? They taught me something the day they attacked me, those bastards. Actually, in a way I'm grateful." With each word of his next sentence he tapped on his desk. "I learned that when opportunity presents itself, you take it, whether it's random or not. Without considering fairness or another person's guilt or innocence. That's the business world's alpha and omega, you understand? Sharpen your weapons and use them constantly. Just go for it. In this case my weapon was being able to influence Kimmie's father."

Carl took a deep breath. It didn't sound especially sympathetic to his provincial ears. He squinted his eyes. "I still don't think I completely understand."

Basset shook his head. He had expected as much. They were from different planets.

"I'm just saying that since it was easiest to go after Kimmie, then she was the one who'd have to suffer my revenge," he said.

"You didn't care about the others?"

He shrugged. "If I'd had the chance, I would have avenged myself on them, too. I simply haven't had that chance. You and I each have our own hunting grounds, you might say."

"Then Kimmie wasn't any more actively involved than the others? Who would you say was the prime mover in that gang?"

"Kristian Wolf, of course. But if all those devils were on the move at once, I believe Kimmie is the one I would stay farthest away from."

"What do you mean?"

"She was very neutral when they began

on me. Mostly it was Florin, Pram, and Kristian Wolf. But when they'd had enough — I was bleeding from my ear, after all, so they were probably scared — *then* Kimmie started in."

He flared his nostrils as if he were still able to sense her proximity. "They wound her up, you see. Especially Wolf. He and Pram groped her until she was worked up and then they shoved her toward me." He clenched his fists. "At first she only tapped a little, then it got worse and worse. When she noticed how much it hurt, her eyes grew wider and wider, she breathed deeper and deeper and hit harder and harder. She was the one who kicked me in the abdomen — with the toe of her shoe. And hard." He stubbed his cigarette out in an ashtray that looked identical to a bronze statue on the roof across the street. Basset's face seemed wrinkled. Only now in the sharp sunlight did Carl notice. Fairly early for such a young man.

"If Wolf hadn't intervened she would have continued until I was dead. I'm certain of that."

"And the others?"

"Yes, the others." He nodded to himself. "I'd say they could barely wait until the next time. They were like spectators at a bullfight.

Believe me, I know a thing or two about *that*."

The secretary who'd given Carl his coffee entered the office. Slender and attractive in clothes that were dark like her hair and eyebrows. In one hand she held a small envelope that she gave to Carl. "Now you have some euros and a boarding pass for the trip home," she said in English, offering him a friendly smile.

Then she turned to her boss and slipped him a sheet of paper, which he scanned quickly. The unbridled anger this document induced reminded Carl of the wide-eyed Kimmie that Basset had just described for him.

Without hesitation Basset ripped the paper to shreds and bombarded the secretary with recriminations. His face looked wild, the wrinkles obvious now. The fierce reaction caused the woman to tremble and cast her eyes at the floor in shame. The scene definitely wasn't nice to witness.

When she closed the door behind her, Basset smiled at Carl, seemingly unaffected. "She's just a stupid little office mouse. Don't concern yourself with her. Will you be able to make it home to Denmark now?"

He nodded silently and tried to express some form of gratitude, but it was difficult.

Kyle Basset was just like the people who'd once done him harm. Devoid of empathy. He had demonstrated it right before Carl's eyes. To hell with him and everyone like him, the dumb prick.

"And Kimmie's punishment?" Carl said finally. "What was that?"

He laughed. "Ah, it was pure happenstance. She'd miscarried and had been seriously beaten up. All in all she was quite ill, so she went to her father for help."

"Which she didn't get, I imagine." He pictured the young woman whom the father wouldn't assist, even when she was in the greatest need. Had this lack of love already left its mark in the little girl's face when she stood between her father and stepmother in the old *Gossip* photo?

"Oh, it was nasty, I've been told. Her father lived at Hotel D'Angleterre at that time — he always does whenever he's home — and she just came bursting in. What the hell had she expected?"

"He got her thrown out?"

"Head first, I can assure you." He chuckled. "But first she was given the chance to fish around on the floor for some thousand-krone bills he'd tossed at her. So she got *something* out of it, but after that it was good-bye and farewell forever."

"She owns the house in Ordrup. Do you know why she didn't go there?"

"But she did. And she received the same treatment." Basset shook his head. He was positively indifferent. "Well, Carl Mørck, if you want to know more, you're going to have to take a later flight. You have to check in quite early here, so if you're going to make your 4:20 flight, you'll have to leave now."

Carl took a deep breath. He could already feel the plane's turbulence arousing the anxiety center of his brain. Then he remembered the tablets in his breast pocket, so he pulled out the teddy bear and then the pills. He set the teddy bear on the edge of the desk and took a sip of coffee so the pills could glide more easily down his throat.

He glanced over his cup at the chaos of papers on the desk, the pocket calculator, the fountain pen, the half-filled ashtray, and finally at Kyle Basset's clenched hands and completely white knuckles. Only then did he look up and see Basset's face. What he saw was a man who probably for the first time in ages had been forced to surrender to the memory of some searing pain, which people are so good at inflicting on others and themselves.

Basset was staring intensely at the guileless, tiny stump of a stuffed animal. It was as if a lightning bolt of repressed feelings had just struck him.

He fell back in his chair.

"Do you recognize this teddy bear?" Carl asked, the pills stuck somewhere between his throat and his vocal chords.

Basset nodded, then for a moment drew strength from the rage that came to his rescue. "Yes, Kimmie always had it dangling from her wrist at school. I don't know why. It had a red silk ribbon around its neck that tied it to her wrist."

For a moment Carl thought Basset was going to give in and cry, but then his face hardened and the man who could humiliate an office mouse as if it were nothing at all was himself again.

"Yes, I remember it all too well. It was dangling from her wrist when she beat me senseless. Where the hell did you get it?"

32

It was almost ten o'clock Sunday morning when she awoke in her room at the Hotel Ansgar. The TV was still flickering at the foot of her bed, showing Channel 2 News reruns of the previous night's events. Even though the police had put in an enormous effort, they hadn't come any closer to explaining the explosion near Dybbølsbro Station, and therefore the episode had faded somewhat into the background. Now attention was directed more at the American bombing of insurgents in Baghdad and Kasparov's candidacy for president of Russia, but primarily it was focused on a body that had been discovered in front of the ramshackle red high-rise in Rødovre.

It was probably murder. Several indicators pointed in that direction, the police spokesman said. In particular the fact that the victim had clung to the balcony railing before falling and had been struck on the fingers with a blunt object — possibly the pistol that had been fired at a wooden figurine in the flat the same night. The police were stingy with their information and still did not have a suspect.

That's what they said, anyway.

She hugged her bundle.

"Now they know, Mille. Now the boys know I'm after them." She tried to smile. "Do you think they're together now? Do you think Torsten and Ulrik and Ditlev are discussing what they should do when Mummy comes after them? I wonder if they're afraid now."

She rocked the bundle. "I think they deserve to be, after what they did to us, don't you agree? And do you know what, Mille? They have good reason to be."

On the screen the cameraman was attempting to zoom in to the ambulance crew who were moving the body, but it was clearly too dark to get decent footage.

"Do you know what, Mille? I shouldn't have told the others about the metal box. That wasn't the right thing to do." She dried her eyes. The tears had come so suddenly.

"I shouldn't have told them. Why did I do that?"

She'd moved in with Bjarne Thøgersen, and

that was sacrilege. If she was going to fuck anyone, it had to be in secret or with the entire gang; there was no other choice. And now this fatal breaking of all the golden rules. Not only had she picked one member over the others, she had also selected the one at the bottom of the hierarchy.

That was completely unacceptable.

"*Bjarne?*" Kristian had thundered. "What the hell do you want with that good-for-nothing?" He wanted everything to remain as it had always been. Wanted their violent forays together to continue, wanted Kimmie to always be available to all of them, and only them.

But in spite of Kristian's threats and pressure, Kimmie held firm. She'd chosen Bjarne; the others would have to settle for living with their memories.

For a while the group continued its orgies. They met about every fourth Sunday, snorted coke and watched violent films, then went off in one of Torsten's or Kristian's huge, four-wheel-drives in search of someone to harass and beat up. Sometimes they made an agreement with the victims and gave them blood money for the humiliation and pain they'd endured; sometimes they simply attacked them from behind and beat them senseless before they were seen.

And there was also the rare occasion, like the time they found an old man fishing by himself at Esrum Lake, where they just knew their victim wasn't going to leave alive.

This last type of assault was the kind that suited them best. When the conditions were right and they could go all the way. When everyone could play out his role to the fullest.

But something went wrong at Esrum Lake.

She saw how excited Kristian was becoming. He always got worked up, but this time his face grew quite dark and determined. Lips pursed tightly and eyes alert. He turned his frustration inward and stood far too quietly and passively, observing the others and watching how Kimmie's clothes clung to her as they hauled the man out into the water.

"Take her now, Ulrik!" he shouted suddenly, as she squatted in the rushes with her knees apart and her summer dress dripping, watching the body float out into the lake and sink to the bottom. Ulrik's eyes glinted at the opportunity, mixed with his fear of being inadequate. Time after time in the period before she went to Switzerland he'd had to give up penetrating her and let the others take over instead. It was as though this cocktail of violence and sex didn't work for him like it did for the others. This letting the pulse rate fall before it could rise again.

"Come on, Ulrik!" the others cried, as Bjarne yelled at them to stop. It was then that Ditlev and Kristian grabbed hold of Bjarne and held him back.

She saw Ulrik unzipping his trousers, for once seemingly very ready. What she didn't see was Torsten, who threw himself at her from behind and forced her to the ground.

If it weren't for Bjarne's cursing and wild punching and the subsequent shriveling of Ulrik's manhood, they would have raped her that day in front of the thicket of bullrushes.

It didn't take long, however, before Kristian systematically began to seek her out. He couldn't care less about Bjarne and the others. As long as *he* could have her, he was content.

Bjarne changed. When he and Kimmie talked together he seemed unfocused. Stopped returning her caresses and was often absent when she got home from work. Spent money he shouldn't have had. Talked on the telephone when he thought she was asleep.

Kristian courted her favor everywhere. In

the Nautilus pet shop, on the way home from work, in the flat she shared with Bjarne after he'd been given a cushy job by the others and was well out of the way.

And Kimmie derided him. Mocked Kristian for his dependency and lack of a sense of reality.

She quickly saw how his anger increased. How the steel in his eyes grew flinty and piercing.

But Kimmie didn't fear him. What could he do to her that he hadn't already done so many times before?

It finally happened that day in March when the comet Hyakutake was visible in the sky over Denmark. Bjarne was given a telescope by Torsten, and Ditlev had made his yacht available. The plan was that while Bjarne drank lots of beers and tried to fathom the enormity of the universe, Kristian, Ditlev, Torsten, and Ulrik would break into his flat.

She never found out how they had managed to get hold of a door key, but suddenly they were standing there with their pupils small and nostrils itching from the coke. They said nothing, just went right at her, pressing her against the wall and tearing at her clothes until she was adequately accessible.

They didn't get her to say anything because she knew it would only make them wilder. As if she hadn't seen it plenty of times when they'd assaulted others.

The boys in the gang hated whining. So did Kimmie.

They threw her on the coffee table without clearing it first. The rape began when Ulrik straddled her stomach and grabbed her knees with his huge paws, forcing her to spread her legs. First she tried pounding his back, but the cocaine frenzy and his layer of fat absorbed the force of her blows. And what was the point, anyway? She knew Ulrik loved it. A thrashing, humiliation, coercion — whatever challenged conventional morality. Nothing was taboo for Ulrik. No fetish went untested. None. Still, he couldn't get it up like everyone else.

When Ulrik climbed off her, Kristian got into position between her legs and pounded his will into her, until only the whites of his eyes were visible and his lips curled with self-satisfaction. Second was Ditlev, who finished quickly with his usual strange, cramplike shuddering, and then came Torsten.

As his lean body was bulldozing her, Bjarne suddenly appeared in the doorway. She looked him straight in the face as recognition of his own inferiority was born inside him and the gang's camaraderie broke his will and took over. She shouted at him to leave, but he didn't.

After Torsten had pulled out of her, their collective deep breathing turned to jubilation when Bjarne took his place.

She stared into his detached, bluish-red face and saw clearly for the first time just what her life had become.

Resigning herself, she closed her eyes and drifted away.

The last she heard before completely disappearing into the protective fog of subconsciousness was their laughter when Ulrik wanted another try and failed once more to get an erection.

It was the last time she saw them all together.

"My little darling, look what Mummy's brought you."

She unraveled the little person from the cloth and gazed at her with the sincerest tenderness. What a gift from God. Such small fingers and toes. Such tiny fingernails.

Then she unwrapped a package and held the contents in the air above the desiccated body.

"Look, Mille, have you ever seen anything

like it? Isn't it just what we need on a day like today?"

She touched one little hand with her finger. "Mummy's very warm, isn't she?" she asked. "Yes, Mummy is very warm." She laughed. "Your mum gets that way when she's really excited. But you know that."

She looked out the window. It was the last day of September. Almost the same date she'd moved in with Bjarne twelve years ago. Except it hadn't rained that day.

As far as she could recall.

When they'd finished raping her, they left her lying on the coffee table and sat in a circle on the floor snorting coke until they were totally blasted. They had screamed their lungs out laughing and Kristian had slapped her hard a few times on her naked thighs. Apparently as a sign of reconciliation.

"Come on, Kimmie!" Bjarne shouted. "Don't be so prudish. It's just us."

"It's over now," she snarled. "Finished."

She could tell they didn't believe her. They thought she was too dependent on them, and that she would come crawling back before too long. But she wasn't. Not ever. In Switzerland she had managed without them. She could do it again.

It took her a while to get up. Her perineum was burning. The ligaments in her hips were sprained, her neck ached, and humiliation weighed her down.

That feeling returned with a vengeance when Kassandra greeted her at the house in Ordrup with scorn in her voice, and the words: "Is there anything in this world you are capable of doing right, Kimmie?"

The next day she learned that Torsten had bought her place of employment, Nautilus Trading A/S, and that she was now out of a job. One of the employees who had been her friend gave her a check and told her that unfortunately she would have to leave the premises. Florin had made the personnel changes, her colleague said. So if she wanted to lodge a complaint, she would have to approach him personally.

When she went to the bank to deposit the check, she discovered that Bjarne had emptied their account and closed it.

Under no circumstances would she be allowed to escape from their clutches. That was the plan.

During the following months she stayed in her quarters in the house at Ordrup. At night she fetched her food from the main kitchen and took it up to her flat. During the day she slept, her little teddy bear clasped in her hand and her legs tucked beneath her. Kassandra often stood outside the door, exercising her shrill voice, but Kimmie was deaf to the world.

For Kimmie didn't owe anything to anyone, and Kimmie was pregnant.

"You have no idea how happy I was when I discovered I was going to have you," she said, smiling at the little one. "I knew instantly that you were a girl and what I would call you: Mille. It was simply your name. Isn't that funny and strange?"

Her hands fumbled a bit as she swaddled the body again. There she lay in the white cloth, like a tiny, wee Jesus child.

"I so looked forward to having you and to our living in our house, just like other people do. Your mother was going to find a job as soon as you were born, and after Mum picked you up from the day nursery, we were just going to be together all the time."

She pulled out a bag, set it on the bed, and stuffed one of the hotel's pillows into it. It looked secure and warm.

"Yes, you and I were supposed to live in that house, just the two of us, and Kassandra just would've had to go."

■ ■ ■ ■

Kristian Wolf began calling her during the weeks before his wedding. The thought of being shackled made him desperate, as did her repeated rejections.

The summer was a gray one, yet it was a blissful time for Kimmie, who began to take control of her life. She had put the terrible things they'd done behind her. Now she was responsible, beginning anew.

The past was dead.

It wasn't until Ditlev Pram and Torsten Florin were standing in Kassandra's living room, waiting for her one day, that she realized how impossible it was to escape the past. When she saw them scrutinizing her, she remembered how dangerous they could be.

"Your old friends have come to visit you," Kassandra chirped, in her nearly transparent summer dress. She protested at having to leave her domain — "My Room" — but what was about to happen wasn't intended for her ears.

"I don't know why you're here, but I want you to leave," Kimmie said, fully aware that that was just the beginning of negotiations over who would be in charge and who wouldn't by the time the meeting was over.

"You're too deeply involved in everything, Kimmie," Torsten said. "We can't have you pulling out. Who knows what you might do."

She shook her head. "What are you talking about? That I'd commit suicide and leave ugly letters behind?"

Ditlev nodded. "For example. There are also other things we could imagine you might do."

"Such as?"

"Does it matter?" Torsten said, coming closer.

If they grabbed hold of her again she would smash them with one of the massive Chinese vases standing in the corner.

"The main point is that we know where we've got you when you're with us. You can't live without it either, just admit it, Kimmie," he went on.

She smiled crookedly. "Maybe you're going to be a father, Torsten. Or maybe you, Ditlev." She hadn't intended to say it, but it was worth it to see their faces tighten. "Why would I want to go with you?" She laid a hand on her belly. "You think it's good for the child, maybe? I don't."

She knew what they were thinking as they exchanged glances. They both had children, and they'd both been through a number of divorces and domestic scandals. Another one wouldn't destroy their reputations. Her insurrection was all that troubled them.

"You'll have to get rid of that child," Ditlev said, unexpectedly harsh.

"Get rid of," he'd said. With those three words, she knew the child was in mortal danger.

She raised her hand toward them to demonstrate the distance between them.

"If you want to protect your interests, then let me be, understand? Just leave me alone — totally."

She noted with satisfaction how her shift in tone made them screw up their eyes.

"If you don't, then you should know I have a box which contains items that could completely destroy you. That box is my life insurance. Rest assured, if anything should happen to me, the box will see the light of day." In fact she'd never planned it this way. Granted, she did have the box tucked away, but she'd never considered showing it to anyone. They were just her trophies. A little object for each life they'd snuffed out. Like the Indian's scalps. Like the matador's bull's ears. Like the hearts of the Incas' victims.

"What box?" Torsten asked, as the wrinkles in his fox-face became more pronounced.

"Just things I've collected from our assaults. With the contents of that box, everything we've done can be exposed, and if you touch me or my child, you'll die behind bars, I promise you."

Ditlev clearly bought it. Torsten, on the other hand, seemed skeptical.

"Name one thing," he said.

"One of the earrings from the woman on Langeland. Kåre Bruno's rubber anklet. Remember how Kristian grabbed him and shoved him off the board? Then maybe you also recall how he was standing outside Bellahøj afterward with the anklet, laughing. I don't think he'll laugh when he finds out it's currently keeping company with a couple of Trivial Pursuit cards from Rørvig, do you?"

Torsten Florin looked away from her. As if he wanted to be certain that no one was listening on the other side of the door.

"No, Kimmie, you're right," he said. "I don't think he will, either."

Kristian visited her one night when Kassandra was passed out cold from drinking.

He stood over her by the bed and said the words so slowly and emphatically that every single one of them bored into her.

"Tell me where the box is, Kimmie, or I will kill you right now."

He pounded her brutally until he almost couldn't raise his arms. Pounded her abdomen and her groin and ribcage until bones cracked. But she didn't tell him where the box was.

Finally he left. Totally drained of aggression. Fully confident that his mission was completed and that Kimmie had simply made up the story about the box and its contents.

When she came to, she was just about able to call the ambulance herself.

33

She awoke with an empty stomach and no
appetite. It was Sunday afternoon and she
was still at the hotel. An hour's worth of
dreams had given her the assurance that
everything would fall into place. What other
sustenance did she need?

She turned to her bag containing the
bundle, which was on the bed beside her.

"Today I'm giving you a present, little
Mille. I've thought about it. You shall have
the best toy I've ever had in my entire life,
my little teddy bear," she said. "Mummy
has thought about giving it to you so often,
and today's the day. Doesn't that make you
happy?"

She sensed the voices lurking, waiting for
her to make a blunder, but then she stuck
her hand into the bag, felt the bundle, and
let the warm feelings take over.

"Yes, I'm calm now, my love. I'm completely calm. Today nothing will be able

to hurt us."

When she'd been brought in with massive hemorrhaging in her abdomen, the staff at Bispebjerg Hospital had asked her repeatedly how something like that could have happened. One of the head doctors even suggested calling the police, but she talked them out of it. The bruises on her body, she assured them, were the result of a fall from the top step of a long, steep staircase. She'd been having dizzy spells sometimes, and she'd had one as she was standing on that top step. No one had tried to kill her, she swore. She lived alone with her stepmother. It was just a foolish and ugly accident.

The following day the nurses had given her faith that the child would survive. It wasn't until they brought her greetings from her old school friends that she knew she needed to be careful.

Bjarne came to visit in her private room on the fourth day. It was hardly a coincidence that he was the one who'd become their errand boy. For one thing, Bjarne, unlike the others, was not a public personality; for another, nobody could bring a conversation down to basics like he could, to where empty rhetoric and offhand lies were unable to take root.

"You say you have evidence against us, Kimmie. Is that true?"

She didn't respond. Simply stared out the window at the pompous, rundown buildings.

"Kristian apologizes for what he did to you. He wants me to ask if you'd like to be transferred to a private hospital. The baby's OK, isn't it?"

She'd given him an angry glare. It was enough to make him avert his eyes. He was well aware that he didn't have the right to ask her anything at all.

"Tell Kristian that it was the last time he's ever going to touch me or have anything to do with me. Get it?"

"Kimmie, you know Kristian. He's not easy to get rid of. He says you don't even have a solicitor. One that you've confided in about us, Kimmie. He also says he's changed his mind and now believes you *do* have a box with those items you claim to have. That it seems like something you'd do. He actually grinned when he told me." Bjarne made an unsuccessful attempt at conveying the impression by grunting like Kristian, but Kimmie was unimpressed. Kristian never laughed at anything that could threaten him.

"And if you don't have a solicitor, then

Kristian's wondering who you've allied yourself with. You have no friends, Kimmie, apart from us. We all know that." He touched her arm, but she jerked it away. "I think you should just tell me where the box is. Is it in the house, Kimmie?"

She turned on him suddenly. "Do you think I'm stupid?"

It was clear that he bought it.

"Tell Kristian that if he just stays away from me, you can keep doing what you do, for all I care. I'm pregnant, Bjarne, haven't you lot realized that? If those items see the light of day, then I will be hung out to dry, and my baby, too. Don't you see that? The box is just an absolute emergency solution."

It was the last thing she should have said.

Emergency solution. If there was anything that could threaten Kristian, it was those words.

After Bjarne's visit she could no longer sleep at night. Just lay there in the darkness, on guard, with one hand on her belly and the other next to the cord to call the nurse.

He came wearing a doctor's white coat on the night of August 2.

She had dozed off for only a moment when she felt his hand on her mouth and the hard pressure of his knee on her chest.

He put it bluntly: "Who knows where you'll disappear to when you're released, Kimmie? We're keeping an eye on you, but still, you never know. Tell me where the box is, and we'll leave you in peace."

She didn't respond.

He punched her hard in the belly with his free hand, and when she still didn't answer he punched her again and again until the contractions began, her legs jerked, and the bed rocked.

He would have killed her if the chair beside her bed hadn't been flung over and filled the dead silence in the room with an infernal racket. If the headlights from an ambulance hadn't lit up the room and nakedly exposed him in all his gruesome wretchedness. If she hadn't laid her head back and gone into shock.

If he hadn't felt certain that she was about to die anyway.

She didn't check out of her hotel. She left her suitcase and simply took the bag with the little bundle and a few other things and walked the short distance to the central station. It was almost two o'clock in the afternoon. Now she was going to fetch the little teddy bear for Mille as she'd promised. And after that she would complete her task.

It was a clear autumn day and the S-train was filled with happy nursery-school children and their teachers. Maybe they were heading home from a museum, maybe they were on their way to the park for a few hours. Maybe the little ones would return home this evening to Mum and Dad with flushed cheeks, brimming with tales of multicolored foliage and flocks of deer on the plains surrounding Eremitage Castle.

When she and Mille were finally reunited, it would be even lovelier than all those things. In the infinite beauty of Paradise. They would gaze at each other and laugh.

For all eternity, that's how it was going to be.

She nodded and stared across Svanemøllen's barracks in the direction of Bispebjerg Hospital.

Eleven years ago she'd got out of her hospital bed and had taken the little child who'd lain under a sheet on the steel table at the foot of the bed. They had left her alone for only a moment. A woman in the next room had gone into labor, and there had been serious complications.

She had risen, dressed, and swaddled her child in the sheet. And an hour later, after she'd been humiliated by her father at Hotel D'Angleterre, she'd taken the exact same route out to Ordrup that she was taking now.

On that occasion she'd known she couldn't stay in the house. That the gang would come after her, and the next time would mean the end.

But she also knew that she needed help bad because she was still bleeding, and the pain in her abdomen felt unreal and frightening.

So she was going to ask Kassandra for more money. Make her give her what she needed.

Once again on that day she'd found out what people whose name began with "K" could do to her.

All that Kassandra had angrily shoved into her hand was a lousy two thousand kroner. Two thousand from her and ten thousand from her so-called father, Willy K. Lassen, was as much as they were willing to inconvenience themselves with. And that was far from enough.

When she'd been asked to leave the house and found herself on the street with the bundle hugged to her chest and the sanitary pad between her legs once again completely soaked in blood, she knew the day would come when everyone who had mistreated her and forced her to her knees would pay for what they'd done.

First Kristian, then Bjarne. Then Torsten, Ditlev, Ulrik, Kassandra, and her father.

Now, for the first time in many years, she stood in front of the house on Kirkevej, and everything looked exactly the same. The church bells up the hill no doubt still called the staid bourgeoisie to Sunday services, and the homes in the neighborhood still towered unashamedly. The door of the house was still just as hard to open.

She recognized not only Kassandra's preserved face when she opened the door, but also the attitude her presence always provoked in her stepmother.

Kimmie didn't know how the hostility between them had begun. It had probably been back when Kassandra, in her misguided attempts at child-rearing, had locked Kimmie in dark wardrobes, bombarding her with torrents of cruel words, the half of which the little girl didn't understand. That Kassandra herself had suffered in this insensitive household was arguably a mitigating factor when taking her behavior into account. But it was no excuse. Kassandra was a devil.

"I'm not letting you in," Kassandra hissed, trying to force the door closed. Exactly as she'd done the day after the miscarriage when Kimmie stood there, injured and in deep despair and need, with the bundle in her arms.

Back then she'd been told to go to hell, and it truly was hell that awaited her. Despite the horrible shape in which Kristian's blows and the miscarriage had left her, she had been forced to walk the streets for days, hunched over, without anyone offering to help her, or even approach her.

People saw only her cracked lips and filthy hair. Edging away from the repulsive bundle in her hands and her sleeves stained brown by dried blood, they didn't see a fever-ravaged fellow human in need. They didn't see a person falling to pieces.

And she'd considered it her punishment. Her own purgatory that she had to endure to atone for all her terrible misdeeds.

It was a junkie from Vesterbro who saved her. Only Tine, that stick-thin waif, ignored the smell that rose from the bundle and the caked-on spittle that had accumulated in the corners of her mouth. She had seen far worse, and she took Kimmie to a room down an alley in Sydhavnen to another drug addict who once, at the dawn of time, had been a doctor.

It was his pills and D and C that got rid of the infection and staunched her bleeding. The price she paid was that she never bled again.

The following week — around the time the little parcel stopped reeking — Kimmie was ready to start a new life on the street.

The rest was history.

Entering the rooms where Kassandra's thick perfume hung heavy, and all the lingering ghosts laughed at Kimmie as they had always done, was like being frozen in the middle of a nightmare.

Kassandra raised a cigarette to her lips. Her lipstick had long ago been sucked into dozens of earlier cigarettes. Her hands trembled slightly, but through the smoke her eyes followed Kimmie watchfully as she set her bag on the floor. It was obvious that Kassandra felt uncomfortable and her eyes would soon begin darting around. This was not a scenario she had planned for.

"What do you want here?" Kassandra asked. Precisely the same words as eleven years before. After the rape and the miscarriage.

"Do you wish to keep on living in this house, Kassandra?" Kimmie retorted.

Her stepmother tipped her head back, but

otherwise remained still for a moment, thinking, her wrist limp, the blue smoke swirling around her graying hair.

"Is that why you've come? To throw me out? Is that it?"

It was refreshing to watch her struggle to remain calm. This person who'd had the opportunity to take a little girl by the hand and lift her out of a cold mother's shadow. This miserable, self-loathing, egocentric woman who'd dominated Kimmie's life with emotional abuse and daily neglect. This woman who'd nurtured in Kimmie all that had led her to where she was today: mistrust, hatred, cold indifference, and lack of empathy.

"I have two questions that you'd be wise to answer nice and snappy, Kassandra."

"Then you'll leave?" She poured a glass of port from the carafe she'd no doubt made attempts at emptying before Kimmie arrived, and took a measured mouthful.

"I'm not making any promises," Kimmie said.

"What are your questions?" Kassandra sucked the cigarette smoke so deeply into her lungs that nothing exited when she exhaled.

"Where's my mother?"

She tilted her head back, her mouth

slightly open. "Oh my God. Is that your question?" She turned abruptly to Kimmie. "Well, she's dead, Kimmie. She's been dead for thirty years, the poor thing. Didn't we ever tell you?" Once again she tilted her head back and made a few sounds that were supposed to express surprise. Then she turned again to Kimmie. This time her face was hard. Merciless. "Your father gave her money, and she drank it. Need I say more? Amazing that we never told you. But now that you know, does it make you happy?"

The word "happy" permeated all the cells in Kimmie's body. *Happy*?!

"What about my father? Have you heard from him? Where is he?"

Kassandra knew that question was coming. She was repulsed. Just the word "father" was enough. If anyone hated Willy K. Lassen, it was her.

"I don't understand why you want to know. For all you care, he could burn in hell, couldn't he? Or do you just want to make sure he is? Because I can assure you, you daft girl, that your father is indeed burning in hell."

"Is he ill?" she asked. Maybe what the policeman had told Tine was true.

"Ill?" Kassandra snuffed out her cigarette and stretched her arms with fingers spread and nails jagged. "He's burning in hell with cancer in all his bones. I haven't spoken to him, but I've heard from others that he's suffering terribly." She pursed her lips and exhaled heavily as if she were expelling Satan himself. "He's suffering terribly and will be dead by Christmas, and that's fine with me, do you hear?"

She smoothed her dress a little and pulled her glass of port on the table toward her.

That meant Kimmie, her little one and Kassandra were the only ones left. Two cursed K's and the tiny guardian angel.

Kimmie lifted her bag off the floor and put it on the table beside Kassandra's carafe.

"Tell me, were you the one who let Kristian in when I was expecting the little one here?"

Kassandra watched as Kimmie opened the bag a bit.

"Dear God! Don't tell me you have that hideous thing in that bag!" She could tell from Kimmie's face that indeed she did. "You're sick in the head, Kimmie. Take it away."

"Why did you let Kristian into the house? Why did you let him come to me, Kassandra? You knew I was pregnant. I'd told you I wanted to be left alone."

"Why? I didn't care one iota about you and your bastard child. What did you expect?"

"And you just sat here in the living room while he beat me up. You must have heard it. You must have known how many times he punched me. Why didn't you call the police?"

"Because I knew you deserved it. Isn't that right?"

"I knew you deserved it," she'd said, and the voices began sounding off in Kimmie's head.

Punches, dark rooms, derision, accusations — all of it making a racket in Kimmie's head, and now it had to stop.

In one bound she leaped forward and seized Kassandra's hairdo, forcing her head back so she could pour the rest of the port into her. The woman stared in confusion and surprise at the ceiling as the liquid drained into her windpipe and made her cough.

So she clamped Kassandra's mouth shut and clutched her head in a headlock as her coughing fit and attempts to regurgitate grew stronger.

Kassandra grabbed Kimmie's forearm and tried to shove it away, but life on the streets creates a sinewy strength that dwarfs that which an elderly woman gets from spending her days ordering people around. Her eyes grew desperate as her stomach contracted, driving gastric acid up to the mounting catastrophe about to take place somewhere between her windpipe and esophagus.

A few, quick, futile inhalations through her nose caused further panic in Kassandra's body, which now flailed with all its limbs to get free. Kimmie held tight and closed off every opportunity for life-giving oxygen to get in, and Kassandra went into convulsions as her chest heaved frantically, drowning her whining.

And then she became still.

Kimmie allowed her to fall right where the battle had been fought, letting the smashed port glass, the coffee table that had been knocked out of place, and the regurgitation that flowed from the woman's mouth speak for itself.

Kassandra Lassen had always enjoyed the good things in life, and now they had taken that life from her.

An accident, some would say. Predictable, others would add.

Those were precisely the words one of Kristian Wolf's old hunting mates had been quoted as saying when they found him with a severed femoral artery down at his Lolland estate. An accident, yes, but predictable. Kristian was known for being careless with his shotgun. One day something was bound to go wrong, the hunting buddy said.

But it was no accident.

Kristian had controlled Kimmie from the day he first laid eyes on her. He had coerced her and the others to participate in his games, and he had used her body. He had pushed her into relationships and pulled her out again. He had gotten her to lure Kåre Bruno to Bellahøj with promises of them getting back together. He had goaded her into shouting for Kristian to shove Kåre over the edge. He had raped her and beaten her, once, then a second time, so the baby didn't survive. He'd transformed her life on multiple occasions, each time for the worse.

After she'd been living on the streets for six weeks, she saw him on the front page of a tabloid. He was smiling, had made some terrific business deals and was about to leave for a few days of relaxation on his Lolland estate. "No animal on my grounds should feel safe," he had said. "My aim is excellent."

She stole her first suitcase, put on impeccable clothes and took the train to Søllested, where she got off and walked the last three miles in the twilight until she reached the estate.

She spent the night in the bushes, listening as Kristian's constant yelling inside finally forced his young wife to flee upstairs. He slept in the living room and after a few hours was more than ready to take out his personal shortcomings and general frustrations on vulnerable pheasants and any other living creature within range.

The night had been ice-cold, but not for Kimmie. The thought of Kristian's blood, which would soon be spilled for his sins, felt like a summer heat wave. It was life-giving and inspiring.

Ever since boarding school she had known that Kristian's restless soul drove him out of bed long before anyone else. A couple of hours before a hunt, he would stroll round the hunting grounds to get a feel for the terrain and to ensure the best cooperation between beaters and hunters. Several years after he'd been murdered, she could still clearly recall the moment when she finally spotted him walking through the gates of his estate and out to the fields. Fully equipped in the manner the upper classes considered fitting for a killer to look: squeaky clean, foppish, and with shiny, laced-up boots. But what did they know about real killers?

Moving swiftly, she had followed him at a distance through the windbreaks, sometimes fearing that the noise of crackling leaves and twigs would alert him. If he saw her he wouldn't hesitate to shoot. An accident, he would call it. A misunderstanding. A false assumption that he'd seen a deer or some wild animal.

But Kristian didn't hear her. Not until the moment she leaped out at him and jammed the knife into his sex organs.

He fell forward and thrashed about, eyes wide open in recognition that the face above him would be the last thing he'd see.

She pulled his shotgun over toward her, and let him bleed to death. It didn't take long at all.

Then she turned him around, tucked her hands inside her sleeves and wiped off the weapon, stuck it in the corpse's hand, aimed the barrel at his groin and fired.

The police report concluded that it was an accidental shooting and the cause of death was given as exsanguination following the severing of a major artery. It was the most talked-about hunting accident of the year.

Yes, it was labeled an accident, but not for Kimmie, and a rare peace settled over her.

Unlike the other gang members. She had vanished without a trace, and they all knew that Kristian would never have died in such a way without assistance.

Inexplicable, people called Kristian's death.

But Kimmie's old friends didn't buy it.

It was at this point that Bjarne turned himself in.

Maybe he knew he would be next. Maybe he'd made a pact with the others. It didn't matter.

She read about the case in the newspapers. About how Bjarne accepted the blame for the Rørvig murders, and thus she could now live in peace with the past.

She called Ditlev Pram and told him that if he, Ulrik, and Torsten wanted to live in peace, too, they'd have to pay her a certain amount of money.

The procedure was agreed upon and they kept their word.

That was smart. At least it bought them a few years before their fates caught up with them.

For a moment she looked at Kassandra's body, wondering why she didn't feel a greater sense of satisfaction.

It's because you're not finished yet, said one of the voices. *No one can feel happiness halfway to paradise*, said another.

The third voice was silent.

She nodded and removed the bundle from her bag, then slowly made her way up to her rooms, explaining to the little one how she'd once played on those stairs, sliding down the banister when no one was watching. How she'd always hummed the same song over and over when Kassandra and her father couldn't hear her.

Small moments in a child's life.

"You can stay here while Mummy finds Teddy for you, my love," she said, laying the bundle carefully on the pillow.

Her bedroom was exactly as she'd left it. It was here she'd lain for a few months, feeling her belly growing. Now this would be her final visit.

She opened the balcony door and felt her way in the fading light toward the loose tile. There it was, right where she remembered it. The tile moved surprisingly easily, which she hadn't been expecting at all. It was like opening a door that had just been oiled. Dark forebodings came over her, making her skin grow cold. Then, when she put her hand in the hollow space and found it empty, the cold became a warm, burning sensation.

Her eyes feverishly scanned the tiles surrounding the loose one, but she knew it was in vain.

Because it was the right tile, the right hollow. And the box was gone.

Now all the nasty K's in her life lined up before her as the voices howled inside her, laughing hysterically as they gave her a scolding. Kyle, Willy K., Kassandra, Kåre, Kristian, Klavs, and all the others who'd crossed her path. Who had crossed it this time and removed the box? Was it the very ones whose throats she'd planned to stuff the evidence down? Was it the survivors, Ditlev, Ulrik, and Torsten? Could they really have found the box?

Trembling, she noticed how the voices had gathered into one. How they made the veins in the back of her hand throb visibly.

This hadn't happened in years. The voices concurring.

The three men had to die. For once the voices were in total agreement.

Exhausted, she lay down on the bed next to the little parcel, brimming with past humiliations and subjugations. Her father's first, hard punch. The alcohol breath behind her mother's fiery red lipstick. The sharp fingernails. The pinches. The yanking of

Kimmie's fine hair.

After they'd given her a thrashing she would sit in the corner, her shaking hands hugging little Teddy. It was someone she could talk to and be consoled by. Small as he was, Teddy spoke with authority. "Take it easy, Kimmie," the stuffed animal had said. "They're just evil people. They will disappear one day. Suddenly they'll be gone."

When she grew, the tone changed. Now the teddy bear would say that she should never, ever let anyone hit her. If anyone was going to do the hitting, it should be her. She mustn't tolerate being mistreated.

And now Teddy was gone. The only thing in her life that called forth small glimpses of happy, childhood moments.

She turned to the bundle, stroked it softly, and, overcome with remorse at not being able to keep her promise, said: "You can't have your teddy bear now, little angel. I'm so sorry."

34

As usual, Ulrik was the one who was best informed of the latest news, but then he hadn't spent the weekend practicing with his crossbow, as Ditlev had. That was the difference between them, and always had been. Ulrik, when possible, preferred to take a more laid-back approach to life.

When his mobile rang, Ditlev stood facing the Sound, shooting a series of bolts at a target. At first he'd shot some right past the target and into the water, but in the last two days hardly any had been launched without hitting their mark. It was Monday and he'd just amused himself by arranging five bolts in the shape of a cross in the target's center when Ulrik's panicked voice put an end to his fun.

"Kimmie killed Aalbæk," he said. "I heard about it on the news, and I just know it was her."

For a split second this information occupied Ditlev's entire being. It felt like a premonition of death.

He listened intently to Ulrik's short and rather disjointed account of Aalbæk's fatal fall and the details surrounding his death.

As far as Ulrik could glean from the media's interpretation of the vague police reports, it was impossible to definitively call it a suicide. Which meant it was equally impossible to rule out murder.

It was very sobering news.

"The three of us have to meet, do you hear?" Ulrik whispered, as if Kimmie had already scented him out. "If we don't stick together she'll pick us off one by one."

Ditlev looked at the crossbow dangling from the strap around his wrist. Ulrik was right. From now on things would have to change.

"OK," he said. "For now, we'll do as we've planned. We'll meet for the hunt early tomorrow morning at Torsten's, and afterward we'll talk things over. Remember, this is only the second time in over ten years that she's struck. We still have time, Ulrik. That's my gut feeling."

He gazed out across the water, his eyes slipping out of focus. There was no ignoring it now. It was either her or them.

"Listen, Ulrik," Ditlev said. "I'm phoning

Torsten to let him know. In the meantime, call around and find out what you can. Call Kimmie's stepmother, for example, and tell her what's going on, OK? Ask people to let you know if they hear anything. Anything at all."

"And Ulrik," he said before they hung up. "Stay indoors as much as possible until we see each other, OK?"

He didn't even manage to put his mobile back in his pocket before it rang again.

"It's Herbert," said the voice without inflection.

Ditlev's older brother never used to call. Back when the police investigated the murders in Rørvig, Herbert saw through his kid brother at first glance, but he never said anything. Never voiced his suspicion, nor did he get involved. But it didn't foster any love between them. Not that there had been any in the first place. Feelings didn't suit the Pram family's style.

And yet Herbert had been there when it counted. Probably because his relentless fear of scandal trumped all else. The fear that everything he stood for would be sullied had suddenly become too overwhelming.

That was why Herbert had been the perfect tool when Ditlev was considering how to get Department Q's investigation put on standby.

And that's why Herbert was calling now.

"I'm calling to tell you that Department Q's investigation is in full swing again. I can't give you any more details because my contact at police headquarters has withdrawn his antennae, but in any case Carl Mørck, the department head, now knows I tried to influence his work. I'm sorry, Ditlev. Keep a low profile."

Now Ditlev, too, felt the panic rising.

He caught Torsten Florin just as the fashion mogul was backing out of his parking spot at Brand Nation. He'd just heard the news about Aalbæk and, like Ditlev and Ulrik, thought it must be Kimmie's doing. But he hadn't heard that Department Q and Carl Mørck were operational again.

"Fuck! It keeps getting worse and worse," the irritated voice on the other end of the line shouted.

"Do you want to cancel the hunt?" Ditlev asked.

The long silence spoke its own language.

"There's no point. The fox is going to die on its own anway," Torsten finally said. Ditlev could just imagine. Torsten had no doubt spent the entire weekend relishing the demented fox's torments. "You should have seen it this morning," he said. "Completely insane. But let me think about it a moment."

Ditlev knew Torsten. At this moment he was fighting an inner battle between his murderous impulses and the basic reasonableness with which he'd managed his professional life and growing empire since the age of twenty. In a moment he would be whispering a quiet prayer. That was another side of him. If he couldn't solve the problem himself, there was always some god or other he could call upon.

Ditlev put his mobile's headphones on, tensed the crossbow's string, and pulled a new bolt from the quiver. Then he loaded the weapon and aimed at one of the wharf piles that still remained from the old pier. The bird had just landed and was busy cleaning the sea fog from its feathers. Ditlev measured the distance and the wind and released the bolt ever so gently — as if it were a baby's cheek he was stroking with his finger.

The bird never saw it coming. Pierced by the arrow, it simply lurched backward into the water and floated there as Torsten prayed almost soundlessly on the other end of the line.

It was this amazing shot that led Ditlev to his decision.

"We'll do it, Torsten," he said. "Get all the Somalis together tonight and instruct them to keep a watchful eye out for Kimmie from now on. Put them on guard, Torsten. Show them a photo of her. Promise them a huge bonus if they see anything."

"OK," Torsten said after a moment's consideration. "What about the rest of the hunting party? We can't have Krum and all those dunces running around."

"What are you talking about? It doesn't matter who's with us. If she appears in the vicinity, we just need witnesses when the bolts go through her."

Ditlev patted his crossbow and looked out at the small white blob that was slowly being pulled down into the waves.

"Yes," he went on softly, "Kimmie's more than welcome to show up. Don't you agree, Torsten?"

He couldn't hear the response over his secretary's shouting from Caracas's terrace. As far as Ditlev could see at that distance, she was waving her hands and raising them to her ears.

"I think there's someone trying to get hold of me, Torsten. I'm hanging up now. See you early tomorrow morning, OK? Take care."

They hung up at the same time, and a second later his mobile rang again.

"Did you turn off the call-waiting function again, Ditlev?"

It was his secretary. Now she was standing motionless on the hospital terrace.

"You shouldn't do that, it means I can't get in touch with you. We have a bit of a problem up here. A man calling himself Deputy Detective Superintendent Mørck has just turned up and is sniffing around. What do you want us to do, Ditlev? Will you talk to him, or what? He hasn't shown us a warrant, and I don't think he has one, either."

Ditlev felt the salty mist settle on his face. Apart from that, he felt nothing. Over twenty years had passed since the first assault, and during all those years a tickling unease and latent anxiety had served as his ever-growing source of energy.

But at this moment he felt nothing, and it didn't feel good.

"No," he replied. "Tell him I'm out of town."

The seagull vanished in the dark waves.

"Say I've gone traveling. And see to it that he's thrown the hell out."

35

For Carl, Monday started ten minutes after he'd gone to bed.

He had been disoriented all day Sunday. He'd slept like a log for most of the flight home, and it had been almost impossible for the crabby stewardesses to wake him. They'd had to drag him out of the plane, after which airport personnel needed an electric cart to drive him to the medics.

"How many Frisium did you say you took?" they asked. But he was already asleep again.

And now, paradoxically, he had woken up the very moment he'd gone to bed.

"Where have you been today?" Morten Holland asked, when Carl came tottering into the kitchen like a zombie. A martini appeared on the table quicker than a soul could say no thanks, and the night grew long.

"You should find yourself a girlfriend,"

Morten purred, as the clock struck four, and Jesper arrived home, offering additional advice about love and women.

Now Carl knew that Frisium was best in small doses. In any case, it wasn't a good sign when one's best advisers on matters of the heart were a sixteen-year-old closet punk and an as-yet closeted homosexual. Next it would probably be Jesper's mother, Vigga, putting in her pennies' worth. He could just hear it: "What's wrong with you, Carl? If something is wrong with your metabolic system, then you should give rose root a try. It's good for all kinds of things."

He ran into Lars Bjørn at the reception desk, and he didn't look too good, either.

"It's those damn rubbish-bin assaults," he said.

They nodded to the officer behind the glass and walked together out to the colonnade.

"You've probably noticed the coincidence between the names 'Store Kannikestræde' and 'Store Søndervoldstræde,'" Carl said. "Are you keeping an eye on the other streets?"

"Yes, we have continual surveillance on both Store Strandstræde and Store Kirkestræde. Plainclothes female officers are out there, so we'll see if that tempts the assailant. Which is why we can't spare any officers to help on your case, but you probably know that."

Carl nodded. At this moment he hardly cared. If whatever it was that was making him feel this worn out, slow-witted, and woolly-headed was anything like jet lag, then he bloody well failed to understand what on earth a "fairy-tale holiday" could be. Nightmare holiday was a far more appropriate term.

Rose greeted him with a smile in the basement corridor, which no doubt he would soon manage to swipe off her face. "Well, how was Madrid?" was the first thing she said. "Did you have time for a little flamenco dancing?"

He simply didn't have the energy to respond.

"Come on, Carl. What did you see down there?"

He fixed his heavy-lidded eyes on her. "What did I see? Apart from the Eiffel Tower and Paris and the inside of my eyelids, I saw absolutely nothing."

She started to protest. *That's not possible*, said her look.

"I'll be blunt, Rose. If you ever do anything like that again, you'll soon be calling yourself an ex–Department Q colleague."

He slipped past her and headed for his chair. The padded upholstery awaited him. Just four or five hours' slumber with his legs up on the desk and he'd be good as new. Of that he was certain.

"What's going on?" came Assad's voice, the instant Carl entered dreamland.

He shrugged. Nothing, other than that he was about to come unglued. Was Assad blind, or what?

"Rose is upset. Were you mean to her, Carl?"

He was about to get riled again, but then saw the papers Assad had under his arm.

"What have you got for me?" he said tiredly.

Assad sat in one of Rose's metal monstrosities. "They haven't found Kimmie Lassen yet. They're searching everywhere, so it's probably a question of time then."

"Is there any news from the explosion site? Have they found anything?"

"No, nothing. As far as I know they're finished now." He pulled out his papers and glanced through them.

"I got in touch with those folks at Løgstrup Fence," he said. "They were very, very friendly. They had to go all the way around

563

in their department before they found someone who could tell us something about the key in the fence."

"OK," Carl said, eyes closed.

"One of their employees had a locksmith come to Inger Slevs Gade to help a lady from the ministry who had ordered some extra keys then."

"Did you get a description of the woman, Assad? It was Kimmie Lassen, I presume?"

"No, they couldn't find out which locksmith it was then, so I didn't get a description. I've told the whole story to the people upstairs. Maybe they would like to know who could have had access to the house that exploded."

"OK, Assad. Fair enough. So we'll cut that string."

"What string?"

"Doesn't matter, Assad. My next assignment for you is to make a case file on each of the other three, Ditlev, Ulrik, and Torsten. I want information about all kinds of things. Tax statements, business ventures, residencies, marital status, and all the rest. Just build up the files bit by bit."

"Who do I start with then? I have some stuff about all of them already."

"That's good, Assad. Do you have anything else we should discuss?"

"Up in homicide they told me to let you know that Aalbæk's mobile many times had been in contact with Ditlev Pram's."

Of course it had.

"That's good, Assad. So there's a connection between them and this case. That means we have a pretext for visiting them."

"Pretext? What kind of text is that?"

Carl opened his eyes and looked into a pair of dark brown question marks. Honestly, every now and then it was a bit much. Maybe a few private sessions in the Danish language could remove a few feet of the language barrier. On the other hand, there was the risk that he'd suddenly start speaking like a bureaucrat.

"And I've found Klavs Jeppesen," Assad said, when Carl didn't react to his question.

"That's good, Assad." He tried to remember how many times he'd already said "that's good." He wouldn't want to overuse the expression. "And where is he?"

"He's in the hospital."

Carl straightened in his chair. What *now*?

"Well, you know," Assad said, making a slashing motion across his wrist.

"Jesus Christ. Why'd he do that? Is he going to survive?"

"Yes. I've been out there. I went already yesterday."

565

"Well done, Assad. And?"

"Not much. Just a man without back-bones."

Backbones? There it was again.

"He's come close to doing it for many years, he said."

Carl shook his head. No woman ever had that kind of effect on *him*. Unfortunately.

"Did he have more to say?"

"I don't think so. The nurses threw me out."

Carl smiled wearily. By now Assad must have become accustomed to it.

Then his assistant's facial expression changed. "I saw a new man up on the third floor earlier today. An Iraqi, I think. Do you know what he's doing here?"

Carl nodded. "Yes, he's Bak's replacement. He's from Rødovre. I met him out at the high-rise early Sunday morning. Maybe you know him. His name's Samir. I don't remember his surname."

Assad lifted his head a little. His full lips parted slightly and a set of faint wrinkles formed around his eyes, which weren't caused by smiling. For a moment he seemed far away.

"OK," he said softly, nodding slowly a few times. "Replacement for Bak. So that means he's staying?"

"Yes, I assume so. Is something wrong?"

Suddenly Assad's expression changed back. His face relaxed and he looked directly at Carl with his usual unconcerned air. "You've got to figure out how to be good friends with Rose, Carl. She's just so hard-working and so . . . so sweet. Do you know what she called me this morning?"

He was no doubt going to find out in a second.

"Her 'favorite Bedouin.' Isn't that just sweet then?" He flashed his overbite and shook his head, pleased as Punch.

Irony wasn't exactly the man's strongest suit.

Carl plugged in his mobile to recharge it and studied the whiteboard. The next step would have to be direct contact with one or more from the gang. Assad would have to go with him, so there would be a witness in case they gave themselves away.

Apart from that, he had yet to meet with their solicitor.

He rubbed his chin and gnawed at the inside of his cheek. It was bloody unfortunate that he'd done that number on Krum's wife. Claiming Krum was having an affair with his own wife! How idiotic could one person be? It certainly wasn't going to make it any easier to arrange a meeting with him.

He looked up at the board where the solicitor's number was listed and punched it in.

"Agnete Krum," said a voice.

He cleared his throat and threw his voice into a higher register. Recognition was good if a person was famous. Not if he was infamous.

"No," she said. "He doesn't live here anymore. If you would like to get in touch with him, I suggest you call his mobile." Sounding sad, she gave him the number.

He called it right away and then listened to the message on Bent Krum's voicemail, saying he was out preparing his yacht for the new season, but could be reached the next day at the same number between nine and ten.

Son of a bitch, Carl thought. He called Krum's wife again. The boat was in Rungsted Harbor, she said.

That was hardly a surprise.

"We're going for a drive, Assad, so get ready!" he shouted across the corridor. "I just need to make one more call, OK?"

He punched in the number to his old colleague and rival at Station City, Brandur Isaksen, who was half Faroese, half Green-

568

lander, and one hundred percent North Atlantic in his very soul. The Icicle of Halmtorvet, he was called.

"What do you want?" he asked.

"I'd like to know about one Rose Knudsen whom I've inherited from your department. I've heard she caused some friction with your lot at City. Can you tell me what it was?"

Carl hadn't expected the uproarious laughter that followed.

"You're the one who got her?" Isaksen howled ominously. Hearing him laugh was about as uncommon an occurrence as hearing him say anything friendly.

"I'll sketch it out for you," he went on. "First she backed her Daihatsu into three of her colleagues' private cars. Then she put her leaky teapot on the chief's handwritten notes for the weekly reports. She ordered all the office girls around. Bossed all the investigators and nosed about in their work. And last of all she shagged two colleagues at a Christmas party, as far as I understand." At this point he seemed about to fall off his chair — it was apparently that hilarious. "Is it you who got her, Carl? Don't give her anything to drink, I'm warning you."

Carl sighed. "Anything else?"

"Yes, she has a twin sister — not an identical twin, but one who's at least as strange."

"Aha, and what about her?"

"Well, wait till she starts calling Rose at work. You've never heard two women do so much yakking. In short, she's clumsy, unmanageable, and sometimes extremely contrary."

In other words, nothing he didn't already know, apart from the bit about the alcohol.

Carl hung up and stared into space while his big ears attempted to decipher what was going on in Rose's office.

He got up and sneaked into the hallway. Yep, she was on the telephone.

He crept up close to the door frame and turned his ear directly toward the open door.

"Yes," she was saying, softly. "Yes, you've got to accept that. Uh-huh, yes, of course. Really . . . ? Well, then, that's lovely . . ." And much, much more in the same vein.

Then Carl put his head in the doorway and gave her a trenchant look. One could always hope it would have some kind of effect.

Two minutes later she hung up. The effect hadn't been too dramatic.

"Well, are you sitting here having a nice chat with your friends?" he asked acidly. His comment apparently bounced off the silly girl.

"Friends?" she said, breathing deeply. "Hmm, I guess you could call them that. It was a department head at the Justice Ministry. He just wanted to say they'd got an e-mail from Kripo in Oslo, in which they praise our department and say that it's probably the most interesting thing that has happened in Nordic crime history in the last twenty-five years. And now the Ministry just wanted to know why you haven't been nominated for superintendent."

Carl swallowed. Were they starting that bullshit again? He'd be damned if he was going back to school. He and Marcus had abandoned that idea long ago.

"How did you respond?"

"Me? I began talking about something else. What would you have liked me to say?"

Good girl, he thought.

"Hey, Rose," he said, gathering himself. It wasn't so easy to apologize when a guy came from a hick town like Brønderslev. "I was a little sharp with you earlier. Forget it. The trip to Madrid was actually OK. I mean, the entertainment value was above average, now that I think about it. In any case I saw a tramp without teeth, had all my credit cards stolen, and held a strange woman's hand for at least twelve hundred miles. But next time, give me a little orientation first, OK?"

She smiled.

"And there's one more thing I just thought of, Rose. Was it you who spoke to a maid that called from Kassandra Lassen's house? I didn't have my police badge, you'll recall, so she called here to check my identity."

"Yes, I did."

"She asked you to describe my appearance. Do you mind telling me what you told her?"

A pair of traitorous dimples planted themselves in her cheeks.

"Weeell, I just said that if it was a guy wearing a brown leather belt and super-worn-out size 10 1/2 black shoes who looked totally unremarkable, then there was a considerable probability that it was you. And if she could also see a bald spot on his crown that looked like a pair of butt cheeks, then there could be no doubt."

She's bloody merciless, he thought, sweeping his hair back a bit.

They found Bent Krum all the way out on pier number 11, sitting in an upholstered easy chair on the quarterdeck of a yacht that no doubt cost more than a man like Krum was worth.

"That boat there is a V42," said a boy in front of the promenade's Thai restaurant. He was certainly well educated.

Whatever enthusiasm Krum might have displayed upon seeing a guardian of the law enter his white paradise, followed by a deeply sunburned and thin-haired representative of Alternative Denmark, was very hard to detect.

But he didn't get a snowball's chance in hell to sling out any professional protests.

"I've spoken with Valdemar Florin," Carl said, "and he suggested I talk to you. He said you would be the right person to speak for the family. Do you have five minutes?"

Bent Krum shoved his sunglasses above his forehead. He might just as well have left them up there the whole time, seeing as there was no sun. "Five minutes is all. My wife is expecting me at home."

Carl smiled broadly. *Fat chance*, the smile said, and Bent Krum, being the sly, old rat he was, recognized it immediately. Perhaps he'd be more careful about lying in the future.

"You and Valdemar Florin were present in 1986, when the youths were brought down to the Holbæk Police Station under suspicion of having committed the murders in Rørvig. He suggested to me that a couple of them stood out from the others in the group, but thought this was something you could better elaborate on. Do you know what he was referring to?"

In the sunlight he was a pale man. Not without pigmentation, but anemic-looking. Bleached and worn down by all the villainy he'd had to defend over the years. Carl had seen it time and again. No one could look paler than a policeman with unsolved crimes in his baggage or a solicitor with all too many solved ones.

"Stood out, you say? They all did, I guess. Fine, young people, I'd call them. Their activities since then have proved that, wouldn't you say?"

"Well," Carl said, "I'm not that much of an expert. But one shoots himself in the private parts, another makes a living stuffing women with Botox and silicone, a third lets undernourished young girls prance back and forth while people stare at them, a fourth is sitting in prison, a fifth specializes in making rich people richer by preying on the ignorance of small investors, and the sixth has been living on the street for just over eleven years. So, really, I'm not sure how to respond."

"I don't think you should make such statements in public," Krum said, already prepared to file a lawsuit.

"In public?" Carl said, glancing round at the teak and glossy fiberglass and chrome. "Is there anything less public than this?" He spread his arms and smiled. A compliment, many would say.

"What about Kimmie Lassen?" Carl continued. "Didn't she stand out? Isn't it true that she was a central figure in the gang's activities? Isn't it the case that Florin, Dybbøl Jensen, and Pram might have a certain interest in seeing her quietly disappear from the face of the earth?"

Vertical wrinkles appeared on Bent Krum's head. Not especially attractive. "I'd like to remind you that she already *has* disappeared. Of her own free will, it should be noted!"

Carl turned to Assad. "Did you get that, Assad?"

He raised his pencil in confirmation.

"Thank you," Carl said. "That was all."

They stood up.

"I beg your pardon?" Krum said. "Got what? What just happened there?"

"Well, you said the gang had an interest in Kimmie Lassen disappearing."

"No, that's not at all what I said."

"Did he not, Assad?"

The little man nodded vigorously. He

certainly was loyal.

"We have all kinds of indications that suggest it was the gang that killed the siblings in Rørvig," Carl said. "And I'm not just talking about Bjarne Thøgersen. So we'll probably meet again, Mr. Krum. You'll also be meeting a number of people that maybe you've heard of, and maybe not. In any case, they're all interesting people with good memories. Like Kåre Bruno's friend Mannfred Sloth, for example."

Krum didn't react.

"And a teacher at the boarding school by the name of Klavs Jeppesen. Not to mention Kyle Basset, whom I interviewed yesterday in Madrid."

Now Krum reacted. "Just a moment," he said, grabbing Carl's arm.

Carl looked disapprovingly at the hand, and Krum swiftly removed it.

"Yes, Mr. Krum," he said. "We're aware that you have a considerable stake in the gang's well-being. For one thing, you're the chairman of the board of Caracas, Pram's private hospital. That alone may be the main reason you can sit here in such gorgeous surroundings." He gestured at the pier's many restaurants and farther out across the Sound.

There was no doubt that in a moment

Bent Krum would be making a few frantic calls.

But then the gang members would be nicely prepared by the time Carl came to visit. Maybe even tenderized.

Assad and Carl walked into Caracas like a couple of narcissists interested in exploring the place before they got a little fat sucked out here and there. The receptionist stopped them, of course, but Carl pushed determinedly on toward what resembled administrative offices.

"Where is Ditlev Pram?" he asked a secretary, when he finally found the sign that read: DITLEV PRAM, CEO.

She already had the phone in her hand to call security when he flashed his police badge and gave her a smile that even Carl's down-to-earth mother would have found irresistible. "Excuse us for barging in, but we have to speak with Ditlev Pram. If you can get him to come here, he'll be pleased and so will we."

She didn't fall for it.

"Unfortunately he's out today," she said authoritatively. "But can I set up an appointment for you? How about the twenty-second of October, at 2:15? Does that work for you?"

So it wasn't Pram they'd be talking to on this trip. A damned shame.

"Thanks. We'll call," Carl said, pulling Assad with him.

She was going to warn Pram, no doubt about it. She'd already stepped out on to the terrace with her mobile. Sharp secretary.

"We were sent down here," Carl said, pointing toward the prep and recovery ward as they passed the receptionist again.

Watchful eyes followed them, and they returned each glance with a friendly nod.

After they'd passed the surgical wing, they stood a moment and kept an eye out in case Pram showed up. Then they headed past a number of private rooms, from most of which classical music came streaming out, and reached the utility wing where less well-preserved people were wearing less prestigious uniforms.

They nodded at the cooks and finally wound up in the laundry, where a lot of very Asian-looking women seemed utterly terrified to see them.

If Pram found out that he had been down here, Carl ventured to guess that these women would disappear within the hour.

On the trip back Assad was very quiet. Only when they reached Klampenborg did he turn to Carl. "Where would you go if you were Kimmie Lassen?"

Carl shrugged. Who could tell? After all, she was pretty unpredictable. Apparently she had truly mastered the art of improvising her way through life. She could be anywhere.

"We both agree that she would have a great interest in Aalbæk not looking for her anymore. I mean, she and the rest of the group weren't exactly the best of chumps."

"Best of chums, Assad. Chums."

"The homicide division says that Aalbæk was at something called Damhuskroen Saturday evening. Did I tell you that?"

"No, but I've heard it."

"And he left with a woman, yes?"

"That, I hadn't heard."

"Which means, Carl, if she killed that Aalbæk, they are probably not so happy, the others in the gang."

That was probably putting it mildly.

"So there's a war between them now."

Carl nodded wearily. The last twenty-four hours were beginning to settle not only into his head, but also his entire nervous system. Suddenly the accelerator seemed impossibly difficult to press down.

"Don't you think she would go back to the house where you found the box so she could get hold of the evidence against the others then?"

Carl nodded slowly. That was definitely one possibility. Another was that he pull over and take a nap.

"Shouldn't we then drive over there?" was Assad's conclusion.

They found the house dark and locked up. Rang the doorbell a few times. Found the telephone number and called. They heard ringing inside, but no one picked up. It seemed rather pointless. In any event Carl couldn't muster the energy to do anything more about it. For God's sake, elderly women were allowed to have a life outside their home's four walls.

"Come on, let's go," Carl said. "You drive so I can take a nap."

Rose was gathering her things when Carl and Assad arrived at headquarters. She wanted to go home, so they wouldn't be seeing her for another two days. She was tired, having worked hard Friday night, Saturday, and part of Sunday. They weren't getting any more for *that* nickel.

Carl felt exactly the same way.

"By the way," she said. "I got hold of the university in Berne, and they found Kirsten-

Marie Lassen's file."

So apparently Rose had made it through her entire list, Carl thought.

"She was a good student, down there in Switzerland. There were no problems, they said. Aside from her losing her boyfriend in a skiing accident, it was a highly successful stay, according to her records."

"A skiing accident?"

"Yeah, it was a little strange, the woman in the office said. The story did get quite a bit of attention. Her boyfriend was a fairly good skier. Not someone who normally skied into an off-piste area with so many crags."

Carl nodded. Dangerous sport.

He met Mona Ibsen in the police headquarters courtyard. She had an enormous bag slung over her shoulder and gave him a look that said no thanks even before he opened his mouth.

"I'm seriously considering taking Hardy home to stay with me," he said, low-key. "But I feel I know too little about how it might affect him psychologically, as well as us at home."

He looked at her with tired eyes. Evidently that's what was needed, because when he followed up by asking her out to dinner so they could discuss what consequences such a big decision could have for everyone involved, the answer was positive.

"Well, I suppose we could," she said, giving him one of those smiles that always hit him so hard in the abdomen. "I'm hungry now, as it happens."

Carl was dumbstruck. Didn't know what to say. He simply looked into her eyes and hoped that his charm would do the trick.

After they'd sat for an hour over their meal, Mona Ibsen gradually began softening up, and his whole being was overcome with such blissful relief and submission that he fell asleep, his head lolling onto his plate with a thump.

Nicely positioned between the tenderloin and the broccoli.

36

On Monday morning the voices were silent.

Kimmie awoke slowly and looked around her old bedroom, confused and empty-headed. For a moment she thought she was thirteen again and had overslept. How many times had she been thrown out of the house with no other nourishment for the day than her father and Kassandra's scolding and door-slamming? How many times had she sat in class in Ordrup with a rumbling stomach, dreaming herself far away?

Then she remembered what had happened the day before. How wide-open and dead Kassandra's eyes had been.

That was when she began humming her old song again.

After she'd dressed, she carried her bundle downstairs, shot a quick glance into the living room at Kassandra's corpse, and sat in the kitchen, whispering menu suggestions to the little one.

She was sitting like that when the telephone rang.

She raised her shoulders slightly and lifted the receiver hesitantly. "Yes?" she said in an affected, hoarse voice. "Kassandra Lassen speaking. To whom do I owe the pleasure?"

She recognized the voice on the first word. It was Ulrik's.

"Yes, my apologies, but you are speaking with Ulrik Dybbøl Jensen. Perhaps you remember me?" he said. "We believe that Kimmie is on her way to see you, Mrs. Lassen. And if that is the case, we ask that you be careful and be sure to let us know the very moment she steps through the door."

Kimmie looked out of the kitchen window. If they came from that direction, they wouldn't see her if she stood behind the door. And the knives in Kassandra's kitchen were exquisite. Could slice through tough as well as tender meat as though it were air.

"I believe you should use the utmost caution if you see her, Mrs. Lassen. But indulge her. Let her in, and keep her there. Then call us. We'll come to your rescue." He laughed cautiously to make it sound plausible, but Kimmie knew better. No man in the world could help Kassandra Lassen if Kimmie showed up. That had already been proven.

He gave her three mobile numbers Kimmie didn't know. Ditlev's, Torsten's, and Ulrik's.

"Thank you ever so much for the warning," she said, and meant it as she wrote down the numbers. "Dare I ask where you are? Would it even be possible for you to get here quickly, if necessary? Wouldn't it be better if I called the police?"

She could just see Ulrik's face. Only a major Wall Street crash could make him look more concerned at that moment. The police! A nasty word in such a situation.

"No, I can't imagine it would," he said. "It can take up to an hour for the police to arrive, you know. That's if they even bother to react. That's how it is nowadays, Mrs. Lassen. It's not like in the old days." He emitted a few mocking sounds designed to convince her of the dubious effectiveness of the police. "We aren't far from you, Mrs. Lassen. Today we're at work, and tomorrow we'll be up in Ejlstrup at Torsten Florin's. We'll be on a hunt near Gribskov Forest, in a grove that belongs to his estate, but we will all have our mobiles on. Call us, no matter when, and we'll be there ten times faster than the police."

"Up in Ejlstrup at Florin's," he'd said. She knew exactly where.

And all three at once. It couldn't get any better.

So there was no need to rush.

She didn't hear the front door open, but she heard the woman calling out.

"Hi, Kassandra, it's me! Time to get up!" the voice boomed, making the windowpanes vibrate and Kimmie freeze.

There were four doors in the hall. One led to the kitchen area, one to the loo where Kimmie was now, one to the dining room, and through that to "My Room" — where Kassandra's stiff body lay — and the fourth door led to the basement.

If the woman valued her life, she would choose any door but the one leading to the dining room and living room.

"Hi!" Kimmie called back, yanking up her knickers.

The steps outside the loo came to a halt, and when she opened the door, Kimmie found herself staring into a pair of confused eyes.

She didn't know the woman. Judging by the blue smock and apron she was busy putting on, she was a home helper or housekeeper.

"Hello. I'm Kirsten-Marie Lassen, Kassandra's daughter," she said, extending her hand. "Unfortunately, Kassandra is ill. She's been admitted to the hospital, so we won't need your services today."

She grabbed the housekeeper's hesitant hand.

There was no doubt that the woman had heard Kimmie's name before. Her handshake was quick and superficial, her eyes watchful. "Charlotte Nielsen," she replied coldly, peeking over Kimmie's shoulder toward the dining room.

"I think my mother will be returning home on Wednesday or Thursday, and I will call you then. In the meantime, I'll look after the house." Kimmie felt the word "mother" burning on her lips. A word she'd never used before for Kassandra, but which seemed necessary now.

"I can see it's a little messy here," said the maid, casting a glance at Kimmie's coat draped over the Louis XVI chair in the hall. "I believe I'll do some tidying up, all the same. I was supposed to be here all day, anyway."

Kimmie blocked the dining room door. "Oh, that's kind of you, but not today." She put a hand on the woman's shoulder and ushered her toward her coat.

When the woman left she didn't say goodbye, but her eyebrows were raised.

Better get rid of the old dear, Kimmie said to herself, vacillating between digging a grave in the garden and cutting up the body. If either she or Kassandra had owned a car, she knew a lake in northern Zealand that surely had room for another corpse.

Then she stopped, listened to the voices, and remembered what day it was.

Why go to all that trouble? they asked. *Tomorrow is the day when everything comes together.*

She was just about to go upstairs when she heard glass shatter in "My Room."

Seconds later she was standing in the living room, matter-of-factly ascertaining that if the housekeeper got her way, she, too, would be lying beside Kassandra in a few seconds with an equally astonished final expression on her face.

The iron bar the woman had smashed the door with whizzed past Kimmie's head. "You killed her, you crazy person! You killed her!" she screamed over and over, tears welling in her eyes.

How in the world could Kassandra, of all the rotten creatures on the planet, have commanded such devotion in a person? It seemed completely unfathomable.

Kimmie backed her way toward the fireplace and the vases. *You want to fight?* she thought. *Well, you've come to the right place.*

Violence and volition go hand in hand. Kimmie knew all about that. They were two of life's elements that she'd mastered to perfection.

She grabbed an art deco brass figurine and weighed it in her hand. Properly thrown, its gracefully poised arms could pinion anything. A human cranium was no match.

So she aimed and threw, and then stared in shock as the woman knocked the statuette aside with the iron bar.

It planted itself deep in the wall and Kimmie retreated backward to the door, hoping to make a dash upstairs to where her pistol was, safety latch off and ready. That would have to be the fate of this proud fool who was challenging her.

But the woman didn't follow her. Kimmie could hear crunching steps on the glass shards and moaning, nothing else.

Kimmie slinked back to the living-room door. Peering through the slightly open door, she saw the woman fall to her knees before Kassandra's lifeless body.

"What has that monster done?" the woman whispered. She might even have been crying.

Kimmie frowned. During the entire time they'd carried out violent assaults on people, she'd never seen signs of grief. Horror and shock, yes, but this soft feeling called grief she only knew from herself.

Kimmie pushed the door farther open to get a better view, and the woman's head shot up as it creaked.

The next instant she charged her, the iron bar raised above her head. Kimmie slammed the door. Totally astonished, she ran up the stairs to get her pistol. She was going to put an end to this. Not kill her, just tie her up and neutralize her. No, she wouldn't shoot her. She simply wouldn't.

Just as Kimmie was running out of steps, the woman behind her screamed and howled and finally flung the iron bar at Kimmie's legs, bringing her facedown on to the landing.

It took only a second to get her bearings, but it was already too late. The stocky young woman stood over her with the iron bar pressed against her throat.

"Kassandra spoke of you often," she said. " 'My little beast,' she called you. Do you think I was pleased to see you in the hall? That I thought your being here meant anything but trouble?"

She put her hand in the pocket of her

smock and pulled out a beaten-up Nokia. "There's a policeman named Carl Mørck. He's looking for you, did you know that? I have his number right here, saved in my directory. He was so kind as to give me his card. Don't you think we should give him the opportunity to come and talk to you?"

Kimmie shook her head. Tried to seem shocked. "But I'm not to blame for Kassandra's death. She choked on her port while we were sitting there talking. It was a horrible accident."

"Really." The woman clearly didn't believe her. Instead she shoved her foot brutally into Kimmie's chest and pressed the end of the bar hard against Kimmie's larynx as she searched for Carl Mørck's number. She almost impaled Kimmie's neck.

"And I bet you did nothing to help her, did you, you slut?" the woman continued. "I'm certain the police would like to hear what you've got to say. But don't think it'll help you. What you've done is written all over your face." She snorted. " 'Admitted to the hospital,' you said. You should have seen yourself when you said it."

She found the number and Kimmie kicked, hitting her squarely in the groin. She kicked again, making the wild-eyed woman lose her grip on the bar and hunch forward as though her back had been broken.

Kimmie didn't say a word as the mobile beeped its way through the digits. She just hacked her heel into the woman's calf and slapped the phone from her hand so it smashed against the wall. Then she lurched back and freed herself of the iron bar, which now lay slack in the woman's hand. Finally Kimmie stood up and grabbed the bar.

It had taken less than five seconds to restore the balance.

Kimmie caught her breath for a moment as the woman tried to pull herself up, her face knotted in anger.

"I won't hurt you," Kimmie said. "I'm going to tie you to a chair, that's all."

But the woman shook her head and snuck a hand behind her until she got hold of the banister. Clearly she was trying to find something to push off from. Her eyes darted back and forth. She was far from defeated.

Then, with outstretched arms, she lunged for Kimmie's throat, digging in her nails. Kimmie backed up against the stairway wall and brought one knee up as a wedge, giving her just enough leverage to shove the woman backward until half of her body swayed over the banister, five yards above the hallway's stone floor.

Kimmie screamed for her to stop resisting, but she wouldn't, so Kimmie reared back and head-butted her. Everything went black for a moment before flashes of light exploded in her brain.

Then she opened her eyes and leaned over the banister.

The woman lay on the marble floor as if crucified, arms outstretched and legs crossed. Completely still and very, very dead.

For ten minutes she sat on the chair in the hall, observing the twisted, dead body. For the first time in her life she saw a victim for precisely what it was: a human being who had possessed a will of its own and the right to live. It surprised her that she had never had this feeling before. She didn't like it at all. The voices upbraided her for having thoughts like these.

Then the doorbell rang. She heard them talking. Two men who seemed impatient. They rattled the door and a moment later the telephone rang.

If they walk around the house they'll see the smashed door. Get ready to run upstairs for the pistol, she urged herself. *No, do it now.*

She bounded up the stairs in just a few soundless steps, found the pistol, and returned to the landing with the silencer aimed at the front door. If the men came in, they wouldn't be leaving again.

But leave they did. Through the window on the landing she could just get a glimpse of them walking to their car.

A tall man with a long stride and a small, dark man shuffling along at his side.

37

The horrible conclusion to the previous evening — Mona Ibsen laughing uncontrollably at the shocked expression on Carl's onion-smothered face — was still festering in him. It was as embarrassing as having the runs the first time you used a potential lover's bathroom.

Oh God, how do I get beyond this? he thought, lighting a morning cigarette.

Then he began to concentrate. Maybe today was the day he could give the prosecutors the final, decisive information they needed to issue an arrest order. The earring from Lindelse Cove, some of the other contents of the box — there was certainly enough to go on. If nothing else, there was the connection between Aalbæk and Pram, and therefore the rest of the gang. Carl didn't care what grounds he used for getting them into the interrogation room. Once he had them there, he'd make one of them talk about what mattered.

What had begun as a double homicide investigation might well bring to light other crimes. Perhaps even murders.

All he needed was a direct confrontation with the gang members. Be able to ask them the questions that would make them panic, maybe even cause a rift in their friendship. And if he couldn't do that with them in custody, it would have to happen on their own turf.

The hardest nut to crack was finding the weakest link. Whom should he focus his attack on first? Of course Bjarne Thøgersen was the most obvious choice, but years in prison had taught him how to keep his mouth shut. Besides, he had shielded himself by being behind bars. Thøgersen couldn't be made to talk to Carl about something he had already been convicted of. If they wanted anything out of him, they would need airtight evidence of new crimes.

So no, he couldn't be the first. Who then? Torsten Florin, Ulrik Dybbøl Jensen, or Ditlev Pram? Which of the three would be easiest to get under the skin of?

To answer this question properly he would first have to have met each of them personally, but his intuition told him this wouldn't be easy. Yesterday's botched visit to Pram's private hospital demonstrated as much. Because of course Pram had been aware of their presence from the very first moment they had shown up at the hospital. Maybe he had been close by, maybe not. Either way, he had known they were there.

And he had stayed away.

No, if Carl were to get one of these men to talk, he would have to take them by surprise. That was why he and Assad were getting such an early start that morning.

Torsten Florin would be the first, and that choice wasn't entirely coincidental. In many ways he seemed literally the weakest, with his slender figure and effeminate profession. His press releases on fashion also gave the impression of there being something beneath the surface that was vulnerable. He seemed to stand out from the others.

In two minutes Carl would pick up Assad at the Triangle, and hopefully in half an hour they would be at Florin's estate in Ejlstrup for a most inconvenient surprise visit.

"I assembled all the information about the ones in the group," Assad said from the passenger seat. "Here's Torsten Florin's file then." He pulled a case file from his bag as they drove out of town on the Lyngby motorway.

"His house I think looks like a fortress," Assad went on. "He has a super-enormous metal gate that blocks the road up to the estate. I've read that when he has parties, people's cars are let in one at a time then. And that's actually true."

Carl turned his head to look at the color printout Assad held up. It was difficult to get much from it since he also needed to keep his eye on the narrow road that wound through Gribskov.

"Have a look at this, Carl. You can see really well everything in the aerial photograph. Here is Florin's estate. Apart from the old building where he lives, and that wooden house there," he tapped a spot on the map, "everything was built in 1992, including this gigantic building and all the tiny houses behind it."

It actually looked rather strange.

"Are those houses all the way inside Gribskov? Did he get permission to build in the forest?" Carl asked.

"No, they're not in the forest. Between Gribskov and his little patch of woods here there is a fire . . . a fire . . . ? What's this kind of thing called, Carl?"

"A firebreak?"

He felt Assad looking at him, sensed his puzzlement. "Well, in any case you can clearly see it in the aerial photo. Have a look. It's a narrow, brown strip. And then he has put up a fence around his property — the lake and hills and all the rest."

"I wonder why he did that? Is he afraid of paparazzi or what?"

"It has something to do with him being a hunter."

"Yes, of course. He doesn't want the animals on his land to escape into the state forest. I know the type." Up in Vendsyssel where Carl was from, people made fun of folks who did that sort of thing. But in northern Zealand this was apparently not the case.

They had reached a point where the landscape opened up, first clearings in the forest and then far-reaching fields where pale brown wheat stubs still poked from the ground.

"Can you see the Swiss chalet over there, Assad?" He pointed at a low-lying house to their right, not waiting for Assad to respond. One couldn't miss it, down there in the glacier-carved valley. "Behind it is Kagerup Station. One time we found a little girl there we thought was dead. She had hidden in a sawmill because she was afraid of the dog her father had brought home."

Carl shook his head. But *was* that really

599

the reason? Suddenly it sounded so wrong.

"Turn here, Carl," Assad said. He pointed at a road sign for Mårum. "Up there at the tophill we need to turn right. There's a couple of hundred yards from there to the gate. Do I call him up first then?"

Carl shook his head. No fucking way. Florin wasn't going to get the chance to vanish, just like Ditlev Pram did the day before.

It was correct that Torsten Florin had fenced in his property good and proper. The name DUEHOLT stood out in oversize, brass letters from a granite boulder next to the cast-iron gate that rose above the windbreak.

Carl leaned close to the intercom that was attached to a post at window height. "This is Deputy Detective Superintendent Mørck," he said. "I spoke to your solicitor, Bent Krum, yesterday. We would like to put a few questions to Torsten Florin. It should only take a minute."

At least two minutes passed before the gate opened.

On the other side of the hedge the landscape spread out. To the right, lakes and rolling hills dotted a meadow that was surprisingly lush, given the time of year. Farther down, scattered groves became forest, and in the distance, Gribskov's enormous colonnade of century-old oak trees was visible, the crowns nearly leafless.

This is a hell of a lot of land, Carl thought. *Given the price of an acre up here, this place would have to be worth millions.*

When they reached the estate that was nestled near the forest, the impression of tremendous wealth was confirmed. Dueholt Manor itself boasted a tasteful alliance of carefully restored cornices and glazed, black-tiled roofs. Several atriums had been added, each one probably facing a point of the compass, and the grounds and driveway were so well maintained as to put the royal gardeners to shame.

Behind the manor was a red wooden building that was probably listed as an architectural treasure. In any case, with at least a couple of hundred years' history, it stood out from the rest. It was undeniably quite a contrast to the massive, yet quite attractive, steel construction towering behind it. All glass and glittering metal, just like the Orangery in Madrid that Carl had seen on a poster in the airport.

Ejlstrup's own Crystal Palace.

A few small houses were clustered near the edge of the forest, like an entire little village with miniature gardens and verandas, surrounded by plots of plowed land, probably for growing vegetables. There were still lots of leeks and green cabbages.

Jesus Christ, this place is incredible, Carl thought.

"Wow, this is really something," Assad said.

They didn't see a single soul in this landscape until they rang the doorbell and Torsten Florin, in person, opened up.

Carl extended his hand and introduced himself, but Florin saw only Assad and stood like a block of granite, blocking the entrance to his home.

Behind him, stairs wound their way up through the hall in an orgy of paintings and chandeliers. Rather vulgar for a man who made his living selling style.

"We'd like to speak to you about a few incidents we might be able to connect Kimmie Lassen to. Perhaps you can help us?"

"Which incidents?" Florin asked drily.

"Finn Aalbæk's murder on Saturday night. We know Ditlev Pram and Aalbæk had a number of conversations. We also know Aalbæk was looking for Kimmie. Did one of you hire him? And if so, why?"

"I've heard the name a few times over the course of the last few days, but otherwise I don't know anything about this Finn Aalbæk. If Ditlev had conversations with him, then he's the one I suggest you speak to. Good-bye, gentlemen."

Carl stuck his foot in the door. "Excuse me a moment. There was also an assault on a couple on Langeland and an attack on Kåre Bruno at Bellahøj back in the late eighties, both of which are connected to Kimmie Lassen. Most likely three murders, actually."

Florin blinked rapidly several times, but his visage was like stone. "I can't help you. If you want to speak with anyone, then speak with Kimmie Lassen."

"Perhaps you know her whereabouts?"

He shook his head, an odd expression on his face. Carl had seen his share of odd expressions, but he didn't understand what this one meant.

"You're certain?" he asked.

"Absolutely. I haven't seen Kirsten-Marie since 1996."

"We have a lot of evidence connecting her to these events."

"Yes, my solicitor told me. Neither he nor I know anything about the cases you're talking about. I must ask you to leave. I'm busy today. Remember a warrant if you come by another day."

His smile was incredibly provocative, and Carl pressed him with additional questions. But Torsten Florin moved aside and three dark-skinned men who must have been waiting behind the door stepped forward.

Two minutes later Carl and Assad were back in their car. Threatened with death and destruction, the media, the public prosecutor, and the whole kit and caboodle.

If Carl had previously thought Torsten was weak, then it was high time he considered revising his view.

38

On this morning, the day of the fox hunt, Torsten Florin had woken as usual to classical music and the light pattering of feet that announced the arrival of the young black woman, bare-chested and with outstretched hands, who stood before him now. As always, she was holding the silver tray. Her smile was stiff and feigned, but Torsten Florin didn't care. He had no use for her affection or devotion. He needed order in his life, and order was created when daily rituals were followed to the letter. That's how he'd lived for eleven years now, and that's how he planned to continue. For some wealthy people rituals were a way of marketing themselves. Torsten used them to survive daily life.

He took the napkin from the tray, enjoying its scent, laid it on his chest and received the plate on which lay four chicken hearts, freshly slaughtered organs without which he remained convinced he would waste away.

He ate the first heart in one bite and prayed for a successful hunt. Then he polished off the remaining three and had his face and hands dried with a camphor-scented cloth, a procedure the woman executed with practiced hands.

Then he waved the woman and her husband — who'd been on guard duty all night — out of the room and savored the emerging day's first rays of sun as they illuminated the forest. In a few hours it would begin. At nine o'clock the pack of hunters would be ready. This time they weren't hunting their prey at sun-up; the animal was too sly and crazed for that. It would have to be done in broad daylight.

He imagined how the rabies and survival instinct would rage within the fox when they set it loose. How easily it would be able to stick close to the ground and wait for the right moment when the beaters were close. A single lunge for the groin and it would be gone again.

But Torsten knew his Somalis; they wouldn't let the fox get that close to them. He was more concerned for the huntsmen. Well, *concerned* was probably the wrong word. Most of them were shrewd enough people who had partaken in his games often before, who burned with a desire to live on the edge. All of them influential men who'd made their mark. Men whose ideas were greater and more far-reaching than those of the man on the street. That's why they were here today. They were folk of the right mold. No, he wasn't so concerned for them, he was more absorbed by a nagging uneasiness.

If it hadn't been for Kimmie and that fucking cop who'd approached Bent Krum, and if those cases that should've been long forgotten hadn't been reopened — like the assaults on Langeland and on Kyle Basset and Kåre Bruno — this day would have been perfect.

These were thoughts he would be revising a few hours later.

How the hell was it that this jumped-up policeman who suddenly appeared on his doorstep could actually know about these things?

He stood inside the glass hall, surrounded by the din of the animals, and stared at the fox as the Somalis pulled its cage from the corner. Its eyes were wild, and it kept lunging at the bars, gnawing at them as though they were living flesh. The thought of these teeth and the deadly bacteria that was slowly killing the animal sent a shiver down Torsten's spine.

To hell with the police, to hell with Kimmie and all other trivialities in this world. Stepping toward the edge of eternity, which was what setting the animal free in their midst would represent, made everything else seem insignificant.

"You'll soon be meeting your fate, Fantastic Mr. Fox," he said, launching his fist against the cage.

He glanced around the hall. It was a sight fit for the gods. More than a hundred cages, containing every imaginable animal. The last addition had been the predator's cage from Nautilus. It had been placed on the floor, and inside it, scowling, was an enraged hyena with a crooked back. It would soon take the fox's spot in the corner, along with the other exotic quarry. The hunting expeditions from now until Christmas had already been arranged. He had things under control.

He heard the cars glide into the courtyard and turned, smiling, toward the hall entrance.

Ulrik and Ditlev had arrived, on time as usual. Yet another detail that separated the sheep from the goats.

Ten minutes later they were down in the

shooting tunnel with crossbows and watchful eyes. Ulrik was in a masochistic mood, quivering blissfully after their discussion about Kimmie and her uncertain whereabouts. Maybe he had taken one line too many of the white powder that morning. Ditlev, on the other hand, was clear-headed, with especially alert eyes. The crossbow lay in his arms like an organic extension of himself.

"Yes, thank you, I slept wonderfully last night. Kimmie and everyone else can bring it on," he said, in answer to Torsten's question. "I'm ready for anything."

"That's good," Torsten replied. He wasn't about to ruin his hunting companions' high spirits by telling them about Deputy Detective Superintendent Mørck and his digging around in the past. That could wait until after they'd shot a practice round. "I'm glad you're ready for anything. I think you're going to need to be."

39

They'd been sitting in the car for a few minutes by the side of the road, discussing their meeting with Torsten Florin. Assad thought they ought to drive back and reveal what they'd found in Kimmie's metal box. He believed it would deflate Florin's self-confidence, but Carl was in total disagreement. They would not mention the box until they had an arrest warrant.

This elicited some grumbling from Assad. Contrary to popular perception, patience apparently wasn't all that widespread in the desert regions he'd trod in his childhood sandals.

Carl looked down the road and saw two vehicles driving toward them at a speed well over the limit. They were four-wheel-drives with tinted windows — the kind of vehicle that teenage boys only came close to when staring longingly at glossy brochures.

"I'll be damned!" he shouted when the

lead car roared past. He started the engine and swung around behind the second one.

When they reached the road branching off toward Dueholt, they were only twenty yards behind.

"I'm certain I caught a glimpse of Ditlev Pram in the lead car. Did you see who was in the rear one, Assad?" he asked, after the two vehicles had turned down the gravel road to Florin's estate.

"No, but I've taken down the registration numbers. I'll check them now."

Carl rubbed his face. Imagine if the two men were on their way to meet at Florin's at this moment. If it were really them, when would he ever have such an opportunity to observe all three together?

And if he *did* get the chance, what would he be able to get out of it?

It only took a moment before Assad had the information from the motor vehicle office.

"The lead car is registered as belonging to one Thelma Pram," he said.

Bingo.

"And the rear car belongs to UDJ Stock Analysts."

Bingo again.

"So the flock is gathered," Carl said, checking his watch. It wasn't yet eight in the morning. What the devil were they up to?

"I think we should keep an eye on them, Carl."

"What do you mean?"

"Oh, you know. Enter the grounds and see what they're doing then."

Carl shook his head. Sometimes he was a tad too creative, this little man.

"You heard Florin," he said as Assad sat there, nodding with big eyes. "We need a warrant, and we won't get that on the basis of the existing evidence."

"No, but can't we get one if we learn more?"

"Of course. But we won't find anything out by sneaking around in there. We don't have a warrant for that either, Assad. We don't have the authority."

"What if they were the ones who killed Aalbæk to cover the tracks after them?"

"What tracks? It's not illegal to hire someone to shadow others."

"No, but what if Aalbæk actually found Kimmie and those men are holding her hostage in there right now? It's a distinct possibility. Isn't that the kind of word you like to use? Now Aalbæk is dead, so they are the only ones who know if they've caught her. She is your most important witness, Carl."

Carl could see he was building up to something, and then it came.

"What if they're about to kill her right now? We've got to get in there."

Carl exhaled heavily. It was simply too many questions.

The man was right, of course; and yet he wasn't.

They parked the car on Ny Mårumvej near the Duemose whistle-stop and walked from the Gribskov train tracks along the paths that bordered the forest until they reached the firebreak. From where they stood, they could see directly across the marsh and up along part of Torsten Florin's woods. They were dense and lush. Way off in the distance, up the hill, the entrance gate was just visible, so that was one direction they wouldn't be heading in. They had seen all the surveillance cameras.

More interesting was the courtyard, where the two enormous four-wheel-drives were parked. From there, their path was clear in all directions.

"I think there are cameras everywhere in the firebreak, Carl," Assad said. "If we want to cross it, we have to go this way."

He pointed at a bog hole where the fence

had sunk so far down it was pretty much invisible. It was the only spot where they could make it over the fence without being detected.

Not exactly encouraging.

Afterward they had to lie on the ground for half an hour with soaking wet, muddy trousers and eyes peeled, before the three men came into view in the courtyard. Behind them walked a couple of lean black men carrying objects that resembled hunting bows or something along those lines. Sounds of conversation carried almost all the way to the hedge where Carl and Assad lay. Toneless voices, partially absorbed by the distance and the slight breeze that swirled coolly around them.

Then the three men disappeared into the main house and the black men continued on toward the small red houses.

Ten minutes later, several more black men appeared and then disappeared into the big hall. A few minutes after that they came out again, bearing a cage that they lifted onto the back of a pickup. Then some climbed into the cab and others onto the flatbed beside the cage, and drove off into the woods.

"If we're doing this, it's got to be now," Carl said, pulling a mildly protesting Assad behind him along the hedge and directly toward the small houses. They heard people inside. Chatter in a foreign language. Babies crying and shouts from older children. It was an entire little society.

They sneaked past the first house and noticed a sign on the door with many exotic-sounding names on it.

"Over there, too," Assad whispered, pointing at a door sign on the next house. "Do you think actually he's keeping slaves?"

Probably not, but it certainly seemed to be something like that. It resembled an African village in the middle of the estate. Or shacks lying in the shadow of some giant Southern-state mansion before the American Civil War.

They heard a dog bark not far away.

"What if he has dogs running loose on the grounds?" Assad whispered worriedly, as if they had already heard him.

Carl glanced at his partner. *Easy now*, his face said. If there was anything he'd learned on the plowed fields of Vendsyssel, it was that unless ten angry fighting dogs were coming at you, the human was in charge. One, well-timed kick usually established the pecking order. If only they didn't make such a bloody ruckus.

They ran across the open stretch by the

courtyard and saw they had a good chance of getting behind the main house that way.

Twenty seconds later they stood with their faces pressed flat against the manor's windows, behind which there was absolutely nothing going on. What they saw resembled a ·conventional office with mahogany furnishings. There were rows of hunting trophies on the shelves. Nothing that suggested anything untoward.

They turned around. If there were any irregularities in the vicinity, they would have to find them fast.

"Did you see there?" Assad whispered, pointing at a large cylinder that extended from the massive glass hall a good way into the forest. It was at least fifty yards long.

What the hell is it? Carl thought.

"Come on," he said. "Let's check it out."

The face Assad made when they walked into the hall ought to have been immortalized. Carl felt something similar. If Nautilus was a shocking sight for animal lovers, then this was ten times worse. Cage after cage after cage containing frightened animals. Bloody, flayed hides in every size hung to dry on the walls. Everything from hamsters to calves. Fierce fighting dogs were barking, probably the ones they'd heard earlier. There were big, lizardlike beasts and hissing minks. House pets and exotic animals in one great menagerie.

But this was anything but Noah's Ark. It was the opposite. No animal would leave this place alive — that much was instantly obvious.

Carl recognized the cage from Nautilus standing in the middle of the hall, a growling hyena inside. A large ape screamed in the corner, a warthog grunted, and sheep baa'd.

"Do you think Kimmie could be in here then?" Assad asked, walking a few paces farther into the hall.

Carl's eyes wandered along the cages. Most of them were too small to house a human.

"What about here?" Assad said, pointing at a row of deep freezers that were humming in one of the side passageways. He opened the first one.

"Ugh!" he exclaimed, with visible shivers of disgust.

Carl stared into the freezer. A stack of flayed animals stared back up at him, empty-eyed.

"It's the same in all these." Assad opened and closed lid after lid.

"I would imagine they're mostly used to

feed the animals," Carl said, sizing up the hyena. Any kind of flesh would disappear in no time down the throat of a hungry creature like that. A gruesome thought.

It took five minutes for them to confirm that there were no humans in the remaining cages.

"Look, Carl," Assad said, pointing inside the huge pipe they had seen from the outside. "It's a shooting range."

It was true. If the police had such a thing at headquarters, people would be lining up to use it all day long. With air nozzles and everything, it was state-of-the-art.

"I don't think you should go in there," Carl warned, when Assad headed into the cylinder. "If someone comes we'll have no place to hide."

But Assad wasn't listening. He had his sights set on the large targets at the far end.

"What is this then, Carl?" he called out, beside one of the targets.

Carl glanced over his shoulder. There was no cause for alarm behind him, so he went to see what Assad was talking about.

"Is that an arrow, or what?" his partner wanted to know, indicating a metal rod that had bored its way through the center of the target.

"Yes," Carl said. "It's a bolt. The kind

used with crossbows."

Assad looked at him, confused. "What did you say just there, Carl? With what? Crossbows?"

Carl sighed. "A crossbow is a bow that's loaded in a special way. It shoots with tremendous force."

"OK. I can see that. And it's precise, Carl?"

"Yes, very precise."

When they turned around, they knew they'd walked into a trap.

Down at the other end stood Torsten Florin, his legs spread, and behind him Ulrik Dybbøl Jensen, and Ditlev Pram. Pram was holding a loaded crossbow, aimed directly at them.

You've got to be kidding me, Carl thought. He shouted: "Get behind the targets, Assad! *Now!*"

He drew his pistol from his shoulder holster in one fluid movement and aimed it at the group of men at the same instant Ditlev fired a bolt.

Carl heard Assad hurl himself behind a target, just as the bolt rammed Carl's right shoulder and his pistol hit the gravel.

Strangely, it didn't hurt. All he knew was that he'd been flung backward half a yard and was now pinned to one of the targets, with only the bolt's fletching visible in his bleeding wound.

"Gentlemen," Florin said, "why are you putting us in this situation? What are we going to do with you?"

Carl tried to force his beating heart into a calmer rhythm. They had pulled the bolt out and sprayed a solution into the wound, which nearly made him faint, but at least it stopped the bleeding, more or less.

It was a dire situation. The three men were not to be swayed.

Meanwhile, Assad was fuming at how they'd been forced back into the hall and down on to the floor with their backs against one of the cages.

"Don't you realize what happens when you do something like this to police officers in action?" he yelled.

Carl carefully nudged Assad's foot. It quietened him for a moment.

"It's very simple," Carl said, each word pounding throughout his upper body. "You let us go now. Then we'll see what happens next. You don't have anything to gain by threatening us or holding us hostage."

"I see!" It was Pram. He still held the crossbow ready in his hand. If only he would point it the other way. "We're not stupid. We know you suspect us of having committed murder. You've named several incidents. You've contacted our solicitor. You've found a connection between Finn Aalbæk and me. You think you know everything about us, and suddenly some so-called truth emerges." He came closer and positioned his leather boots in front of Carl's feet. "But that truth involves more than just us three. If you're lucky enough to convince people that your suspicions are correct, thousands will lose their livelihood. Nothing's simple, Carl Mørck."

He pointed round the hall. "A vast number of assets will be frozen. Neither we nor anyone else wants that. So I repeat Torsten's question: what are we to do with you?"

"We have to make it very clean," said the big man, Ulrik Dybbøl Jensen, in a quivering voice, his pupils enormous. There was no mistaking what he meant. But Torsten Florin was hesitating, Carl could tell. Hesitating and thinking.

"How about we give each of you a million kroner and let you go? Just like that. As soon as you drop the case, the money's yours. What do you say?"

Of course they had to say yes. What else could they do? The alternative certainly wasn't much fun to think about.

Carl looked over at Assad, who nodded. Wise man.

"And you, Mørck? Are you as amenable as Mustafa here?" asked Florin.

Carl gave him a hard look. Then he, too, nodded.

"But I am sensing that it's not enough. So we'll double the amount. Two million to each of you for your silence. We'll do it discreetly. Are we agreed?"

They both nodded.

"There's just one thing I need to have clarified. I want an honest answer. I'll know if you're lying, and then there will be no deal. You got it?"

He didn't wait for an answer. "Why did you mention a couple on Langeland to me this morning? Kåre Bruno I can understand, but the couple? What does that have to do with us?"

"Meticulous investigation," Carl said. "We have a man at headquarters who's followed cases like this for years."

"That has nothing to do with us," asserted Florin.

"You wanted an honest answer. Meticulous investigation *is* the answer," repeated Carl. "The character of the assault, the location, the method, the time frame. It all fits with you."

It was at this point that the gang remembered what it was capable of.

"Answer me!" Ditlev Pram shouted, slamming the shaft of the crossbow into Carl's wound.

He didn't even manage to scream before his throat contracted in pain. Then Ditlev struck again. And again.

"Answer me! Exactly why do you think we're connected to the assault on Langeland?" Pram yelled.

He was about to hit Carl even harder when Assad put a stop to it.

"Kimmie had the one earring," he exclaimed. "It matched the other one found on Langeland. She had it in a box, in which there were other things from your assaults. I guess you know that."

If Carl had had any strength left in his body he would have made it crystal clear to Assad to keep his mouth shut.

Now it was too late.

They both recognized it in Florin's face at the same moment. Everything the three men feared had suddenly become reality. There was evidence against them. Concrete evidence.

"I take it there are others at police headquarters who know of this box? Where is it now?"

Carl said nothing. He just looked around.

From where they sat, it was about ten yards to the gate. From there to the edge of the woods was at least an additional fifty yards. Through the woods was almost another mile, and behind them loomed Gribskov Forest. That would be the best hiding place. But it was just too far away, and there was nothing, absolutely nothing, around them that could serve as a weapon. Two men with crossbows stood over them. What could they do?

Absolutely nothing.

"We've got to do it here and now, and do it clean," Dybbøl Jensen sniffled. "I'll say it again: we can't trust these two. They aren't like the others we bought off."

At this Pram and Florin's heads turned slowly toward their friend. *Not smart to let that slip out,* their faces clearly said.

As the three men conferred, Assad and Carl exchanged glances. Assad apologized, and Carl forgave him. What the hell did it matter if Assad made a little mistake when their deaths were being decided at this very moment by three thoroughly unscrupulous men?

"OK, we'll do it, but we don't have much time. The others will be here in five minutes," Florin said.

And with no further ado, Dybbøl Jensen and Pram threw themselves at Carl, while Florin covered them at a few yards' distance with his crossbow. Carl was taken totally unawares by their efficiency.

They placed gaffer tape over his mouth, pulled his hands behind his back, and taped them, too. Then they yanked his head back and stretched the tape over his eyes. He twisted a bit so the tape caught on his eyelids and pulled them up a fraction. It was through this narrow slit that he saw how Assad began protesting violently a moment later, kicking and punching so one of the men fell to the ground with a hard thump. It was Dybbøl Jensen, he could see, now completely paralyzed by a karate chop to the neck. Florin tossed aside his crossbow and came to Ulrik's aid. And while the two were busy subduing Assad, Carl got up and began running toward the light coming from the entrance.

The way he was bound, he wouldn't have been able to help Assad in a fight. He could only help by escaping.

He heard them shouting to one another that he wouldn't get very far. That their work crew would catch him and bring him back. To share the same fate as Assad. Inside the hyena cage.

"Look forward to the hyena!" they yelled.

They're insane, Carl thought dizzily as he tried to orient himself through the narrow slit of light.

Then he heard the cars up at the main gate. There were a lot of them.

If the people in the cars were just like the ones in the hall, he was done for.

40

As soon as the train lumbered out of the station and the sound from the railway sleepers settled into a regular rhythm, the voices in Kimmie's head started up. Not noisy and insistent, but persevering and self-assured. By now she was used to it.

The train was streamlined. Not at all like the old, red Gribskov "rail bus" that had brought her and Bjarne up here last time, many years ago. Much had changed.

Those had been wild times. They had drunk, snorted, and partied all day, from the moment the landscape changed as Torsten had proudly showed them around his new acquisition — forest, marshland, lakes, and fields. The perfect spot for a hunter. So long as one made sure wounded game didn't cross into state land, it simply couldn't get any better.

They had laughed at him, her and Bjarne. To them, nothing was more comical than the thought of a man trudging about in green, laced, rubber boots. But Torsten didn't notice. The forest was his, and here he ruled over every kind of wild creature in the Danish countryside worth shooting.

For a couple of hours they had hunted and killed roe deer and pheasants and finally a raccoon she herself had procured for him at Nautilus. A gesture he'd appreciated. And afterward they had followed the ritual and watched *A Clockwork Orange* in Torsten's home theater. An average, mind-numbing day where too much coke and even more alcohol made them sluggish and sapped them of the energy needed to go out and find new victims.

That turned out to be the first and only time she ever went to Torsten's. She remembered it as if it were yesterday; the voices made sure of that.

They're all there today, Kimmie, you realize that? This is your chance. The opportunity has arrived, they chanted incessantly.

For a moment she studied her fellow passengers. Then she slipped her hand into her duffel bag and touched the hand grenade, the pistol and the silencer, the shoulder bag, and her beloved bundle. Everything she needed was in that canvas bag.

■ ■ ■ ■

At the Duemose whistle-stop she waited until the other early-morning passengers had been picked up or had ridden away on their bicycles that were parked by the red shelter.

One motorist asked her if she wanted a lift, but she simply smiled. A smile could also be used that way.

When the platform was clear and the road was as deserted as before they'd arrived, she walked to the end of the platform, hopped down onto the gravel, and continued along the tracks by the edge of the forest until she found a place where she could leave her duffel bag.

Then she packed her shoulder bag, slung the strap over her head, tucked her jeans into her socks, and stowed the larger bag behind a bush.

"Mummy will be back, my love, don't be afraid," she said, as the voices implored her to pick up her pace.

The public forest was easy to navigate. Just a few yards up the road, past a small business establishment, and she was already on one of the paths that would lead her to the rear of Torsten's property.

She had plenty of time, in spite of the voices telling her otherwise. She raised her eyes to catch a glimpse of the last splatters of color hanging in the branches, and sucked in the autumn air, taking in all the season's strength and beauty.

It had been years since she'd been able to do that. So many years.

When she reached the firebreak, she could tell it had been widened since she'd been there. She lay down at the edge of the forest and looked across the cleared area toward the fence that separated Torsten's forest from the public one. Having lived on Copenhagen's streets for so long she was well aware of how inconspicuous surveillance cameras could be. She scanned the trees and the fence and took her time finding out where they were. From where she was she could see four cameras. Two that were stationary and two that rotated back and forth continuously on a 180-degree axis. One of the stationary cameras was aimed directly at her.

She retreated into the thicket and considered her situation.

The firebreak itself was nine or ten yards wide. The grass was freshly mown, so the space was quite open and level. She looked in both directions. It was the same everywhere. There was only one way to get over the firebreak undetected, and that wasn't by crossing the grass.

It was from tree to tree. Branch to branch.

She thought hard. The oak tree on her side of the clearing was taller than the beech on the other side. Sturdy, gnarled branches that stretched five or six yards across the clearing, compared to the beech's smaller, skinnier branches. If she leaped from the tall tree to the low one, the drop was a couple of yards, but at the same time she would have to throw her body forward to land closer to the trunk of the beech tree. Otherwise the branches wouldn't support her.

Kimmie had never been good at trees. Her mother had forbidden her to play wherever she risked getting her clothes dirty, and when her mother had gone, so too had her desire to climb trees.

It was a fine specimen, this huge oak. Crooked branches that jutted out a good distance, and the bark was rough. Actually quite easy to climb.

It was a good feeling. "You'll have to try it, too, sometime, Mille," she said softly, and began pulling herself up.

Not until she was sitting in the tree did she begin to have second thoughts. The distance to the ground was suddenly so real, the leap over to the beech's smooth branches seemed daunting. Could she really do it? From the ground it had looked easy, but not from here. If she fell, she was done for. She would break bones. They would see her on the surveillance cameras. They would capture her, and then everything would be out of her hands. She knew them. Revenge would then be theirs, not hers.

So she sat for a while, trying to calculate how to make her jump. Then she rose carefully, her arms behind her, clinging to the oak's branches.

When she sprang, she knew she had made too strong a takeoff. Knew it as she flew through the air and watched the tree trunk beneath her come far too close. She felt one of her fingers breaking in her attempt to avoid the collision, but her reflexes took over. Even if one finger didn't work, she had nine others that did. She would have to deal with the pain later. As she clung to the tree, she noted that beeches have fewer branches on the lower portion of their trunk than oaks.

She climbed down the first bit, then clutched at the lowest branch, estimating that she still had three or four yards before she reached the ground. Then she slung herself out across the branch and hung there a moment as the broken finger did its own thing. She gripped the branch closest to the trunk, wrapped an arm around it as well as she could, and then let go. Scars and knots in the tree bloodied her forearms and neck as she slid to the ground.

Examining her twisted finger, she yanked it back in place, sending waves of pain through her entire body. But Kimmie remained silent. She would have shot it off, if necessary.

Then she wiped the blood from her neck and moved into the forest shadows on the far side of the fence.

The vegetation was mixed. She remembered that from their previous hunt. Evergreens in clusters, small clearings with newly planted deciduous trees, and long stretches of birch, brambles, beech, and scattered oaks.

It smelled strongly of rotting leaves. More than a decade spent in the asphalt jungle made one extra sensitive to these kinds of scents.

The voices now demanded that she hurry up and finish the job. And that the confrontation be on her terms. But Kimmie didn't listen. She knew she had time enough. When Torsten, Ulrik, and Ditlev played these gory games, they never finished until they were satiated. And that didn't happen quickly.

"I'm walking along the edge of the forest and the firebreak," she said aloud, so the voices would back off. "It's a longer route, but we'll still reach the estate."

That was how she came to see the dark-skinned men standing around, facing the woods and waiting, and how she saw the cage with the enraged animal. It was how she noticed the leather leggings the men wore over their trousers, all the way up to the groin.

It was why she ducked back into the forest to see how things would develop.

She was in the land of the hunter.

41

He ran with his head angled backward, catching glimpses of the ground beneath him in flickering alternation between dry leaves and treacherous branches. Far behind him he could hear Assad's enraged protests, until finally everything grew quiet.

He slowed down. Struggled with the gaffer tape on his back, his nostrils dry from gasping for breath. He craned his neck to try to see.

He had to get the tape removed from his eyes. Before anything else. In a short while they would be coming at him from every direction. The hunters from up by the estate, the beaters from God knows where. He turned his body all the way round and saw only trees and more trees through the narrow slit in the tape. Then he ran again for a few seconds before a low-hanging branch knocked him on the head and flung him backward.

"Damn it," he muttered. God fucking damn it.

He stood up with difficulty and felt around for a branch on the tree, which was broken at shoulder height. Then he moved up to the trunk, positioned himself so the branch stump got under the gaffer tape right next to his nostril, and forced his body steadily downward. This caused the tape to tighten around his neck, but it didn't get it away from his eyes. The tape was stuck too tightly to his eyelids.

He pulled his head downward again, trying to keep his eyes closed, but could feel how his eyelids once more stuck to the tape, turning the whites of his eyes outward.

"Fuck, fuck, fuck!" he cursed, and began swinging his head from side to side as the branch scratched one of his eyelids.

Then he heard the beaters' cries for the first time. They weren't as far away as he'd hoped. Maybe only a few hundred yards; inside these woods it was hard to judge. He raised his head, watched the stump release the gaffer tape, and noticed he could now see more or less freely with the one eye.

The dense forest spread out before him. The light fell unevenly and, truth be told, he had no idea which direction he was facing. That alone made him realize it could soon be all over for Carl Mørck.

The initial shots came after Carl had gotten past the first clearing, and now the beaters were so close that he was forced to lie on the ground. As far as he could tell, the firebreak was just ahead and behind that were the paths through the state forest. He was no more than seven or eight hundred yards, as the crow flies, from where his car was parked, but what use was that when he didn't know what direction it was in?

He saw birds flap their wings and scatter above the treetops, heard the underbrush shifting. The beaters were shouting and knocking pieces of wood together. Animals fled.

If they have dogs with them, they'll have no trouble at all finding me, he thought, dropping his eyes to a pile of leaves that the wind had swept into a heap, caught by a couple of forked branches on the ground.

When the first roe deer leaped, the shock of it made him jerk involuntarily and he rolled instinctively toward the cluster of leaves, twisting and turning and burrowing his body down into the heap.

Breathe calmly and slowly now, he told himself, resting in the humus-scented pile. Damn, he hoped Torsten Florin hadn't given his beaters mobiles so he could warn them that they were approaching an escaped policeman who absolutely mustn't get away. How he wished Florin hadn't! But was that likely? That a man like him would fail to take such precautions? Hardly. Of course the beaters had to know who and what they were chasing.

It was while he was under the pile of leaves that he noticed how his wound had reopened, how the seeping blood was making his shirt cling to his body. If there were dogs, they would sniff him out in an instant. And if he lay like that for very long, he would bleed to death.

So how the hell could he help Assad? And if against all the odds he survived and Assad died, how could he ever look at himself in the mirror again? He simply wouldn't be able to. He'd lost a partner before. He had let down a partner before. That was a fact.

He breathed deeply. He couldn't let it happen again. Even if he burned in hell. Even if he landed in jail. Even if it cost him his life.

He blew the leaves away from his eyes and heard a kind of hissing sound that slowly grew louder, turning into a huffing and a muted barking. He felt his pulse rise and the wound in his shoulder throb harder. If this was a dog, it was all over now.

Farther away, the beaters' determined steps grew louder. They were laughing and shouting; they knew exactly what they were doing.

Then the brittle, crunching noises the animal was making in the underbrush stopped, and he suddenly knew it was standing there, looking at him.

He blew a few more leaves from his eyes and found himself gazing directly into the distended muzzle of a fox. Its eyes were bloodshot and there was froth ringing its mouth. Panting as though it were deathly ill, and quaking in every muscle as if it were freezing.

It hissed when it saw him blinking there among the leaves and hissed again when he held his breath. Bared its teeth in a demented growl and slunk toward him with its head lowered.

Suddenly it stiffened. Raised its head and looked back as if sensing danger. Then it turned again toward Carl, and suddenly, as if the animal possessed the capacity for reflective thought, it crawled along the ground toward him and settled at his feet, digging itself under the leaves with its dripping snout.

There it lay, breathing shallowly and waiting. Completely hidden by leaves. Exactly like him.

A flock of partridges was gathered in a shimmering ray of light a little way off, and when it took flight, frightened by the beaters' rumbling through the woods, there was a volley of gunfire. Every single round fired sent shivers through Carl as the fox trembled at his feet.

He watched the hunters' dogs fetch the birds, and soon after he saw the hunters themselves, like silhouettes against the leafless thicket.

There were nine or ten of them, all wearing laced-up boots and plus fours. As they came closer, he recognized several of them as members of society's elite. *Should I stand up and identify myself?* he wondered for a moment, before catching sight of their host and his two friends, both of whom were holding loaded crossbows. If Florin, Dybbøl Jensen, or Pram spotted him, they would shoot first without hesitation. They would claim it was an accident. They would get the others in the hunting party to go along with the story. Their camaraderie was tight, he knew. They would remove the tape from him and make it look like an accident.

Carl's breathing grew shallower and shallower, like the fox's. What about Assad? And what about himself?

Now they were standing a few yards from the pile of leaves, the dogs growling and the animal at his feet breathing audibly. Suddenly the fox sprang straight for the nearest hunter, tearing at his groin with all the power it could muster. The young man emitted a blood-curdling scream. A cry of mortal dread. The dogs snapped at the fox, but the animal made a furious stand against them, pissing with legs spread before springing for its life. Ditlev Pram took aim.

He didn't hear the bolt whistling through the air, but he heard the fox howl in the distance and then its whining death throes.

The dogs sniffed around the fox's urine and one stuck its muzzle where the fox had lain at Carl's feet, but it didn't pick up Carl's scent.

God bless the fox and its piss, Carl thought to himself, as the dogs clustered around their masters and the injured man lay screaming on the ground a few yards away, writhing with cramp in both his legs. His hunting buddies bent over him and attempted to attend to his wound. They tore their scarves into strips, bandaged him, and lifted him up.

"Good shot, Ditlev," he heard Florin say, when Ditlev returned with his bloodied knife and the fox's tail in his hand. Then Florin turned to the men behind him. "The hunt's over, my friends. I'm sorry. Would you please make sure Saxenholdt gets to the hospital immediately? I'll call the beaters over so they can carry him. See to it he's vaccinated for rabies; you can never tell, can you? Keep your finger pressed down hard on the artery the whole time, OK? Otherwise you'll lose him."

He shouted something into the woods and a flock of black men appeared from the shadows. He sent four with the hunters and asked the last four to remain. Two of the men had slender hunting rifles just like Florin's.

When the hunting party had disappeared with the whimpering man, the three old school chums and the four dark-skinned men gathered in a circle.

"We don't have a lot of time, understand?" Florin said. "This policeman is relatively strong and fit; he's not much older than we are. We mustn't underestimate him."

"What do we do with him when we find him?" asked Dybbøl Jensen.

"You pretend he's a fox."

He listened for a long time until he was certain the men had spread out and were

642

headed to the far end of the woods. Which meant there was an open route back to the estate, provided the other black men didn't return to join in the chase.

Run! he told himself, and stood up, leaning his head back so that his relatively free eye could lead him through the thick underbrush.

Maybe there's a knife in the menagerie I can slice the tape off with. Maybe Assad's still alive. Maybe he's alive. Thoughts whirled through his head as the thicket yanked at his clothes and blood trickled from the wound in his shoulder.

He was cold now. His hands shook behind his back. Had he lost so much blood already that it was too late?

Then he heard several SUVs roar to life somewhere close by and zoom off. That meant he must be getting close.

Just as he realized this, a bolt whistled past his head, so close that he could almost feel it. It pounded into the tree trunk in front of him with such force that it would be impossible to pull out.

He twisted his body round, but saw nothing. Where were they? Then there was another shot that tore up the bark of a second tree.

Now the beaters' calls suddenly grew

clearer. *Run, run, run!* his brain screamed. *Don't fall. Get behind a bush, then the next one, so you'll be out of range. Isn't there somewhere I can hide?*

He knew they would catch him now. Knew that dying wasn't going to be a simple matter. After all, this was how they got their kicks, the bastards.

His heart was pounding so hard in his chest that he could hear it plainly.

He leaped over a creek, his shoes almost getting stuck in the mud. The soles grew heavy as lead, and his legs began giving out. *Just run and run.*

Then he detected a clearing off to the side. Probably where he and Assad had entered, since the creek was just behind him. So he needed to head to the right. Up and to the right. It couldn't be far now.

The next shot was way off target and suddenly he found himself standing in the courtyard. Completely alone, heart hammering, and with only ten yards to the hall's broad entrance.

He'd made it halfway when the next bolt plowed into the ground right next to him. It was no coincidence that it hadn't struck him. It was only to let him know that if he didn't stop running, another would follow.

All his defense mechanisms shut down.

He stopped running and stood there staring at the ground, waiting for them to fall upon him. This lovely, cobblestoned courtyard would become his sacrificial altar.

He inhaled deeply and turned around slowly. It wasn't just the three men and the four beaters standing there silently observing him. There was also a little crowd of dark-skinned children with curious eyes.

"That's good, right there. You can go now," Florin commanded. The black men left, shooing their children before them.

At last there was only Carl and the three men. They were sweaty and wore strange little smiles. The foxtail dangled from Ditlev Pram's crossbow.

The hunt was over.

42

They prodded him forward as he stared at the floor. The light in the hall was glaring and he didn't want to see Assad's remains in any detail. He refused to be witness to what a hyena's powerful jaws could do to a human body.

In fact, he didn't want to see anything more of anything. They could do with him whatever they pleased. But he wasn't going to watch as they did it.

Then he heard one of the men laugh. A laughter from deep within, which spread to the other two. An eerie, rolling chorus of merriment that made Carl close his eyes tight — as tight as the tape would allow.

How could a person laugh at another person's misfortune and death? What had made these people so sick in the head?

Then he heard a voice spitting out curses in Arabic. Ugly, guttural sounds meant to provoke anger, but for a brief moment the direness of the situation was supplanted by an indescribable joy that made him raise his head.

Assad was alive.

At first he couldn't tell where the sound was coming from. He saw only the shiny steel bars and the scowling hyena. Then he craned his neck and saw Assad, who had wedged himself like an ape into the top of the cage, his eyes wild, bloody lacerations showing on his arms and face.

Only then did Carl notice how badly the hyena limped. As though its rear leg had been slashed with a single stroke. The animal whimpered with each weak step and the three men's laughter gave way to silence.

"Pig animals!" came Assad's disrespectful yell from above.

Carl almost smiled under the gaffer tape. Even this close to death, the man remained true to form.

"You'll fall down sooner or later. Next time the animal will know what you're like," Florin hissed. Assad's disfiguration of the zoo's prize specimen had stung and enraged him. But the bastard was right. Assad couldn't hang on forever.

"I don't know," Pram said. "That orangutan up there seems pretty fearless. If he falls down on top of the animal with that great body of his, it won't be good for it."

"Then fuck the hyena. It hasn't accomplished what it was put on this earth to do, anyway," Florin said.

"What are we going to do with these two men?" The question came softly. An entirely different tone to the other's. It was Ulrik Dybbøl Jensen again. He seemed less under the influence than before. More vulnerable. That's how the come-down following a cocaine high often affected people.

Carl turned to face him. If he had been able to say anything, he would have said they should just let him and Assad go. That killing them would be meaningless and dangerous. Rose would send every department in the land into action when they didn't show up the following day. The police would be all over Florin and his establishment, and they would find all the evidence they needed. Setting Carl and Assad free and then hauling their backsides over to the other side of the globe to hide for all eternity was their only chance.

But Carl was unable to say anything. The tape was still stretched far too tightly across his mouth. Besides, they wouldn't fall for it. Torsten Florin would use every available means to erase all traces of his involvement, even if he had to burn the whole fucking place down. Carl knew that now.

"We'll throw him in there with the other one. I don't care what happens," Florin said calmly. "We'll look in on them tonight, and if it's not over we'll let some other animals loose in the cage. We have enough to choose from."

Carl started kicking and making noises. He wasn't going to let them get close to him without putting up a fight. Not again.

"What the hell are you doing, Mørck? Is something bothering you?"

Ditlev Pram was standing right beside him, avoiding his clumsy kicks. He raised his crossbow and aimed it directly at the eye Carl could see out of.

"Stand still," he commanded.

Carl considered kicking again so that at least it would all be over with quickly. But he did nothing, and Pram reached out with his free hand, grabbed the tape covering his eyes and yanked.

It felt as though his eyelids had been ripped off. As if his eyes were suddenly hanging loose from their sockets. The light flooded into his head and blinded him an instant.

Then he saw them. All three of them. Their arms opened wide, as if for an embrace, their eyes telling him this would be his final struggle.

And in spite of the loss of blood and the weakness in his body, he kicked out at them and growled from behind the tape over his mouth that they were a bunch of cocksuckers who would get what they deserved.

In the midst of this, a shadow darted across the floor. Florin had noticed it, Carl could tell. Afterward they heard a clattering farther down the hall that was repeated again and again. Then cats began brushing past them and out toward the daylight. And the cats became raccoons and weasels, and birds that flapped their way up toward the aluminum braces under the glass ceiling.

"What the hell is going on?" Florin shouted as Dybbøl Jensen's eyes followed a potbellied pig's short-legged race through the passageways and around the cages. Pram's body language changed; his eyes sharpened as he carefully picked his crossbow up from the floor.

Carl stepped back. He noticed how the noise in the depths of the hall was growing more and more intense. How the sound of freed animals became louder and louder.

He heard Assad's laughter at the top of the cage. Heard the three men's curses and more pattering sounds and grunts and yelps and hissing and beating of wings.

But he didn't hear the woman until she stepped forward.

She was suddenly right there, her jeans tucked into her socks and the pistol with its silencer raised in one hand, a hunk of frozen meat clutched awkwardly in the other.

There was something rather fine about her as she stood there with her bag slung over her shoulder. Something beautiful, actually. She wore a peaceful expression, and her eyes were shining.

Seeing her, the three men fell silent. They let the animals wander around the hall and paid them no attention. They seemed stunned. Not because of the pistol or the sight of the woman, but because of what the woman stood for. Their fear was palpable. Like that of the lynch victim in the clutches of the Klan. Like the atheist standing before the Inquisitor.

"Hi," she said, nodding at each in turn. "Drop that thing, Ditlev." She waved at Pram's crossbow and asked them to take a step back.

"Kimmie . . . !" Ulrik Dybbøl Jensen attempted. There was both affection and anxiety in how he pronounced her name. Maybe more affection than anxiety.

She smiled at a pair of agile otters as they sniffed one of the men's legs before escaping to freedom.

"Today's the day we all get freed," she said. "Isn't that marvelous?"

"You there," she said, looking straight at Carl. "Kick that leather leash over to me." She showed him where it was, shoved halfway under the hyena's cage.

"Come here, little one," she whispered into the cage, where the injured animal was breathing heavily, not once letting the three men out of her sight. "Come and have a snack."

She threw the meat into the cage and waited for the animal's hunger to overcome its fear. When it approached, she picked the leash up from the floor and inserted it carefully between the bars, so that its noose encircled the slab of meat.

Confused by all the people and the empty silence they created, it took some time before the hyena gave in.

When it dropped its head to the meat she pulled the strap so the animal was caught in its noose. Ditlev Pram took off, running toward the door to the angry protests of the other two.

She raised her pistol and fired. Pram dropped heavily, his head banging against the stone floor. He groaned loudly. With some difficulty she tied the strap to the bars, and the animal twisted its head from side to side, trying to get free.

"Get up, Ditlev," she said quietly, and when he couldn't, she led the other two over to him and made them carry him back.

Carl had seen shots halt a fleeing man before, but nothing as clean and effective as the wound that had split Pram's hip socket in two.

His face was white as a sheet, but he said nothing. It was as if she and the three men found themselves in the middle of a private ceremony that no one was permitted to leave. Something silent and unspoken, yet understood by all.

"Open the cage, Torsten." She looked up at Assad, still hanging from the top. "You were the one who saw me at the central station. You can come down now."

"Allah be praised!" he said, as he unhooked his feet from the bars. When he landed he could neither stand nor walk. Every part of his body was numb, and had been for some time.

"Get him out, Torsten," she said, following his every movement until Assad lay outside the cage on the floor.

"Now you three get in," she said quietly.

"Oh God, no. Let me go," Ulrik whispered. "I never hurt you, Kimmie, don't you remember?"

He tried to arouse pity by pulling a pathetic face, but she didn't react.

"Move," was all she said.

"You might as well kill us," Florin said, as they heaved Ditlev Pram inside. "None of us will survive in prison."

"I know, Torsten. I hear you."

Pram and Florin said nothing, but Dybbøl Jensen whined, "She's going to kill us, don't you get it?"

When the cage door slammed shut, she smiled, leaned back, and threw the pistol as far behind her in the hall as she could.

It landed with a smack, metal against metal.

Carl looked down at Assad, who lay rubbing his legs, smiling. Except for the blood still dripping slowly from his hand, this was a truly welcome turn of events.

It was at this point that the three men began shouting at once.

"You there, get her!" one shouted to Assad.

"Don't trust her," Florin urged.

But the woman didn't move an inch. Just stood observing them, as if an old film was playing that had long been forgotten but had now somewhat reluctantly resurfaced.

She went over to Carl and pulled the tape

from his mouth. "I know who you are," she said. Nothing else.

"I know who you are, too," Carl said, and took a deep, liberating breath.

Their exchange of words made the men cease with their protesting.

Florin came up right beside the bars. "If you two policemen don't do something now, she's the only one here who'll be breathing in five minutes. Do you realize that?" He looked Carl and Assad in the eyes, one after the other. "Kimmie's not like us, OK? She's the one who kills people, not us. It's true that we've assaulted people, that we've beat them senseless, but Kimmie is the only one who has killed."

Carl smiled, shaking his head. Survivor types like Florin were like that. No crisis was to be viewed as anything other than the beginning of a success. No one stayed down forever, until the day the Grim Reaper paid a visit. Florin was used to fighting, and he did so without scruples. Hadn't he and his friends just tried to kill Carl? Hadn't they thrown Assad into the hyena's cage?

Carl turned to Kimmie. He had expected to see a smile, but not this joyous, icy grimace. She stood there as if in a trance, listening.

"Yeah, just look at her. Is she concerned?

Does she look like she has any feelings? Look at her finger. It's dangling. Does it make her whine? No. She won't whine about anything, including our deaths." The words came from the floor of the cage, where Ditlev Pram lay with his fist stuck into his nasty wound.

For a moment the dreadful events the gang had called forth filed past in Carl's mind. Could they be speaking the truth? Or was it just part of their fight for survival?

Then Florin spoke again. He wasn't a king now. Wasn't a leader. He was simply himself. "We acted on Kristian Wolf's orders, you understand? We found the victims according to Kristian's instructions. And we beat them all together until we weren't having fun anymore. And all the while that evil woman stood there with her head back, waiting for her turn. Well, naturally, once in a while she took part in the punishments, too." Florin paused and nodded, as if he could see it all before him. "But she was always the one who did the killing, you've got to believe us. Apart from the time Kristian had an issue with her old boyfriend, Kåre, it was always Kimmie. We prepared the way for her, nothing more. *She* was the killer. Only her. And that's how she *wanted* it."

"Oh God," Dybbøl Jensen groaned. "You've got to stop her. Can't you see that Torsten's telling the truth?"

Carl could feel the mood shifting in the room — and deep within himself. He watched Kimmie open her shoulder bag quite slowly, and he could do nothing, bound and exhausted as he was. The men held their breath. Carl saw that Assad was now closely following events in anticipation of what was to come, and with all his strength was trying to get to his knees.

She found what she wanted in the bag and pulled out a hand grenade. She held the safety latch and pulled out the pin.

"*You've* done nothing, my little friend," she told the hyena, looking directly into its eyes. "But you can't very well live with that leg, you know that, don't you?"

She turned to Carl and Assad as Dybbøl Jensen screamed his innocence from inside the cage, promising he would accept the punishment he deserved if only they would help him.

"If you value your lives," she said, "you'll step back a bit. *Now!*"

Carl protested, but did as he was told, with his hands bound behind his back and his pulse racing. "You, too, Assad," he said, and watched as his partner crab-walked backward.

When they were far enough away, she stuck the hand holding the grenade into her shoulder bag and in one movement slung it through the bars into the furthest corner of the cage, then leaped aside as Florin threw himself on the bag in a vain attempt to toss it back through the bars of the cage. It exploded, leaving the hall an inferno of fearful animal cries and endless echoes.

The blast threw Carl and Assad against a number of smaller cages that fell on top of them and which a moment later shielded them from a downpour of glass shards.

When the dust had finally settled and only the noise of the animals remained, Carl felt Assad's arm reach out and touch his leg through the wreck of metal cages.

He pulled his boss toward him and made certain that Carl was OK before reporting that he, too, was OK. Then he tugged the tape from Carl's wrist.

It was a dreadful sight to behold. Where the cage had once stood there were now metal pieces and body parts, a torso here, arms and legs there. Frozen expressions in dead faces.

Carl had seen a lot in his time, but never anything like this. Usually by the time he and the crime-scene techs arrived on-site, the blood had stopped flowing and the bodies lay lifeless.

Here the border between life and death was still visible.

"Where is she?" Carl said, turning his eyes from what had once been three men in a stainless-steel prison cell. Forensics were certainly going to have enough to rummage through. "I don't know," Assad said. "She's probably lying here somewhere."

He hoisted his boss to his feet, and Carl's arms were like two dead appendages that had nothing to do with him. Only his throbbing shoulder had a life of its own.

"Let's get out of here," he said, moving toward the doorway with his friend.

That's when they saw her standing there, waiting for them. With wild, dust-filled hair and eyes so deep they seemed to convey the sorrows and unhappiness of the entire world.

They told the dark-skinned men to withdraw. That they wouldn't be held responsible for any of this and were out of danger. That they should concentrate on getting the animals out. And extinguish the fire. The women pulled their children close while the men stared at the hall, from which smoke now poured, black and threatening, above the shattered glass roof.

Then one of them shouted a few words, and suddenly they were all in motion.

Kimmie walked along voluntarily with Assad and Carl. Showed them the path to the firebreak. Pointed at the hasps that opened the lock. She was the one who, with few words, led them down sun-splashed forest paths to the train tracks.

"You can do with me as you wish," she had said. "I'm no longer alive. I admit my guilt. We'll go down to the train station. My bag is there. I've written down everything I remember."

Carl tried to keep pace with her as he told her about the box he'd found and about the terrible uncertainty that relatives of the victims had lived with for years, which could now be put to rest.

She seemed remote when he spoke about people's sorrow at having lost a loved one. About how not knowing who had murdered their children or how their parents had disappeared had scarred them for life. People Kimmie hadn't known. The others who had suffered besides the victims themselves.

None of this seemed to register with her. She simply wandered ahead of them through the forest, her arms limp at her sides and her broken finger jutting out. The killing of her three former friends had clearly also meant the end for her as well. She had said as much herself.

People like her don't survive long in prison, he thought to himself. He just knew.

They reached the railway a good hundred yards from the platform. Here the tracks sliced through the forest as if drawn with a ruler.

"I'll show you where my bag is," she said, heading toward a bush close to the rails.

"Don't pick it up, I'll do it," Assad said, forcing his way ahead of her.

He gathered up the duffel bag and walked the last twenty yards to the platform, holding the bag away from his body as if some mechanism inside would spear him if he shook it too much.

Good old Assad.

When they reached the end of the platform, he unzipped it and turned it upside-down, despite her protests.

Sure enough, there was a notebook inside. A quick riffling through it revealed that the first few pages were packed with descriptions of locations, incidents, and dates.

It was an incredible sight.

Then Assad reached for a small, cotton bundle and yanked at its corner as the woman gasped and raised her hands to her head.

So did Assad when he saw what was inside.

A tiny mummified person with empty eye sockets. Its head completely black, its stiff fingers sticking out. Dressed in clothing scarcely bigger than a doll's.

They saw her rush to the child's corpse and made no move to stop her from snatching it up and clutching it tightly.

"Little Mille, little Mille. Everything's OK now. Mummy's here and she will never leave you again," the woman sobbed. "We'll always be together. You'll get a little teddy, and we'll play together every single day."

Carl had never experienced that definitive, interconnected feeling people have when they hold their offspring in their arms immediately after birth. But he'd felt the absence of that feeling, at least theoretically. At a slight distance.

Now he looked at the woman and felt a sharp pang of regret and loss, so deep in his heart that it made him able to understand. And he raised his injured arm to his breast pocket, pulled out the small talisman — the teddy bear he had found in Kimmie's metal box — and handed it to her.

She said nothing. Stood as if paralyzed,

staring at the toy animal. Slowly she opened her mouth and cocked her head. Stretched her lips as if she were about to cry, vacillating for an endless moment between a smile and tears.

At her side stood Assad, uncharacteristically disarmed and vulnerable. With a wrinkled brow and an inner stillness.

She reached cautiously for the teddy bear. As soon as she felt it in her hand, she loosened up, filled her lungs to capacity and threw back her head.

Carl wiped his nose, which had begun to drip, and tried to look away so he wouldn't surrender to the tears. Glanced down the tracks to where a group of travelers was waiting for a train, and where Carl's car was parked beside the whistle-stop's shelter. He turned around and saw the train creeping toward them from the other side.

He focused again on the woman, who was now breathing calmly and hugging the teddy bear and the child's corpse close to her.

"Well," she said, exhaling a sigh capable of loosening decades of emotional knots, "now the voices are completely silent." She gave a short laugh as tears streamed down her cheeks. "The voices have ceased, they're gone," she repeated, raising her eyes up to the sky. Suddenly she radiated a peacefulness Carl didn't understand.

"Oh, little Mille, now it's just you and me. It has finally come to pass." A sense of release sent her spinning around and around, embracing the corpse in a dance without steps that seemed to make her levitate.

And when the train was ten yards away, Carl watched as her feet danced to the side and hit the edge of the platform.

Assad shouted a warning just as Carl raised his head and gazed directly into Kimmie's eyes, which were full of gratitude, her mind now seemingly at peace. "Just you and me, my beloved little girl," she said, stretching out the one arm.

A second later, she was gone.

Only the frantic screeching of train brakes remained.

EPILOGUE

It was a twilight lit up by columns of blinking blue lights coming from the train crossing and along the road heading toward the estate. The entire landscape was awash with this blueness and the air rang with the yowling sirens of fire engines and police vehicles. Police badges were everywhere, along with ambulances, a sea of journalists and cameras, and inquisitive locals standing on the fringes as people received crisis counseling. Down on the tracks themselves, crime-scene techs and paramedics were busy, all getting in each other's way.

Carl was still dizzy, but his shoulder wound was no longer dripping blood; the medics had made sure of that. It was inside that he was bleeding. The lump in his throat was still large.

He sat on the wooden bench at the Duemose whistle-stop, leafing through Kimmie's notebook. Her notes disclosed the gang's deeds — they were mercilessly honest. The assault on the brother and sister in Rørvig. How they'd been selected at random. How they had humiliated the boy and undressed him after the fatal blow. The twin brothers whose fingers they'd chopped off. The couple that had vanished at sea. Kåre Bruno and Kyle Basset. Animals and people, one after another. Everything was there. Plus the fact that it was always Kimmie who had committed the murders. The methods were different, and she'd documented each one in detail. What was incredibly difficult for Carl to comprehend was that this was the same person who had saved his and Assad's lives. The same woman who lay there, under the train, together with her dead child.

Carl lit a cigarette and read the final pages. They spoke of remorse. Not in Aalbæk's case, but in Tine's. That she hadn't wanted to give her an overdose. There was a tone of tenderness in the ugliness of the words, a kind of presence and insight that was missing in her descriptions of all the other atrocious acts. She'd used words like "farewell" and "Tine's last, heavenly high."

This notebook would send the media into a frenzy and stock values plunging, once those men's complicity was revealed.

"Take the notebook to headquarters and make copies immediately, OK, Assad?"

He nodded. The aftermath would be hectic, but short. With no one else other than this trio implicated, apart from the man who was already in prison, it was primarily a question of informing bereaved relatives and ensuring proper distribution of the no doubt enormous damages to be paid by the estates of Pram, Florin, and Dybbøl Jensen.

He gave Assad a quick hug and waved off the crisis psychologist who had decided it was now Carl's turn.

When the time came, he had his own crisis psychologist.

"I'm driving to Roskilde now, so you go with the crime-scene techs back to headquarters, OK? I'll see you tomorrow, Assad. Then we'll talk about all of this, eh?"

Assad nodded again. He'd already resolved it all in his head.

At that moment things between them were good.

The house on Fasanvej in Roskilde seemed so dark. The blinds were shut and all was quiet. On the car radio they were reporting on both the violent events in Ejlstrup and the arrest of a dentist whom the police were convinced was behind the rubbish-bin assaults downtown. He had been arrested during an attempted attack on an undercover female officer on Nikolaj Plads near Store Kirkestræde. What the hell had the idiot been thinking?

Carl glanced at his watch and then again at the darkened house. Old people go to bed early, he knew, but it was only half past seven.

Then he nodded at the nameplates that read JENS-ARNOLD & YVETTE LARSEN and MARTHA JØRGENSEN and rang the doorbell.

His finger was still on the bell when the frail woman opened the door and attempted to shield herself against the cold with her thin kimono.

"Yes?" she said sleepily, looking up at him in confusion.

"I'm sorry to disturb you, Yvette Larsen. It's Carl Mørck. The policeman who came to visit you recently. You remember, don't you?"

She smiled. "Oh yes," she said. "That's right, now I remember."

"I have some good news, I think. I would like to share it personally with Martha. We've found her children's killers. Justice has been served, one could say."

"Oh," she said, placing a hand to her breast. "What a shame." Then she smiled an unusual smile. Not simply sad, but also apologetic.

"I should have called, I'm very sorry. You could have saved yourself the long drive here. Martha is dead. She died the same night you were here. Though not because of your visit, of course. She simply didn't have any more strength."

She put her hand on Carl's. "But thank you. I'm sure that it would have been an immense relief for her to know."

For a long time he sat in his car, staring out across Roskilde Fjord. Lights from the city showed way out over the dark water. Under other circumstances it would infuse him with calm, but just now there was none to be found.

The phrase "Don't put off till tomorrow what you can do today" rotated ceaselessly in his head. Don't put off till tomorrow what you can do today, because suddenly there are no tomorrows.

Had it been just a few weeks earlier, Martha Jørgensen could have died with the knowledge that her children's executioners were dead. What peace of mind it would have given her. And what peace of mind it would have given Carl, knowing that she knew.

669

"Don't put off till tomorrow what you can do today."

He looked at his watch again, then picked up his mobile. Stared a long while at the display before he finally punched in the numbers.

"This is the spinal clinic," said a voice. In the background the television was on at high volume. He could make out the words "Ejlstrup," "Dueholt," "Duemose," and "comprehensive animal-rescue mission."

Yes, the news had even reached there.

"Carl Mørck speaking," he said. "I'm a close friend of Hardy Henningsen. Would you be so kind as to tell him that I'll be visiting him tomorrow?"

"Of course. But Hardy's asleep right now."

"OK, but please tell him first thing tomorrow morning."

Staring out over the water again, he bit his lip. He had never made a bigger decision in his life.

And misgivings settled in him like a knife to the abdomen.

Then he breathed deeply, punched in the next number, and waited year-long seconds before Mona Ibsen answered.

"Hi, Mona, it's Carl. I'm sorry about how things ended last time."

"Never mind that." She sounded as if she

meant it. "I heard what happened today, Carl. It's on every TV station. I've seen pictures of you. Lots of pictures. Are you badly hurt? That's what they're all saying. Where are you now?"

"I'm sitting in my car, looking out over Roskilde Fjord."

She was silent a moment, probably trying to gauge the depths of his crisis.

"Are you OK?" she asked.

"No," he said. "No, I can't say that I am."

"I'll come right away," she said. "Stay where you are, Carl. Don't move an inch. Look at the water, be calm. I'll be there in no time. Tell me precisely where you are, and I'll be there."

He sighed. That was sweet of her.

"No, no," he said, allowing himself a little chuckle. "No, don't worry about me. I *am OK*. I just have something to discuss with you. Something I'm not sure I can handle on my own. If you can meet me at my place, that'll make me very, very happy."

He had spared no pains. Neutralized Jesper with money to be spent at Pizzeria Roma and Allerød Cinema. More than enough for two people, plus a shawarma down at the station afterward. He had called the video-rental store and asked Morten to go straight

671

down to the basement when he got home from work. He'd made coffee and boiled water for tea. The sofa and coffee table were as tidy as they'd ever been.

She sat beside him on the sofa, hands folded in her lap. Her eyes were intense. She listened to every single word he said, nodding when his pauses were too long. But she said nothing herself until he was as finished as he possibly could be.

"You want to take care of Hardy in your house, and you're afraid," she said, nodding once more. "Do you know what, Carl?"

He felt his whole physical presence shift gear, slipping into slow motion. Felt as though he'd been shaking his head for an eternity. That his lungs were working like a leaky bellows. "Do you know what, Carl?" she'd said. Whatever her question would turn out to be, he wouldn't know the answer. He just wanted her to sit there forever, her unasked question hanging on lips he would die for to kiss. Once she received an answer, there would be all too little time before her scent became just a memory, the sight of her eyes fading into unreality.

"No, I don't know," he said hesitantly.

She laid a hand on his. "You are simply gorgeous," she said, and leaned herself against him so that her breath met his.

She's wonderful, was what he thought, just as his mobile rang. She insisted he answer it.

"Hi, it's Vigga!" came the strongly provocative voice of his runaway wife. "Jesper called. He says he wants to move in with me," she said, as the feeling of Paradise that had just begun to settle in Carl's body was torn from him.

"But that won't work at all, Carl. He can't live with me. We have to talk about it. I'm on my way over. I'll see you in twenty minutes."

He was about to protest. But Vigga had already hung up.

Carl met Mona's enticing gaze and smiled apologetically.

This was just his life in a nutshell.

ACKNOWLEDGMENTS

A warm thanks to Hanne Adler Olsen for her daily encouragement and tremendous insight. Thanks, too, to Elsebeth Wæhrens, Freddy Milton, Eddie Kiran, Hanne Petersen, Micha Schmalsteig, and Henning Kure for indispensible and thorough commentary, as well as Jens Wæhrens for his consultation and Anne C. Andersen for all the juggling and her eagle eye. Thanks to Gitte and Peter Q. Rannes and the Danish center for Writers and Translators at Hald Hovedgaard for their hospitality when the urge struck, and to Poul G. Exner for being uncompromising. Thanks to Karlo Andersen for his all-round knowledge of hunting, among other things, and to Police Superintendent Leif Christensen for his generosity with his experience and for his sharp corrections on police procedures.

Thanks to you, all the fantastic readers

who've visited my Web site, www.jussiadler
olsen.com, and encouraged me to keep writ-
ing.